The Maidstone Chronicles
Book Two

Beyond the Hollowtangle

Shane Trusz
— and —
Darryl Frayne

The Maidstone Chronicles Book Two:
Beyond the Hollowtangle
Copyright © 2018 by Shane Trusz and Darryl Frayne

Published by: Fairbay Publishing
Text & Cover Design by: Darryl Frayne

ISBN:
978-1-9995495-5-8 (Hardcover)
978-1-9995495-0-3 (Paperback)
978-1-9995495-1-0 (eBook)

To Ty.
Thanks for adding so much color to this world.
Shane

To Mom and Dad,
who give, inspire, believe, and love unconditionally.
Darryl

CONTENTS

BEYOND THE HOLLOWTANGLE

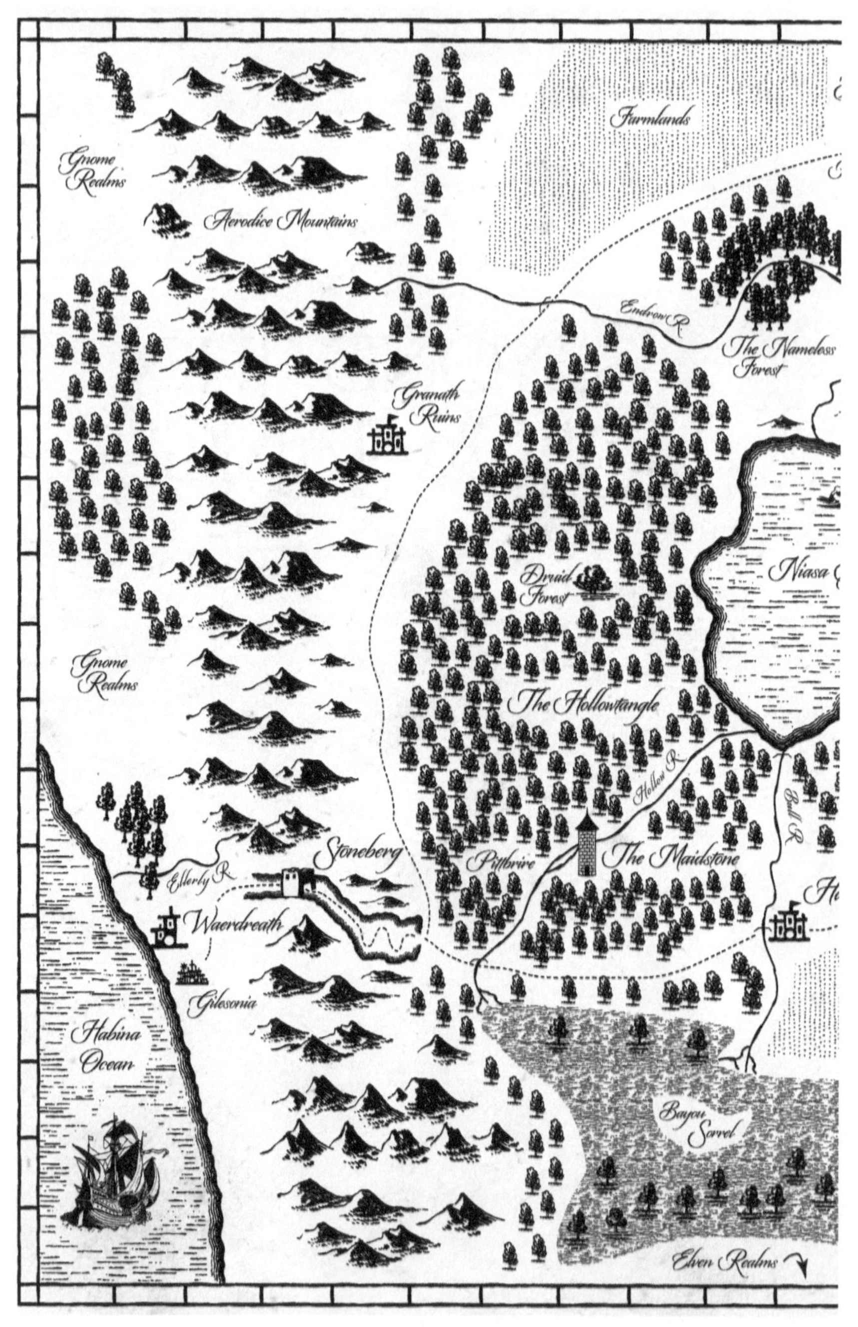

THE FOURWINDS
MAIDSTONE CHRONICLES MAP

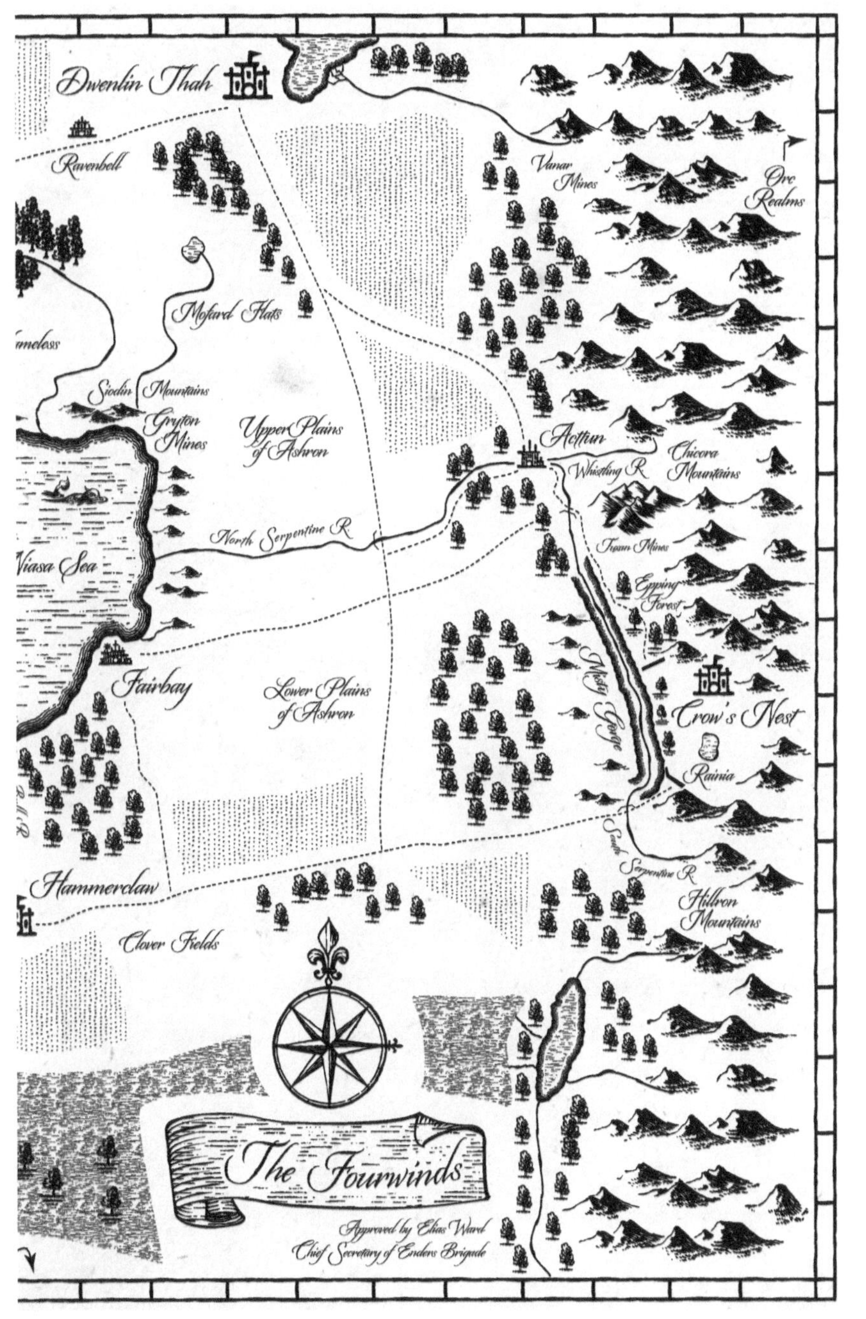

Dwenlin Thah
Ravenbell
Mofard Flats
Nameless
Siodin Mountains
Gryton Mines
Upper Plains of Ashron
Vanar Mines
Orc Realms
Acttun
Whistling R.
Chicora Mountains
North Serpentine R.
Tiwan Mines
Epping Forest
Viasa Sea
Misty Gorge
Crow's Nest
Rainia
Fairbay
Lower Plains of Ashron
South Serpentine R.
Hammerclaw
Hillron Mountains
Clover Fields
The Fourwinds
Approved by Elias Ward
Chief Secretary of Enders Brigade

Prologue

High above the Hollowtangle, a great eagle circled. Its twenty-foot wingspan sliced the clear, crisp morning air, bleeding altitude. The ancient forest below stretched like a woolly green blanket between the Niasa Sea and the Aerodice Mountains. A few months earlier, snow had covered the entire land, making sleeping forest, barren fields, and frozen falls indistinguishable from above. Now in early summer, the Hollowtangle was a prominent patch of deep green. The forest was discolored only by a single river, swollen with spring runoff, that fed the seven waterfalls beside the enigmatic Maidstone tower. North of the river, the great eagle circled in silent descent. Only a few scattered clearings in the forest offered a safe landing area for such a large creature.

On the eagle's broad back, clinging to the rear saddle horn behind Shaey, the renowned elven eagle rider, General Raric focused on a darker-green patch in the Hollowtangle. At the center of the forest, visible only to a well-trained eye, was a manicured grove known as the Druid Forest.

Raric adjusted his position in the saddle as Shaey tugged the reins, guiding the eagle in a smooth banking motion. They descended in ever-tightening circles toward a tiny clearing at the edge of the mythical Druid Forest. Raric tightened his stomach muscles and pursed his chapped lips. The general was comfortable in a horse's saddle, but this was a unique experience for him.

The flight had begun as a terrifying thing, but after several hours behind an elf who seemed as comfortable soaring as he did walking, Raric relaxed, if only a little. He eased a hand from the horn and stretched his aching fingers. The palm of the light-brown leather glove was stained with a wet dark patch. Raric's life-threatening injuries had been cured in the elven healing tent, but the scars on his hands and feet remained tender and prone to bleeding.

The general brushed his fingers across his freshly shaven head. When he had awoken in the healing tent, only a few patches of hair remained, reminders of the unspeakable brutality he'd endured while imprisoned in the Waerdreath castle. The Dark Queen's minion, Uluk the Shadowfallen, had been merciless. Raric traced a few of the deeper scars on his scalp, wondering if his hair would eventually grow back. Some scars were old, some were still healing. In the meantime, he would keep his old straw hat close at hand to hide the ugly patchwork.

The wind whistled in his ears as the eagle increased speed on descent. Raric shivered and adjusted the leather vest he wore over a long-sleeved wool sweater.

Shaey looked back at the general through the large leather goggles covering half his face. The elf rider's shoulder-length blond hair whipped over the tips of his pronounced ears.

Raric pointed to the small clearing. "Can we land there?"

"No problem, no problem." Shaey's accent was gentle and melodic.

"Are you certain?" Raric shouted against the wind.

The huge trees surrounding the clearing made it look even smaller the closer they came. Raric wondered how they would be able to land in such tight quarters, let alone take off again.

Shaey fired another glance at Raric. "No problem, no problem."

Raric did not appreciate the eagle rider's wild-eyed look.

The eagle banked left, causing Raric to tighten his grip on the saddle horn. He winced, knowing he had split more cracks in his scabbed palms. Round and round they descended as the trees loomed up before them. Shaey tugged on the reins until they were within a few feet of the outstretched branches. Flocks of multicolored birds flew from the safety of the trees and trailed the great eagle like the adoring subjects of a returning king. It was both terrifying and beautiful.

From a distance, the forest had appeared overgrown with hundreds of trees. But as they glided just above the canopy, Raric caught an occasional glimpse through the fluttering leaves and was surprised to count only a few dozen trees with expansive trunks. Each was topped with branches the size of regular large trees, spreading out like the giant, gnarled fingers of outstretched interlocking hands. Together, the trees formed a leafy covering that shaded two acres. The largest among them bore dappled leaves as big as a half-orc's hand. In all his journeys across the Fourwinds, Raric had never seen such unusual trees.

Shaey leaned, applying pressure against the right side of the eagle, and it turned in the direction of the small clearing. Raric leaned back, trying to avoid glimpses of the dizzying blur of green grass beneath him. The ground flew up to meet them but stopped suddenly when the eagle flared its massive wingspan in an upward motion. The roar of the wind ceased. The eagle landed in the tall grass, folded its wings, and preened its feathers as if such landings were routine events. Raric released his grip on the saddle horn and clutched his queasy stomach.

Shaey ripped off his goggles and smoothed his hair into a ponytail. "Be quick about it, General."

Raric nodded as he released his restraining belt.

From the dark borders of the Druid Forest, a few bold animals ventured toward the great eagle and its strange passengers. At first, Raric noticed only a few, but as he watched, dozens more appeared. Everything from badgers to bears to bees waited in silent anticipation. It was an eerie thing, and even the eagle shifted its considerable weight as if expecting an attack.

Between two stately bucks, a large man stepped from the forest, long dark hair flowing around nine-point antlers protruding proudly from his temples. He wore a vest of green moss and loose-fitting trousers of thin tree bark. His feet were bare, and his arms were covered with dark fur. From a distance, Raric couldn't tell if the fur was clothing or actual hair. Carrying a long walking stick with sprouts of bright-green leaves, Druid Margrave glided through the tall grass. The animals remained at the tree line.

Raric stumbled from the saddle and rubbed his aching thighs. His simple brown homespun pants were tucked neatly into tall leather boots laced tightly to support his weakened ankles. Pinpricks of pain jabbed at the scabs on his feet as his circulation returned to his extremities. Doing his best to keep from hobbling, General Raric straightened his back and walked out to greet the druid.

Margrave had an ancient quality to him despite his smooth brown complexion. His short, well-groomed beard could have been construed as dark-brown fur rather than hair. He had long eyelashes and eyebrows the color of birch bark, which arched above his wide-set bright-green eyes.

"My, my, Raric. Has it been a hundred years since our last meeting?" Margrave stopped three yards from Raric and leaned on his walking stick.

"By appearance only," Raric said. "Twelve years, if memory serves."

The druid shook his head and knit his brows. "With a hundred years of living in that time, I see."

Raric blinked away a tear. The sudden emotion came less from painful memories of the Waerdreath than the restorative power of the elven healing tent. The experience in the tent had partly mended his physical wounds, but it had also softened his heart. Although he was unfamiliar with such sentimentality, neither was he ashamed of it. "It is good to see you, Margrave."

"I was in the throes of an enjoyable day, Raric, but seeing you here like this…" He trailed off, thin lips forming a tight line.

"I would not have come if—"

"Your need is obvious, Raric. There is so little of you left." Margrave took one step closer. "To be honest, I am surprised you survived your captivity in the Waerdreath."

"I will spare you the details." Raric spat the words, the bitter taste of Sidara's grim castle still fresh in his memory. "You still have it?"

Margrave sniffed. "Of course I do." His eyes narrowed. "It took me three years to form the armor. My hands are pained to this day, dragon hide being what it is. It's a wonder there is any magic left in the Fourwinds. Shades! If the process took much longer, I might have used it all up."

"Scarlas, the Red Dragon." Raric's weakened knees bent as an image of the Dragon War flashed in his memory.

"I spoke to him once, Raric. A vile thing he was. Although I do not condone violence, killing that dragon is an exception I am able to sleep with."

"No one thought it possible to bring him down, but we did."

"I remember seeing you shortly after, full of fresh wind and fire. You stood a solid…what, two hundred and twenty pounds?"

Raric nodded.

"What are you now? One fifty? Shades, lad! You even look like you lost some height."

"This"—Raric tapped his temple—"is what killed Scarlas. Not physical strength."

"So true. They may have broken your body, but it was that hurricane of a mind that made you a force of nature. Never have I met someone who could command a thousand men in the throes of battle with the ease and grace of a bard strumming a lute. And yet, here you are. Have they broken your mind too?"

Raric raised his wounded hands. "If the dragon armor can make me whole again…"

"If you wanted full restoration, Raric, you should not have left the healing tent so soon. The Elf Queen could have done wonders beyond my capacity."

"There was no time for that, Margrave. The Shadowfallen threatens to destroy the Fourwinds. If I'd waited to be fully healed, there would be no army left to command." Raric dropped his hands to his sides and cast an intent gaze at the druid. "I need my strength back."

"Although the dragon armor is complete, what comes next… well, that is something else." Margrave scratched his beard, and a few flying insects escaped. "You mustn't think of it as a suit of armor. Instead, it is something that is melded to you. In fact, it would replace your skin."

"Can you do it?"

Margrave's eyes widened. "So eager, my old friend!" His gaze fluttered down Raric's body to his feet, then back again. "Well, the answer depends on you. Although this has never been done before, my theory is sound. And I am confident wielding the magic required for the melding. The uncertainty lies in the strength of the subject. We will not know until you either survive or perish. There was a time when I was confident in the probability of success, but seeing you now, I confess my doubt. What have they done to you, Raric? And why attempt something like this now, when there is so little left of you?"

"The Shadowfallen had his way with me for a long time." Raric ground his teeth. "I wake up screaming ten times a night from nightmares more real than you standing before me. And…" His voice faltered. "And the tears…they come without warning. There are times I can hardly manage a sentence. I am not the man I was and probably never will be again. One day I might come to terms with that, but not before I tear the Shadowfallen limb from limb—starting with his wings!"

Tiny flakes fell from the druid's raised eyebrows. "Surely you are wise enough not to stick your hand in the same fire twice? Nevertheless, times being what they are, I suspect that if you were to survive the melding—and looking at you, I cannot see how you could"—the druid leaned forward on his staff and pointed a long, bony finger at the general—"you would need to fight for your soul."

"I destroyed Scarlas, and I endured Sidara's torture. I can—"

"To destroy a dragon, you first must kill it, certainly. But then you must annihilate the creature's hide. A difficult task."

"Annihilate its hide?"

"It is a commonly accepted theory that a dragon's soul resides in its hide, which is stronger than the most durable alloys ever created. Once the dragon armor is melded to you, I believe that your soul will fight with the soul of Scarlas for supremacy. After all, there can only be one soul."

A gust of wind rustled through the long grass. Raric folded his arms across his chest and shook off a chill before it crept down his spine.

"If you survive that fight, you will possess much of what makes a dragon, well, a dragon. You would be a daunting foe on—or above—any field of battle. However, if the soul of Scarlas proves stronger, you will cease to exist. And then the Fourwinds will have yet another problem."

Margrave sighed and transferred his staff to the other hand, shifting his weight. "I have told you all I know. Would I be willing to perform the deed? Absolutely. Dragon melding has long been the subject of speculation, but never has there been a dragon's hide available. And if one were, few would be willing to try. That being said, Raric, imagine the possibilities."

"How much time would you require if I decide to go through with the melding process?"

"Most of the work has long been completed. On the heels of this conversation, three days should suffice."

Raric nodded. "I am prepared. But let us hope it does not come to this. My task now is to stop Uluk the Shadowfallen from destroying the Fourwinds. I hope the army is strong enough and there will be no need for your dragon armor, but I had to know if it was an option. It is possible Uluk has weapons more powerful than the mightiest army."

"Are you referring to rumors on the winds?" Margrave asked.

"In these dark days, there are more rumors than truths."

"What about the rumor of Sidara's latest experiment called Phyriad? Is *that* true?"

Raric shuffled his feet to relieve the tingling sensation. "It is."

Margrave chortled. "I have heard tales of her infectious elixir, but they all sound preposterous."

Raric glared at the druid. "I witnessed many horrors during my time at the Waerdreath, but none as dire as Phyriad. Those who become infected transform into the image of Natas, a brutally painful process that destroys the victim's former identity."

Margrave's smirk dissolved. "Can it be stopped?"

Raric offered a simple shrug. "That may be for you and me to determine, Margrave. Perhaps the Fourwinds needs someone willing to sacrifice his former identity by transforming into the image of another dragon."

CHAPTER 1
THE CABIN

Will Owens stumbled through the doorway of the ancient cabin into the shadowy stillness of the Arden Forest. He swayed like a drunkard, crunching through shriveled leaves as he struggled to keep his feet beneath him. He squeezed his dark-brown eyes shut to stop the desolate forest from swirling around him, his mind reeling from the frightening yet familiar journey through the Gateway.

A sapling branch slapped his boyish face as he bent over, both hands on his knees, gulping the stagnant air of the murky forest. He scanned the shadowy clearing, dreading any sign of the monsters he had last seen here. About a month ago, he and Morgan had tumbled into the cabin, leaving Inspector Joe Cheechoo and a hideous creature—which Will had later learned was a harvester named Eurynome—encased in an icy spell. Will's breathing slowed. There was no sign of life in the forest now, only a lingering scent of death.

With his crimson Trannalun cloak draped over his lean body, Will did a quick check for broken bones. Surprised but grateful to find none, he lifted the cloak's hood onto his head. The spinning sensation slowed, but the ringing in his ears grew louder. He opened and closed his mouth, trying to release the pressure that filled his ears as if he had descended from a mountain too quickly. He stood as tall as his stiffening muscles allowed and pulled his cloak around his aching body. Running a hand through his shaggy, sweat-soaked hair, Will faced the ghastly cabin that stood still and sinister in the failing light of day. He was back in Cochrane, but he had never felt so far from home.

As the Trannalun cloak worked its healing magic on Will's aches and nausea, he waited in the spectral stillness of the Arden Forest. One moment drifted into the next as he stared at the vile membranes covering the window openings of the cabin. Rowe and Morgan should have come through the Gateway by now. Morgan had not fared well the last time she'd traveled through the Gateway, so Rowe had promised to use his warding magic to shield her this time. Traveling close together must have slowed their journey, Will reasoned.

Will had been the first of the three to enter the Gateway through the Records of Time, the library tower connected to the Crow's Nest castle. After they'd returned from the elven healing camp, Rowe had led Will and Morgan from the West Hall rooftop to the Records of Time, slipping past the duke's guards undetected. The day was a blur in Will's memory. He wanted to know more about the magic orb used to hide the tower, but Rowe was more concerned with avoiding the duke's guard.

The political affairs of the Crow's Nest remained fuzzy in Will's mind, but Rowe had been clear about the corrupt Duke Renaldi. Over the last few months, the duke had been allowing harvesters into the castle to gain favor with the Dark Queen Sidara. Once inside, these creatures assumed human form so they could attempt to enter the Records of Time and travel through the Gateway into Will's world. A few had succeeded. Despite his recent adventures across the Fourwinds, and the boost to his self-confidence after facing Sidara, Will remained doubtful he could ever wield magic or be as strong as Rowe. He accepted the fact that he was a Callum Sage, like Rowe, but how could he ever live up to such high standards? Would anyone trust him the way Morgan—and many others throughout the Fourwinds—trusted Rowe of the Nest?

Pushing aside his melancholy thoughts, Will noticed that the black cauldrons had been returned to their places at the four corners of the cabin, beneath the eaves. He specifically remembered knocking over one of them before the enraged harvester had attacked him, their bloody contents a nightmarish memory. While they were in the Fourwinds, someone—or something—had returned the cauldron to the large hook on the cabin. Strange umbilical-like cords connected the contents of each cauldron to the cabin, as if feeding the aged structure with sustaining energy. Will stared, mesmerized by the dark pulsing veins within the logs.

A sharp crackle sounded from within the cabin, followed by a flash of dazzling light. Instinctively, Will covered his eyes. A gust of warm wind flowed through the yawning front doorway of the cabin, and a red-cloaked figure emerged.

With one hand clutching a long, bloodstained dagger and the other supporting Morgan beneath the shelter of his Trannalun cloak, Rowe of the Nest hesitated at the cabin doorway. He pulled his cloak from Morgan's shoulders and she staggered onto the hard ground. Her wide eyes met Will's, and the color from her tanned face drained as she sheathed her sword. She took two steps before convulsing. Leaning over, she swept her long auburn hair from her face, anticipating the imminent loss of her meager evening meal.

Rowe crept from the cabin, his penetrating blue eyes searching the area. His broad shoulders hunched as he tensed like a coiled snake, ready to strike. He brushed a long crop of sandy hair from his hawkish face. Will thought he looked like a hunter who had been lost in the woods for a month.

"It's okay, Rowe," Will said. "We're alone. We made it."

"No harvesters?"

"Not yet."

Although Rowe possessed the strength and magic to destroy a harvester, only Will had the ability to discern the deadly creatures, especially when they assumed human disguises.

Rowe let out a hoarse huff before drawing in a deep breath of air that immediately sent him into a fit of coughing. Will turned his head away from the cabin, suddenly aware of the acrid air that reminded him of diesel exhaust. Far beyond the trees, a semitruck rumbled down the Arden Road. Rowe shifted his head, trying to identify the strange sound.

Will resisted the urge to smile at the guarded look in Rowe's eyes. "It's okay; that's a familiar sound, Rowe. I've had a look around and there's nothing to worry about. For now."

Morgan straightened to her full height, hands on hips, sword at her side. Taller than most women, she had a confident, athletic stance and ease of movement about her that betrayed the present anxious look in her eyes. Today was not one of her better days. She brushed her tangled hair from a high-boned cheek that was unusually pallid. Turning, she grimaced at the sight of the cauldrons and quickly distanced herself from the cabin.

"That trip through the Gateway wasn't as bad as I remembered,"

Will said, his voice cracking. "Rowe, are you sure no one can follow us now that you've restored the Records of Time?"

"Impossible," Rowe said between coughs. "The duke and his guard will now be able to see the stairwell entrance, but I have protected the tower using magic none of them could possibly know. The secret runes carved into the stone walls require a unique combination of tracing with a sunstone and speaking ancient words."

Will nodded as he raised his eyebrows and shared a confused look with Morgan.

"I can't believe we're back in this dreary forest, Will," Morgan said. The disoriented look in her hazel eyes faded as she stood next to him. "I hope we can find my mom."

"We'll find her, Morgan," Will said. "And I hope the Elf Queen was right about Ryowyn being in Lake Commando. As clean as that lake is, I don't know how foreign water will affect a mermaid." He looked up at the gray sky. "Let's get out of this cursed forest before it gets dark."

Rowe raised his blade, stress lines deepening in his forehead as he searched the clearing like a hunted stag.

Will flashed a smile. "I've been looking forward to this, Rowe. Boy, do I have a world to introduce you to." He pointed to the outline of a small path amid the sickly spruce trees and decaying brush. "We need to head due west along that trail there. When we get to my house, I'll grab my scuba gear and then you can ride in my horseless carriage."

Rowe cleared his throat. Each breath sounded gravelly and strained. "How far is it?"

Before Will could respond, a distant but powerful explosion rippled through the forest. Rowe wrapped his arm around the trunk of a spruce to steady himself. Will and Morgan caught each other to keep from stumbling. A bright-orange fireball lit the sky north of the forest, then faded to a steady glow.

"Was that a familiar sound too?" Rowe asked, walking toward them.

"Not sure," Will answered, pulling his cloak tighter. "But I do know we've got to get to Cochrane—right now."

CHAPTER 2

A Terrible Business

At the Esso bulk fuel station five miles north of Cochrane, Abaddon leapt off the vintage 1973 fire truck with a heavy thud and claimed the ground as his own. Under the human guise of Pastor Grant Finley, the harvester examined the stolen pumper truck, his demon-wild eyes eclipsing the gentle spirit of the former man of God. The steady droning of the pumps, long past their scheduled service date, disturbed the calmness of dusk while forcing 87 octane into the thousand-gallon holding tank.

It had been a week since the Dark Queen Sidara had inexplicably cut off contact with the harvesters, Abaddon and Eurynome. She had been giving them strict instructions regarding their responsibility to maintain her powerful connection to this strange world. Not a night went by without a vision from her. But after six days of silence, the harvesters had agreed to return to the Fourwinds.

An unexpected vision from Uluk the Shadowfallen, who commanded Sidara's armies, changed everything. With no explanation of Sidara's silence, Uluk's arresting presence left no doubt about who was in control. While Sidara had dictated their every action in Cochrane, Uluk had given the harvesters their heads. Their leashes severed, they were now free to pour out their pent-up rage on the sleepy town.

The two harvesters had no trouble embracing the order from Uluk. Despite their adherence to Sidara's wishes, they had always suspected she was a means to an end, much like they were. The only creature who might command either Sidara or Uluk was Natas, the mythical creature of chaos. But had Natas really returned to the Fourwinds? Had he always been the one silently controlling the ebbs and flows of war? The harvesters suspected Uluk had murdered Sidara and usurped her rule, but they couldn't care less. It was their nature to respond to strength. And if Uluk the Shadowfallen's shackles had indeed been loosed, violence would reign.

The station's fuel pumps came to a clanking, grinding halt. From the main pump shack, Eurynome appeared in the form of a well-built, leathery-skinned man with long black hair tied back in a ponytail. He wore faded blue jeans, a long-sleeved plaid shirt, and an odious smile. The harvester kicked up the dust as his heavy steel-toed boots crunched the fine gravel. Despite his confident pace, there was no mistaking his limp left arm: a lingering injury from his battle with Johanissan, the Callum Sage that the humans called Joe of the Mushkegowuk.

Eurynome approached the controls at the side of the pumper truck and turned two heavily pitted stainless-steel valves before detaching the four-inch hose. He stepped away and nodded at Abaddon, who climbed into the truck's cab. Abaddon stomped the clutch to the floor, turned the key, and pushed the start buttons in the rusting dashboard. The engine clunked and rattled as black smoke spewed from what remained of the exhaust system. Little by little, the diesel engine sputtered until it finally roared to life. Abaddon wriggled the reluctant shifter until the transmission yielded first gear, then he eased out the clutch. With both hands, he cranked the large steering wheel and maneuvered the pumper truck toward the Arden Road.

Eurynome heaved the end of the four-inch hose between the fifty-foot-tall storage tanks. He followed the length of the hose back to the pump shack and restarted the pumps, which hummed to life in a bunker beneath him. After about thirty seconds of idling, he pushed two long red levers forward and grinned when gasoline gushed from the hose, splashing between the storage tanks. A third smaller lever brought the pumps to their maximum rpm, sending hundreds of gallons per minute around the tanks. Eurynome had already doused the top of the tanks, so there was only one thing left to do. Careful to avoid the spraying hose, he leapt from the pump shack and sprinted toward the fire engine as it slowly pulled onto the rutted pavement.

Once on the Arden Road, Eurynome stopped to take a red road flare from his back pocket and cracked the cap. He struck the top of the flare against the cap several times until it erupted in a brilliant flash that illuminated the harvester's broad smile. Eurynome took several quick steps and launched the flare in a high arc toward the tanks as Abaddon shifted into second gear. With a loon-like laugh, Eurynome sprinted after the lumbering pumper truck, caught the rail along the passenger-side door, and flung the door open. The truck grudgingly whined into third gear.

When the flare hit the gasoline vapors between the storage tanks, a deep, thunderous blast thrust Eurynome into the cab. Billowing clouds of smoke blackened the silvery-blue evening sky as flames leapt hundreds of feet in the air, enveloping both storage tanks in a matter of seconds. Abaddon pressed the accelerator to the floor, turning the steering wheel left and right to keep the sputtering fire engine between the ditches on either side of the road. The harvesters would only have a few minutes before the storage tanks exploded. Once they did, the heat of the secondary blasts would certainly catch the fire engine's full tank of gasoline. Unfortunately for the people of Cochrane, the old pumper truck escaped the blasts.

Five miles away, residents of the isolated community rushed outside to see what had shaken their homes. Flames and rolling smoke defaced the northern horizon. Before anyone could dial 9-1-1, sirens blared as a dozen volunteer firefighters sprang into action.

Less than a mile outside the town limits, Abaddon veered the pumper truck off the Arden Road and down a narrow dirt side road. At the entrance to an old gravel pit, he swung the large vehicle in a wide circle and stopped. With a clear view of the Arden Road, Abaddon shut off the diesel engine and killed the lights. The harvesters waited quietly as the cooling engine crackled.

They didn't have to wait long before the first police car raced past them toward the Esso bulk station. Two network news vans followed. Moments later, another police car sped past with sirens roaring, and before the sound dissipated, all three of Cochrane's active fire trucks drove by.

When the caravan of lights faded, Abaddon fired up the engine and steered the truck back onto the Arden Road. When they reached town, he turned right onto Eighth Street. Working through the gears, he drove past two streets before turning left onto Seventeenth Avenue where he slowed to a near stop. Despite nearly everyone being outside watching the glowing sky to the north, none thought it strange to see a fire truck turning onto their avenue until someone recognized the driver.

"Pastor Finley?" A woman pointed as a few people walked toward the truck.

Abaddon shot an angry glare that stopped the crowd in their tracks. "Run to the lake! You will be safe there," Abaddon lied.

Eurynome climbed out of the passenger side and started the main pump from the rear controls. He scrambled up to the forward-facing water cannon and checked a small gauge, which told him the pressure was holding. Abaddon eased the truck past the stunned onlookers. Eurynome opened the pitted control valve of the cannon and sent a blast of gasoline in a high arch toward the nearest rooftops. Once he had the range figured out, he shifted the cannon back and forth to make sure he hit every house.

At first, the noxious smell confused people. But when gasoline rained on them, panic spread like the impending inferno. Shouts filled the air as some people ran into their homes while others ran for their lives. Most smelled of gasoline. Eurynome fired up another road flare. The harvester bounded off the fire truck as it turned at Third Street. Eurynome took a few quick steps and grunted as he threw the flare at a large house on Seventeenth. The moment it hit the front porch, a gut-wrenching *whoosh* blew out windows for several blocks and the entire avenue erupted into a fiery nightmare.

Abaddon navigated the truck along several other streets as they worked to create a blazing perimeter around the most densely populated section of town. Their intent was to corral the humans to Lake Commando in the center of town.

After igniting a dozen more infernos, they reached the south end of the lake, blaring the siren to get past several swerving vehicles. They turned onto Sixth Avenue and sprayed the two-story commercial buildings on both sides of the street. Now that the western perimeter was about to go up in flames, soon the only place to go would be the lake. Abaddon flicked the truck lights and blasted the siren to clear away the growing number of panicking drivers. They bathed the shops in gasoline, then continued along the northern part of town along Seventh Street.

Throughout town, citizens took to the streets, some on foot and some in cars, adding to the congestion. Ash and red-hot coals rained down, causing the commercial buildings behind the truck to burst into flames. Barely ahead of the fires, Abaddon pushed the accelerator down a little farther.

As traffic snarled to a standstill, many drivers abandoned their vehicles. With much of the town now surrounded by raging infernos, people fought their way on foot toward the perceived safety of Lake Commando. Abaddon cursed the vehicles littering the streets, driving across several lawns to the beach where a growing crowd gathered. As the heat of the flames intensified, many waded into the cool water.

After navigating a virtual sea of abandoned vehicles, Abaddon steered the pumper truck across a sidewalk, through the small parking lot in front of the beach, and over a curb. He parked on the grass at the crest of the small hillside. Abaddon watched large flakes of hot ash float down on the frenzied crowd. A broad, contented smile spread across his face as he breathed in the human fear. With enough fuel left to douse the crowd all the way to the lake, he exhaled a satisfied, sensual groan. Whatever had happened to the Dark Queen, regardless of the fate of the Fourwinds, this night would be a historical victory.

Abaddon secured the brakes, turned off the sirens, and opened the cab door. Turning to step out, he came face-to-face with the cold polished steel of a Springfield 1911 handgun.

"This is for Joe!" Will shouted, firing a single round straight between Abaddon's narrowing eyes.

The report raised the pitch of screams as people pushed away from the fire truck. Will fired the remaining nine rounds in rapid procession, spattering the cab with chunks of flesh and black ichor. He holstered the handgun and, with a painful grunt, pulled himself onto the top step of the cab.

Will saw through the human form to the hideous creature it was. He grabbed one of Abaddon's flailing feet, placed a boot against the seat, and heaved backward with all his might, his red Trannalun cloak flapping in the evening breeze. Will jumped off the steps, dragging the stunned harvester with him.

Despite the hysteria caused by the gunshots, a few people pointed in horror. In their eyes, the troubled Owens boy—who had claimed to have had visions of evil creatures—was pulling the bloodied body of Pastor Finley from the fire truck. A CTV News cameraman bravely focused his lens at the unfolding terror. One part Pastor Grant Finley, one part beast: it was their worst nightmares come to life.

Abaddon's head thumped down each metal step before his body hit the ground with a heavy thud. He rolled onto his side, growling as his girth suddenly tore his clothes, revealing patches of tight dark-gray hide pulled over an enormously disfigured muscle mass. He was about to push himself up with a clawed hand when Morgan suddenly let out a short scream as she slid to a stop beside the transforming creature.

"D-dad…is that…*you?*" Morgan stood motionless, her mouth open and glazed eyes bulging. A large tear rolled down her cheek. Despite the bloody mess of her father's face, she froze.

"Kill it, Morgan! Kill it!" Will shouted as the harvester rolled

onto its knees. The face of Morgan's father glared at Will, who saw only the evil creature beneath the human facade.

Morgan's arms remained limp at her sides.

Will grabbed her by the shoulders and spun her to face him. "It's not your father, Morgan! It's a harvester!"

Abaddon raked a massive claw across the back of Will's brilliant-red cloak, and Morgan's eyes focused on Will's face. The vicious attack and the sound of Will's voice shattered her shocked state. She sprang into action. Her long, thin sword, awash with an ethereal green magic, sliced Abaddon's arm off before its claw could find a gap in Will's cloak. With a desperate, pain-filled battle cry, Morgan shifted and thrust her blade beneath the harvester's armpit and through its chest. The force of her attack drove the creature to the ground and buried her blade into the soil.

Will watched in awe as Morgan's face radiated like it had when she'd faced harvesters in the Fourwinds. Tiny sparks of energy flared from her shoulders and down her arms, hands, and through the steel blade like a high mountain waterfall. Morgan gasped as the magic lanced through the hideous, transforming body of the harvester. The beast buckled, green flashes shooting from its eyes and mouth, as Morgan leaned all her weight on the hilt. Before the harvester could transform from its human shell, its innards crackled and burned. Morgan squeezed her eyes shut, weeping as she turned her head to avoid a final look at her father's closed eyes.

When Will's first volley of bullets had slammed into Abaddon, Eurynome had clambered out of the cab and up to the water cannon. As Abaddon writhed on the ground, transforming from his human guise, Eurynome followed suit. The moment his clothes tore, skin fell away to reveal gray scales beneath. A new wave of terror spread through the people unable to distance themselves from the truck. The CTV cameraman slid the camera from his shoulder and attempted to flee with the remaining onlookers. But there was nowhere to go.

By the time the fire engine's tank system pressurized, Eurynome had transformed into a gator-like monster with lanky clawed forearms and powerful hindquarters bulging with uneven muscle mass. A long tail provided balance. The creature raised its bear-size head, testing the air with a three-split tongue emerging from a gaping maw of jagged teeth. Narrow yellow eyes scanned the crowd as the beast flexed leathery wings while feeding on the spreading screams.

The burgeoning crowd inched away from the fire truck; there was no room to run. Eurynome grasped the water cannon with three long, crooked fingers. The creature moaned in delight as it directed a short burst of gasoline forty feet over the crowd, dousing dozens of people. Immediately, the pumps idled and sputtered before shutting off altogether. Eurynome glared at Will and Morgan, then roared at the sight of Abaddon's burned-out carcass lying next to them. The harvester slashed in anger at the water cannon and turned at the sound of a soft, fluttering noise at the back of the truck.

Wrapped in his protective Trannalun cloak, Rowe faced Eurynome, sword ready. Eurynome lunged but Rowe dodged, thrusting his blade into the creature's side. Blue flames licked Eurynome's rough hide. Somehow, the harvester managed a desperate backhand that connected with Rowe's cheek.

The Callum Sage's sword clanged against the edge of the truck as he stumbled over a pile of coiled fire hoses. He rolled onto his side and wrapped his cloak around himself seconds before a bone-chilling roar filled the air. Eurynome dropped onto Rowe.

Dagger-sharp claws scratched harmlessly off the red fabric that radiated with powerful warding magic.

Will left Morgan to finish off Abaddon and jumped onto the back bumper of the truck. He slammed a fresh clip into his 1911 and climbed the ladder. Peering over the edge, he took aim and squeezed the trigger. The slug caught the harvester high in the temple and jerked its head back, allowing Will to fire the next round beneath its long snout. That hobbled the creature long enough to expose a broad chest. Will never hesitated, firing two more rounds point-blank.

Forced back a step, Eurynome turned and crouched awkwardly, wings unfolding. With a terrific grunt, it leapt off the truck before Rowe could gain his feet. Will cried out and sprang after Eurynome without thinking. He caught the harvester's foot and tried to get a solid grip, but his hands slid from the smooth, hard scales. Eurynome forced down a powerful gust of air with its wings, causing it to shoot up above the fire truck while swinging a leg forward in a long kicking motion. Unable to secure his handhold, Will flailed through the air. He closed his eyes a second before crashing into a small crowd. Fortunately, two men had been watching and raised their arms to break his fall.

Rowe stood on top of the fire truck, cursing under his breath as Eurynome disappeared into the night sky. The hard angles of his face darkened as a bruise formed across his right cheek. Morgan appeared at his side, breathless but radiating energy. Rowe pointed at Will, who was struggling to get back to them, but the crowd carried him in the opposite direction.

"Where's that harvester going?" Morgan asked over the chaotic shouts on the congested beach. She leveled her sword at the creature's dark shape as it fled. "Can we follow it?"

"That's strange," Rowe answered, sheathing his sword. "Harvesters are not known to run from battle. No telling where it's headed."

"It's heading toward my house!" Morgan shouted, wide-eyed. She rushed down the ladder without looking to see if Rowe followed.

"Morgan, wait!" Rowe called, darting after her. He jumped from the truck and grabbed Morgan's arm. "We cannot leave Will!"

"We'll catch up to him later." The words tumbled from Morgan's trembling lips. "This is the lake Ryowyn might be in. He'll be here. We need to find my mom. If she's at home and that… that *thing* is going there…"

"Very well." Rowe's voice remained calm, his eyes a steady beacon in the turbulent storm of events. "You lead the way, Morgan. This is an unusual place for me."

Morgan placed her hand on Rowe's, easing his grip. "Believe me," she said. "This place has become unusual for me too."

CHAPTER 3

LAKE COMMANDO

Will pushed and prodded through the confused crowd, which swirled in random directions like fallen leaves caught in a whirlwind. He ventured occasional glances back at the fire truck but saw no sign of Morgan or Rowe. The evening sky was a glowing, smoky haze, but at least the winged harvester was gone. Wherever it went, it might buy him time to search the lake for Ryowyn.

When his impatience with the sluggish crowd boiled over, Will drew his gun and waved it in the air. People near him dodged and shoved, trying to get out of his way, but with dozens of people pressing in from all sides, it was nearly impossible.

"Out of my way!" Will shouted, squeezing off a desperate round into the sky. Those nearest him covered their ears and pushed away, but some stopped and stared at Will.

"It's the Owens boy," someone muttered. More eyes turned in his direction, but everyone backed away.

Will swallowed, trying to relieve the sudden tightness in his throat. The depressing loneliness that he thought had left when he'd first met Morgan and Joe now had a firm hand around his neck. He swallowed again and holstered his gun.

"It's okay," Will said, raising empty palms. "I'm not—"

Before he could finish his explanation, three Lessers scurried between the legs of a family huddled together. Will stood unblinking with his mouth agape. He had not seen these small dark creatures in the Fourwinds, but they seemed alive and well here in Cochrane. One of the Lessers flashed a mischievous grin at Will before following the others away from the crowd.

Will pulled out his gun. "Get out of here!" he shouted, chasing the ugly, twisted creatures. Because only Will could see them, people screamed and fell over one another, creating a gap for Will to follow the Lessers. "Ya! Ya!" he cried as the Lessers joined a group of six others before disappearing into a cluster of cedars.

Will spun in a quick circle. The Lessers were gone, and the crowd was still moving away from him toward the beach. Fortunately, Will was now only a few yards from where he had parked his Land Cruiser shortly after he, Morgan, and Rowe had returned from the Arden Forest.

Will threw off his cloak and jumped into the driver's seat, gasping for breath. He slammed the door shut and muffled the chaos outside. Checking the rearview mirror, and peering into the shadows outside, he sighed in relief; no one had followed. As usual, neither the Lessers nor the townspeople had any interest in him. He had just saved Cochrane from an unthinkable fate, yet people still thought him a freak. And after the incident with the gun, they might even think he was ultimately responsible for all the death and destruction.

Lines of sweat streaked his forehead. He brushed a forearm across his brow and grasped the rearview mirror, studying his face for a moment. His eyes looked weary, older, and sad. And yet, something had changed. The Fourwinds had changed him. Although his boyish features remained, now there was iron in his eyes that had replaced the persistent, anemic fear. Life had meaning and purpose again, as bleak as the present situation appeared. He focused on Ryowyn.

Will rolled down the window, started the engine, and did a quick shoulder check. He had hoped to stay with Rowe and Morgan, but he had to assume the pair would stick together and try to find Morgan's mom. Will would need to search for Ryowyn alone.

A cloud of smoke drifted in through the window as he eased the clutch out until it engaged. He coughed and wiped his eyes, jerking forward and bumping into a minivan. The steering wheel whirled in his hands. He clunked the shifter into reverse and made a tight turn and crashed into a garbage bin. The Land Cruiser rumbled over a curb and across the park lawn. Will leaned on the horn, scattering frightened pedestrians. He found a space between two parked cars barely wide enough for the Land Cruiser and raced up Eighth Street to access the other side of the lake.

As he passed Sixth Avenue, the intense heat from the rows of shops suffering some of the largest fires forced him to roll up his window. Moments later, he approached the yellow bars that formed a guardrail where the road snaked between the lake and the steep hillside. He sped past the bars and over the sidewalk, skidding to a stop a few feet from the water's edge.

Will rushed around and opened the back of the truck, trying to catch his breath. Sweaty clothes clung to his trembling body. At least the air was a bit cleaner on this side. He unloaded his scuba gear and dropped it on the grass near the water. Several vehicles raced past on the other side of the yellow bars, their tires barking on the pavement as the mad exodus continued. Will flinched each time, but no one slowed or glanced his way.

He peeled off his T-shirt and green cargo pants, then took a few quick steps into the water and dove over the sharp drop. The cool water helped to calm his frazzled nerves despite the screams that ebbed and flowed across the lake. To have any chance of success, he needed to get his breathing under control before he dove with the scuba tanks. He breathed deeply, treading water for a moment longer, focusing on the task at hand. Ryowyn's need drowned out the surrounding pandemonium.

Will returned to the grass and pulled on his wet suit. Even on a warm summer night, full gear was necessary in the cold depths of Lake Commando. He entered the water and bounced along the sandy bottom toward the drop-off. Leaning back, he dipped his head into the water before pulling the dive mask in place. He gulped a few deep breaths to relax his breathing, then placed the regulator into his mouth. The rubber button on his flashlight clicked softly and a million candlepower flared to life. Under his feet, the sandy bottom fell away and Will sunk beneath the surface. Moments later, the stillness enveloped him.

After about thirty minutes, the cold and dark seeped into his mind, arousing despair. The oxygen tanks were running low. If he failed to locate Ryowyn soon, he would need to drive to Timmins to have the tanks replenished. With his spotlight shining several feet in front of him, he expanded his grid pattern to no avail. Soon the light's battery would also fail. He had swum past three sunken cars along this section of the lake and discovered several shopping carts and more than a dozen bicycles: all familiar objects from previous dives. But no sign of Ryowyn.

Will checked the gauge. His breathing had finally calmed, but he was still using more oxygen than necessary. He allowed the gentle current to carry him. A sudden thought occurred to him like the voice of someone trying to waken him from a dream: *Turn off the light.* He clicked it off and darkness shrouded the area, reminding him of the passages beneath Queen Sidara's castle, the Waerdreath. Seconds later, a soft glow appeared in the distance.

He clicked the light back on and slowly kicked forward. Through the turbid waters, a body took shape. Flowing white hair danced in the depths around Ryowyn's slender, teal-skinned body. Her arms stretched above her head. She floated in suspended animation, but her face was strikingly restful, her delicate body relaxed. Will stopped breathing. He lowered his light, and dozens of shades of blue and green sparkled from her long tail swaying in the murky waters.

Ryowyn was clearly alive, but she didn't react when Will brought the light near her face. He clipped the flashlight to a D-ring on his shoulder strap, removed his gloves, and carefully but firmly grasped her wrists. He pulled her gently toward him, and her limp form moved with little effort. When she didn't respond, Will wrapped his arm around her waist and kicked toward the surface.

CHAPTER 4

A WEATHERED WELCOME MAT

Morgan gripped Rowe's hand and pulled him through the flow of people converging at the beach. In their eyes she saw fear, confusion, and despair. Mothers and fathers held children close. Morgan longed to stop and offer words of encouragement, but right now she had none to give. Most people provided them a wide berth, casting wary looks at Rowe's long red cloak and the dangerous swords at their sides.

Seconds later, Morgan and Rowe broke free from the worst of the crowds and quickened their pace down Fourth Street. Dozens of rooftops on Third Street were ablaze, sparking many secondary fires throughout the small town. The streetlights had all turned black, but there was enough of a fiery glow above to light their way. Morgan watched about a dozen people on the other side of the street heading to the lake.

"Why is everyone going to the lake?" Morgan wondered aloud.

Rowe coughed, choking on the spreading smoke. "They will need many hands to carry buckets for these fires."

Morgan considered explaining how people dealt with fires here, but the familiar face of a man in the group across the street stopped her in her tracks. Rowe bumped into her. The wind shifted suddenly, enveloping them in a cloud of thick smoke. Morgan squeezed her burning eyes, coughed, and breathed into her sleeve. When the smoke cleared, the man was gone.

"What is it?" Rowe asked as soon as he had taken a full breath of air.

Morgan scanned the group scurrying toward the lake. Two pickup trucks rushed past, horns blaring. "I thought I saw…"

"Saw what, Morgan?" Rowe planted his feet and grasped the hilt of his sword. "Eurynome?"

Morgan stayed his hand before he could draw his sword. She peered across the street. "No, it was…"

Rowe's face was tense. Drying blood from a cut on his cheek mixed with grime. He held his left arm tight against his ribs, and most of his breaths were short.

"No. I thought I saw Joe," she said quietly, eyes shifting from his face to those in the crowd. "But it couldn't have been him. The person I saw was too old."

"Johanissan?" Rowe asked as a man and woman brushed past them. "Are you certain?"

"The person looked like Joe, but his hair was…almost white. If you told me it was Joe's grandfather or some relative, I'd believe it. It sure looked like him."

"If Johanissan had seen my Trannalun cloak, he would have come to us."

Morgan shrugged, uncertain. She shook her head in frustration. "You're probably right; let's keep going. My house is only a few blocks away."

By the time they were approaching her house, Morgan's breath was coming in short, painful gasps. The acrid smoke stung her eyes, and tears streaked her dirty cheeks.

She led Rowe through a back alley. "That's it," she said hoarsely, pointing to a split-level brick house with steep roof lines.

Rowe barely managed a nod as his shoulders drooped and his coughing increased.

Morgan's entire street was dark. The eerie quiet was interrupted only by distant cries, honking horns, and the crackling of flames on the next street. She wondered if the whole town was now without power.

"Your world is so different," Rowe said. "Steel carriages that move without horses, homesteads made of material I have never seen before, roads covered with a smooth, hard material…."

"We've got to keep moving, Rowe." Morgan was about to rush toward the house when Rowe caught her by the shoulders and spun her to meet his somber gaze. To anyone else, he had the look of a killer, but Morgan saw weariness and urgency mingled in his eyes. He released his grip and held out his hands.

"Rowe, you're bleeding!" She grasped his wrists. "Is this from the harvester?"

"I'm fine, Morgan. Some of those creatures got the better of me when we passed through the Gateway." Despite his fragile state, his voice remained strong. He leaned closer, and the healing warmth of his cloak radiated against Morgan's cheeks. "We know little of what we might find in your house. And my strength is failing. Your mother *might* be inside, but so might Eurynome."

Morgan balled her hands into fists. The night sounds grew distant. "I know, Rowe. But I just helped destroy my father's killer, and if there's something inside threatening Mom, it will face the same fate." She grasped her sword with a trembling hand.

Rowe studied the house for a moment. "A great evil has lived here. It lingers…heartless and unmerciful."

Morgan nodded, both terrified and angry at the thought of what they might find in her family's home. If her mother was dead because of her, she wasn't sure she could recover.

"I sense it too, Rowe." Morgan shivered. She had been away from this place for so long, the sudden presence of evil caused her skin to crawl. She drew her sword, crossed the street, and strode through the overgrown lawn to the front door.

"It's locked," Morgan whispered.

"A harvester would not need to lock a door."

Morgan sheathed her sword and bent down to lift the weathered *Welcome* mat. She retrieved the spare key and turned the deadbolt with a soft clunk.

As dark as the streets were, inside the house was a shadowless tomb. Morgan drew her sword again and eased the door open, hoping her eyes would adjust to the gloom. A soft glow appeared from behind her, and for a split second she thought a fire had ignited nearby. She turned to see Rowe's sunstone in the palm of his hand, filling the room with a dim light as he stepped in behind her.

Morgan inched her way past the living room into the kitchen. The streaks of blood she had discovered last time she was home were now dark stains in the shadows. Morgan shivered and avoided them. She opened a drawer as Rowe watched her from the shadows, sword held high despite his obvious exhaustion. He followed her into the kitchen. Morgan pulled a small LED flashlight from the drawer and shone it on the blood-spattered floor at Rowe's feet.

Rowe recoiled from her bright light, dousing his sunstone as he gaped at the flashlight.

Morgan glanced at the flashlight in her trembling hand. "It's… like a sunstone," she explained.

"Shades!" Rowe whispered. "So bright. You said this place was void of magic."

Morgan hitched her right shoulder. "Science," she said. "And here's a clean rag for your cut." She tossed him a dish towel, then shone the light around the kitchen and into the living room.

Despite the open floor plan, there were plenty of places for a harvester to hide. Morgan shuddered, realizing that if Eurynome shot out from a dark place, it would be a terrible thing to fight in such close quarters. The flashlight flickered in her shaky hand, but something deep within her dared the harvester to attack. The creatures had murdered her father, and she resolved to do everything in her power to stop them from destroying more families.

An explosion from somewhere in town rattled the kitchen window. "Give me your sunstone," Rowe whispered as he took the flashlight from Morgan. "We have little time."

The flashlight revealed two closed white doors behind Morgan. Rowe took three quiet steps and opened the nearest door. Morgan's heart quickened at the sight of her mom's old Buick in the garage. Rowe quietly closed the garage door and opened the other door to the small bathroom, but there was no one there. Morgan pointed to the stairs with her sword and led the way up the plush brown carpeted steps. Rowe followed, tracing the back of his hand along the smooth drywall in the narrow stairway, shaking his head.

Morgan stumbled on the top step when she saw the spring-loaded ladder hanging from the opening to the attic. The back of her hand ached as she tightened her grip on her sword. After a quick search of the three upstairs bedrooms, they returned to the hallway at the base of the rickety attic steps.

Rowe shone the light through the attic opening, then climbed the ladder, which shifted and creaked with each step. Sword raised in front of him, he paused when he crested the dark opening. He tilted his head and looked at Morgan, bringing a forefinger to his lips. When he did, the flashlight illuminated his bleeding cheek. Sweat beaded on the tip of his nose and dripped past her to the hallway floor. Lifting the flashlight, he eased himself through the opening. He still had one foot on the top step when Morgan climbed behind him. When he didn't move, she tapped his leg.

In one smooth motion, Rowe pushed himself up. He knelt beside the opening and lowered his sword. When Morgan was through, she followed the steady beam of the flashlight.

At the far end of the attic knelt a woman holding a serrated kitchen knife. Long strands of gray-streaked auburn hair veiled her face and tight jawline as she hunched over a large gap in the floorboards. Even from a distance, the resemblance to Morgan was obvious, and the look in Rowe's wide eyes said as much.

"Mom?" Morgan whispered.

The woman stared blankly into the light, her eyes shimmering.

"Mom? Is that…really you?"

Julie Finley stared at Morgan with dark-etched eyes and flaring nostrils, a dreamlike span of time drifting between them. Her head slumped, and she blinked at the knife clenched beneath white knuckles as though seeing it for the first time. Morgan took a hesitant step forward, but Rowe stopped her.

"Wait," he whispered. "Harvester…. It might be a trap."

"Mom, it's me," Morgan said, a warm tear rolling down her cheek. "Please be you, Mom. Please."

Julie blinked, a slow recognition returning as her eyes softened. Her voice cracked when she spoke. "Mor…gan. Can it…really be you?"

"Ask her something only she would know," Rowe whispered.

Morgan cleared her throat. "I need to ask you a question, Mom."

Julie's fixed gaze was impossible to read. Rowe reached for his sword.

"Is that okay?" Morgan asked.

Julie sat motionless and unresponsive.

"How much do you love me, Mom?"

The ensuing silence was deafening.

"Please, Mom, just answer the question." Morgan tried to stifle the desperation in her voice.

Julie blinked several times.

"How much do you love me?" Morgan repeated.

Julie closed her eyes and slouched. "To the moon and back," she answered.

Morgan rushed forward. She knelt and wrapped her arms around her mother. There was a rawness to their cries, emotions swirling like ocean currents, deep and powerful.

"Where have you been, Morgan?" Julie said. "It's been weeks… I thought I lost you…"

"I'm sorry, mom. I didn't know we'd be gone so long. There's… so much to tell you, and most of it will be hard to believe."

Rowe joined them and gazed at the gap in the floor where one wide plank was missing. A smile spread across his cracked, swollen lips.

"This is where I found my sword, Rowe, lying on top of this cloth—" Morgan said.

Before she could finish, Rowe reached between the joists and pulled out a large, crisply folded swath of crimson fabric. Morgan gasped, seeing how closely the color and material matched Rowe's Trannalun cloak. He gently stroked the surface and unfolded it in a grand, sweeping gesture.

Morgan pulled away from her mother's tight embrace and stood. "I thought that was just a blanket wrapping the sword."

"I believe this belongs to you, Morgan," Rowe said. He lifted the cloak. Even before it touched her, the magical warmth reached out soothingly. "Take a deep breath," Rowe said as he draped the cloak over her shoulders.

Morgan shuddered, and a soft moan escaped her lips. The sensation reminded her of the sword's energy, but it was far less intrusive. Morgan felt safe and protected. She indulged a soft smile as her confidence swelled. The magic embraced her like Coach's hug after she had won the World Fencing Championships. The throbbing in her right calf muscle subsided and the low-grade headache from smoke inhalation faded.

For the first time since the elven healing camp, Rowe was smiling. But it didn't last long. "We need to find Will," he whispered.

Morgan helped Julie to her feet. "This is Rowe, Mom. I can't wait to tell you about him and about these cloaks, but first we need to leave. Can you walk?"

Julie's head bobbed as she gawked numbly at the two cloaked figures. Morgan took her hand and followed Rowe across the dusty floor to the attic opening. When they reached the edge, the soft whomp of the front door closing stopped Rowe midstride. A tingling chill raced down Morgan's spine.

After a hushed moment, Rowe crouched with a raspy groan and lay on his stomach. He lowered his sunstone and poked his head through the opening for a look into the hallway toward the stairs.

A moment later, he pushed himself into a sitting position. "I cannot hear or see anyone, but something is down there."

Julie's wide eyes flitted around the attic as if looking for another way of escape. Morgan felt like a caged animal, needing to hunt. With her sword poised before her, she stepped toward the opening, but Rowe held his arm out to stop her.

"You're in no shape to fight," she said, removing his hand from her arm.

"Morgan, let me—" He stopped short when their eyes met, and Morgan didn't budge. "Yes, I know. You are right."

The attic ladder creaked as the three descended, announcing their presence to who- or whatever was downstairs. With her flashlight in one hand, sword in the other, Morgan led the way downstairs to the main floor. Rowe was on her heels, limping and breathing heavily.

Morgan stopped short of taking the final few steps.

"I feel it too," Rowe whispered.

Rowe pressed a hand against his ribs and drew in a staggered breath. He winced as he descended the final steps behind her.

Morgan leaned on the narrow railing and crouched low to survey the room. As the light drifted to the front entry, they stiffened at the sight of a man standing like a statue by the closed front door.

"Joe?" Morgan said, her voice cracking.

The man's long, straight hair was charcoal black, his skin weathered. His chiseled face was expressionless, stiff and unreadable.

"Is it really you?" Morgan asked, casting a glance at Rowe.

"It is good to see you, Morgan Finley." The man spoke in Joe's familiar, rhythmic tone.

Morgan grinned and stepped forward, her arms opening wide.

The man raised his arms to accept the embrace, but Julie reached out to catch the edge of Morgan's cloak.

"Stop!" Her shrill cry brought all movement to a standstill.

"It's okay, Mom. It's Joe. We know him."

"Wait!" Julie stood on the bottom step, arms outstretched in warning. "Don't take another step, Morgan."

Rowe's eyes narrowed.

Julie glared at the man. "When they brought Joe into the emergency room, I was there, helping to put him back together. He should've been dead a hundred times, but somehow his heart kept beating. We put nine units of blood into him and dozens of stitches."

"He fought off a demon to save us, Mom," Morgan argued. "It's okay."

Julie shook her head sternly. "We had to put him into a medically-induced coma to give him a chance to survive. When I checked on him at the start of my next shift, his hair had turned white as snow and the number of wrinkles tripled. He'd somehow aged a generation in twelve hours."

The man froze, his eyes flicking from one person to the next.

Rowe inched forward. "The only way for Johanissan to keep himself alive for nearly two hundred years," he reasoned aloud, "was through magic." Rowe glanced at Morgan as his voice intensified. "After he gave his Trannalun cloak to Will, he would have had to increase the level of magic needed to keep himself alive. But without the cloak to help preserve his age—"

Before Rowe completed his train of thought, the man lunged at Morgan so fast her mother barely had time to scream. Instinctively, Morgan sprang back as a clawed hand swept a few inches from her face. Her sword came up sharply, and the severed hand thumped to the floor.

Rowe lowered his head and dove into the transforming harvester before it could recover. Eurynome caught Rowe with his remaining hand and launched him across the room. Rowe careened over the couch and smashed through a large coffee table before bowling into a rocking chair. His sword jangled across the hardwood floor, out of reach.

Eurynome sprang over the couch, but not before Morgan shot forward. Julie screamed again. Morgan's sword bit deep into Eurynome's side, sparkling with green light as the harvester's flesh sizzled.

Unfazed by the brush with the sword's deadly magic, the harvester snatched a wooden leg from the coffee table and pinned Rowe to the floor. As Morgan rushed in to attack again, Eurynome hurled the table leg, grazing her left eyebrow.

Julie lunged for her daughter as Morgan's body collapsed on the floor.

Eurynome dragged Rowe to his feet by the hair and, with a terrific grunt, picked up the Callum Sage and pitched him through the massive plate glass picture window. Rowe bounced onto the front lawn with a heavy thud. The wind exploded from his lungs. Unable to gain his feet, he barely had the wherewithal to roll over, enveloping himself in his cloak in a desperate defensive maneuver. Eurynome's sizable mass shook the ground next to him. Rowe braced himself for a pummeling, but his weakened body slackened, and everything went black.

Morgan jolted conscious, then rose to her knees before her mother found her voice.

"Easy, Morgan, you may have a concussion." Julie's voice sounded distant and muffled.

Morgan struggled to her feet and snatched her sword, staggering toward the window opening. Eurynome stopped slashing at Rowe's still, cloaked form and growled at Morgan as her feet crunched the broken glass in the flower bed beneath the window. She assumed an attack position, but a slight movement beyond the harvester caught her eye. Behind her, Julie gasped as an elderly man strolled across the lawn.

"Now *that's* Joe!" Julie cried out.

Recognition struck Morgan like a bucket of icy water. It was Joe! His hair was nearly white, but his easy smile and broad shoulders, slightly hunched now, were unmistakable. He walked slowly, leaning on a thick, shoulder-high walking stick. The fight between Joe and Eurynome in the Arden Forest, which seemed like years ago now, flashed in Morgan's memory. Joe was unable to destroy the beast at that time, so how could he dare challenge it now in his diminished state?

Eurynome whirled to face the old man. The beast roared and crouched low, its long tail almost tripping Morgan as it thrashed and scattered shards of glass from the flower bed.

Morgan opened her mouth to scream as a waft of smoke blew across the yard. "Run, Joe!" She choked out. *"Run!"*

Joe remained still. Instead of fleeing, his wrinkled face came alive in a warm, doting smile as he held Morgan's gaze.

She was aghast. Did he not see the harvester readying itself to pounce on him?

"All is as it should be," Joe said soothingly, his gentle voice somehow drowning out the threatening fires, blaring horns, and the snarling harvester.

Morgan felt paralyzed.

Eurynome took a quick jabbing step toward Joe, as if trying to gauge his reaction time. Joe never so much as twitched as his eyes nonchalantly moved from Morgan to Eurynome. The harvester's growls intensified as it clawed at the soft earth.

"A dog might look like a wolf," Joe said with a wink. "But they are not the same thing."

Eurynome was shaking but lowered several inches before springing forward. Joe bent his knees as though locking himself into the earth. As Eurynome bore down on him, Joe shifted and lunged to meet his much larger attacker. Before the harvester could react to Joe's sudden motion, Joe drove an ice-encased fist into Eurynome's throat. The creature dropped so fast it looked like its legs had disappeared. The harvester drew a short breath, and Joe slapped the palm of his other hand over Eurynome's jowls. He whispered a few words that Morgan could not discern, and a great blast of frigid air shot forth from Joe's palm into Eurynome's mouth. The creature bounced a foot off the ground before flopping in a heap.

Joe stood, looming over the quivering harvester. With a quick nod, he raised his knee and drove his foot into Eurynome's frozen chest, shattering it like a wrecking ball through the windows of a condemned building. Joe removed his foot from the harvester's lifeless remains with another satisfied nod.

The silence that followed was a great, cavernous thing. Joe's chest rose and fell. Morgan blinked unbelieving eyes. Rowe slowly rolled free of his cloak.

"Is it…really you, Joe?" Morgan asked.

Joe flashed a familiar captivating smile. "It is so good to see you again, Daughter of Nations."

CHAPTER 5

DARK WATER

Morgan steered her mother's Buick Century around the yellow guardrails near the edge of Lake Commando, hitting the curb harder than she had intended. Rowe's head bumped against the passenger-side ceiling, and in the back seat, Joe and Julie grunted as they bounced off their seats.

"Sorry, guys," she mumbled.

"Is that Will's carriage?" Rowe asked.

Morgan shut off the engine and turned to Rowe. Her stomach did a nervous flip. One of Rowe's eyes had swollen shut and the bruise on his right cheek was purple and bloody. Before she could answer, he leaned his head out the window and spat another mouthful of blood.

Morgan nodded. "Will's probably already in the water. There's nothing you can do, Rowe, so please stay in the car and rest a minute."

Julie was the first to open her door, inhaling the fresh breeze from the lake. Morgan met the anxious look in her mother's eyes. They had usually been able to share everything with each other, but

Morgan wondered how she would begin to explain where she had been for the past few weeks, and how it had changed her life. She wanted to tell her mother about the incredible journey through the Arden Forest and into another world, of Trannalun cloaks, Callum Sages, harvesters, and other strange creatures. And of the evil powers that planned to destroy the Fourwinds and bring their terrible poison into our world. But those conversations would have to come slowly. Her mother was strong, Morgan reasoned, and she had seen trauma in her life, both here and in the war-torn regions of Africa. Morgan sighed. Her mom knew what it meant to travel to a foreign place, to see new lands, new customs, new creatures… and new enemies. Maybe that would help her understand the Fourwinds better. But for now, they had to focus on finding Will and somehow get Ryowyn back to the Fourwinds.

Morgan stepped out from behind the wheel and ran around to the passenger side of the car. The healing magic of her cloak coursed through her body, energizing her. But for some reason, Rowe was not responding as well to his cloak. She flung the door open and reached beside Rowe's seat and pushed the seat-back lever. Rowe flinched as his seat tipped back.

"It could take Will a couple hours to find Ryowyn," she said. "So, please, Rowe, just lay back and close your eyes." She placed her hand against his left cheek, wiped a drop of blood from the corner of his swollen lips with her thumb, and offered a tender kiss to his forehead.

"That sounds good," he said, giving her elbow a soft squeeze.

Morgan closed the door and fell into step with Joe, who was hobbling toward Will's Land Cruiser parked near the dark shore of Lake Commando. She stopped beside him and followed his gaze across the lake.

Piercing screams from the growing crowd echoed across the water, drowning out the gentle, persistent lapping of waves. North of the beach, several yards up the steep embankment, some of the largest buildings in Cochrane were in flames, including the Swan Castle Best Western Inn across from the train station. Ash fell from the sky like late-autumn snowflakes, and a few hot coals sizzled and hissed upon the surface of the cool lake.

Joe tapped the rear window of Will's Land Cruiser and pointed at the empty scuba tank bracket. His red Trannalun cloak was stuffed behind it.

"Like an onion," Joe murmured.

"I beg your pardon?" Morgan kicked her shoes off and rolled up her pants as she searched the moonlit surface of the lake.

"Will. I didn't know he could scuba. Many layers to the boy, like an onion."

"You have no idea," Morgan said, wrapping her cloak tighter around her body.

"Tell me about your cloak," Joe said.

"Rowe found it in my attic. It was there when I first found the sword—before we went to the Fourwinds—but I thought nothing of it at the time."

Joe arched his bushy gray eyebrows.

Julie shuffled next to Joe, her lips parted in wordless awe. Her glistening eyes reflected the horrific scene in the helpless town. Morgan draped an arm across her mother's shoulders. "Actually, Mom found the cloak *and* the sword."

Over the forested ridge behind them, a helicopter suddenly dipped toward the lake, the roaring *woop-woop-woop* of the rotors causing Morgan to start.

The Buick shook as Rowe scrambled in his seat and slammed

the door open. He tumbled to the ground and Morgan was by his side in seconds. She cupped her hands over his ears to soften the roar of the helicopter as it hovered over the lake. A large red bucket dangled beneath it.

Morgan tucked his head into the crook of her neck and pressed her lips to his ear. "Easy, Rowe. It's okay. It's a helicopter. It's okay."

"Wha-what is that?"

Morgan thought a moment. "You know how Will's truck and mom's carriage can move without horses? Well, we also have carriages that can fly without wings."

Rowe sat up and leaned against Morgan as she ran her fingers through his hair. "Amazing," he said.

"That's one of Expedition's choppers with a water bucket beneath it," Morgan explained. "Watch. It will fill that bucket from the lake."

The helicopter lowered the bucket to the water, and the engine screamed to a fever pitch to generate enough lift to pull the bucket from the water. As it flew toward the burning town, a second chopper appeared over the trees with a similar bucket. Again, Morgan covered Rowe's ears as he pressed into her.

When both helicopters flew away over Cochrane, Rowe gaped at Morgan. "Was the Fourwinds this frightening to you?"

"Some of it was worse." Morgan smiled.

"I'm so sorry, Morgan. I did not understand how different your world is."

"The helicopters are loud and frightening, but they're a good sign. Devin is the guy who flies the Bambi Buckets, and he lives up on Eighteenth Avenue." Morgan looked toward town, wondering aloud. "Will's house might survive this nightmare."

"I understand now why your world has no magic," Rowe said.

"Why?" Morgan asked.

"You have no need of it."

Julie stood nearby, looking like a mother who suspects a teenager of hiding something. Morgan understood her confusion. Her first few days in the Fourwinds had been overwhelming. In the Records of Time, Morgan had the benefit of rest, Ellywick's healing potions, and Rowe's patient explanations. But there was no time for any of that now as the avalanche of events crashed into her mother's world. Even so, Morgan was amazed how strong her mother was, considering the disappearance of her husband and daughter, the deadly harvesters, swords and healing cloaks, a strange young man who appeared to have a connection with her daughter, and the miraculous, mysterious return of Inspector Joe Cheechoo.

Without a word, Julie helped Morgan guide Rowe back into the front seat of the car.

"I'm sorry, Mom. You must have so many questions."

Julie examined Rowe, evading eye contact. His cloak radiated. "We need to get him to the hospital, Morgan. He's burning up with fever."

"No, the heat is in his cloak. It's… I don't know how to explain it." She met her mother's gaze. "It's…it's magic. And it's healing him." The corner of Morgan's mouth twitched, and she released a quick, nervous laugh. It still sounded crazy, even after all she had been through in the Fourwinds, but she had to give her mother some kind of explanation.

Julie furrowed her brow. "I will not pretend to understand any of this, but I've always trusted you." She waited a moment, then looked down at Rowe. "I still think he needs medical attention."

"I imagine it must be hard for you as a trauma nurse, but I honestly think he'll be fine. He needs to sleep so he can heal."

Morgan and Julie joined Joe who was surveying the lake. "Oh, Mom, I have so much to share with you." Morgan stepped toward Julie for a hug. "Most of it's gonna sound crazy."

"Whenever you're ready to tell your story, I'll listen. But I'm having trouble processing what I've heard and seen since you found me in the attic. So, maybe the stories can wait."

"Nurse Julie," Joe said in a quiet voice that resonated with kindness, "I remember you." He smiled at Morgan. "Your mother has steady hands. Great at stitching."

"You remember that?" Julie asked. "We put enough drugs in you to knock out a moose."

"You stitched up my right calf, and I think you did the cut across my shoulder here." He pointed along the top of his left shoulder.

"I can't believe you remember that," Julie said.

Joe reached out and took her hand. "Your perception of what is sane or otherwise is about to change, Julie Finley."

"Look!" Morgan exclaimed, pointing to a small cluster of bubbles on the lake.

About twenty feet out, from deep beneath the surface, a small soft glow appeared, growing larger and clearer by the second.

"There he is!" Morgan could not contain her excitement as Will broke the surface and slipped off his mask. She waded out to meet him, ignoring the goose bumps that instantly covered her limbs. "Will! Over here! You found her!"

As Will approached the shallows and found his footing, he carefully lifted Ryowyn to keep her from dragging across the rocks. "Bring my cloak," he said. "And a towel for me."

Morgan reached down beneath Will's arms for additional support as he cradled Ryowyn against his chest. Julie rushed into the water to help but stopped short and let out a startled cry at the sight of a mermaid in Will's arms.

"Pull them off," Will said as he lifted his flippers from the water.

Julie's mouth hung open as she fumbled with the flippers. Joe spread Will's Trannalun cloak over the grass, and Will and Morgan laid Ryowyn on it. In the blink of an eye, Ryowyn's tail melted away, replaced by slender, teal-skinned legs.

Joe let out a soft whistle. "Is this…a child of Ryodan Ayoust?"

Will glanced up at Joe, then turned to Morgan, blinking in disbelief.

Morgan suppressed a grin as Will gawked. "Yes, Will. It's Joe."

"It is good to see you again, Will Owens," Joe said, tossing him a towel. "It appears we have a few stories to exchange."

"And, Will," Morgan said, "this is my mom, Julie."

"Hi," Will's voice cracked. He wiped the towel across his face.

"Good to finally meet you, Will." Julie's face wore a confounded look similar to Will's, but she knelt to help wrap Ryowyn in Will's cloak. Instantly, she jerked her hands away as if touching a hot stove.

"Your cloak responds to her need as it would to yours, Will," Joe observed. "It seems she has become one with you."

Will cleared his throat and swallowed hard as he unzipped his wet suit. *"One with me?"*

"I don't know what happened to you two in the Fourwinds, and we do not have time for details now." Joe pointed to the gold chain around Will's neck. "What can you tell me about that necklace?" Joe's head tilted.

Will brought his hand to the chain and the small dewdrop-shaped pendant sparkled in the half-light. "What does this have to do with anything?"

"More than you know," Joe said thoughtfully. "When you marry a woman here, what do you present to her as you exchange vows?"

Will shrugged as he sat on the grass, drying his hair with the towel.

Joe pointed to his left ring finger. "You exchange rings," he explained like a patient grandfather. "In Ryowyn's culture, by accepting the necklace she offered you, you accepted her as your wife. If she accepted you as her life partner, that means—"

"Will saved her life at Fairbay, Joe," Morgan interrupted.

Joe scratched his jaw. "That explains the exchange of the necklace. But she is here now…" He fell silent, as if processing the implications. "Something happened to you, Will. You…you must have been close to death, and she brought you back…which is why she's.…" He fell short with a nod. "I believe I understand."

"Yes," Morgan confirmed. "Will was shot with a gnome arrow. Rowe explained to us that Ryowyn exchanged her life for Will's. But the Elf Queen said she was still alive, in a suspended state… or something like that."

"I beg your pardon?" Julie managed. "Shot with *what* kind of arrow? And did you say *Elf* Queen?"

"I am sorry, Nurse Julie," Joe said. "You have my word that, when time allows, I will answer as many of your questions as I am able."

"Speaking of Rowe," Will said, looking around the area.

"He's in the car," Morgan said, pointing to the Buick. "He's badly injured but resting."

"Well," said Julie, rising to her feet and smoothing her hands on her thighs. "I'm not sure what's going on here, or what to think about magic cloaks and mermaid necklaces, but I do know we now have two injured people needing immediate medical attention."

"We cannot take them to the hospital," Joe said. "There would be too many questions."

"And it's likely overrun by now," Julie added. "I have medical supplies at home, but the fires were so close to our house. I doubt our home will last the night."

"Will's house is farthest from the fires," Morgan said.

"Can either of you drive a stick?" Will asked, lifting Ryowyn.

Joe walked beside Will to the Land Cruiser. "I will drive that death trap of yours, but only if you can assure me that the brakes are operational."

"I'm so glad you're here, Joe." Will sniffled as he adjusted Ryowyn in his arms. "And the brakes were good enough to keep the truck out of the lake."

"Very good, then." Joe turned to Morgan. "I'll take Will and Ryowyn in the tin can, and you two take Rowe and follow us to Will's house."

CHAPTER 6
SHOWERS OF QUESTIONS

Will rode in the back seat of his Land Cruiser for the first time since he was a child. His parents always used to sit in the front seats, laughing together as his father told stories. The memory tightened in his chest like a vise; those days were gone. The pressure increased as he gazed at Ryowyn's fragile form in his arms. Joe was taking the long way to Will's house, keeping to the quietest streets to avoid heavy traffic and the threat of fires. In the dim light, Joe's eyes narrowed as he adjusted the rearview mirror.

"What is it, Joe?"

"Julie just turned left back there." Joe eased off the accelerator.

"They're probably heading home to grab what they can before they lose it all," Will said. Ryowyn was completely unresponsive to the sound of their voices. "But don't worry about them. You can't imagine the warrior Morgan's become. I pity anyone who messes with her tonight."

"And now she has a Trannalun cloak," Joe said.

"Doesn't surprise me. Mind telling me why you look like you've aged a hundred years in the last few months?"

"It required much to keep my appearance…youthful," Joe answered. "But after that go-around with Eurynome at the cabin, well, I just about had my dance card punched."

"Are you able to keep yourself the way…I mean, the age you are now?"

Joe shook his head as he turned onto Nineteenth Avenue. "We won't discuss my actual age, but from this point forward, I'll be aging like everyone else."

Will chuckled. "Well, at least now you *look* like my great-grandpa."

By the time Morgan, Julie, and Rowe arrived at Will's house, Ryowyn was settled in bed and Will was emerging from the shower. Dressed in a pair of gray track pants and a T-shirt with a faded Coca-Cola logo across the front, he joined Joe at the front door.

Morgan guided Rowe into the kitchen. His face had taken on an ashen tint. Pulling a chair away from the table, she motioned for him to sit. Large drops of blood spotted the tile floor beneath him.

"Why isn't your cloak healing you, Rowe?" Will asked, pulling a first-aid kit from a kitchen drawer.

"Believe it or not, it actually is working," Rowe moaned. "But my injuries are too extensive, and I need rest and nourishment to speed the process."

Everyone bustled around the small kitchen to help. Joe filled a large glass of water from the sink and handed it to Rowe. Morgan took the Coleman lantern that Will had lit earlier and positioned it on the floor beside Rowe's bleeding leg. Julie found clean dish-cloths in a drawer. Will opened the first-aid kit for Julie and then lit another lantern.

Kneeling beside Rowe, Julie carefully rolled up his bloodied pant leg. "I've never seen such thick work pants," she muttered.

"Yeah…they're, um, Carhartts," Will said.

Julie shot a cynical glance at him and pointed to the knife sheath sewn into one of Rowe's leather boots.

"There's no point trying to hide things, Will," Morgan said. "She's in too deep now."

"Pull the laces right out," Julie told Morgan, sliding the lamp closer. "A lot of the blood has dried already. I suspect it'll be a nasty bit of business getting his boot off before we can stitch him up." Julie dabbed a wet cloth around a deep gash, careful to avoid the exposed muscle tissue.

Morgan turned her head. "Should I run a bath for him, Mom?" Morgan asked.

"Good idea. Will, do you have a showerhead mounted on a flexible hose?"

"The shower downstairs does," Will answered.

"Good. Rowe, I'll clean and stitch this up, then I want you to rinse all the grime off the rest of your body before we give you a thorough once-over." Julie pushed aside Will's first-aid kit and pulled a suture set from her large medical bag.

"Ah," Joe said. "So that's why you stopped at your house."

Julie shrugged. "Well, he needs more than a few Band-Aids."

Morgan stood and placed a hand on Rowe's shoulder. "Can you handle a shower? A bath?"

Rowe managed a nod, but Will was doubtful. Rowe's eyes were drawn and glossy, with dark lines beneath them. The nasty bruise across his right cheek was now bleeding freely. The healing magic of his cloak was barely keeping him from failing altogether.

"You're in for a treat, mister." A wry but gentle smile formed across Morgan's lips as she helped her mom cut the thread.

Will observed the familiar, loving exchange between Morgan and her mother with mixed emotions. He smiled to see them reunited but had to suppress the memory of his recent encounter with his own mother in the fiery vision at Sidara's castle. Was that even real? Would he ever see his mother again?

Rowe coughed and wiped a trickle of blood from his mouth. "Dare I ask what you mean by a shower?"

"A long, hot bath," Morgan said. "Perhaps even better than the one at the Recovery Inn at Fairbay."

Will huffed. "Now don't set his hopes too high!"

"The Recovery Ale House and Inn." Joe had a faraway look in his eyes. "Good to know that place is still standing."

As Julie finished stitching Rowe's leg, Will fumbled through a drawer and found an extra flashlight. He grabbed a Coleman lantern and plugged his nose mockingly. "You guys reek; no more talking. C'mon, I'll show you where the bathroom is. There should be a few clean towels down there, an extra flashlight, and plenty of soap."

"Is there a bed down there?" Julie asked Will.

"Two spare bedrooms."

"Good. Get Rowe settled on a bed after his shower, and I'll come see what else might need stitches."

<hr>

Morgan set the lantern on the sink counter, instantly brightening the large downstairs bathroom. She pulled the shower curtain to the side and lifted the main lever. Water sputtered from the old faucet, and Rowe dropped his cloak onto the floor. "Ingenious," he breathed.

Morgan held her hand beneath the faucet, making slight adjustments with the tap. "Turn it this way to make it hotter, and that way to make it colder." She removed the handheld showerhead from the wall clip and the pulled the top lever. As the steaming water pattered against the smooth metal tub, Rowe's good eye widened.

"Shades!" he breathed.

"Here's a towel," Morgan said, dropping it on the toilet seat. "Try to keep the water in the tub, eh?" She fumbled through some drawers and found the flashlight Will had mentioned. "Toss your clothes outside the door and I'll do a load if the power comes back on. And I'll find us something to eat that doesn't require a stove or microwave."

Morgan hung the showerhead back on the wall, making sure Rowe understood how to remove it. As she brushed past him, he caught her wrist. She had been trying to avoid his weary, bloodshot eyes, but now the flickering firelight of the small red lantern revealed the depth of his pain. Her stomach lurched and caught in her throat.

"Are you sure you're able to do this on your own, Rowe?"

He loosened his grip and held her hand. "I need…I'm not sure how…how do I stop the water?"

"Push that lever straight down when you're done, and the water will stop."

"But…how long will it flow?"

"As long as you want it to." She squeezed his hand. "I'll ask Will to find something for you to wear until your clothes are ready."

Upstairs, Morgan found Will and Joe in quiet conversation as Will started a portable camp stove. Joe had found some canned soup, a jar of salted peanuts, and some bags of dried fruit. Julie was sorting through her medical bag, but her face came alive when Morgan entered the kitchen.

"I sure missed you, kiddo."

"There's so much I want to tell you, Mom, but the smoke is giving me a headache. Will, can I use the shower up here?"

"Sure thing. It's down the hall, and to the right—not sure how much hot water will be left with Rowe showering as well. And I've got some old track pants and a T-shirt that should fit Rowe, although he might look like a flood victim."

Morgan grabbed a flashlight and the pack she'd brought from home and found her way to the main bathroom. She resisted a long shower, knowing they would need to conserve what little time and resources they had.

The aroma of chicken noodle soup cooking over the camp stove and the murmur of casual conversation greeted her return. The comforting smells and sounds were the perfect complements to her favorite light-blue cotton shorts and simple white T-shirt. Morgan couldn't help but smile.

"That was incredible!" she said, wringing her hair with the towel. "I sure missed hot showers in the Fourwinds."

"I can still hear the shower downstairs," Will said.

"That would be…" Julie began.

"His first hot shower. Ever," Joe finished, the creases on his face bunching up into a smile.

"I'll go check on him," Morgan offered, taking the track pants and T-shirt from Will.

When Morgan was halfway down the stairs, the shower stopped, and she called out: "Are you alive in there?"

Rowe opened the door a few inches. Morgan eased it open a

bit more and stood outside. Steam billowed from the room. "It's just me," she said. Inside, the lantern glowed like a beacon in the fog, and she slipped into the room.

A large green towel covered Rowe from his waist to his ankles. He shook his head to clear the wet hair from his face, spraying water against the vanity mirror. Morgan laid the fresh clothes beside the sink, aware of his gaze on her every movement. Pretending not to notice his expression, she produced a new toothbrush and some Crest toothpaste.

"How did that feel?" she asked, pulling the shower curtain all the way closed as her mother had taught her when she was young.

"If there are words, I am unaware of their existence." His warm tone wrapped around her like a comforting blanket, and she turned to catch his eyes flicking upward to meet hers.

Morgan flashed a smile and tucked a strand of hair behind her ear as she stepped close to him. Rowe leaned back, bracing himself on the sink counter with both hands behind him. Morgan traced a dark bruise on his ribs with her fingertips. She avoided touching several new scratches on his toned abs. Rowe flinched but kept his hands on the counter. Morgan understood that he must be in pain, but she longed for him to hold her. She combed her fingers through the light tufts of hair covering his chest. His hand touched her side, and she moved closer.

Rowe dipped his head toward her face. His eyes were weary and bloodshot, but kind and inviting. Morgan lost herself for a moment in the wild sea of blue, then lowered her gaze down his cheek. She pressed her lips against the corner of his mouth, careful to avoid his cut and swollen lip. He pulled her closer, and she rested her head on his shoulder. His heart thumped in rhythm with hers. Morgan breathed deeply, hands pressed against his firm, warm back. If only this moment could last…

She brushed her cheek against his bristled jaw and whispered in his ear: "Let's get you stitched up so you can sleep."

Will sat on the edge of his bed, holding Ryowyn's hand as he watched Julie, hoping she might have something helpful in her medical bag.

"She's so beautiful," Morgan said, keeping the lantern steady.

"I don't understand what you mean by the cloak responding to her need," Julie whispered.

Wrapped tightly in Will's cloak, Ryowyn lay motionless on his bed, her long, exotic white hair spread like a fine veil over the pillow. There was no need to whisper, Will thought: Ryowyn was in a deep sleep. Julie leaned in and placed a gentle finger on her neck in search of a pulse.

"She has no pulse, no retinal response to light, and yet there are no signs of rigor mortis." Julie turned to Joe, who sat at the foot of the bed. "Rowe said this cloak cannot help a lifeless body, but clinically speaking, Ryowyn's dead."

Joe's head bobbed thoughtfully. "Merpeople are born with an innate ability to heal. I suspect this has served her well as she drifted in the foreign waters of Lake Commando, which would have otherwise polluted her body."

Joe leaned on his walking stick and pushed himself to his feet with a low groan. "These old bones of mine." He led them back into the kitchen, lantern in one hand, walking stick in the other as he shuffled along.

"Isn't there anything we can do for her, Joe?" Will asked, almost pleading, as he sat across from Joe with his elbows on the table. "Some kind of magic, or…"

Joe eyed him as if unperturbed by Ryowyn's state. "What say you, Will Owens? What does your heart tell you?"

"We need to find a way to break the spell that binds her," Will said without hesitation. He grabbed a shaky handful of peanuts from the bowl on the table and popped a few in his mouth.

"How do you propose we do that?" Morgan asked.

Will sensed all eyes on him. He shifted uncomfortably in the wooden chair as he munched on the nuts.

"Speak freely, Will," Joe said. "Do not be concerned about how odd it might sound. We will work through the details together."

Will picked at a callous on his palm for a moment. "The Maidstone," he blurted.

"What about it?" Morgan asked.

"The way to break Ryowyn's spell is waiting in the Maidstone," Will said.

Morgan cocked her head to one side, and Will held up his hands. "I have no idea how or why I know this, but I do."

"A bold statement," Joe said.

"Was there something in that dream of yours that might help?" Morgan asked.

"You have dreamed about the Maidstone?" Joe asked, folding his hands on the table.

"Sorry, Joe. It's something I never had time to tell you about before Morgan and I landed in the Fourwinds."

Will summarized the recurring dream that had not disturbed his sleep for the past couple of weeks. "The dream always began with me falling through an icy river, then standing on a high ridge overlooking seven waterfalls. There was a tall dark tower nearby.

The dream always ended with an obscure vision of a dark horse standing next to me, in my peripheral vision."

Joe listened intently until Will finished.

"Rowe was quite sure the tower in my dream is the Maidstone," Will added. "We had hoped to go back to the seven waterfalls after our trip to the Waerdreath, but we had a change of plans when we learned that Ryowyn was trapped here in Lake Commando." Will lowered his eyes and wrung his hands. "After she saved my life."

"I agree with Rowe about the tower being the Maidstone," Joe said. "And I have a hunch about the dark horse, but that will be for you to confirm."

"I need to go to the Maidstone," Will said, placing his hands flat on the table.

Joe nodded. "Indeed. Your path seems to be leading there; dreams and dark horses and fate, as it were."

Will released a long sigh and looked up at the others, who watched him in silence.

"Too bad Bremer couldn't be here," Will said with a smirk, trying to shake the heaviness slowly settling on his spirit like falling ashes. "I really wanted to get him back for throwing me off that cliff into the Misty Gorge."

"I beg your pardon?" Julie said. Her face twisted with questions.

"Oh, Mom…the stories we have," Morgan said.

"It seems we've all been part of some unbelievable stories," Julie said. "You especially, Will. Not long ago, you were the subject of some strange rumors here in Cochrane. I remember seeing a fearful young man whenever you ventured into town. Now I understand why, but you're not the same boy people gossiped about."

"I don't know how much I've changed, but I know I'm not the same. There was a time when fear ruled my life, but now there's a… I don't know. It's kinda like that lamp there: it only lights a few feet ahead, but that's all I seem to need. I wish I could see farther out, but I can't, and that's okay."

Joe's chair creaked as he leaned back. His eyes twinkled with an appraising gaze that filled Will with confidence.

"What about your vision on the altar in the Waerdreath?" Morgan asked. "Any chance of you finishing that story?"

A helicopter flew overhead, reminding Will their time was short. "I saw her," he said. "I saw my mom in the flames with me. I… you just…well…" He trailed off, struggling for the right words.

"Did she say anything to you?" Morgan asked.

"She said a lot, but…" Will scratched the back of his neck. "You won't ever be the same if you hear what she said."

"It's up to you, Will. We're here for you either way," Morgan said.

"It is always difficult to carry a burden alone," Joe added.

Will drew more courage from Joe's compassionate eyes. "I keep remembering more and more—like a dream. Or a nightmare, I suppose."

Morgan glanced at Joe.

Will straightened in his chair. "Mom said Natas has found a way to subvert…" He turned his gaze to the large kitchen window.

"Subvert who?" Morgan asked.

"Everyone," Will answered.

"Come again?" Joe said.

Will stared out into the night sky, recalling his vision from the Waerdreath flames. "I saw an image of a wild horse being led in chains to a corral as vast as an ocean. Millions of horses had already been corralled, and there was no more fight in any of them. The hopelessness that hung over the corral was depressing." Will's voice sounded distant and dreamlike in his ears. "I wonder if the massive war effort Sidara was leading was only a distraction to keep us from recognizing the real danger. That elixir called Phyriad will mean the end. Few will be spared, regardless of race or creed."

Will waited for the impact of his words to settle upon each of them. Naming Sidara's potion aloud sounded like the word for the unwelcome emotion he saw reflected in their eyes: fear.

"Can we stop it?" Morgan asked.

Will shook his head. "I hope so, but between what my mom said and my vision, it seems bleak. If it's all true, only a remnant will remain to begin again—in the Fourwinds."

"I don't understand," Morgan said.

"It's hard to explain. But I don't think more than a few hundred people will survive what's to come. Once Phyriad is introduced into a densely populated area, it's impossible to stop the spread. Humanity will be forced to the edges of existence."

Morgan slumped in her chair. "What do we do?"

"Mom said our only hope lies in the Rainia Valley," Will said.

Joe sat quietly, his eyes fixed on Will. "I see," he said.

"See what?" Morgan asked.

"If we shore up the defenses of both the North and South Crow Gates, it's possible we could remain segregated from the rest of the Fourwinds indefinitely," Joe said.

"Can we do it in time? Before a single infected person steps foot into the valley?"

"Could we bring people here?" Julie asked.

Will shook his head slowly, staring at the floor.

"Why not?" Morgan asked.

Will shrugged.

"You have the look of a man who has said almost everything on his mind," Joe said.

"We cannot bring people here," Will said, "because something much worse is gonna happen here."

"Here? In Cochrane?" Morgan asked.

Will shook his head. "Here in the world. I don't think there will be anything left to come back to." His chair scraped the floor as he pushed away from the table and stood. "And it will happen soon. We need to get back to the Crow's Nest—for Ryowyn, and for all of us."

CHAPTER 7

Assembling

The small trading village of Ravenbell was located between the Hollowtangle and the capital city of Dwenlin Thah. The inhabitants of this unassuming town were a mixed basket of former soldiers, poor fishermen, and failed craftsmen from across the Fourwinds. Most people ended up in Ravenbell because they couldn't find work in the capital. A growing number were casualties of war. But what they lacked in skilled labor or physical strength, they made up in their ability to trade with passing visitors willing to make a deal. The best traders in Ravenbell developed a keen sense of strangers who preferred not to barter with them. Experience taught the residents to keep their noses out of military affairs or the mysteries of magic wielders. They preferred simple business transactions and strong ale.

General Raric walked through Ravenbell with a pronounced limp. He concealed his face beneath the cowl of a heavy brown traveling cloak. The people of Ravenbell knew he was not there to trade, but they were curious nonetheless. Raric paid little heed to the eyes that followed his labored steps. The cloak effectively hid his form, but not his presence. It was as if people could sense who he was, and word spread like a midsummer brushfire.

Raric's feet ached in his stiff boots and were likely bleeding again. His stomach growled, and his throat was parched. He considered stopping at the Spicy Toad Inn and Tavern, down along Market Lane, but cursed his weakness. If he stopped now, the ensuing crowds would make things difficult, and time was not his companion. So, he pressed on toward Dwenlin Thah.

As Raric approached the final few homesteads at the outskirts of town, a company of riders galloped in from the north. He lifted his hood above his eyebrows for a clearer view and was surprised to see a group of villagers nearby watching both Raric and the approaching horsemen. The lead rider caught Raric's eye, stood in the stirrups, and yanked on the reins.

"Company, halt!" The dust of the riders rose in a thin cloud around the lead rider, who sat motionless in his saddle, his lips parted.

"Twell Heno—" Raric tasted a few words on the tip of his tongue, but the rest caught in his throat. His eyes burned, and not from the dust.

"Shades!" Twell Henowing, first lieutenant of Enders Brigade gaped at his commander general. His stallion stamped and huffed. After an awkward moment, Twell raised his arm, signaling the company to form a protective perimeter. As the horses encircled Raric, Twell slid from his mount.

Like all the soldiers with him, the first lieutenant wore a heavy brown vest with the Enders Brigade's insignia of a wolf's paw print burned into the thick leather. Unlike the others, Twell was broader and stood a few inches above six feet. He adjusted his scabbard and dipped his head of gray hair, peering with fierce dark eyes into Raric's shadowy hood. Twell's hard features softened.

"You look like an old cracked dish," Raric said, his throat raspy.

"Commander General?"

A murmur arose from the curious crowd that had been following Raric through town. "The Dragon Killer has returned," someone said, but a hard glance from Twell quashed the rumor, for the moment at least.

Raric stepped toward Twell to remove any doubt as to his identity, but he had no intention of removing his hood. His gaunt face and bald head might be too much to take for the soldiers.

"With all due respect, General, you look—"

"Was it ever my body that our enemies feared?" Raric asked.

"No, sir."

"Well and good. Now if you would stop looking at me with blubbery cow eyes, perhaps we could get to the tasks at hand."

Twell straightened. "Yes, sir." He stepped forward and extended a hand in greeting.

Raric kept his leather gloves on to conceal the nail wounds. As the men clasped hands, Raric was thankful that his old friend offered little in the way of a squeeze.

"Is Enders Brigade still stationed at Dwenlin Thah?" Raric asked.

"Aye, Commander General. After Hammerclaw fell, your sister ordered a full retreat."

"Understandable. How long to assemble?"

"I have the men on a six-hour call to arms."

"Exercise the call immediately, Lieutenant, and inform First and Second Ranger Companies to expect hard travel for long days without resupply. And keep the tongues short."

"Aye, Commander General."

"Is Tonna still with us?"

"Aye, Commander General, and still riding Interrupted."

"Is that mare still as fast as she was during the Dragon War?"

"Seems to get faster as she ages, sir."

Raric's throat tightened. "Good to hear. I need Tonna sent to the Crow's Nest to deliver this message to Rowe of the Nest." Raric handed Twell a tightly bound parchment. "And he needs to leave now."

"Aye, Commander General." Twell gave a short nod before snapping orders that sent two riders galloping north. At Twell's command, another soldier dismounted from his towering black mare and offered the reins to Raric.

The horse huffed and nuzzled Raric. "Shilo," Raric whispered as he patted its shoulder. "I've missed you too, old girl."

Raric grasped the saddle horn with his right hand. With his left, he guided his foot into the stirrup. With a deep breath, he grunted and hoisted himself up in one smooth motion. Despite the excruciating jab of pain in his foot and a mild spinning sensation in his head, Raric slumped, grateful to be off his feet. Apart from his strange journey with Shaey the elven eagle rider, he had not been in a saddle for over a year.

Without another word, the entire procession closed in around their commander general as he spun Shilo around and led the way north to Dwenlin Thah.

⚜

There was blood everywhere; the room smelled of iron and earth. The exotic white satin sheets on the festooned bed were beginning to crust. Beside the bed, a small pool of bright red surrounded a toppled bucket on the seamless white marble floor. A set of bloody footprints leading from the bed to the royal bedroom's double doors suggested a hasty retreat. A second bucket lay near the foot of the bed with a tiny, partially formed arm intermixed with indiscernible matter.

Alarra of the House of Aldor, High Queen of Dwenlin Thah, lay still, her breathing shallow and labored. One leg, smeared with blood, was visible from beneath the sheet. Wet tangles of the queen's black hair fanned across the sweat-stained pillow. Brynlee Mason, the queen's governess, stood next to the bed. She had cared for the queen since infancy while her mother tended to matters bestowed upon the wife of a king.

Brynlee watched the young queen in quiet contemplation. Never had she met a woman with the lustful appetites of a man hell-bent on selfish ambition. Despite thirty years of Brynlee's patient, loving council, the queen had conspired against—and often executed—anyone who stood in her way. Her two brothers, Harroc and Raric, were the primary targets of her zeal. And now she had terminated her own bloodline. At great personal risk to his own life, the surgeon responsible had suggested that any future thought of childbearing would be misguided. Brynlee stood trembling, a failure to her life's work.

The queen's bloodshot eyes flickered opened. "What…is it?" Queen Alarra mumbled.

"Oh, child, please allow me to clean you."

"Something has happened, Brynlee. Tell me, even as I lie here in the blood of my unborn child."

Brynlee raised her misty eyes to the high ceiling and sighed. For many years, she had hoped to help birth the queen's first child. Instead, she had watched helplessly as the surgeon had reached into the queen's womb with sharp metal instruments. Still numb from the trauma, Brynlee shuddered, wondering if she would ever hope again.

Alarra propped herself up on one elbow, craning her neck toward the window. "Brynlee, what has happened?"

Brynlee averted the queen's narrowing eyes but could not ignore the sounds of excitement from the city beyond the palace.

A great sadness clouded Brynlee's heart as she looked down at her queen. "The High Council decided to wait until you were better before informing you—"

"I…will not…ask again," Alarra said.

Despite the queen's pain and the lingering effects of the tevan root, Brynlee knew she would not be able to withhold any information from her. "Your brother has returned to the capital, Your Highness."

Alarra blinked. Her face contorted into a weak sneer. "Harroc is dead," she breathed.

Brynlee shook her head. "No, ma'am. I mean Raric."

Alarra's body stiffened. She smacked her dry lips but was unable to speak.

Brynlee dipped a cloth into a basin of cool water and brought it to Alarra's lips. The queen sucked on the cloth like a babe at the breast.

"Of course he has," the queen spat. "The Dragon Killer." Her fiery eyes flicked at Brynlee. "The High Council. Summon them… at once."

Brynlee nodded but didn't move.

"I would do it myself, but…" Alarra tried to sit up but fell back against the pillow. "Curse this tevan root." She clenched her teeth. "What was…my brother's command?"

"I beg your pardon, ma'am?" Brynlee said, despite knowing what she was being asked.

Alarra scoffed. "His *beloved*?"

"You're referring to Enders Brigade, ma'am?"

Alarra nodded, eyes narrowing.

Brynlee suppressed a knowing smile. "What about Enders Brigade?"

"Have them…pulled from the curtain wall…or wherever we have them…stationed."

"But—"

"I want them all on a leash…until we bring Raric in…in chains. He needs to understand…who rules."

Brynlee bit her lip. "That will be difficult."

The queen's pale visage flushed. "Why, Brynlee?" she groaned.

"By all accounts, ma'am, your brother has just left the city with the entire Enders Brigade in tow." Brynlee turned to the open window as sunlight streamed into the room, offering her a ray of hope. "And more are heeding his call clear across the Fourwinds."

CHAPTER 8

THE BATTLE WAGON

Twenty miles southeast of Dwenlin Thah, Enders Brigade moved in a steady, unchallenged procession away from the capital city. The central command for the brigade was a large horse-drawn carriage simply referred to as the Battle Wagon. But the carriage was far from simple. Eight feet wide and twenty feet long, its sides rose five feet off the deck, with bows arching to ten feet in the center. The wagon bows were covered with two tight layers of canvas and a layer of fine chain mail capable of deflecting lances or heavy bolts fired from any range. The wheels were a foot wide, doubled up on each of the massive iron axles. The jockey box spanned the front of the wagon beneath the driver's seat, which was surrounded by short, crenellated walls to provide cover for the four men that rode up front. Narrow planks lined both sides, each strong enough to support five armed soldiers. More than a dozen quivers of bolts and arrows were strapped to both sides.

Pulled by a team of six armored draft horses, the Battle Wagon rolled along on heavy leaf springs that smoothed the ride over rougher terrain. The captain in command, clad in light plate armor, sat beside the wagoner, with lancers to either side of them. Two crossbows lay at their feet. Eight soldiers stood watchful along both side planks, the midday sun gleaming off their tall oval shields. The soldiers wore plate chest guards, banded armor on their shoulders and arms, and bowl helmets with visors open. Some held bows, arrows notched, while others carried over-under crossbows with quick-load levers. There was no shortage of lances, crossbow bolts, or arrows. The soldiers scanned the forest in silence, ready for battle.

First Dragoon Company of Enders Brigade, consisting of fifty armored cavaliers on heavy warhorses, traveled in close proximity to the Battle Wagon. Second Dragoon Company had fifty light armored cavaliers riding out as far as a mile away in highly organized patrols.

From the rolling hillside, a single messenger rode toward the Battle Wagon, accompanied by two Second Dragoon cavaliers.

"Make way!" bellowed the captain in command. He stood and raised a hand, and the messenger slowed his mare.

"Kinlan Barrett, from Second Silver Hawks, reporting from the remnant of Marauders Brigade returning from Hammerclaw."

A cavalier grasped the messenger's reins and led him through the First Dragoon ranks until they were close enough to the Battle Wagon for clear communication. The captain in command leaned with his ear next to a narrow opening behind the driver's seat. After receiving word from within the wagon, he nodded and faced the messenger.

"Number?"

"4-9-4-9-5-3," Kinlan replied.

"Father's name?"

"Orphaned at birth."

The Battle Wagon continued at the same pace while the captain waited for orders from within.

"Send him in," the captain said after a long pause.

The cavalier lead Kinlan to the back of the wagon. "Dismount and await further instructions on the landing," he said, pointing to the steps at the back of the rolling wagon.

Kinlan slid from his saddle and, in a few quick steps, was on the landing. He grasped the handrail to steady himself and met the watchful glare of the side soldier riding closest to the back. Kinlan removed his riding hat and smoothed his shoulder-length black hair with a trembling hand.

"Remove your cloak and tunic as well," came a voice from behind the heavy canvas that covered the rear entry of the wagon.

Kinlan shrugged off his riding cloak, and then his short coat, draping both neatly over his left arm. He picked at his damp chemise, which clung to his chest, and inhaled a deep, shaky breath.

"Enter," said the voice from inside.

Kinlan rubbed his sweaty palms over his riding britches. He lowered his head and stepped through a break in the canvas, eyes fixed on his feet. The glaring soldier stepped in behind him.

"Get on with it, lad," said the voice that had invited him in.

Kinlan raised his eyes, adapting from the full sun outside, and his breath caught in his throat. The room was larger than he'd expected. Detailed maps lined the inside walls of the Battle Wagon, and a complete map of the Fourwinds was inked onto the arching canvas roof. In the center of the room was a large wooden desk laden with parchment and massive leather-bound volumes. Seated behind the desk was a plump man with thick spectacles, thinning gray hair that had not seen a comb in days, and a wispy white beard. Kinlan immediately recognized the man as Chief

Secretary Elias Ward. On both sides of the desk were filing shelves with stacks of well-organized parchments. Behind Elias was a wide table covered by another map. When the two men hovering over the map looked up, Kinlan straightened, and lost his voice entirely.

"Mr. Barrett," Elias said after some silence, "we've been anxiously awaiting word from the Marauders."

Kinlan recognized one of the two men behind the table as Brigadier Arman Bayard, commander of Enders Brigade. Bayard was tall, with a chiseled look that could intimidate the most seasoned soldier. Kinlan knew who the other man was, although he didn't recognize the commander general, whom he had met three years ago during the Dragon War. Wearing a straw hat, a long-sleeved wool sweater buttoned to his neck—despite the heat within the wagon—and brown homespun pants tucked into tall leather boots, General Raric might have been mistaken for a humble farmer. But there was no mistaking his fixed and penetrating yet sympathetic gaze.

"What word do you bring, son?" Raric asked, his tone deep and commanding.

"Pardon the intrusion, Commander General," Kinlan said.

"Your timely arrival is hardly an intrusion," Raric said.

Kinlan collected his thoughts. "Marauders Brigade was in the midst of a full-scale retreat when the Dark Queen unleashed—"

"We are well aware of the unfortunate events and tragic loss at Hammerclaw," Elias interrupted.

"Yes, sir. Marauders Brigade was marching north on orders to retreat to Dwenlin Thah and was set to arrive in two days—until we heard of your return, Commander General."

"And what of your orders now?" Raric asked.

"We have halted our retreat to Dwenlin Thah and await your charge, Commander General."

Raric held his stern gaze, but his eyes glistened.

"Have the Marauders make haste to the Pine Hollow Grange," Brigadier Bayard said, tapping his knuckles on the table. "We have soldiers en route to reestablish you to full brigade strength."

"Shades," Kinlan gasped before he could stop himself, the excitement getting the better of him.

"The commander general is reforming the Marauders, and turning them into a sledgehammer," Bayard added.

"It was a terrible thing that happened at Hammerclaw, son," Raric said, returning his attention to the map before him. "But vengeance will be the business of the Marauders at the South Crow Gate. Since passing through Hammerclaw, the gnome army has split in two. The North Gnome Army is on their way to Dwenlin Thah. The South Gnome Army, made up almost entirely of bush gnomes, is traveling due east, with plans to turn north along the high mountain ridge toward the Rainia Valley and the Crow's Nest. It will be a race to shore up our defense of the South Crow Gate before they arrive. The South Gnome Army cannot be allowed to breach that valley—no matter the cost."

With that, the armored soldier behind Kinlan held open the slit in the canvas. Alive with pride and unable to find his voice, Kinlan bowed low and stepped back through the opening. On the landing, he squinted at the afternoon sun and took a deep breath that felt like his first since the slaughter at Hammerclaw. The mere thought of returning the Marauders to its former glory was more than any of his brigade had dared to hope. Kinlan could not get word to them fast enough.

Brigadier Bayard brushed a hand over his thick gray-streaked hair and adjusted the scabbard at his side. General Raric nodded to him and settled into a cushioned leather wingback chair. Bayard grimaced as he watched Raric remove his thin gloves with considerable effort. The nail wounds were scabbing over, but each time the general flexed his hands, the scabs cracked anew. His feet were probably worse, which explained why Raric took advantage of each opportunity to sit. Despite his time in the elven healing tent, the general was but a shadow of his former self. And that was only his outward appearance. Bayard also recognized the inner frailty of the one responsible for killing Scarlas, the only dragon ever killed by man.

"How did you manage to hold on to hope?" Raric asked, brushing the corner of his eye with his index finger.

"What do you mean?"

"For almost two years, you planned my return, adjusting how you would—" Raric's voice cracked and faltered. He took a cup from the table and sipped his tea. "How you would send word, and in what order you would do so, while war scattered the army throughout the kingdom. You refurbished the Battle Wagon and stockpiled arms, all while taking orders from my sister, Alarra, who you knew had handed me over to the Shadowfallen." Raric swiped at another tear.

Bayard felt no condemnation for his commander; he had seen what war could do to a man.

"Planning is my responsibility, General. As for hope, well, suffice it to say there were times when hope was a fleeting friend."

"We've already accomplished in days what I had suspected would take weeks."

"All those hours you and I spent pouring over battle plans…" Bayard smiled. "I've learned more than a few things from you."

Raric didn't return the smile.

"Still the long face?" Bayard said.

"I'm tired of feeling like an old dog that's been beaten too much."

"We both know men who have taken years to recover from a fraction of what you've had to endure." Bayard sighed as he sat on the edge of the chair next to Raric. "Yet here you are, planning a war instead of speaking with one of the healers about your injuries. Those scars," Bayard said, pointing to the exposed skin between the general's sleeve and glove, "are nothing compared to *those* scars," he finished, pointing at Raric's forehead. "Perhaps you should consider—"

"Time's being what they are, Bayard, it's quite possible we're already too late. Our way forward will be paved with unimaginable violence. Humankind will either live on, or it will not. Such are the stakes."

"I will follow you to the end, Raric. But I fail to understand why you need to rush headlong into a brawl with the Shadowfallen. The capital has been in dire need of leadership since your sister stole the crown—" Bayard winced as the words left his mouth, hoping he had not crossed a sensitive boundary.

Raric shrugged. "I understand such sentiment. But Uluk the Shadowfallen has—"

"You were betrayed by your own blood! We should be hanging your sister from a tower!"

Raric sipped his tea, unfazed by Bayard's emotional outburst. "Perhaps you are right. But for the moment, I'm in charge of this army, and Uluk commands the North Gnome Army that marches toward Dwenlin Thah." Raric flinched as he slipped off his other glove. "There's a part of me that feels like those gnomes are as much a victim as I was."

"Why would you say that?"

"I'm not so sure the gnomes are willing participants in this war—at least not the highland gnomes." Raric set his cup down and leaned forward. "Let's cut the head off the snake and see what happens, Bayard. I suspect that once the Shadowfallen is dead, the highland gnomes will lose their taste for fighting."

Bayard folded his thick arms and cocked his head. "You sound serious."

Raric nodded. "I certainly am. When you get to the heart of who the highland gnomes are, you come face-to-face with hard-working farmers."

"Maybe so," Bayard said with a frown. "But what about the bush gnomes?"

"A ruthless lot, but no one cares for them—not even their cousins. The Marauders will cut down the bush gnomes at the South Crow Gate and probably kill every last one of them. But the highland gnomes are another matter altogether."

"Do you really believe their hands are clean in this?"

"The bush gnomes have blood on their hands, no question. But I suspect most gnomes long for their farming communities as much as we long for peace. If I'm right and we manage to kill the Shadowfallen, I suspect the worst part of this war will be over."

Bayard unfolded his arms and leaned back. "You have a way of seeing things that others do not, General."

"Elias," Raric said. "How are the numbers looking?"

The chief secretary had not lowered his quill since Kinlan had left. He paused and cleared his throat. "Enders Brigade was at forty-seven hundred this morning, and I suspect we'll have a full brigade of five thousand on the morrow. We have them staging along the Mofard Flats just north of the Niasa Sea. Latest reports have the staging area for the Marauders Brigade nearing two thousand men. Adding those who fought at Hammerclaw, the numbers are promising. Promoting Twell Henowing to brigadier of the Marauders is also being met with excitement."

"Twell is an aggressive commander," Raric said, squeezing his hand into a fist. "And those who survived the battle of Hammerclaw will want revenge." Raric dabbed at some pus in his palm with a cloth. "Soon they will face the same bush gnomes that sacked Hammerclaw. Only this time, the gnome army won't have Sidara's dark magic."

"I have scribes registering men as quickly as they arrive," Elias continued. "It will not be long before your army is as organized as it once was."

"Any updates from Striker Company, Elias?" Raric asked.

"Staging near the North Crow Gates."

"They've never lost their ability to move," Bayard added. "I wish I could have been there when they heard you were reforming the Strikers."

"If all goes well, they should pass through the North Crow Gates tomorrow morning," Elias said. "But I would be more comfortable if we could hang Duke Renaldi before the Strikers set up to defend the South Crow Gate. Our men can ill afford to face trouble from both sides."

"Rowe of the Nest will kill him as surely as I will kill Uluk," Raric said.

Bayard stared at the general, wondering how he planned on killing a creature that could kill ten men at a time. Knowing that Raric still had his wits about him, he could only suspect that there was more to the plan than Raric wished to share. After all, the man had slain the Red Dragon.

"Once Rowe dispatches the duke," Raric continued, "we should have an additional four hundred soldiers from the garrison to join Striker Company at the South Crow Gate. That should be enough to hold it until the Marauders arrive." Raric leaned back and pointed to a small area on the ceiling map. "That valley is very important to us."

"And you were right about Josson," Elias said, shuffling parchments. "He withdrew his command of the Hennen Outpost and accepted the captaincy of Striker Company."

"How long before he joins them?" Raric asked.

"The parchment containing rank changes and official orders reached the staging area this afternoon, about an hour before his arrival to assume command," Elias said.

"You only get better with age, Elias," Bayard said.

"Not unlike a fine mead," Elias said, reaching for a chalice with his free hand without slowing the quill that danced across the parchment before him. "And now that Queen Alarra is withdrawing every soldier she can from the field—as you expected she would—most suppliers have signed new contracts with us. We've already started receiving food shipments at the Pine Hollow Grange, if you can imagine. And with the way you structured our supply stores, Bayard, our lines will be short and easily managed." Elias drained his chalice and reached for another parchment. "I have every smith registered on this sheet. We already have thirty-five arrow smiths, fifty weapon smiths, and fifty-two armor smiths setting up workshops as we speak."

"And what about materials supply?" Raric asked, reaching for his teacup.

"The Vanar Mines are sending us all the alloys they're producing," Elias said.

"Impressive, Elias. I wasn't sure how you were going to make that happen."

"Most of our suppliers believe in you, General. But in the end, they're merchants seizing an opportunity. Everyone suspects you will have charge over the royal coffers before long. And judging by your sister's recent negligence, she's terrified of the possibility."

"I don't think it's going to matter who controls the coffers," Raric said, slowly rising to stretch his legs.

"Why not?" Bayard asked.

Elias set down his plume and turned.

Raric shrugged. "Because it's likely we'll all be dead before any payments are due."

Bayard glanced at Elias, then back at Raric as if the general had tossed cold water in his face. But Raric was silent, gazing into his empty cup as the Battle Wagon lumbered along.

CHAPTER 9

UNWELCOME RETURN

Will stumbled from the Gateway into the Records of Time. His Trannalun cloak clung to his shoulders and draped over Ryowyn's limp form in his arms. Seeing that Joe had arrived safely in the library ahead of him, Will opened his cloak and checked Ryowyn. She appeared unharmed and slept without a hint of worry on her delicate face. A line of sweat from his drenched hair tickled his ear, and he brushed it away with his shoulder. His arms ached from fighting to keep Ryowyn safe through the Gateway. He couldn't see the threats in the darkness of that place between worlds, but many claws had tried to tear the princess of the Niasa Sea from his arms.

A sharp pain jabbed Will's left calf muscle. He turned his leg, and a small line of blood soaked through the brown fabric of his pants where an unseen creature had slashed. He limped across the floor to the same settee that Morgan had recovered on after their first journey through the Gateway. That seemed like years ago instead of weeks. He lowered Ryowyn onto the cushioned fabric and shrugged the bulging hockey bag off his back. He groaned as he massaged his throbbing shoulders and biceps, then found some gauze to wrap his leg.

In contrast, Joe appeared well rested despite the brutal journey through the Gateway. Will imagined it must have been very difficult for the aged Callum Sage, expending enough warding magic to protect the six travelers on their brief journey from Cochrane. Even so, Joe stood tall with a tight grip on his walking staff and a broad grin on his face. If not for his denim shirt and faded jeans, he would have fit in like a wizard in a high tower. Joe inhaled, as if breathing in the aroma of his grandma's fresh-baked apple pie for the first time since childhood. His eyes twinkled with delight.

"Ah, the memories, Will," Joe said. "So many decades since…" His dark eyes drifted around the great library's circular walls lined with towering, handcrafted shelves, each laden with books and parchments. A dark shadow crossed his face, erasing his smile. "I'm home, but those I left are now ghosts. And I suspect the Fourwinds will never be the same."

Rowe arrived through the Gateway with a bulky green duffle bag across his back. His slender blade dripped with blood. He had stayed close to Will and Ryowyn, protecting them from the creatures that lived in the chaos between worlds. Rowe slapped his sword into its scabbard and shifted the strap over his head so he could drop the load. He removed his Trannalun cloak with a flourish and wiped his damp forehead with his sleeve but didn't look quite as weary as Will felt. Rowe had slept for about forty-eight hours in Will's spare bedroom, wrapped in the healing power of his cloak. The light-brown color had returned to his face and his injuries were fading memories.

Morgan entered a moment later, her bloody blade outstretched and her cloak shielding Julie. Morgan heaved her large North

Face backpack from her shoulders, dropped it on the floor, and stumbled to her knees. With her left hand, she pried the fingers of her right hand from the hilt of her sword.

She gazed at Rowe as she spoke between breaths. "Such violence… Don't know what I killed in there.…"

Between Joe's warding magic and Morgan's formidable sword, Julie had fared well. She wore a distraught look, which softened as she glanced at each familiar face in the room.

Joe shuffled over to check the main door locks. "Apart from stress and fatigue, is everyone all right?"

No one spoke, but everyone nodded.

Will slumped to the floor, resting his head against the soft edge of the settee. He closed his eyes as exhaustion overtook him. After what seemed like several minutes, he jerked awake. Morgan stood next to him, placing a small pillow beneath Ryowyn's head. She smiled despite the lingering trauma of their journey.

"How long was I out for?" Will asked, his voice raspy.

"A minute, maybe two." Morgan found a small green blanket and covered Ryowyn.

"Here," Will said as he unfastened the brooch at his neck. "Cover her with my cloak."

"You will need that," Rowe said. "And besides, she will be safe here."

"It's okay, Will. She's fine," Morgan said, patting his shoulder.

Will studied Ryowyn's tranquil, beautiful face. He wanted to argue Morgan's opinion, but he had little fight left. As his eyelids grew heavy, he noticed Joe lying on another settee several feet away, an arm draped across his eyes. His mouth opened as his breathing slowed.

"Is Joe all right?" Will whispered.

Rowe didn't seem concerned with Joe. "His power is remarkable, but his age is weighing on his endurance." He paced the room, neck stretched and head cocked as if expecting footsteps beyond the reinforced door.

Suddenly aware of the distinct possibility of danger lurking beyond the Records of Time, Will scrambled to his knees and unzipped the hockey bag. He pulled out his Remington short-barreled shotgun with a short pump below the barrel. Five bright-red shells lined the black synthetic buttstock. A clip held another seven shells opposite the ejection port.

"What are those small red objects?" Rowe asked.

"These are super magnum, double-aught buckshots, and I brought a few more," Will said, opening one of the five boxes of shells he had in the hockey bag.

"There are similarities between that weapon and the small one you carry on your hip. I assume you load those red objects—buck-shots—into the weapon like bolts in a crossbow?"

Will smiled. "Imagine the choice between throwing a rock at someone and firing a heavy crossbow at close range. That's the difference between the power of my handgun and this shotgun."

Rowe's eyebrows arched. "How is such a thing possible? I've seen what that handgun has done to men and harvesters."

"This shotgun will cut an armored soldier in half, and let's just say I wouldn't want to be the unlucky guy standing behind him," Will said. "The problem is, I only have five shots before I have to reload."

"How long does that take?"

Will placed five shells on the floor and slid four into the tube before pushing one in the barrel.

"That was not long," Rowe said, shaking his head.

"And it's gonna be loud—much louder than the 1911—especially if I fire it indoors."

"Let us hope it doesn't come to that," Rowe said, watching Morgan as she wrapped a wool blanket around her mother.

Will stood. "How many soldiers will be down there?"

"I would offer much for that answer. The moment the duke discovered that I had sealed the door with warding magic, I can only imagine he shifted his attention to our eventual return. You can be sure they are expecting us." Rowe approached a tall, narrow embrasure that had an iron ladder against the wall beneath it. After he had climbed several rungs, the breeze ruffled his hair as he peered out the opening. His eyes narrowed. A moment later, he let out a low whistle and descended.

"What is it?" Morgan asked as Rowe stepped off the ladder.

"The patrols are scant on the battlements, and they are the duke's personal guard," Rowe said with a sigh. "I did not see a single member of the garrison."

"Does that mean Dench hasn't returned?" Will asked.

"Judging by the presence of the duke's guard, it's unlikely. I had hoped to have the strength of the half-orcs to help take back the Crow's Nest."

"What about your friend on the inside, the councilman?" Will asked.

"And what about the people—the workers and the refugees? What about Gloriana and Lillie?" Morgan added.

"If the duke suspected that Councilman Tranas had betrayed him, Tranas would have led as many people as possible into the safety of the caverns beneath the castle." Rowe glanced at Morgan. "Lillie and the others will be fine in the caverns, Morgan. They had enough supplies to keep them fed for months, and Tranas knows the caverns better than any of the duke's men. So, don't spend another moment worrying about them." Rowe rubbed the back of his neck. "As for us, it's best to assume we're on our own for the time being."

"Sounds like a lot of people may need our help." Julie stood in front of a tall shelf packed with leather-bound tomes that made up the Histories. She shrugged the wool blanket off her shoulder and replaced it with her large medical bag.

"Lillie's the orphan I was telling you about, Mom," Morgan explained. "And Gloriana…well, I think you'll like her."

"I can't wait to meet them." Julie sounded calm, but her face was rigid. Her breathing was slow and deep, and her wide eyes constantly flickered toward the Gateway. Despite the two days they had in Cochrane discussing and preparing for the Fourwinds, Julie looked out of her element.

"I suspect you'll have your chance soon enough," Rowe said. "But for now, we need you to care for Ryowyn."

Will knelt beside the settee and pulled the coverlet up to Ryowyn's neck. He brushed his hand across her cheek, allowing his fingers an extra moment to weave through the wonderful softness of her exotic white hair that spilled across her pillow. Leaving her in this helpless state was the furthest thing from his mind, but he sensed Rowe was eager to leave. He leaned close and kissed her eyelids, willing them to open.

"What's the plan, Rowe?" he said.

"I suspect most of the duke's personal guard are patrolling the battlements, so I do not expect to see many below. I imagine they have specific orders to report our presence to the duke the moment they discover we've returned."

"So, all we have to do is stop them from reporting to the duke and we're good," Will said, drawing deep for a feigned smile.

Rowe glanced at him and nodded, then turned to Morgan. "Can you remain here to care for your mother and Ryowyn?" He lowered his voice to a whisper. "As much as I could use your skill and your blade, you should stay with your mother. She is not ready to leave this room. Perhaps some quiet time to recount some of your experiences here would be helpful for her." He cleared this throat. "I need you to lock the door the moment we leave. Don't open it until you are certain it is us."

"I'll be ready, but why don't you take a few minutes of rest before charging headlong into Lord knows what?" Morgan asked while she and Julie walked with them to the door. "Or at least until Joe can go with you?"

Rowe unlocked the door. "Time is not our friend," he said. "Remain alert in the event that we need to make a hasty retreat. We shall return as soon as we learn what has happened in the Crow's Nest during our absence."

Rowe and Will stepped through the door into the stairwell, and Morgan replaced the locks. She leaned back against the door and released a long sigh. Smoothing her hair from her perspiring forehead, she gazed up at the lofty ceiling. Through an embrasure, a butterfly fluttered into the Records of Time. Morgan watched it glide along a massive timber spanning the length of the room twenty feet above and settle atop a bookcase. The butterfly's incredibly large wings were like stained-glass works of art: bright green with deep purple edges and symmetrical patches of yellow, ruby red, and black. Morgan could not see the butterfly's tiny eyes but sensed it was staring at her. A shiver scurried down her spine like a dozen insects and stopped when her mother touched her shoulder.

"What are you looking at, kiddo?"
Morgan pointed to the bookcase, but the butterfly was gone.

CHAPTER 10
SACKED

Rowe tightened the brooch at the neckline of his Trannalun cloak as he neared the bottom of the narrow, spiraling stairwell. He gripped the hilt of his sword and grimaced at Will.

"What did you call that weapon?" Rowe asked. "In case I need to call on you to use it."

"It's a Remington—well, let's just call it a shotgun."

"Shotgun. Got it."

On the last step, Rowe leaned forward for a glimpse into the hallway, straining his ears. It was not unusual for this hallway to be quiet, but the complete absence of sound and movement was unnerving. He had expected Duke Renaldi's personal guard to be standing by, but the place was like a deserted outpost. Staring, he noticed that the shadows seemed to be moving like a dark fog, obstructing most of the floor.

"Where is everyone?" Will whispered.

Rowe shook his head. "Something isn't right."

The moment Rowe stepped from the stairwell, a brilliant flash erupted behind them. An unseen force struck their backs like a gale wind, launching them across the hall. Rowe grunted as he careened into the far wall. Will landed against the same wall, a dozen feet from Rowe. Fortunately, their cloaks had absorbed the brunt of the collision.

Rowe leapt to his feet, sword flashing in a wide arc, watery eyes searching the low-lying shadows for their attacker. But there was none. Instead, a translucent, shimmering wall spanning the hallway cut off his access to the stairwell to the Records of Time. A second wall between him and Will also cut off Will's access to the stairwell. A rush of panic coursed through Rowe's veins as three dark forms emerged from the shadows, clustering around Will's crumpled form.

As the first attacker lunged at him, Will rolled onto his hands and knees, clawing for the shotgun that had spun away from his grip when he'd hit the wall. Unable to reach it, he stretched his leg and grasped the smaller weapon strapped to his thigh—the *nineteen-eleven*, Rowe recalled. As Will extended his leg, the attacker kicked below his knee. Through the shimmering wall, Rowe heard a gut-wrenching snap. Will hit the ground face-first, his leg at an odd angle. The attacker kicked Will's hand, and the weapon scraped across the floor into the shadows. A second attacker grabbed the edge of Will's cloak and punched his face. Blood gushed from Will's nose. Rowe shouted and slashed at the magical wall with his sword, searching in vain for a way to reach Will.

A dark form rose to attack from the swirling shadows dissipating around Rowe like a morning fog. Rowe shifted to his left, his body snapping like a steel spring, sword arching. Arms outstretched, the attacker lost both arms below the elbows. Rowe drove his right boot into the man's chest, cracking several ribs before sending him crashing to the floor. Another attacker swung a quarterstaff at Rowe's knees, but Rowe stomped on it, crushing the wielder's fingers against the floor. In one fluid motion, Rowe drove his sword deep into the dark form, recognizing the person as a slave runner.

Rowe turned to see a rope being tightened around Will's neck as another man ripped Will's Trannalun cloak from his back. Will's mouth opened wide in a silent gasp for air. His face turned red as his fingers clawed at the rope digging into his neck. The first attacker jabbed his fist into Will's cheek and thrust a black hood over his head. Vulnerable and weakening, yet still conscious, Will grappled with the hood. His attacker kicked his ribs, and Will went down hard.

As Rowe watched helplessly, an edged weapon struck his back but didn't penetrate his cloak. Rowe spun, bellowing a furious battle cry. Leading with his elbow, he caught his would-be assailant across the jaw, spraying blood and teeth. Rowe extended his arm and jabbed with his hilt, splitting his toothless attacker's forehead. Enraged, he drove his sword deep while cursing traitorous nobles, spit flying with every venom-filled word.

Rowe slashed at the magic wall again, desperate to help Will, who slumped to the floor, one hand gripping the rope that bound him. Will's captor yanked the rope, and Rowe saw Will's shoulder pop as he was jerked to his feet. This time, a grating scream burst from Will's mouth when his weight settled on his broken leg. An instant later, Will collapsed on the floor and stopped moving.

Heavy boots clomped the floor behind Rowe. He pivoted as two men sprang forward. The first caught Rowe's long knife in the back of the neck and dropped lifeless to the floor. In a smooth swish of his sword, Rowe opened the second man's chest. As he checked both men for movement, a bolt glanced off the back of Rowe's cloak. He turned to see the shooter lower his crossbow, and before the man could reload, Rowe lunged with a screaming curse and drove his sword into a gap in the archer's armor.

Rowe spun around and rushed past the moaning, bloodied bodies toward the magical wall. Three men with rusted and chipped swords, dressed in the familiar rough banded armor of slave runners, dragged Will's drooping body down the far stairway.

Two creatures stepped from the unnatural shadows between the magical walls, as if from thin air. Rowe grew light-headed as he gaped. There was powerful magic at work here, and his stomach churned as if an orc had just driven a club into his gut.

The creatures were tall and lanky, with narrow heads and flat faces. They wore dark-brown leather robes and carried long swords. One turned to look at Rowe, milky eyes blinking slowly. The creature's narrow mouth opened in an evil grimace, revealing two rows of tiny serrated teeth. Its scorpion-like tail suddenly slammed into the magic wall, startling Rowe. The smile widened as the creature brought its long, skinny tail back behind it.

"How are you called?" The guttural voice made Rowe's skin crawl. "Or perhaps a better question is: Who is in the library?" There was a short pause. "Ah, someone dear to you, I see."

Rowe flinched.

"If you tell me how you are called, Rowe of the Nest, I promise that someone will be spared."

"Why are you doing this?" Rowe asked.

The second creature turned and raised a large leather satchel. "If you tell us how you are called, I will show you what's inside."

Rowe's mind raced. They clearly knew his name, but he could not figure out what game they were playing. The creature opened the satchel a crack before turning toward the stairwell.

"Wait!" Rowe shouted.

"Who dares speak to us in this manner?"

There was a long moment of hesitation. When the creature turned once again, Rowe realized he had no choice.

"It's Rowe," he said. "Open up that bag."

"That was not so difficult, was it?" The creature opened the satchel wide and lifted it toward the translucent wall. Rowe stepped forward. Inside the satchel was a large flask filled with something so dark Rowe couldn't tell if it was a gas, a liquid, or a solid.

"This form of Phyriad will spread throughout the land beyond the Gateway like a midsummer wildfire." With each word, the voice morphed until it sounded exactly like Rowe's. Then it repeated Rowe's phrase, and Rowe suddenly understood their game. "It's Rowe," the creature said. "Open up." And with that, both creatures turned and disappeared into the stairwell.

"Stop!" Rowe pounded the shimmering wall several times as the creatures disappeared up the stairs. "No! No! No!" Rowe stumbled to one knee. For years he had fought to defend the Gateway. For years he had watched the influence of the Callum Sages dwindle. Hope had resurfaced when two gifted Callum Sages, who had also become Rowe's closest friends, had appeared. Johanissan had returned to the Fourwinds to offer his wisdom and strength. But now, in a matter of minutes, hope dangled from a frayed rope over a yawning abyss.

Terrifying images of Morgan, Julie, Johanissan, and Ryowyn being deceived and then torn apart by the harvesters—or whatever the two creatures were—flashed in his mind's eye. After killing them, the creatures would step through the Gateway and usher in a wave of mass destruction in Morgan and Will's world.

Rowe struggled to his feet. "No," he whispered. He would not go down without fighting for his friends, their homeland, and for all that was good and true in the Fourwinds.

Rowe spun on his heels and charged down the hallway. There was no breaching the magic wall, but there was still a chance he could save Will. He would need to go the long way around, but he would never give up.

Bounding off the last five steps of a sprawling stairwell, Rowe skidded against a wall as he raced through the Crow's Nest, propelling himself onward, chest heaving. A few clusters of servants slowed his pace, all of them crying out as they leapt clear of the blazing Callum Sage. Rowe hoped the slave runners were experiencing similar delays. If they left the castle with Will, they would disappear for the slave camps of the Clover Fields.

Rowe sprinted down several more stairs and through the busy hallway outside the castle kitchen, pushing aside any who stood in his path. Fortunately, he did not see a single soldier before he burst from the keep. Outside, the courtyard was empty save for the wall walks. He pulled his hood over his head and charged toward the yawning main gates, heedless of shouting soldiers.

Several arrows ricocheted off his cloak before he ducked around the gates. The slave runners must have had a good head start. They would be impossible to catch on foot, so Rowe doubled back to the main stables. He burst through the door and collided with a stableman who tumbled back into the stall he was mucking out. In front of the next stall, a slack-jawed boy stood holding the reins of a beautiful chestnut stallion. Without a word, Rowe leapt into the saddle, leaned hard on the reins, and kicked the stallion's flanks.

"Ya! Ya!" Rowe shouted as he exploded from the stables. Arrows whizzed past his covered head. Most bolts deflected off his cloak, but two struck the horse just behind the saddle. With renewed vigor, the stallion kicked up clouds of dust as its thundering hooves echoed off the courtyard walls. Rowe leaned forward in the saddle as his brave mount galloped through the main gates and down the Gauntlet at breakneck speed.

Rowe dared not raise his head as he rode through the narrow passage of the Gauntlet, but the rotten stench would not be ignored. He risked a single glimpse that revealed the blur of dead bodies—garrison soldiers—hanging from the walls. He groaned. The image of hope slipping a few inches farther into the abyss clouded his vision. He chased it from his mind and whipped the stallion's flanks.

The horse raced past the outer curtain wall and down the narrow road overlooking the Rainia Valley. Rowe eased his grip on the reins as his shoulders slumped, tears forming from more than the dry wind lashing his face. Two miles ahead, a trail of billowing dust followed four horses. Three riders hunched forward on their mounts, while the fourth horse carried a figure draped across its back.

It would take a miracle to catch them, but Rowe kicked the horse's flanks, refusing to allow the crushing weight of desperation to slow him. "C'mon, boy, dig!" Rowe shouted. "Dig!"

By the time Rowe reached the other side of Rainia Lake, the slave runners were approaching the distant wall that shored up the southern defense of the valley. Rowe hoped the gates would be closed, allowing him time to catch up. But hope disappointed once again.

The South Crow Gate was a formidable boundary between the towering cliff face of the Hillron Mountains to the west and the Misty Gorge to the east. Rowe scanned the wall walks and despaired. The gates were wide open, without a garrison soldier in sight.

Rowe kicked his horse anew, but the animal snorted and swayed. Blood flowed down its hind leg, likely from an arrow that had pierced the animal's thigh. It was amazing the horse had made it this far. After the final hundred yards to the South Crow Gate, Rowe slid from the saddle before the stallion lost its footing and collapsed to the stony ground.

Rowe bounded up the steep wooden steps and ran onto the wall walk. The battlements were deserted. He held his breath and gazed beyond the wall. Despite the nearly cloudless sky above the majestic gorge, Rowe's day digressed from depressing gloom to a raging tempest.

The view from the lofty battlements of the South Crow Gate was among the most breathtaking in the Fourwinds. The sprawling depths of the Misty Gorge, with its strange, jagged rock formations, stretched north to south. Along the section near the South Crow Gate, the gorge was three hundred yards wide and a half mile deep.

Parallel to the Misty Gorge, on the eastern border of the Rainia Valley, the peaks of the Hillron Mountains cut hard lines into a blue sky. Dark granite ledges streaked the cliff faces like fine brushstrokes in the slate-gray mountains. Between the stunning landscapes was a narrow mountain ridge that formed a natural thoroughfare to the southwest. The ridge was a key trade route that offered safe passage from the Rainia Valley to the Southlands. Well traveled and maintained, the route was usually protected by those stationed at the South Crow Gate.

The slave runners veered off the main thoroughfare and disappeared around a cleft in the rock face. Rowe wondered why they would not keep to the easier open road, but then he noticed a distant rectangular mass filling the winding thoroughfare. Still miles away, the dark shape crawled northeast. Rowe squinted in the midmorning haze, refusing to believe what he was seeing. At first, he thought the shape might be a shadow cast by the approaching storm clouds. But there was no mistaking the massive shape: it was an army. And in all likelihood, it was the army that had sacked Hammerclaw. With the South Crow Gate unoccupied, and the Crow's Nest in the hands of a duke bent on its destruction, the army would face little resistance.

Rowe dropped to his knees and cried out at the top of his lungs, hands balled into fists. He had never felt so helpless and indecisive. One dear friend was being carried off to face the horrors of the slave camps, and the other probably lay dead in the Records of Time with the others he'd sworn to protect. How many more had the duke executed or exiled? And now an enemy army approached the Crow's Nest, unchallenged. Rowe buried his face in his trembling hands and wept.

"Rowe of the Nest?" came a sudden voice.

Rowe jumped to his feet, brandishing his sword.

On the top step stood a young man with black ponytailed hair beneath a messenger's hat. His knee-length riding cloak flapped in the breeze.

"Never thought the Crow's Nest would see so many problems," the man said, raising his hands in defense. "I am Tonna, first messenger of Enders Brigade." He looked up and down the vacant wall walk. "I was told there were two Callum Sages."

"We are three, actually." Rowe sheathed his sword and rubbed his eyes with the palms of his hands. "The other one you expected to find has been captured and carried away," Rowe said, "while the other is probably dead in the Records of Time."

Tonna let out a long slow breath. "I am most sorrowful for your loss, Rowe of the Nest. These have been arduous times for many."

"It only gets worse," Rowe said, pointing to the approaching army.

Tonna glanced at the dark mass in the distance but was unruffled. "Yes, we had hoped for more time to prepare."

"You knew they were coming? That must mean—"

"Commander General Raric sends his regards, along with orders." Tonna handed him the sealed parchment from Raric. "These orders may seem difficult to fulfill, considering what has happened to Hammerclaw, and what is coming to the Rainia Valley."

The parchment quivered in Rowe's hand as he read. "What kind of gnomes are they?"

"The gnome army broke into two commands after destroying Hammerclaw. Half the army—that half—are bush gnomes. We are referring to them as the South Gnome Army. The other half—the North Gnome Army—are highland gnomes marching toward Dwenlin Thah as we speak."

"I don't like bush gnomes," Rowe said, scowling at the mass of soldiers.

"The commander general's plans are being set into motion throughout the kingdom. Your orders are to hold this wall at any cost."

"That's a heavy yoke."

"The general believes this valley is the linchpin to the war effort," Tonna said. "Please take my words with the deepest respect I can afford at the moment, Rowe of the Nest."

Rowe lowered his eyes and nodded.

"Your brother being carried off is beyond your reach, at least for the moment. As for the one you spoke of in the Records of

Time, even if luck has not completely forsaken you this day, he would not survive if that army breaches this wall."

"She," Rowe corrected.

Tonna raised his eyebrows. "My apologies. Your difficulties are not lost on me, sir, but I must return to the commander general with a full report. How many of the garrison remain at the Crow's Nest?"

Rowe was quiet, uncertain whether to laugh or cry. "They're either dead or they've deserted."

"The commander general expected four hundred."

"I do not know what happened to the rest, but at least fifty bodies hang along the Gauntlet. I assume the rest fled when the duke started the executions."

Tonna removed his hat. "Again, my sympathies."

"Any chance of reinforcements?" Rowe asked.

"Striker Company has been reinstated with some interesting additions and heavy equipment. They will arrive shortly."

"Shortly? How strong are they?"

"Two hundred."

Rowe raised his voice. "Look out there, Tonna! How many do you see?"

Tonna hung his head. "The commander general said to expect the advance force of the South Gnome Army to number twenty-five hundred."

"And on the heels of the advance force?"

Tonna swallowed. "The main force is four days out, and over twelve thousand strong—"

"Mind telling me how Striker Company—all two hundred of them—is expected to defend this stronghold?" Rowe interjected.

"The Marauders will be here within seven days, at full brigade strength."

Rowe nodded. "Seven days. So, it comes down to one giant race."

"How so?"

"If that advance force breaches this stronghold and makes it to the North Crow Gate before the Marauders arrive, all the gnomes need to do is hold it until the rest of the South Gnome Army arrives," Rowe said. "If the gnomes secure both gates, the entire Rainia Valley will be lost."

"Your assessment is correct. The commander general said you were working at drawing reinforcements for our cause?"

"I had someone trying to unite the half-orcs and barbarians in the high country of the Hillrons, but I've heard nothing."

Tonna was quiet for a moment. "Have you ever seen a Rock Pincer?"

"I beg your pardon?"

"A Rock Pincer?"

"Of course I have," Rowe said.

"Have you ever seen one after its handler has lost control of the beast?"

Rowe shook his head.

"After it has killed once, massive chains are needed to contain its fury. Even the strongest handlers have great difficulty restraining the beast. I've seen a Rock Pincer tug so hard that the iron collar sliced its neck."

Rowe scrunched his face and shrugged his shoulders. "What are you trying to say?"

"Well, sir, Striker Company just snapped its chains and they're coming with one thing in mind, and one thing only."

"I hope you're right, Tonna." Rowe gazed at the approaching

gnome army. "There is a great need for a single-minded effort in the Fourwinds. We've been torn apart by corrupt and selfish leaders for too long."

⁂

"It's Rowe. Open up."

"That was fast," Morgan said as she unlocked the door.

The moment she twisted the iron handle, the door slammed open, sending Morgan tumbling across the floor of the Records of Time. Julie screamed and leapt from the chair she had been resting on next to Ryowyn as two heinous creatures dressed in dark-brown robes walked into the room.

Morgan sprang to her feet. Her sword glowed a dull green hue and hummed in her hands, its magic vibrating down her arms and throughout her body. She established an en garde stance and glared at the creatures. One carried a large leather satchel over its shoulder, and both were brandishing swords. The creature carrying the satchel was farthest from her, close to her mother and the opening to the Gateway. Morgan squinted at the leather bag, trying to see its contents, but the creature moved it behind its back protectively. She instantly surmised that whatever was in the satchel was important and meant to pass through the Gateway. If the creatures were successful, they would likely wreak havoc in her world.

No one moved for long moments.

Morgan glanced at Joe, who was sleeping soundly, his arm draped over his eyes. "Joe!" she shouted. When he didn't respond, Morgan wondered if he was dead, because no one could sleep through this.

The creature nearest Morgan turned to square up to her, baring its teeth. It glanced back at its companion and nodded toward the Gateway before lunging at Morgan with its sword outstretched.

Morgan shuffled back a short step, her beat parry so strong it almost knocked the sword from the creature's hand.

Julie let out a short yelp as the creature with the satchel swung its sword, forcing her back against the settee Ryowyn was lying on. It raised its sword to strike again but turned back to the Gateway.

Morgan shot forward at the first creature. Its lanky body shifted, narrowly deflecting her attack. Morgan recovered instantly, lunging a second time in an effort to get in under the creature's guard. It blocked her attack and swung its long, skinny tail toward her face. The tip dripped with acid that sizzled on the floor, but Morgan severed it clean and attacked a third time.

The creature bellowed in pain and blocked Morgan's sword, but her attack had been a feint. She shifted her footing and swung her sword in a series of attacks that had the creature rushing backward as it struggled to block her assault. Fighting for position, Morgan swung a bit too wide, opening herself up to a quick counterattack. The creature's sword rushed past Morgan's, but that, too, had been a feint. When the creature's sword deflected harmlessly off her cloak, Morgan's sword whistled through the air before passing through the creature's neck with little resistance.

Before its head hit the floor, Morgan pounced toward the second creature just as its long tail pulled away from Julie, whose eyes were unnaturally wide. The stinger had struck her shoulder, narrowly missing her neck. The creature scowled at Morgan, then disappeared through the Gateway.

"Nooooooo!" Morgan screamed.

Julie drew in a harsh breath. Her eyes rolled back, and in that moment, time seemed to stop. She had been sitting protectively in front of Ryowyn, and now slumped down on top of her.

Morgan rushed to her mother's side. Julie's eyes flickered. Her breathing was coming in short gasps. Sweat beaded on her forehead. Morgan raised her hands, unsure of what to do.

Julie tried to say something, then drew in enough breath to form the words. "Seal the door…in case more demons come."

Morgan stared, paralyzed with panic as Julie's eyes closed. "Mom!"

Julie's eyes fluttered open, then closed again. "It's…" she managed. "It's gonna be okay. I just need to rest my eyes."

"But the—"

"Morgan! Go…seal the door." Julie's breathing slowed and her body went limp.

CHAPTER 11

STRIKER COMPANY ARRIVES

From the majestic vantage point on the ramparts of the South Crow Gate, Rowe observed the advancing gnome army. Beneath a backdrop of gathering storm clouds, the scene grew more ominous by the minute. Rowe estimated a few short hours before the army disappeared behind the last curve in the mountains. The final bend in the road would conceal their approaching force until they reappeared along the final one hundred yards to the South Crow Gate. Rowe had received General Raric's orders to defend the Gate, but he was conflicted.

"Tonna, can you give me a moment alone?"

"I believe my business here is finished, sir. General Raric will be expecting me with a full report. I'll let him know of your intentions to make those bush gnomes pay dearly for their trespass." Tonna paused at the top of the stairs. "And may the Fourwinds bless you…and your two friends."

When Tonna was gone, Rowe brushed the corner of his eye with the back of his hand. Loyalty to his friends—fellow Callum Sages—tugged at his heart. He longed to follow the slave runners and rescue Will from certain death in the Clover Fields. It was too late to rescue Morgan and the others in the Records of Time from the two disguised harvesters. But Tonna was right: if the gnome army breached the South Crow Gate, any effort to save his friends would be wasted.

"I'm so sorry, Will," Rowe whispered to the western horizon. He turned to face the Crow's Nest. "Morgan, I…" He trailed off as a new emotion boiled within him: an insatiable desire to kill the duke.

Rowe stomped down the stairs. As he gazed at the Crow's Nest castle in the distance, fifty riders approached from the western border of the Rainia Valley. Each rider had a packhorse in tow and maintained a gallop, despite heavy loads. When they were ten yards away, the riders slowed. Dressed in leather riding britches and matching red-and-gold military tunics, the men dismounted and immediately unpacked.

A tall, lanky man broke from the group and held out a hand to Rowe. "My name is Captain Josson of Striker Company."

"Rowe of the Nest," Rowe responded as they clasped hands.

Josson bounded up the stairs. "How long do we have, Rowe?"

"Difficult to say; they could be here by nightfall, but they appear to have stopped."

Josson whistled. "Look at that view." He leaned against a battlement, pointing. "Does the road narrow at that bend?"

"Yes," Rowe said. "The stretch around that cleft is only two wagons wide."

Josson jogged back to the north guardrail and barked orders: "We make our first stand at the closest bend! I want four wagons filled with as much hardwood as they can carry. Get them out around the bend and flip them on their sides. I need that road blocked!" His words stoked a fire under the men, sending them toward the old wagons lining the cliffs next to a group of stables and other weathered structures.

Josson tilted his head toward Rowe. "I met Tonna moments ago on the road, and he informed me that the duke is still alive." He squared to meet Rowe's eyes. "He also mentioned that you may have fallen comrades in the Records of Time?"

Rowe nodded.

"Best guess on the strength of the duke's private guard?" Josson asked.

"Less than forty."

"The commander general mentioned the bad blood between you and the duke." He squinted at Rowe. "I suppose recent events have that blood boiling."

Rowe sized up the captain. "Renaldi is responsible for what ails this valley."

"Well, we need access to the Crow's Nest to shore up our supplies and we need it now."

"Give me your fastest horse and send wagons to the Crow's Nest as soon as you can."

Josson grinned. "Planning to take on forty of the duke's private guard on your own?"

Rowe clenched his teeth and scowled at the captain.

"The commander general was right about you. Take my horse, Rowe, and good hunting."

<hr>

Will drifted in and out of consciousness, dreaming of the seven waterfalls, the Maidstone tower, and the mysterious black horse. His recurring dream always ended with the snort of the horse, but this time a real snuffling sound awakened him. He opened his left eye and realized he was draped over the saddle of a dark-brown horse. He tried to touch his throbbing right eye, but rope bound his arms to the horse. Blood trickled down the horse's legs as the animal stretched to climb a steep embankment. Will assumed it was his own blood.

As the horse climbed, it slipped on the rocky path. The sudden jarring motion popped Will's dislocated shoulder back into place. Blood and spittle sprayed from his mouth as he cried out. The pounding in his head reverberated through his naked body. His plugged nose made it difficult to breathe. Memories of his attackers in the Crow's Nest hallway flashed in his mind. The fist to his face must have broken his nose. The pain in his shoulder dissipated, but the sharp stabbing in his broken leg was excruciating. Each time the horse slipped along the path, the rope around Will's legs tugged at the broken bone, sending nauseating jolts of pain through his body when the bone slid back into place.

Will lifted his head slightly, trying to open his swollen right eye to get an idea of where he was. As he craned his neck, a heavy metal object slapped his back. His body bounced off the saddle from the impact, and for a moment he thought his back was broken. Before darkness overtook him, his foggy mind filled with images of Ryowyn in the Records of Time. He clung to the hope that Rowe had found a way back to help her and the others.

※◈◈◈☀

A half mile from the Crow's Nest, Rowe knelt in a narrow cleft at the base of a towering rock face. With the dense cover of the Epping Forest at his back, he worked his shaking hands to release a hidden latch that opened a small stone door. He stepped inside the darkness of the mountain and ignited his sunstone. As soon as the door's lock clicked behind him, he began a steady pace through the tight, jagged confines of the winding passage. The single-minded purpose with which he ran allowed him to burn up the distance. With each step, the Callum Sage struggled to control the rage brewing in his chest. He had learned to be mindful of hatred, fear, and anger, and the importance of evading their dark paths. Now, for the first time in years, the road to hatred looked irresistibly inviting.

Rowe considered alternatives to assassination, but now that Sidara was out of the picture, all the destruction and sorrow in the Fourwinds bore the duke's stench.

Sidara. Will had faced her in the Waerdreath castle, but he had been reluctant to destroy the evil queen, preferring to offer forgiveness. And where had that path lead? Was Sidara truly gone, or had she escaped? Was the Fourwinds better or worse off as a result? Surely forgiveness was the preferred path for Callum Sages. But so was protecting the innocent and vulnerable. And that duty often led to war, to death. Rowe clenched his jaw and quickened his pace. He searched his heart but found no space for forgiveness. Instead, every thumping heartbeat enlivened his rage as he ran. His throat grew parched in the stale underground air, but the deep pools of vengeance slaked his thirst.

At the end of a narrow path, Rowe slipped from the secret passage into an obscure hallway within the Crow's Nest. He rose to his full height and stretched his stiff back. The hallway was empty and silent. Rowe scrambled up a narrow flight of stairs, then turned right at the intersecting corridor. He passed only a few people, which was odd because this was normally a busy part of the castle. Hopefully the innocent masses had escaped into the caverns. Outside the largest hallway in the keep, Rowe paused beneath the high vaulted ceilings and wall tapestries. Idle chatter mingled with the faint grating and clanking of banded armor.

Rowe peeked around the corner. Four red-caped soldiers stood guard outside the duke's private chambers. Rowe ducked back. He couldn't believe his luck: the duke would typically have at least twenty of his private guard posted outside his bedroom. Renaldi must think he was either dead or had been carried off by the slave runners. But still, only four guards? They must think him dead.

Rowe shot around the corner and burst into a sprint, his cloak flapping behind him. Four twelve-foot glaives whipped around as he closed the gap. The guards stole an incredulous glance at one another, as if seeing a ghost, and Rowe understood that he'd been right about their mistaken assumption.

"Halt!" The youngest of the four guards' voice cracked as two other guards spread apart. The fourth raised his arm, preparing to pound on the massive door chamber. Rowe drew his long knife and threw it midstride. The blade struck the guard at the door beneath his arm and plunged deep, driving the soldier into the doorjamb. His body crumpled to the floor.

Shouts of rage intermingled with cries of confusion. Rowe drew his sword a heartbeat before his chest touched the nearest outstretched glaive. He dropped to his knees and leaned back, avoiding the glaive by mere inches as the guard thrust a second too late. Sliding across the polished stone floor, Rowe plunged his sword into the soldier's abdomen and leapt to his feet. As he did, the blade sliced through the soldier's backplate. Rowe thrust his shoulder into the guard's chest, throwing him back into the soldier behind him.

Another glaive swooshed toward Rowe. He parried effortlessly, the sound of clashing steel resounding in the great hallway. His momentum unhindered, Rowe seized the wooden handle of the glaive and jerked the guard sideways. In a fluid sweeping motion, Rowe's sword sliced the guard's neck as he stepped over the headless guard and faced the glaive of the only surviving challenger. Rowe lunged past the flailing glaive and drove his sword through the man's breastplate with little resistance.

Chest heaving, Rowe retrieved his dagger from the lifeless body at the foot of Renaldi's chamber door. He wiped it clean on the guard's sleeve. Ignoring the dying moans of the guards, Rowe hammered the door several times with the hilt of his sword.

"Renaldi!" Rowe bellowed, his voice cracking. "I'm going to kill you and feed your foul carcass to the crows!"

Thump! Thump! Thump!

"If there's anyone inside who doesn't want to die, open this door! *Now*!"

The only response from behind the door was the faint cry of a young woman.

Thump! Thump! Thump!

"Open this door now!" Rowe screamed, his voice shrill. He stepped back, his body shaking. "All right, then! Everyone is going to die!"

⁂

Curled up in the corner of his private chamber beside a massive armoire, Duke Renaldi sat wide-eyed, staring at the door, willing it to hold. Sprawled on the floor between the king-size four-poster bed and the door Rowe was beating on lay a naked girl in a swelling pool of her own blood, arms outstretched toward the door. The duke's dagger was lodged in her back. The young courtesan had given her body to the duke but had withheld her heart. When she responded to Rowe's demands to open the door, Renaldi made her pay for her disloyalty.

Two soldiers shifted their weight from one foot to the other, glaives pointing to the door. The pounding had stopped.

Despite the size of the palatial bedroom, Renaldi felt the walls pressing in on him. The only exits were the door and a single large window.

"Kain," Renaldi whispered to a guard. "See if there's a way we can escape through the window." He pointed to the other guard. "Rok, you stay by the door!"

Kain drifted over toward the sitting area. He opened the glass window and leaned his head out, examining all four sides. Turning to the duke, he shook his head.

"We're thirty feet up, sir. High enough to kill a man, but not with certainty." He locked the window, gripped the handle of his glaive, and joined Rok by the door.

"Rowe was supposed to be dead," Rok whispered.

"They all were," Kain hissed.

"The emissary said one sage had been carried off, and the other killed!" Renaldi's voice cracked. "You were both there when he said it!"

"What do we do?" Rok said, lowering his glaive.

"Don't you dare open that door!" Renaldi screamed.

The three men fell silent, their heavy breathing the only sound.

One quiet moment drifted into the next as the guards' trembling increased. Kain and Rok glanced back at the duke, and he tried to mask his despair with a scowl.

Renaldi crawled to the dead girl and pulled his knife from her body. The guards exchanged disgusted looks.

"He's hardly worth dying for," Rok whispered.

"I heard that!" Renaldi said.

"But Rowe gave us a chance, sir, and we stood here like defenseless scullery maids."

"It's too late now!" Renaldi shouted. "You open that door and we all die!"

"You make it sound like there's a scenario where we don't die," Rok said.

The duke pointed the bloody dagger at Rok. "Listen here, you—"

The enormous chamber window shattered inward, scattering glass shards across the room. Rowe careened through the opening, releasing a heavy swinging rope before tumbling into a roll. The three other men scattered: Kain lunged back, tripped over a footstool, and landed with a thud on the stone floor; Rok launched his glaive at Rowe and sprang for the door; and Renaldi scrambled behind the bed, clutching his dagger.

Rowe was on his feet in an instant. Kain leaned up on his elbow, reaching for his glaive, but Rowe kicked the weapon away and thrust his hand in an iron grip around the guard's throat. Eyes wide with terror, Kain slashed a dagger at the Callum Sage, but Rowe knocked it away and drove him down hard, slamming his head into the floor. Kain's eyes rolled back as blood seeped through his hair.

Rok threw the first lock open but was fumbling with the second lock when Rowe drew his sword with the conspicuous sound of steel against leather. The guard spun around and threw his hands up.

Rowe pointed his sword at the trembling guard's chest. "Forsake your cape or die!"

Rok whipped off his cape and tossed it at the duke.

Sheathing his sword, Rowe turned, his cloak sweeping in a

wide arc. He took two strides toward the duke, who crouched and quivered beside his bed.

Renaldi wept, but his pathetic state failed to temper Rowe's fury. The Callum Sage reached for the duke's collar but jerked his hand back at the sudden flash of the duke's short dagger. Rowe backhanded Renaldi's wrist, and the dagger clanged against the wall.

"This is for betraying Ellywick!" Rowe drove his fist into Renaldi's face.

The duke's head bounced off the wall, and before he could recover, Rowe's well-placed knee smashed his chin. Renaldi's mouth sagged open, leaking blood and three broken teeth. Rowe drove his knee again into Renaldi's shattered nose. The duke gasped for air and squeezed his eyes shut.

Mad with rage, Rowe clutched the duke's collar with both hands, hoisted him to his feet, and launched him across the bed. Renaldi crashed into the side table, limbs flailing. He had barely struck the floor when Rowe was upon him again. The Callum Sage rolled the duke onto his back, slapped a hand from his cowering face, and unleashed a hailstorm of punches until the once-proud face was unrecognizable. He stopped the flurry when he realized the duke's body was limp.

Rowe stood and grabbed Renaldi's ankles. He dragged his body across the broken glass and stood in the window opening. Three dozen of the duke's private guard gathered along the wall walks, staring up at him.

"Forsake your capes and report to the South Crow Gate at once!" Rowe shouted. "The gnome army is upon us!"

Although none of the seasoned soldiers responded, they showed no sign of defying his order.

Rowe grasped a handful of the duke's hair in one hand and

his collar in the other. He propped the bloodied body onto the window ledge for all to see. Renaldi croaked incoherently. Rowe shoved, and a second later the duke's body hit the courtyard with a sickening thud.

"South! Crow! Gate! *Now*!"

Rowe stood in the window opening for a few minutes until the soldiers dispersed.

"What is your name?" he said to the guard.

"Rok, sir."

"Go and rally the rest of the guard. We will need as many of you as possible to help defend the Crow's Nest."

Rowe's neck throbbed with each heartbeat as adrenaline coursed through his veins. *The duke is dead!* Hope sparked within him as his thoughts turned to Morgan and the others in the Records of Time. Maybe there was a chance....

He rushed to the door. Rok released the final lock and threw open the door. Rowe raced through the castle, determined to fan that flicker of hope into flame.

CHAPTER 12

REUNITED

Rowe ran through the castle keep, his cloak rustling behind him. The hallways were filling with people. *They're coming out of hiding,* he thought. He wanted to stop and share the news about the duke, but by the looks on their faces as they pointed at his bloodied shirt, they understood what had happened. There might be time to give them details later, but Rowe focused his thoughts on the Records of Time.

Outside the keep, Rowe didn't need to look up to know the wall walks were unguarded: red capes littered the courtyard. Smart soldiers. Better to die with honor defending the South Crow Gate than to die in shame defending a traitor to their homeland. Two brave servants loaded the duke's corpse onto a rickety trash cart as a dozen more servants stood by, staring up at the smashed window of the royal chamber. All eyes suddenly turned to the Callum Sage as he sprinted toward the West Hall.

Rowe paused at the side door, his shaking hand hovering over the iron handle. He felt the servants' eyes on him. They needed a new leader to guide them through this transition, to prepare them

≒ 119 ≒

for the threatening tides of war. But if he lingered too long, the Crow's Nest wouldn't need a leader. Without another thought, Rowe swung open the door and charged toward the legendary library above the Upper West Hall.

At the end of the hall, Rowe was relieved to find no trace of the magic walls that had cut off access to Will and the stairwell to the Records of Time. The great hallway was silent.

Near the stairs, Will's shotgun lay where it had fallen against the wall. Rowe bent to pick up the heavy weapon, holding it in an awkward yet similar way he had seen Will carry it. He wished he had learned to wield it, but it would hinder rather than help him. Still, he couldn't leave it here for someone else to find. With a slow, careful movement, Rowe shifted the shotgun to his right hand and drew his sword. If he had to confront the two creatures that he assumed were harvesters, Will's weapon would be useless, especially in his hands.

As he ascended the steps, Rowe strained his ears, but the stairwell was silent. He rounded the final bend at the top and faced a closed door. His stomach tightened. The shotgun rattled lightly in his trembling hands. He leaned the weapon against the wall and tested the door. It was locked.

The knot in his stomach rose to his throat. He fell to his knees and swallowed hard, trying to block out images of what was waiting for him behind the door. Harvesters were capable of unspeakable atrocities. Something gave way deep within the Callum Sage, and he wept desperate tears. A scream of anguish escaped his lips as sorrow commingled with rage. It was then he heard the first lock release.

A harvester would not need to lock a door, he had told Morgan back in Cochrane.

He scrambled to his feet, sword flashing in front of him. His breathing quickened as a glimmer of hope shone on the horrific images he had imagined a moment ago. The sound of the second lock releasing was like the last thunder after a storm. The iron door handle slowly turned.

"Rowe?" The familiar whisper caused his legs to quake. "Is that *really* you?"

Drawing a deep breath, Rowe blurted out the first thing that came to mind: "That first night you arrived from Cochrane, we drank elven mead when you woke in the wee hours. Your hands were shaking so badly, I had to help you with the goblet. You said you loved your mother to the moon and back—a phrase I had never heard before."

Morgan flung the door open. "It's really you," she said, tears welling in her wide eyes. She glanced at the blood spattered across his green homespun shirt.

"It's not mine," he mumbled as she threw her arms around his neck. His sword clattered on the floor as he wrapped his arms around her, scooping her off her feet. Morgan dipped her head, kissing him hard on the lips. Relief unbound the knot in his stomach.

"I knew you'd come for us," Morgan whispered, the soft warmth of her lips pressed against his ear.

Rowe lowered her to her feet and stepped back, if only a little, to soak in her dazzling smile.

The place had a strange smell about it. Rowe peered over her head and saw a creature's body and head lying against the far bookshelves. The floor was a bloodied mess.

Julie was sitting up beside Ryowyn, a pained look on her face. Her eyes flared at the sight of the blood on Rowe's shirt and hands.

"Are you sure none of that blood is yours?" she called as the couple walked into the library.

Rowe shook his head, feeling his smile dissolve. Judging by the way Julie's right shoulder hung limp and the small bloodstain on her light shirt, he realized she had been wounded.

Morgan interjected before he started with the questions. "One of them stung Mom before it slipped through the Gateway. I thought it had killed her, but it only paralyzed her for about twenty minutes."

"I'm fine, Rowe," Julie said as she stood, massaging and rotating her shoulder.

"I'm so sorry, Rowe," Morgan said. "But one got through! They sounded just like you, and when I opened the door, we went at it pretty good, but there was no way to stop both, and I thought Mom was dying and—"

"Easy, Morgan," Rowe said. "You're both alive because of you," Rowe placed a hand on her arm.

"Wait…" Morgan said, peering back at the door. "Where's Will?"

"They have him."

"Who does?" Morgan asked.

"Right after we left you, we were sacked by slave runners and—"

"How did you survive?" Morgan interjected. "Are you hurt?"

Rowe's long hair brushed from side to side as he shook his head. "I killed as many as I could, but they took Will."

Morgan and Julie groaned in unison.

"We were separated by an impenetrable magic wall," Rowe continued. "I took the long way through the castle and chased them across the valley, but they made it through the South Crow Gate before I could catch them. I wanted to pursue them, Morgan, but they fled to the safety of an approaching army of gnomes."

"Safety?" Morgan asked. "Where are they taking him?"

"I'm guessing the Clover Fields, near Hammerclaw."

"Clover Fields?" Julie asked.

"Huge slave camps were set up there after Hammerclaw was sacked," Rowe said.

Morgan stepped closer and touched his arm. "He's resilient, Rowe. We'll find him."

Julie leaned against a bookcase. "Sorry, I'm having trouble grasping all this. I don't understand what you mean by *gnomes*, but are you referring to the bush gnomes you were telling me about, Morgan?"

Morgan nodded. "I tried to explain more things about the Fourwinds to Mom while you were gone, Rowe."

Julie rubbed the back of her neck, her face contorted as if Morgan and Rowe were speaking another language. "So, they're different from *highland* gnomes, right?"

"Yes. The valley is under attack by an army of bush gnomes," Rowe explained as he picked up his sword and returned it to its scabbard. "Before we can even think of rescuing Will, we need to hold the South Crow Gate—the wall protecting the southern border. If we fail, the castle—and likely the Fourwinds—will be lost."

Julie straightened. "How long do we have to hold it for?"

"General Raric has sent the Marauders Brigade to help us, but they won't be here for seven days. Until then, we have about two hundred men to defend the wall against twenty-five hundred gnomes."

"My word," Julie breathed. "What can I do to help?"

"I see where your fire comes from," Rowe said to Morgan. He glanced around the room. "Where is Joe?"

Morgan rubbed her hands together. "I've never been so scared,

Rowe. The moment I opened the door, a big fight broke out, and Joe never moved from the couch. I thought he was dead, but he was in some kind of a trance."

"The journey through the Gateway drained him. His power has increased, but his stamina seems to have suffered. Where is he?"

"He woke about an hour ago as if he'd just enjoyed a nice Sunday-afternoon nap. But then something weird happened. After you left, a beautiful butterfly flew in from that open window. Well, this is gonna sound crazy, but the butterfly turned into a man—or part man anyway—antlers and all."

Morgan paused to catch her breath.

"Margrave." Rowe said.

"You know him?" Morgan asked.

"He's a druid. No one has seen him in years."

Morgan shared an excited look with Julie, who continued the story.

"The moment Margrave appeared, he had a short private conversation with Joe, then they left."

"Did Margrave say anything to you?" Rowe asked.

"Not at all," Julie said. "He ignored us and went to Joe. We only caught bits of the conversation, but apparently Margrave required Joe's help to perform something called a melding. Does that make any sense?" Julie exchanged a quizzical look with Morgan. "Something about Joe having the ability to freeze someone during this melding process."

"The dragon armor," Rowe whispered, raking his fingers through his hair. The two women gaped at him. "I'll explain later."

"The creature that made it through the Gateway," Rowe said. "Was it carrying anything?"

"It all happened so fast," Morgan said. "But, ya, it had a large satchel."

Rowe nodded. "There was a flask inside with a form of Phyriad that the creature said would spread through your world like a brushfire."

"Sounds like an airborne contagion," Julie said.

Rowe stared at the Gateway.

"It went through hours ago," Julie said. "It could be anywhere by now."

Rowe nodded.

"What are you saying, Mom?"

"I can tell you want to go back and try to stop that demon, Rowe, but whatever it was planning to do has probably already been done," Julie said. "People here need us, and these bags are full of medical supplies from the hospital."

"What about the duke?" Morgan asked. "He won't be too happy to see us."

"I killed him," Rowe said in a low voice.

"Oh, child," Julie said. There was genuine concern in her voice, but Rowe sensed fear as well. Morgan was studying his bloodstained shirt, nodding her understanding.

"Is there anyone else who can help us?" Morgan asked. "What about Tranas? And Dench? Or Bremer?"

Rowe stole another glance at the Gateway, then moved to the cluster of bags they had brought from Cochrane. "I never put my faith in Bremer, Morgan. He follows his own path, and I can only hope he never turns against us. I've heard nothing from Dench. As for Tranas, news will have reached the caverns by now, where I expect to find him and Gloriana caring for Lillie and the refugees." He slung one of the large bags over his shoulder. "Let's head down there before setting out to the South Crow Gate." He picked up another heavy bag, leaving Will's bag of weapons. "I wish I knew how to use those weapons."

Morgan heaved her father's old goalie bag full of medical supplies onto its back wheels and followed Rowe to the door.

Julie stood by the settee, her palm on Ryowyn's forehead.

"I can lock her in here, so she will be fine," Rowe said.

"Will I be able to come back and check on her?" Julie asked.

"Yes. If we don't lock the door from the inside, there's a way to work the locks from outside the room. I'll show you."

Rowe found Tranas helping a steady flow of people as they emerged from the main entrance to the caverns beneath the Crow's Nest. The councilman was a bear of a man with a barrel chest and the burly arms of a hardened farmer. A thick black beard covered most of his face and neck. Anywhere else, his presence would have intimidated a band of soldiers. But here, the people smiled warmly at him, offering words of gratitude as they moved in an orderly fashion out of the dank caverns. The moment Tranas met Rowe's eyes, his face wrinkled into a heartfelt smile.

"Shades, lad!" Tranas said as Rowe approached. "That really you?"

"The rumors were true," Rowe offered as they clasped hands.

Tranas frowned. "You've aged, Rowe."

"I expect we'll both be aging quickly over the next few days," Rowe said.

A child's squeal echoed through the hallway as Morgan ran to meet Lillie. Julie followed, grinning.

Tranas's smile returned. "We've kept a close eye on that little one. I can hold my own in a fight, but I wouldn't want to face Morgan if something happened to Lillie."

Rowe chuckled. "Any word from Dench?"

"Not a thing."

"How many soldiers were in the caverns with you?"

"Twenty-four."

Rowe felt his shoulders sag. "This nightmare keeps getting worse."

"We heard about the South Gnome Army and the advance force they sent. Can we hold the wall?" Tranas asked.

"We have little choice," Rowe said. "Best blow the dust off that old ax of yours."

"I'm told Illious is planning to join Striker Company at the gate."

"Interesting," Rowe said. "Well, that's good news. Perhaps he has some magic up his sleeve."

"I see a lot of your father in you, lad. There were times when he would get so low it was all I could do not to step on him." Tranas dropped a heavy hand on Rowe's shoulder. "The darkness before the dawn was like pitch for him—as it is for you. I understand this, and it pains me to see the weight you carry. But believe me, sometimes our plight was every bit as dark as this seems to be, and still he would rise." He squeezed his shoulder. "Know this: when the fighting starts, you will be a force on that wall."

Rowe drew strength from Tranas's confident gaze. "My father was fortunate to have a friend like you."

"Hmph! I was the fortunate one, lad." Tranas stepped away. "Now, if it pleases you, I have to ask Gloriana to find several maidens to go to Rainia to bring back any of the townsfolk not able to help with the war effort. After I see them off, I'll meet up with you at the South Crow Gate."

Tranas disappeared in a crowd down the hallway, and Rowe

turned to see Morgan clutching Lillie's wrists as she spun her around in circles. The hall was filled with more squeals and the rare sound of a child's laughter. As fierce as Morgan could be in a fight, she had a gift for caring for people that Rowe admired. She had only briefly befriended the orphan girl when she and Will had first arrived in the Fourwinds, but Lillie had taken to Morgan as if she were family. Rowe allowed himself a small smile as he joined them. *The warmth of light,* he thought. *Even when all seems cold and dark.*

"Aren't you a pretty little flower," Julie said as Morgan lifted Lillie into her arms.

"Lillie, this is my mother," Morgan said.

Lillie rested her head on Morgan's shoulder. "This is my muvver," she said.

CHAPTER 13

In the Absence of Hope

A crack of thunder muffled Will's agonized cry as someone jerked his legs, pulling his body from the saddle. His chest burned, raw from the constant rubbing against the old, cracked leather. His shattered and swollen nose bashed against the saddle horn as his bound body splashed to the muddy ground. Will gasped for breath, struggling to lift his head, but his elbows slipped and sank into the mud. A heavy boot pressed the back of his neck, driving his face into the muck. Will thrashed in vain until the pain became debilitating.

"Two, there were." The thick accent reminded Will of Ellywick, the first gnome he had met in the Fourwinds. This gnome, however, sounded dark and seething.

The boot lifted, and Will spat a clump of mud from his mouth as he listened.

"We tried to take the other alive, but he left us no choice," said a growly human voice.

Will turned his head for a better view, and the pouring rain washed mud from his cheek. His entire body shivered. Out of his left eye, he noticed a gnome pull his Trannalun cloak from a sack before the boot forced his head down again.

"Which one be this?" To Will, the gnome's voice was a cross between a surly pirate and a sinister version of Yoda.

The booted man coughed. "Rowe of the Nest."

"Good news this is. And where be the one called Will, and where be his cloak?"

"He fought back," the man lied. "And my men killed him. By that time, the garrison was descending on us, and we didn't have time to collect his cloak."

There was a lull in the conversation as thunder rumbled across the evening sky.

"Payment for service rendered."

A sack of coins jingled.

"Feels light."

"Contract we have, slave runner. Payment for bodies presented, or for cloaks in lieu. Only one sage have you."

"What if Rowe here attests to Will's death? He was there; he saw it clearly." The boot pressed Will's face deeper in the mud. "Didn't you, Sage?"

"Half dead he is, fool, and tell you anything he would. Of course, if return you do with the other cloak, full payment will you receive."

"Is this the payment for Rowe?"

"A gnome of my word I be. And you of yours?"

The sound of sloshy footfalls was quickly drowned by the splattering of the heavy rain. A pair of strong hands grasped Will's armpits, pulling him to his unstable feet. He was dragged several yards and then tossed onto a musty wooden floor. Rough hands untied the ropes that bound him: with his leg broken, there was no need to restrain him. Almost numb from the chill and pain, Will curled into himself, too frightened to open his eyes. He tucked his chin against his chest and sobbed, shaking uncontrollably.

Brusque, unintelligible voices swirled around him, their words garbled by booming thunder, clanking chains, and creaking leather. A whip cracked. Will's body jerked backward and then rocked back and forth. He opened his good eye and realized he was on a wagon. The steady jostling dispatched a fresh round of stabbing pains through his leg as the broken ends of his bones ground against each other.

Will drifted in and out of consciousness, unsure of how long he had slept, or if he had slept at all. He squinted his good eye in the dull light. The night had passed, but the rain continued its relentless drizzle. The slatted roof might help to keep the sun off on a good day but did little to stop the rain from seeping through. A chilly north wind whistled through the rusty metal bars that caged him.

His thoughts turned again to Ryowyn. She had sacrificed her life to save him, but he had failed to save her. Despair settled over him like a heavy, itchy blanket. His body ached. The sharp pains had subsided, which made him aware of the potential for life-threatening numbness. He had to find a way to fight the chill.

Blinking away a tear, Will scanned the small wagon. A pile of burlap sacks lay in the corner, just out of reach. Will inched his hand toward the pile, but a searing pain shot through his wrist. He groaned, forcing his arm to full extension. As the tips of his fingers brushed the soggy material, a meaty hand clasped his wrist and pulled. Will's face slammed against the bars. He opened his mouth to cry out, but his parched throat produced no sound.

"Let him be!" A stick cracked against Will's wrist and the hand that gripped him. "Not be telling you again, you filthy dog."

"Just passing time."

Will curled up and sneezed. Dried blood and yellow mucous sprayed from his broken nose. His head snapped back against the floor of the wagon. Tears burned his cheeks as he struggled to stay conscious. He was losing the battle. *I'm so sorry, Ryowyn.*

The wagon slowed to a stop. Footsteps and gruff gnome voices approached. Will closed his eyes and braced for the worst. Before he lost consciousness, someone draped a wet wool blanket over him.

CHAPTER 14
STAGING

The Mofard Flats was a patchwork of large, grassy meadows north of the Niasa Sea. A long, lazy river ran through the central fields, feeding a small, shallow lake. The Flats, as it was commonly known, had served as an effective military staging zone throughout the recorded history of the Fourwinds. Seven outpost towers established on the highest knolls protected the area; a sizable army would have ample warning in the event of an enemy attack.

Enders Brigade stationed the Battle Wagon in the middle of the central field and surrounded it with covered supply wagons. Beyond the wagons, soldiers set up tents all the way to the tree lines. A steady influx of recruits flowed into the camp. At the north end, the field narrowed and opened to another large field where more soldiers tended hundreds of horses in massive corrals. Blacksmith sheds along the outskirts of the field were operating day and night, producing everything from horseshoes to arrowheads. The war machine was coming to life.

General Raric sat with his feet on his desk, listening to the bustle of activity outside the Battle Wagon. He peeled off his wool socks and rested in his chair for a few moments of solitude. His swollen and infected feet relaxed in the cool air. The nail wounds had been scabbing well but still generated thick pus. Despite the healer's prediction that he would walk without a limp by the end of the week, Raric thought such optimism misguided. He sipped his tevan root tea to ease his pain. Would he even be standing a week from now?

Raric examined his hands, which were faring better than his feet. He scratched his beard that was coming in thick and dark, masking several scars that otherwise would shock many battle-hardened soldiers. He massaged his scalp, feeling the short stubble where barren patches had prevented growth until a few days ago. His entire body was benefitting from his new diet of fresh vegetables, eggs, and meat. The minute amount of tevan root the healer had prescribed soothed his waking hours and diminished his nightmares.

Footfalls thumped on the steps to the wagon, and resentment jabbed at Raric's heart. *Oh, to walk without constant pain like that.* He slipped his feet from the desk to the smooth floor and rubbed his knees.

"Enter," he said before the person voiced the request.

"You're looking rested, General." Brigadier Bayard strode into the room, poured himself a cup of tea, and sat on the stool across from Raric's desk. He raised his cup in salute.

"I was just thinking about First and Second Ranger Companies," Raric said, returning the salute.

"And I was just coming to report that they've successfully retaken the Stoneberg for the first time since Sidara stole the key from you. It is locked down and guarded once again."

Raric set his cup on the table and sighed. "Excellent news, Arman. Thank you."

Bayard scratched the back of his head. "I understand that closing the Stoneberg will terminate the gnome army's main supply line, but cutting off their only means of retreat makes no sense to me. I've always assumed that our best hope of coming out of this war alive was to give them reason to retreat. Now it's not so easy for them, and we don't have the numbers to defeat them."

"There are many reasons I want to keep that gate closed, Arman. But my primary concern goes deeper than cutting off Uluk's supply line or means of retreat. Those are important side benefits. My goal is to stop Sidara's plan to spread Phyriad throughout the Fourwinds."

Bayard tilted his head sideways. "You've mentioned that their army carries the deadly elixir to Dwenlin Thah. So, hasn't Phyriad already made it past the Stoneberg?"

Raric leaned forward. "Let me tell you what happened after Rowe and his friends rescued me from the Waerdreath. We all spent time in the elven healing tents, but I spent the longest. When I awoke—even though I still needed more time to heal—the only member of Rowe's group left was Bremer."

"Not surprising," Bayard said. "The rogue has a long list of crimes to atone for."

"That may be true. But Bremer told me what happened when they passed through the Stoneberg the day before they arrived to find me in Sidara's castle. While he was trying to help dozens of tortured soldiers on the west side of the wall, three strange creatures attacked. They had dragon-like features and launched a vicious assault on the dying men. Bremer killed the creatures, but not before they had slashed a few soldiers. Those soldiers began to transform into the likeness of the three creatures."

"What sort of beasts were they?"

Raric sipped his tea. "Bremer believes they were humans who had been infected with Phyriad."

"Was Bremer able to contain the spread of the disease?"

Raric narrowed his eyes. "We hope so, but we cannot know for certain. If Phyriad has spread throughout the gnome lands in the west, it will only be a matter of time before more dragon creatures reach the Stoneberg. If they do, the threat of plague will overtake that of war."

Bayard sat still, his lips parted and eyes wide.

Raric propped his elbows on the desk, rubbing his hands together. "Now, let's consider the capture of the Stoneberg from the gnome army's perspective. Despite what many people think, gnomes—especially highland gnomes—are at least as smart as we are. And they have some wise commanders. When Uluk discovers the Stoneberg is closed, he will be rattled. But more importantly, the news will unnerve the commanders of the North Gnome Army. It's the last thing they will expect. And once their food supplies begin to dwindle… Well, have you ever tried to command an army that is hungry *and* frightened?"

"I have, but not for as long as the gnome commanders have done since Hammerclaw."

Raric paused for another drink. "The use of brute strength alone is a losing proposition for us. We need to give Uluk and his commanders cause for concern. They are advancing so boldly across our lands because Uluk is unchallenged and fearless. His supply lines have been sound—until now—and my sister, the queen, has been calling for one retreat after another. So we slam the Stoneberg shut. What would *you* do if you were leading the gnome armies? How do you think those commanders will respond knowing they're cut off from their homeland?"

Bayard stared at the map on Raric's desk. "I would certainly want to investigate the Stoneberg."

"And what would you find?"

"Four hundred rangers dug into that stronghold like ticks."

Raric shifted his weight, resting against the arm of the chair. "And what would it take to root out four hundred rangers in said stronghold to reopen their way home?"

The brigadier puffed his cheeks and exhaled. "Time and a whole lot of muscle. An army of their size would eventually break through, but they would sacrifice thousands to do it."

Raric bobbed his head, leaning forward again. "Would *you* do it?"

"Not if my orders where to reach Dwenlin Thah, especially if I knew I had to punch through a full brigade with you at the helm to get there."

"And with the loss of your main supply line, what would you do?"

"I suppose I would tell the army to pillage and forage for themselves. But I would also rush our advance before the food ran out. By then the gnomes would realize the supply lines were compromised, that they would be out of food during the final siege of Dwenlin Thah, and that their way home is blocked."

Raric tapped his fist on the desk. "Exactly. No commander worth his post wants to be pressed between starvation and an iron-handed general like Uluk."

Bayard furrowed his brow. "Is their best hope to push north and use Phyriad against Dwenlin Thah?"

Raric looked into his empty cup and nodded. "Without such a powerful weapon, Uluk and his commanders know they would never be able to lay waste to our capital. The highland gnomes are not soldiers, Arman. They are farmers. I have no idea how they were coerced into war, but I believe their desire to fight is flickering."

"So why fight at all?"

Raric pointed to the map and ran a finger along lines marking the shores of the Habina Ocean. "The lands beyond the Stoneberg are dry and rocky. But there was a time—before the Stoneberg was built, and long before the bush gnomes grew in number—when the highland gnomes inhabited the rich and fertile lands farther north. My guess is that Uluk offered to return those lands to their control in exchange for military services."

"And so Uluk has been driving the highland gnomes toward Dwenlin Thah," Bayard said.

"All just pawns, I suppose," Raric said. "Which brings us to the reason you stopped by."

"Yes. In addition to the report from the Stoneberg, I've dispatched scouts to investigate the Gryton Mines, as you ordered."

"I want to know the moment they return. Something's going on along the shores of the Niasa Sea. I can't for the life of me figure out why Uluk is so interested in that mining town."

"He's taking a huge risk. Ryodan Ayoust and his mer army could wipe them out."

Raric nodded. "I agree. Any word on the Marauders Brigade?"

"They're pushing hard toward the Rainia Valley. We haven't heard from them, but it will be close. There is an advance force of twenty-five hundred bush gnomes set to arrive long before the main South Gnome Army. If that force arrives at the South Crow Gate before the Marauders, Striker Company will be alone in the defense of that wall. They will have their hands full."

Raric sucked in a sharp breath between his teeth. "They must hold that wall."

Bayard stood. "Against the advance force of twenty-five hundred bush gnomes, that will be a brutal battle." He turned to exit the wagon, but hesitated.

Raric met his gaze when he turned.

"How long have we known each other?" Bayard asked.

Raric nodded. "Been a few seasons."

"I've always held your trust, but something's changed."

"Is that so?"

"You're up to something, Raric. And the fact that you carry the burden alone is disconcerting."

Raric lowered his eyes.

"I have my suspicions," Bayard said. "But, shades, old friend, I hope you're not considering what I think you are. I know the legend of dragon armor as well as you. Even if half the tales are true, the only druid I would ever trust is yet to be born."

Raric stood and leaned against the desk. "Now that our army is mobilized, Commander, your job is to find out how the gnomes are transporting Phyriad. When you do, you must destroy it. My job is to make sure you can do yours." He turned his gaze to the ceiling map. "If Uluk destroys Dwenlin Thah, his final target will be the Crow's Nest."

"So why don't you look nervous?"

Raric returned to his chair and scanned the ceiling map again. "My mind has caused me more grief than anyone should have to bear. It's tested every relationship. It got me kicked out of the Military Academy in Dwenlin Thah three times despite being the son of a king. And it's rarely allowed me a peaceful night's sleep, or the simple pleasures of daily life. Whether alone or in a large gathering, my mind never lets up. A ruthless thing it is."

Raric reclined in his chair, lifting his infected feet off the floor. "I cannot remember a time when I was genuinely happy, Arman.

I second-guess everything I see. Some men make plans, but I am a planner. I take any problem, large or small, and consider it from every possible angle, then formulate a variety of solutions with dozens of variables. And yet, this curse is helpful in times like these. I have seen the battlefield, Arman, and it makes perfect sense. I have established a plan that takes many possibilities into account. There will be no surprises for me in this battle." He met Bayard's intense gaze. "So, to answer your question, I remain calm because I know I am doing all I can. Will it be enough for us to save Dwenlin Thah and the Fourwinds?" Raric sighed. "Time will tell."

"And if we cannot save Dwenlin Thah from Phyriad?" Bayard asked.

"We could be front-row spectators to the end of the Fourwinds," Raric said. "Should we fail, the capital will be an easy target for their forces. And so, we plan, and we initiate said plan to ensure the best possible outcome for the final leg of this war."

"My heart aches for you, old friend," Bayard said.

Raric nodded. "I appreciate your empathy, Commander, but it's time to blow the trumpet."

"And what of you?"

"There is so little of me left. The infection is spreading. The fevers are getting worse. Shades, Arman! I don't even think I could ride out with you to battle if I wanted to."

"So, what then?"

Raric shook his head as Chief Secretary Elias entered, followed by a young woman carrying clean bandages and a pail of fresh water. "I'm not quite ready to be put to pasture, Commander."

Raric winced as the young woman finished wrapping his feet. The grave look and greenish tint to her face confirmed the smell of rot that Raric had grown accustomed to. His infection was spreading, and it was only a matter of time before someone walked in to inform him that they would have to cut off both his feet to save his life.

The only sound in the Battle Wagon was the secretary's relentless writing. Elias lifted his quill and peered above his spectacles as the young healer walked past him on her way out. She moved with a gentle sway, her white robe clinging to her lithe form as she slipped through the canvas doorway.

Raric caught Elias staring and cleared his throat.

Elias raised his eyebrows and sighed. "Makes me long for my youth, General."

Raric offered a smile, a rare thing these days.

"Do you think I would've had a chance with a woman like that?" Elias spun around in his chair. "You know, back in the day?"

Raric nodded. "My father shared a few stories of your exploits."

Elias scowled. "*My* father used to curse me up and down—something about a *misspent youth*. But a night with a woman like that felt never misspent." A reminiscing smile erased his frown.

Raric forced his legs over the edge of the cot. Bright-white bandages covered both feet. "What I wouldn't do to hear my father's voice right now."

Elias grimaced. "Alas, we no longer have the benefit of such wisdom. But I say: trust your gut, General."

Raric leaned back on his elbows. "Do you think I should do it?"

"Not my place to answer."

"Dragon armor," Raric mumbled. "The things I could do."

"Let us not spin stories here," Elias said. "The best you can hope for at the moment is to survive the procedure. Beyond that, well, who's to say? It might help you lead Enders Brigade to victory. But the flip side to that shiny coin is that you destroy us all."

"I have considered both sides," Raric said.

"Even if you maintain your identity, such power would bring temptations. I suspect it would only be a short time before you went after your sister. Shades, you could end up *destroying* Dwenlin Thah rather than saving it."

Raric was unfazed by the secretary's dark scenarios; he had already explored those paths. "Melding seems an impossible thing to survive," he said.

Elias bent forward with his elbows on his knees. He folded his hands. "When you first came to me after you slew Scarlas, the Red Dragon, I visited the Crow's Nest. I sat with Rowe of the Nest for several hours discussing the Histories and the Druid Margrave. The earliest accounts of the druid date back nearly four hundred years. Rowe has met Margrave on three occasions, so his council did not come from books alone. To be clear, I did not mention you were considering dragon armor, but as surely as we sit in this Battle Wagon facing one another today, Rowe knew I wanted to learn about the melding process. And he knew *why*."

Raric swallowed, his palms suddenly sweaty. "Does *he* believe it possible?"

Elias nodded. "I suspect that Rowe believes it's possible, and that Margrave would be your best hope in this. But Rowe was concerned about what might happen if you survive the process. The will of a dragon is a powerful thing."

Raric nodded as he poured some water into his cup. "That explains why he risked so much to travel to the Waerdreath and rescue me from Sidara's spell."

"Precisely. Rowe believes that if there was ever a person who could survive the melding, it would be you. He didn't come out and say it, but he implied as much. And although he would never condone such a thing, he understood that times being what they are…"

Raric sat on the edge of the cot, rubbing his hands together.

"I knew your father a long time, Raric. And I've known you since your first breath. When you decide on a matter, the deed is done. I also understand the gravity of this decision. It is a heavy yoke you wear."

The men sat in silence until Elias returned to his work.

Raric sipped his water, alone with his thoughts. His body was failing, but the fire that burned within was blazing hot. He understood what lay ahead as much as any man could, and still his resolve was set like iron. He was left with no other choice. If the gnome army was to be stopped, killing Uluk the Shadowfallen was the best option. And no mere human could defeat such a powerful foe.

The general stood on shaky legs. "Have Shilo readied, Elias. I'm leaving."

CHAPTER 15

IN DEFENSE

The town of Rainia and the Crow's Nest castle were alive with activity. For three days, a steady line of heavy-laden supply wagons lumbered toward the South Crow Gate where soldiers and support workers rushed to prepare for the invasion. All able-bodied—and many disabled—men, women, and children offered whatever services and supplies they had. Most wagoners were too old to help with loading and unloading, but there was no lack of hands. As the wagons approached the South Crow Gate, a soldier directed them to a group of aged buildings built along the cliff face of the Hillron Mountain Range. Four barns had been cleaned out and their large doors were now open to receive stores. Two blacksmith shops billowed smoke from their stacks for the first time in a dozen years. In the adjacent woodsheds, boys and girls stacked wagonloads of hardwood. A group of elderly women from Rainia carried piles of bedding into the two-story barracks.

Morgan directed several wagons in various directions before calling over a wagon she had been waiting for, one stacked with clean linens that would be required at the wall. She walked next to the wagon and noticed her mother silently counting a row of cots beneath the wall walk.

Julie straightened and knuckled her lower back, then brushed strands of tangled hair from her face. "I think this makes the most sense," she murmured.

"Pardon me?" Morgan asked as she approached.

"Hey, kiddo—oh, you found the linens. Thank you." Julie slid an arm around Morgan and squeezed. "We'll have the injured brought down those stairs there." She released Morgan and pointed to the wide staircase leading up to the massive wall walk above them. "We'll use these cots for basic procedures, but only for those who can get right back into the fight."

"That wagon there," Morgan said, pointing to an approaching wagon about a hundred feet away, "is filled with medical supplies. I'll send it over, so take what you need, and I'll get the rest unloaded at the barracks. How are you for water? I have a wagon coming with eight barrels of clean water."

"We'll need all eight, and more if you can find some." Julie flashed a wide smile.

"What was that look about?"

"Look at you, Morgan. My goodness, you never stop amazing me. How are you able to procure all these supplies? There's hundreds of wagonloads coming and going, and you seem to know what's in each."

Morgan smiled. "I've seen you in action at the Lady Minto Hospital, Mom. I come by it honestly."

"And your idea about turning the first floor of the barracks into a hospital was genius."

"That's where my ideas end, Mom. I can't imagine how things are gonna be when the fighting starts."

"We must be ruthless about the rules, Morgan. It will be brutal, but we can only afford to treat soldiers who we know will return to the fight."

Morgan's stomach clenched like it always did before a championship fencing match. "This feels surreal."

Two young boys unloaded a table from a nearby wagon and approached Morgan with questioning looks.

"How many do you want, Mom?" Morgan asked. "And where do you want them?"

"I want two tables between each of these cots," Julie told them. She kissed Morgan's forehead. "Just keep putting one foot in front of the other, kiddo. You're amazing."

Morgan nodded as another wagon approached. "There's my load of bed frames. I'll be in the hospital," she said, running to meet the wagoner.

※

The South Crow Gate was forty-five feet high, twenty feet thick, and just over two hundred feet long. Battlements lined the south edge, protecting the wall walk, which provided ample space from which to fight. Where the wall met the sheer cliffs of the Hillron Mountains, the east tower—housing the main war room—rose another fifteen feet. A second tower was located midspan, forming the gatehouse. Besides protection for the gate controls, this tower accommodated a secondary room for planning in the heat of a siege. At the west end of the wall was a smaller watchtower built on the edge of the gorge. The end of the wall doglegged along the gorge for an additional twenty feet.

Rowe of the Nest and Councilman Tranas worked their way up the crowded steps near the gatehouse where they found Captain

Josson of Striker Company. An even stubble of graying hair covered Josson's scalp, face, and neck. His intense blue eyes measured the work around him as he barked orders. "Heave, men, heave!" Josson shouted to eight soldiers as they hoisted a large ballista to the top of the east tower. He spun around and pointed at a dozen carpenters adjusting a redesigned catapult near the gatehouse tower. "Fire another test round! We need to get a flatter trajectory!" Instead of launching projectiles in a high arc, the catapult fired them toward the midfield below with the velocity of a ballista. Josson leaned against the wall and shouted at a wagoner: "Get those weapons unloaded and up to the watchtower!" Four old men rushed to the wagon.

Josson turned to Rowe and Tranas. "Is that all the weapons you have?" he asked.

Rowe smiled. "Don't worry, Captain, there is more on the way. We've plundered the Crow's Nest of its weapon stores."

Josson flashed a grin. "And you plundered the former duke's guard, I see! Well done, Rowe."

"How are your numbers?" Tranas asked.

"We've added twenty-two soldiers from the Crow's Nest to our company," Josson said.

"More will come," Tranas offered, adjusting the bag of tools slung over his shoulder.

Josson raised an eyebrow at Tranas.

"I've sent riders into the hill country to search for Dench and the half-orcs," Rowe said as the three men walked to the south side of the wall. "But that will take time." He leaned against a battlement and scanned a flat section of rocky ground below, trying to imagine it filled with twenty-five hundred bush gnomes.

"How long before they attack?" Tranas asked.

"Bush gnomes have no patience, which may or may not be helpful," Rowe said. "But they have not advanced for the past three days; I imagine they will be well rested."

Josson nodded his agreement. "When they're ready, I suspect they'll rush their attack. If we can ward off their initial assault, they won't have the infrastructure to sustain the onslaught. Shades! Look how long their caravan is." Josson pointed at the column of gnomes snaking from the Misty Gorge to the mountain pass.

"I hope they're enjoying the view," Rowe said.

Tranas huffed. "It's the last thing they'll see in this life," he said. "Well, I've got some reinforcements to make on the gatehouse," he added, leaving Rowe and Josson.

"Is that who I think it is?" Rowe asked.

Across the wall walk, a group of soldiers stacked bundles of arrows against a wall. Near them stood an odd-looking man wearing a soot-smudged yellow traveling cloak and baggy brown trousers tucked into knee-high leather boots. A single gray streak parted his coal-black hair pulled tight into a high ponytail behind his large head. Deep creases etched the parts of his weathered face not covered by bushy eyebrows and a dark-gray beard. His eyes twinkled when he caught Rowe staring at him.

"Look who has finally emerged from his wagon," Josson said while closing the gap, his smile broadening with every step.

"I would not have missed this." The man's voice was gravelly but full of energy, as if he had inhaled the fumes of too many experiments over the years.

"Rowe of the Nest, meet master alchemist Illious."

"I was told your kind had been killed off," Illious said, shaking Rowe's hand.

"At some point that rumor may prove correct, but not—" Rowe managed before Illious cut him short and addressed Josson.

"Anyway, when word touched my ears that Striker Company was being reformed from the ashes, I thought someone was dealin' me false iron." Illious twirled once, arms outstretched. "Now I see that was an understatement!" He held a bony finger up to Josson. "My additional wagons will be along shortly. How many of these ruffians can you spare to help me unload?"

"I'll see what I can do," Josson said, winking at Rowe.

"And make certain not to send me any of these old crows. My goodness, Josson! I've scaled mountains younger than some of the workers around here."

"I'll find you my best," Josson said.

"Very good. Now, how long before those vile creatures start droppin' ladders against yer wall?"

"Could be as soon as tomorrow," Josson said.

"And how long must we hold the wall?"

Josson held up an open hand. "Five days before the Marauders arrive."

"Five days," Illious echoed. He let out a short whistle. "No wonder you were so happy to see me."

"Believe it or not," Josson said with a grimace, "we expect the Marauders to arrive about the same time as the main body of the South Gnome Army."

Illious seemed to ignore the captain, gazing northward with his hand above his brow, as if he were blocking the sun that was already obscured by dark clouds. "Aha! I can see my wagons now." Illious pointed at the procession of wagons going back and forth through the valley. Rowe assumed the purple-and-yellow-striped covered wagon belonged to the master alchemist.

"Tell me, Captain," Illious said. "What do you require of me? Oh, and how does one go about getting a nice cup of tea?"

Josson led Illious and Rowe to the south side of the wall. "We dumped three giant piles of wood around that ridge, and we need to light them up at a moment's notice. Aside from that, picture this area swarming with gnome soldiers." Josson placed a hand on Illious's shoulder. "Surprise me."

Illious grinned like a stableboy who had just been told he could ride any horse he chose, wherever he pleased. "I have a new blend of incendiary powder I've been meaning to try. I'll send a small barrel to each of your blockades. As for surprises, I have two students arriving with my wagons."

Josson's forehead crinkled as his eyebrows rose. "Students? Never thought I'd see the day when Illious traveled with students."

"So true, Captain. So true." Illious said. "How I *loathe* most students… But these two! I couldn't leave them at the Alchemist Hall if I ever hoped to step foot in it again. If they're not blowing things up, they're burning things down!"

"Sounds like their talents might be useful here," Rowe said.

Illious's eyes lit up as he patted Rowe's chest. "Aye, lad! I'm curious to discover what they've been up to these past few days in the town of Rainia."

"You mean you have no idea?" Rowe said.

"It's a difficult leash to hold, Rowe." Illious wagged his head as he walked away. "I'm startin' to wonder if they can help themselves."

"Someone hasn't changed much," Josson said. "I think he's getting crazier with age. I just hope I can keep myself from throwing him off the wall for the next few days."

Rowe watched the master alchemist disappear down the stairs.

"After tonight, Captain, we'll be thankful for anyone who offers us the slightest advantage."

CHAPTER 16

BAD DAYS ROLLING

The wagon wheels creaked and crunched on the stony road in a continuous, discordant rhythm. Will had been awake for a few minutes but was afraid to move or open his eyes. He clung to a tolerable yet far from comfortable fetal position that slipped through his fingers when the wagon hit a pothole and lurched forward. His broken leg scraped the hard floor, and he gritted his teeth.

Now forced to seek relief in another position, Will opened his left eye, then tested his swollen right eye. Dim and blurry beams of light peeked through the broken roof, but he could see. It was dusk, which meant he had slept most of the day. Or maybe two; it was impossible to tell, because most of his waking hours were delirious. The wool blanket that someone had thrown over him was now dry, and actually warm, albeit filthy. He groaned as he massaged the thigh of his broken leg. The slightest movement re-ignited multiple points of pain throughout his body. The wagoner pushed a hard pace, and Will's hope of complete healing waned as they burned up the miles.

Despite his misery, Will fought off despair by focusing on simple blessings: he could see, he had not frozen to death, and his plugged nose blocked most of the odor issuing from the pile of rotten sacks in the corner of the wagon. He rubbed his previously dislocated shoulder that had popped back into place while strapped to the horse. He could move his arm, but it still ached. As he stretched, his left hand passed between the bars of his traveling cell. Without warning, a long walking stick cracked his hand. Will cried out and withdrew his hand so fast he rolled onto his back. Excruciating pain shot through his leg. He closed his eyes and clenched his jaw as the pain pushed him over the edge of consciousness.

The full moon cast its pale-blue light around the wagon, washing the grim scene with varying shades of indigo and black shadows. Through slit eyes, Will watched an owl hovering over an open field, and he longed for the freedom it enjoyed. He flinched when a large hooded figure appeared outside the iron bars, filling his vision.

Beneath a broad leather cowl, the gnome glared at him, walking in step with the slow-moving wagon. Through the shadows, Will glimpsed a dirty face streaked with a cruel sneer. Three short hairs stemmed from the center of a prominent wart on a thick upper lip. The moonlight revealed no white teeth. The gnome's ragged cloak hung in tatters over a wide frame and swept the earth with each stiff and labored step. He growled at Will and made a sudden punching motion through the bars. Will squeezed his eyes shut and braced himself, but the mocking punch fell short. The gnome hooted with laughter.

"Tough you be with the caged ones, Grudum," came a female voice that Will found surprisingly melodious.

Will tried to open both eyes, but the right one had swollen shut again. Grudum glared at the other gnome as she approached. He left the road in a huff to the tall grasses of the meadow they were crossing.

In the distance, beyond a copse of gnarled trees, mountain peaks reflected the moonlight. For the first time, Will noticed that his cell was the third in a long caravan that lumbered along at an unrelenting pace, taking him farther from the Crow's Nest. Starving, scared, and in more pain than he could manage, he tried to find a comfortable position on the cold, splintered planks, but found no relief. Darkness descended over the world and seeped into his heart.

The female gnome was much shorter than Grudum, with long, almost-white hair spilling from the front of her hood. Although her cheeks were smooth, her thin mouth drooped, and hairline wrinkles framed her glassy eyes. Beneath a traveling cloak, she wore a shabby leather vest over a plain gray shirt. As she fell into step with the wagon, she shoved a dirty waterskin between the bars.

Despite grumblings from his stomach and parched throat, Will hesitated.

"Drink you need," she said in a slow, soft voice. "No harm will come to you for taking."

Will opened his hand, but the moment she let go, the waterskin fell to the floor. He opened and closed his hand several times to get his blood moving. This time, he lifted the skin and, removing the stopper with his teeth, took a cautious sip. The cool water soothed his dry mouth and sore throat. He breathed a sigh as the healing power of simple water eased his tense muscles. With an effort, he shifted position and enjoyed a longer pull from the waterskin.

"Dead we thought you were, Callum Sage," the gnome said in her gentle tone.

Will drained the skin and gave her a wary glance, uncertain if his being a Callum Sage was a good thing or a bad one. He tried to pass the skin to her but dropped it, then shrank back as she casually reached in and retrieved it from the floor. Will cleared his throat and swallowed hard, wondering if his voice would cooperate. He drew a deep breath, and his lungs protested with a sharp pain and a crackling sound. "Where…are you taking me?" The words were hollow in his ears, as though the voice belonged to someone else.

"The Clover Fields," the gnome answered, her eyes fixed on the road.

"Why?"

"Labor," she sniggered, as if he were an alien from another planet.

"Labor?" Will echoed, his voice coarse and strained. "I have a broken leg and hand."

"Work the soil or fertilize the soil with your remains. Those be your options." She made a scrawling motion with her hand. "Can you write?"

"Write? I can hardly breathe," he whispered. "You're taking me to a labor camp?"

"Managed by bush gnomes the Clover Fields are. Vile they be but serve the Shadowfallen well they do."

Will's mind filled with questions, but he could not draw sufficient breath to speak.

"Rest now, but know that once this wagon stops, value you must provide or kill you they will."

"I…I can write," Will managed.

The gnome nodded. "Fortunate you are. Illiterate are many of those captured and brought to the Clover Fields. Make certain they know that write you can."

"Thank you."

She raised her bushy brows and her eyes softened as if she were both surprised and touched by his gratitude.

Will made a feeble attempt at puffing out his chest with confidence, but he knew he looked as terrible as he felt. It would take a miracle for him to sit up, let alone be able to sit at a desk and write.

"Why are you doing this?" he asked.

She tilted her head to one side as if surprised by the question. "A time there was when every highland gnome farmed the fertile lands and tended orchards and sugar maples west of the Aerodice Mountains. Warring you humans did with bush gnomes. So ignorant you are of the difference between bush and highland that attack us you did. Farmers we are, not fighters! More in common we had then with humans than with bush gnomes." She sighed. "But swept up in the war we were, forced to settle on lands that were dry, rocky, and barren. Lost everything we did. Started new lives too close to bush gnomes."

A patrol of gnomes trudged past the wagon, and Will lowered his head. When the commotion faded, he propped himself on an elbow. "So, you're a highland gnome?"

The gnome threw up her hands. "See! You humans cannot tell the difference."

She walked in seething silence for a few moments. "Scourges be humans and bush gnomes alike. Better without them the Fourwinds would be."

"But isn't your queen a human?" Will asked.

The gnome eyed him as a gust of wind rustled the tall grass. "Her Excellency, Queen Sidara, is human in body only. Left the cruelty of her people behind she did when she came to us in search of a better way to live. But starving our people were, and help us she did."

Will was silent. The Sidara he'd encountered in the Waerdreath castle did not strike him as someone interested in finding a better way to live. And certainly not one to help others. He decided to skirt the topic to minimize conflict.

"If you've recaptured your lands, why push farther east?"

The gnome raised her voice. "Because regroup you will, and war will ensue. Humans cannot help themselves from attacking and taking what is not their own."

"Not all humans want war. Some—" Will launched into a fit of coughing, the harsh barking sound ringing alarm bells in his mind. Infection was spreading to his lungs.

"But too many of you want war. Eradicate you we must if peace we will ever enjoy."

"We don't deserve this," Will said, waving his good hand over his battered body.

"Large prisons you need to stop from killing each other. Orphans and widows you make when fathers go to battle. Some humans live in poverty while others live like kings. Humans hoard, consume, and wage war. Destroy the world they could."

Will watched the gnome as she ambled next to the wagon. He wanted to argue, to offer a defense, but the jumbled words sounded like weak excuses in his head.

"What's your name?" he asked instead.

The gnome wheeled around and gaped at Will. "A human who cares about the name of a gnome?" She stopped walking and pulled back her hood, revealing wide eyes and a hint of a smile. As Will's rolling prison entered a wooded section of the road, the gnome raised her arm to wave and said, "Panigim."

CHAPTER 17
WAR

Morgan stood in the flickering torchlight at the base of the South Crow Gate. She marveled at her mother, who stood between the makeshift infirmary cots, ushering two dozen people closer. The volunteers had worked tirelessly the entire day and into the night, but fire and determination danced in their eyes. Julie smoothed her hands on her full-length apron as all eyes turned to her.

Gloriana limped close and spoke in a low voice to allow the soldiers on the wall walk a few more minutes of sleep. "We are grateful for the Callum Sages and particularly Morgan, whom some of you have met on her first visit to the Crow's Nest. Morgan has offered her support as we aid the wounded.

"Many of you have already formed deep relationships with Julie…" Gloriana's eyes glistened. She cleared her throat and wrapped her arm around Julie's waist. "This remarkable woman has come from Dwenlin Thah with special training. I am placing her in charge of our efforts, so please give her your complete attention."

The wide-eyed look Julie gave Gloriana reflected Morgan's

surprise. Gloriana took a step away from Julie and waited for her to address the volunteers.

"Well, as we know," Julie said, "less than three hundred soldiers stand between us and an army of twenty-five hundred gnomes. The cots along the wall here," she said, pointing at the thirty-five cots beneath the wall walk, "are for those we can quickly get back into the fight. We'll treat their wounds, feed and water them, then we must get them back on the wall.

"Soldiers with more serious injuries we will send to the hospital. For those of you working there…" Julie paused, biting her lower lip. "Your only objective is to get the injured back into battle. When you determine a soldier is unable to fight, get the wounded on a wagon to Rainia to make room for more. We have to keep things moving. You will need to make some difficult decisions, and there won't be time to second-guess yourself. Once you decide, call for a porter and move on. Porters are those helping us move the wounded. They will have a red kerchief tied around their upper right arms, so you can easily identify them. Any questions?"

"What about those cots at the side of the hospital, beneath the canvas?" someone asked.

"Thank you," Julie said, pausing before she continued. "Those are for soldiers who will not see the sunrise. We have some older volunteers who will sit with them in their final moments…to help them die well."

A murmur arose from the group, so Gloriana stepped in. "It will be difficult, but this wall must hold for four days until additional soldiers arrive to help. The outcome of this battle will depend on how well we do our jobs. For those of you in charge of getting water and food up to the wall walk, do so with urgency. Move quickly and do your best to keep soldiers in the fight. Morgan will direct your efforts from the wall walk, but remember: you do not have the protection of her cloak, so stay low."

Gloriana's face softened as she scanned the group. "I've known each of you since you were children. And I'm very proud to be here with you."

It was Julie's turn to relieve Gloriana. "There are two main stairs to the wall walks." Julie pointed as she explained. "We'll bring the injured down those stairs. The other stairs are for resupplying the soldiers. Once the fighting starts, it will be difficult to manage, but do your best to control the flow. The more organized we are, the more lives we save. Gloriana will be stationed at the bottom of the steps to decide where the injured are to be taken. In order for this to work, it's imperative that we keep the wounded moving along as quickly as possible. We have plenty of stitching, bandages, and water. If the soldier you're working on cannot return to the fight, call for transport and get them moved along. Make the call and do not be timid about it."

"Does anyone have any questions?" Julie asked.

There was a long silence.

"Looks like we're ready," Gloriana said.

As the volunteers spread out, stationed two per cot, Morgan stretched and released a low groan. She breathed in the cool night air. The South Crow Gate was alive with the dancing light of the massive watch fires. The fires were necessary, Morgan had recently learned, because gnomes could see as well in the dark as humans could in daylight.

Along the battlements, soldiers moved into position. There was little conversation. At last count, the garrison was a scant 229, and the air was electric.

Through the bustle, Morgan caught sight of Rowe's Trannalun

cloak as he moved in step with Captain Josson, with Councilman Tranas following closely. Rowe was midsentence when their eyes met. His lips closed in a thin line and curled upward, creating deep dimples in his scruffy cheeks. Morgan returned a small smile, and the men continued along the wall.

"I always wondered what kind of man it would take to win your heart." Julie was leaning against the wall, arms folded. "Now I know."

Morgan felt her cheeks warm.

The mother-daughter connection was shattered when a soldier burst through the yawning gate, shouting. Josson ran from the wall walk to meet him, with Rowe and Tranas close behind.

"Something's coming up the thoroughfare!" The soldier bent with hands on his knees, gulping air.

"What is it?" Josson asked.

"It's bright as a forger's fire," the soldier said, shaking his head. "And walking."

"How far out?" Josson asked.

"A mile, probably less by now."

Rowe brushed past Josson, gazing beyond the gates.

"You know what it is?" Josson asked.

"No." Rowe shook his head. "But pray it's not a moonwalker."

"Is this possible?" Josson said.

The messenger soldier stood, eyes wide. "What do we do?"

Josson watched Rowe, who stood motionless. The South Crow Gate grew quiet. Flickering fires intermixed with the distant thrumming of the approaching army. Suddenly, a steady booming reverberated from the thoroughfare, like the beat of a huge drum. Or heavy footfalls.

"We know nothing for certain." Josson ran through the gate

and shouted over his shoulder: "Have the heavy loads ready at the catapults!"

"And ropes!" Rowe shouted. "Gather as many as you can find—the thicker the better!" He raced after Josson to the narrow road between the cliff face and the sheer drop into the gorge. They scaled two of the massive piles of timbers the soldiers had prepared when they had first arrived. A dozen archers greeted them at the third pile.

Armed and ready, the archers stared into the darkness beyond their torchlights. The flames illuminated the rock wall about a hundred feet up but revealed nothing on the thoroughfare.

The booming footfalls grew louder.

Rowe considered rushing to the fourth wagonload of wood about fifty yards out, but a blast of wind extinguished the torches stationed around it. The gust swept up the road, warming his face. A moment later, from around the mountain cleft, the creature appeared.

"May the gods show mercy!" Josson whispered. "What is *that*?"

Dozens of metal plates shifted at a blurring rate around the broad torso and thick limbs of the massive humanoid creature. Molten lava glowed in the gaps between the plates as it moved forward with unrelenting strides. A massive dragon-like iron helm topped the beast's eight-foot-tall frame. The only weapon it carried was a large steel bar linked to a giant spiked iron ball by a three-foot chain.

In unison, the archers drew their bows and waited for orders.

"Thought I'd seen the last of the moonwalkers," Rowe muttered. "This is unfortunate."

"*Unfortunate*?" an archer echoed.

"Ignite that pile of timber and let's see if it slows the creature,"

Josson commanded. "We need to determine how long we have before the army arrives."

The three massive piles of timber were set up to offer a short-term fiery roadblock against the first gnome attack, providing the garrison precious hours with minimal casualties. But the moon-walker threatened to derail that plan.

An archer dipped his arrow into a nearby torch until the oil-soaked arrowhead ignited. Turning, he fired in a low trajectory. The moment the arrow struck the timber, flames erupted thanks to master alchemist Illious's incendiary powder.

"If the creature passes through that inferno," Josson said, "pull back and let it pass the next pile before lighting it. Maybe we can slow the gnomes. Send word if the gnome army is directly behind it, or if that thing is alone."

Rowe ran behind Josson and stopped in the clearing before the South Crow Gate. From this view, the imposing wall towered into the night sky. At the top of the wall was an expansive stone battlement with evenly spaced merlons for at least two soldiers to hide behind. The merlons were divided by crenels wide enough for a single archer. A secondary battlement above the gatehouse provided an added vantage point. The main catapult near the gatehouse and the large ballista at the top of the east tower were well stocked. Huge watch fires burned at strategic points in the clearing. *It's a stronghold if ever there was one*, Rowe thought. *But will it be enough?*

"You've fought moonwalkers?" Josson asked.

"Yes." Rowe wiped his sweaty brow with his shirtsleeve. "But no weapon can destroy it."

"How do we defeat it?"

"That depends on whether it clears the fires and arrives with an army on its heels or if it comes alone."

Josson cocked his head.

"Think of it as an attack dog, Commander. When you send it to kill, it doesn't understand the greater plan. It simply rushes in to obey the command. If we have time to deal with the moonwalker alone, I have an idea, but we have to work fast."

⁂

The moonwalker materialized around the final cleft in the rock, and 229 soldiers tensed. Heavy footfalls shook the earth and silenced every gaping mouth.

Ten mounted soldiers at the base of the wall near the Misty Gorge reined in their stamping horses. Six soldiers stood near the gorge holding log peavies—spiked metal poles topped with a sharp hook that were usually used by woodsmen to move heavy logs. The six soldiers looped a length of heavy rope through metal rings at the end of their poles. Behind them, several soldiers worked feverishly at the edge of the gorge to fill four heavy nets with rocks. High above, along the wall walk, the remaining soldiers stood armed and alert as their companions prepared to engage the nightmare before them.

Rowe did his best to keep the riders focused on carrying out his crude plan. But the moonwalker was a terrifying distraction.

When the creature was halfway into the clearing, Josson shouted and led his mare forward, javelin raised. The other nine riders fanned out behind him. The moonwalker ignored them. The riders maneuvered through the shadowy clearing toward the mountain wall, keeping the creature between them and the gorge.

Josson launched his javelin and struck the moonwalker across the side of its head. As he galloped past, Josson raised his arm to shield his face from the intense heat of the creature. Another javelin struck it high in the chest, and the moonwalker slowed. The wooden shaft jammed between two plates and instantly erupted into flames before the shifting plates shattered it to pieces. The soldier who threw the second javelin circled around, but the moonwalker swung its weapon toward him. Glowing red, the spiked ball streaked through the air. Soldiers cried out their warnings, but the rider was struck in the side and thrown from his saddle. There was little left of his smoldering body when it hit the ground in a heap. The meager garrison was reduced to 228.

The remaining riders widened their approach and heaved javelins at the moonwalker, then circled around to the wall where soldiers supplied them with more javelins. One rider leapt from his saddle a second before the moonwalker's spiked ball slammed into the side of his horse. The smell of burning flesh filled the air as the animal burned in a mangled mass.

Josson's second javelin snapped in two when it struck the moonwalker's head. The creature stopped. Its glowing eyes followed Josson as he kicked his horse's flanks and broke for the gorge. The moonwalker unleashed its deadly weapon. Josson leaned to dodge the blow, jerking on the reins, and the horse nearly lost its footing as it turned. The spiked iron ball whistled over the commander's head.

The moonwalker pursued the riders toward the gorge where Rowe and five other soldiers ventured to meet it. Once again, the spiked iron ball struck a rider, and only 227 soldiers remained. Rowe rushed forward and drove the hook of his log peavey into the creature's body. It bounced off a plate, but he lunged a second time and the hook caught another shifting plate. Rowe leaned back and slammed his feet into the ground, heaving the pole with all his strength. The peavey shook wildly and glowed orange near the tip as the moonwalker tried to free itself.

"Drop the rocks!" Rowe shouted.

A soldier hacked through a supporting rope, sending five hundred pounds of rock over the cliff. Tied to the net was the length of rope attached to the end of Rowe's pole. He gave a final tug, and the hook prevented the plate from shifting. As the rocks fell, the moonwalker reared against the sudden force that almost pulled it off its feet. It leaned back, sliding several feet as three more javelins found their way into the gaping cracks in its armor.

The six soldiers carrying the log peavies hesitated.

"Get more hooks into it!" Rowe bellowed.

As Rowe ran to the edge of the gorge for another pole, the rope snapped. Soldiers cried out as the moonwalker swung the spiked iron ball in a wide circle a few feet from the ground. One soldier dove over the weapon, but the next soldier jumped too soon and was clipped in the hip. Rowe was at his side at once. In the dim light, blood pooled beneath the disjointed leg and gaping wound. *226.*

As the moonwalker reeled in its weapon, two soldiers heaved large barbed chains at both sides of the creature. One chain dropped across the creature's shoulder and the man pulled the chain, hooking it firmly. The other chain swung around the creature's midsection and caught a shifting plate. The spiked iron ball flashed toward the first soldier, who released the chain and dove to safety. Sparks flew as the spiked ball slammed into the rocky ground.

Rowe dove for the loose chain. "Drop the rocks!" he shouted again.

Two more nets were cut free. As the rocks tumbled over the edge of the gorge, the ropes fastened to the chains on the moonwalker sprang from the ground. The first chain jerked against the weight of the falling rock, dragging the moonwalker several feet. Somehow, the creature dug its feet in, resisting the weight. The second chain ripped a plate from the creature's body and disappeared with the rocks into the gorge.

Josson called for a log peavey. A soldier tossed him the hooked pole as he rode toward the flailing moonwalker. When he was six feet from the red-hot creature, Josson jerked the reins and leapt from his saddle, driving the hook into the moonwalker's exposed chest. The spiked iron ball exploded into the side of Josson's mare a second after he jumped from the saddle.

"Drop the final net!" Rowe shouted.

As the net of rocks fell away, Rowe held his breath. The creature fought against the weight that was inching it toward the cliff. Josson's hooked pole spun the creature and knocked it off its feet. The moonwalker drove the spiked iron ball into the ground, halting the sliding motion toward the edge. Josson grabbed a broken javelin and ran to the spiked iron ball so fast he nearly lost his footing. He drove the shaft beneath the chain and heaved with a terrific grunt. The ball rolled loose, and the moonwalker scrambled and clawed the earth as it hastened toward the cliff.

Less than ten feet from the edge, one of the hooks pulled a plate free from the moonwalker's body. With only one net of rocks now pulling it toward the gorge, the moonwalker caught itself on a large boulder. Rowe grabbed another peavey, hooked it around one of the creature's fingers, and pried like a woodsman freeing a jammed log. The moonwalker lost its hold on the boulder. As it resumed its slide to the edge, soldiers rushed in to break any handhold the creature found, crying out against the unbearable heat.

When the great beast vanished over the edge, a victory shout exploded from the wall walk. Morgan burst through the opened gate, leading Julie and several volunteers carrying stretchers.

Rowe walked to the cliff's edge and peered down. Hundreds of feet below, molten lava splattered over a large area and was already cooling.

"How to take down a moonwalker," Josson said between gasping breaths as he stepped beside Rowe.

"That was close," Rowe said as they walked back to the South Crow Gate. "And we're only beginning."

A sudden commotion erupted near the thoroughfare, and Josson grunted as a bolt struck him in the back. Rowe lunged to catch him as another bolt deflected off his cloak. He whirled around to see the eight riders engaged in a skirmish with a dozen gnome soldiers that had somehow got past the fires and the archers. A rider fell from his mount with a bolt through his neck, reducing their number to 225. But what alarmed Rowe more was a glimpse of gnomes darting throughout the shadows, much closer than he thought possible.

Morgan and Julie ran and knelt beside Josson and Rowe.

"Get under his other arm," Rowe told Julie. "We need to get out of here!"

Rowe wrapped Josson's limp arm around his shoulder, and Julie slid beneath Josson's other arm. Together they jogged toward the yawning gate as it closed. Bows hummed overhead as the clashes of metal continued at the mouth of the thoroughfare.

Morgan moved between them and the gnomes to shield their retreat from further bolts. "Hurry!" she shouted as dark forms rushed toward her.

Rowe stopped and turned, wanting to help her, but the confrontation was over in seconds. Morgan deflected the gnome's attack with ease, driving her sword deep into his chest as a bolt ricocheted off her cloak. Spinning, she defended herself against two more gnomes who seemed to appear out of nowhere, her sword clashing loudly against theirs. Before Rowe could find someone to help with Josson, Morgan had cut down both gnomes with a series of fluid attacks. She ran for the gate as the cavaliers raced to safety with her.

The remaining foot soldiers outside the wall made a final run for the gate. Arrows flew from the wall at an ever-sharpening angle and several soldiers with large shields rushed out to protect their retreat. One foot soldier was hit with a gnome bolt. *224.*

Beneath the bright lantern light in the triage area, Rowe and Julie carried Josson to a cot. Julie gently probed Josson's chest and abdomen. "It didn't go all the way through," she said. "Let's get him on his stomach." She slipped on a pair of latex gloves as Gloriana cut the clothes from the commander's back.

Morgan joined them, her hair clinging to the edges of her sweating face. She looked at Rowe and her mother, and released a deep sigh, then gasped when she saw Josson.

Julie pulled the garments free and grimaced at the amount of blood. The bolt had torn into the center of his lower back. "Looks like it hit an artery," she muttered. "And possibly his spine." She pressed a clean cloth on the gushing wound and held a bloodied finger to his neck. After a moment, she lowered her head.

Gloriana wore an anxious look on her weary face.

The air was suddenly filled with the sound of thundering horse hooves and chain rattling through pulleys as the portcullis lowered. The heavy gates slammed shut. Soldiers up in the gatehouse and those below worked quickly to secure the locks.

Julie waited a moment before looking up at those gathered around her. Her eyes met Morgan's, flickered to Rowe, then back again.

Morgan tugged Rowe's arm. "Come with me," she said.

Rowe followed numbly as she handed him a towel to wipe the blood from his hands. When they moved away from the crowd, she stepped close to him.

"I'm so sorry Rowe, but Josson won't make it," she said.

Rowe sighed, but he knew it was the truth. *223.* Even if Josson survived, there would be little left of him.

Morgan hugged him and whispered in his ear: "It's up to you now."

Rowe was silent.

"The soldiers will look to you as their new commander, Rowe."

Rowe looked around as he absorbed the truth of her words. Already, many soldiers were watching him.

"The gnomes will attack before the sun comes up, right?"

Rowe slouched as the burden of leadership settled on his shoulders.

"How long before sunrise?" Morgan asked.

"Four hours."

"I know in my heart you can hold the wall, Rowe," she said as Tranas ran toward them. "I believe in you," she added, rushing back to the triage area.

"Our riders fended off the first dozen gnomes," Tranas reported. "But the army is staging right around the corner." He grimaced at the somber scene around Josson's body. "I'll inform Striker Company about Josson and meet you up top."

Rowe nodded.

Tranas grasped his shoulders and held his gaze. "Are there any changes to the plan?"

"Nothing has changed," Rowe answered. "Except that we're down to 223 soldiers."

"Then it begins," Tranas said as he bounded up the stairs.

CHAPTER 18

In the Absence of Options

After traveling all day at a steady pace with six rangers from Enders Brigade, General Raric slowed Shilo near a tall thicket deep inside the Hollowtangle. The worn leather saddle creaked as he carefully removed his feet from the stirrups to stretch his aching legs. A towering knot of thorny bushes, the thicket marked the edge of the Druid Forest. It was alive with watchful creatures.

Giant wasps patrolled the border, buzzing past layers of sticky webs guarded by a cluster of deadly spiders. Snakes hissed and slithered beneath the thorns as small rodents scurried out of their paths. Colorful birds darted between the low-lying branches of the surrounding forest, splashing the deep-green canvas with a blur of red, blue, yellow, and purple. A fox was the largest creature visible. The thicket appeared to be a densely populated haven of diverse creatures, but General Raric had been to the Druid Forest before and knew their purpose. If anyone—or anything—wanted to penetrate this wall, they would need to go through these small guardians.

A ranger gasped at the sight, and Raric smiled despite himself.

He knuckled his stiff back and noticed the fox staring at him. It cocked its head, then disappeared into the thicket. No light shone through the impenetrable tangle, but beyond the wall the sound of barking, huffing, and growling increased. Raric imagined the fox spreading news of the human presence to wolves, bears, and other beasts. The Druid Forest was both beautiful and deadly.

"Set up camp and wait for me," Raric said as he coaxed Shilo forward. "If I do not return after two days, go back to the Battle Wagon and let Commander Bayard know what I have done."

The rangers hesitated, but they were veteran soldiers who understood orders. Each one nodded and slid from their mounts.

Raric tugged Shilo's reins slightly as he neared the thicket. When they were less than three feet from the thorny wall, vines untangled and withdrew, forming a doorway large enough for Shilo. A pack of large timber wolves waited beyond the entrance. Two rangers called out in warning, but Raric and Shilo continued, and the vines closed behind them as fluid as the waves of an emerald sea.

The wolves bounded away into the dense undergrowth, leaving Raric and Shilo in unexpected silence. A moment later, a large man emerged from the forest. He was tall and broad, but aged, slouching as he leaned on the support of a thick, shoulder-high walking stick. His smooth white hair pulled back into a ponytail contrasted with his wrinkled and weathered face. Brown trousers and a fitted long-sleeved green shirt alluded to a toned frame that had once been strong and dangerous. The man kept a steady eye on Raric until the gap between them was only a few feet.

"My name is Johanissan of the River Country, but you may call me Joe." The stranger's voice was deep and full of confidence. Despite his friendly manner, Raric remained wary. But there was something familiar about his name…

"Johanissan…of the River Country," Joe repeated slowly, as if reading Raric's confusion.

Shilo nuzzled Joe, who stroked the mare's cheek.

Raric gaped, his mind racing. He had expected Druid Margrave and no others. Gradually, his memories connected with the name.

"Are you—" Raric cut himself short.

Joe nodded, his features unreadable. Yet there was a kindness to the man that allowed Raric to relax, if only a little.

"—a Callum Sage?"

Joe's nodding increased, and he added a smile. "Without the Trannalun cloak."

"I remember my father speaking of you when I was a child."

"Your father was a good man, Raric. It pained me to hear what had befallen him." Joe turned away from Raric and ambled back toward the dense forest. Shilo followed without waiting for Raric's command. Over his shoulder, Joe added: "He would be proud of what you've become."

Raric straightened in the saddle. "And what is it I've become?"

"A leader willing to sacrifice his life for his people."

"I'm hopeful it will not come to that," Raric said.

"So is the Druid Margrave. In fact, the moment he learned of my return to the Fourwinds, he came to seek my help with the melding." Joe paused at the edge of the forest beneath a low oak branch and glanced at Raric. "He usually works alone."

Raric wondered how the old man could help with such a rigorous procedure. His face must have revealed a skeptical look because Joe stopped and explained. "I've always had an affinity with the elements, General." A warm breeze rustled the oak leaves and cooled Raric's clammy skin. "I can freeze objects."

"How would that help me?"

Joe followed a narrow footpath that ran parallel to the dense forest, planting the staff on firm ground before each step. "I could freeze your entire body, which may numb your senses to the painful process of melding."

"That sounds much better than what the druid described: fusing my skin and the dragon hide together." Raric took a pull from his waterskin.

"Oh, the process has not changed, Raric. The road ahead remains a terrible one for you. But I might help alleviate your misery by freezing your body as Margrave works through the melding."

"I understand the risk," Raric said, hope fortifying his tone. "But do you think it might increase the odds of success?"

Joe slowed his pace and turned again. "Unfortunately, my friend, creating dragon armor is pure theory. No one has ever attempted the task we are about to do."

The forest, which had been alive with the exotic dissonance of various species of birds, grew silent. From a copse of pine trees ahead of them, Margrave appeared on the back of a massive elk, its rack dwarfing the druid's own large antlers.

"Have times become so desperate that Raric returns to the Druid Forest?" Margrave raised a furry arm and combed back his long, wild hair with his clawlike fingernails.

As the elk drew nearer, Shilo came to an uneasy halt. Raric nodded at Margrave, his throat suddenly as dry as the Plains of Ashron.

Margrave led the way through a field of tall grass, joining the conversation as though he'd been part of it from the beginning. "There was a unique regality to your father that I enjoyed, Raric. Despite the office he held, King Malaqui was a simple, common sense man—something in short supply in the human realms."

As they crossed the open field, a family of large hares frolicked in the grasses, hopping from their path. Raric inhaled deeply. The lack of underbrush made it easier to breathe, but it was the perfect place to become hopelessly lost. Raric had been through parts of the Hollowtangle, but the Druid Forest was an anomaly. His somber purpose there darkened his mood. Hearing the others talk of his father awakened a futile longing for the king's wise council.

Raric brooded in silence as they passed beneath the shade of an enormous solitary oak. "We have yet to discuss cost," he said.

"I have long considered this," Margrave answered. "The desperation that brought you to me is not a sound platform from which to negotiate. I suspect I could ask for anything and you would happily agree."

"It seems I have little choice," Raric said. "Uluk's strength is too great for our army. I need something beyond military might to match his power." He raised his throbbing palms as he shrugged. "Name your price."

Margrave didn't hesitate. "Prevent the spread of Phyriad in the Fourwinds and I will consider your debt paid."

A long silence followed.

"I fail to understand how that benefits you," Raric said. "You seem unaffected by events in the Fourwinds."

"There was a time when I owed a great debt to Johanissan of the River Country." Margrave's green eyes twinkled as he glanced at Joe. "He has negotiated on your behalf, Raric. And I must say that Callum Sages, with their blasted love of the Histories, can wield their knowledge with as much grace as you once wielded your sword."

"And I, of course, have a vested interest in protecting the Fourwinds," Joe said.

"The cost should not be too great for someone like you, General," Margrave continued. "And I agree with you: you have little choice. Besides, what are your aspirations should you survive this madness?"

"I plan to build a cottage on a remote lake and live out the rest of my days in peace," Raric said. "And maybe find myself a good woman—someone able and willing to see past this cursed exterior. Someone to grow old with," he added before considering his words.

Margrave raised his bristly eyebrows and dipped his head toward Joe. "You were correct, Johanissan."

"You see?" Joe said. "Not all humans share a lust for power, Margrave."

The druid lifted his head and stuck out his short beard. "I'll believe that the moment Raric steps away from the crown—should he be fortunate enough to be presented with such an opportunity."

Raric simply rode in silence, considering his dwindling options. His cottage dream was a fantasy. And as damaged as he was—and was about to be—what woman would want him? But he could not give up now. In truth, Margrave's asking price aligned with his own purposes. Bringing an end to Sidara's plan for using Uluk and the gnomes to spread Phyriad had been his goal from the start. In truth, the druid's fee was no more than he was already paying.

"How does this melding process work?" Raric asked.

Margrave kept his steady gaze forward. "I traveled deep into the ethereal to seek council from the druids who came before me. They granted me the means to place you in the Druid's Slumber while I perform the melding."

"Will I feel anything?"

Margrave shook his head, and several butterflies flittered from his antlers. "The Druid's Slumber is powerful, and good news for you. I was uncertain how to keep you alive while I fuse the dragon armor to your skin, but the Druid's Slumber should accomplish that. The problem, however, comes when you awaken. The shock to your heart will be significant. I cannot imagine the suffering you will endure."

"Would tevan root help?"

Margrave's eyes narrowed. "You clearly underestimate the extent of the pain. You will think yourself engulfed in flames. Your skin will be covered with the heat of dragon armor, and I possess no salve to soothe your melted flesh. Such healing is beyond my reach."

Raric's neck pulsed to the quickened beat of his heart. "So, what then?"

"You are fortunate that Johanissan returned when he did," Margrave said.

"I will do what I can to freeze the melded skin," Joe said. "I have given this much thought. If I can freeze you in a way that the melding occurs over a few days, then the pain might be tolerable. But I cannot say for certain how this will work."

"I suspect you will scream until you lose your voice," Margrave said.

Joe waved a hand in the air. "There is little to be gained by speculating, Margrave, or by fanning the flames of fear. We know nothing about the other side, General. But we will do all that is within our power to ensure a successful outcome."

Raric was suddenly grateful for Joe's role, not only in the melding process but also in tempering the druid's harsh manner.

"Any other questions, Raric?" Margrave asked.

Raric thought for a moment. "Do you know why Uluk the Shadowfallen is so interested in the Gryton Mines? I've sent scouts to investigate but have yet to hear a word."

Margrave tilted his head. "As a matter of fact, I had three feline friends investigate that a week ago. Their findings interest me so much that I plan to see it for myself if time allows."

"What did your spies report?" Joe asked.

"By all appearances, the Shadowfallen has reopened the Gryton Mines. Considering the requirements of war, I understand the need for mining," Margrave said. "Except Uluk is not mining."

"What's he doing?" Raric asked.

"I am uncertain. But dozens of bush gnomes are working there, and Uluk often flies in and out. By all appearances, the mine is fully operational, yet no new digging has taken place. They are more interested in the tailings than in finding new deposits of ore."

"What could he want with tailings?" Raric said.

The druid shrugged while directing them along an intersecting path.

"There has to be a tangible reason for Uluk to leave the gnome army—even for a few hours at a time," Joe said.

"Lately, in fact, he spends more time at the mines than he does with the gnome army," Margrave added.

The druid stopped in a small patch of mossy grass surrounded by a semicircle of dense holly bushes. "Perhaps Johanissan might also consider investigating? The Shadowfallen is going to great lengths to keep his activity at the Gryton Mines a secret."

Joe's forehead wrinkled as he frowned and nodded. "I think I will."

In the middle of the grassy opening was a giant flat block of wood with thick braided vines rooted to the four corners. The slab was large enough to accommodate an outstretched man.

Raric swallowed hard as the horrors of Sidara's crucifix flashed in his mind.

"You are free to leave," Margrave said quietly. "The choice is still within your grasp."

Raric shook his head, drawing deep for courage. "If the pain becomes too great, would you kill me if I asked?"

Margrave scattered more flying insects from his antlers with a brisk shaking of his head. "Once I begin your transformation, there can be no turning back. This will not reassure you, Raric, but unless Johanissan can produce a miracle, the moment you wake you will beg me to kill you through your screams." The druid pointed to the slab. "Thus, the chains."

Raric drew a sharp breath and dismounted from Shilo. He gingerly removed his gloves, then proceeded with the rest of his clothing.

WAR – PART 2

From her vantage point atop the main wall walk stairway, Morgan peered through the shadowy stillness of the clearing beyond the South Crow Gate. Along the wall walk, archers targeted the opening to the thoroughfare where the slain bodies of the first dozen gnome soldiers lay. On the other side of the wall, at the foot of the stairs, her mother and Gloriana waited with the small group of restless volunteers. Rowe stood beside Tranas and the archers with his sword drawn, preparing to signal the initial volley of arrows. The rhythmic march of the South Gnome Army reached an ominous crescendo.

Morgan expected a wild rush of foot soldiers to burst into the clearing, but the first gnomes entered in groups of four, each soldier carrying the corner of a heavy canvas. They scurried through the shadows, draping the canvases over each of the watch fires.

"Hold!" Rowe commanded. "Save your arrows for the attack."

"Wool blankets saturated with fire retardant," Illious murmured. "Clever."

The canvases quickly doused the watch fires, and darkness smothered the clearing near the thoroughfare.

In the blackness beyond the wall, the shuffling of hundreds of rapid footsteps, the clangor of metal, and the scraping of wood over rocky earth painted a clear picture of the assembling gnome army.

"Keep calm, lads," Tranas said as he paced the vast expanse of the wall walk carrying a massive double-edged ax. "How would you like to be facing such a mighty fortress guarded by fierce warriors? We have the advantage here!"

Illious sauntered over to the wall near Rowe and leaned over the edge.

"Some light out there would be welcome, Illious!" Rowe said.

"To what end? The only way up here is by ladder, and I suspect you've seen a ladder before."

Illious's deadpan tone left Rowe gaping. "If *you* don't have an idea, what about those infamous students of yours?"

Illious smirked. "As a matter of fact, while you were fighting that moonwalker, I mentioned to my student, Dadore, that there would come a time when light at the base of this wall would be most appreciated."

Rowe nodded slowly. "I think I almost tripped over him when I was running back to the gate. He was burying something…"

Illious's eyes darkened. "He calls it an *ordinance*, and even *he* took great care in handling it—reckless as he is. It's not much to look at. Simply a crude iron pitcher with four holes evenly spaced around the perimeter three-quarters of the way to the top. I noticed that each hole was angled up and away from the pitcher." Illious stroked his beard. "Dadore half filled it with a liquid he'd been working on for the past year. He had the nerve to suggest his formula was similar but more volatile than my renowned Illious

Fire." The master alchemist wagged his head and hissed through his teeth.

"Go on, Illious," Rowe said. "We haven't much time."

"Yes, yes, of course. After burying the ordinance so the top was level with the ground, Dadore placed a round sphere containing another liquid inside the pitcher. The liquid within will disintegrate the sphere, and once both liquids touch…well, it will be interesting." Illious wandered away, shaking his head. "May the gods have mercy! If those blasted kids don't blow up this wall, it will be a testament to my tutelage."

Morgan caught Rowe's eye, and he shrugged his shoulders. Apparently, she wasn't the only one confused by the master alchemist's quirky manner.

Tranas continued his pacing, offering words of encouragement to the soldiers. In the flickering firelight, he looked larger than usual. With a thick beard and a shock of unruly curly hair, he could have been mistaken for a simple farmer if not for his fierce, steely eyes.

"I would much rather be up here with both hands on my ax than down there with one hand on a ladder and the other on me jewels," Tranas shouted.

Soft laughter rippled across the wall walk. Morgan marveled at the soldiers' sense of humor, while she could barely speak.

Tranas adjusted his studded leather vest and ducked behind one of the battlement's tall merlons. "All the same, lads, best be keeping low. Bush gnomes are excellent craftsmen, especially when it comes to making crossbows."

The opening volley of gnome bolts shot from the darkness but failed to strike the soldiers, who had followed Tranas's lead and ducked behind the safety of the large stone merlons. A full minute of silence passed before a deafening roar erupted and the South

Gnome Army swarmed into the dim light cast by the torches on the wall.

Morgan gasped at the size of the army. Among the hundreds of howling gnomes racing toward the wall, it looked as though some carried three huge birchbark canoes upside down.

Rowe raised his sword for an instant, then slashed downward. The archers' bows hummed. Most arrows pinged off metal shields, but a few found their mark. The massive army surged forward.

A second volley of gnome bolts quickly followed, and this time three soldiers were too slow to duck behind the merlons. *222. 221. 220.*

"Clear!" A soldier pulled a long lever and released a catapult. Over twenty skull-size rocks disappeared into the night sky in a high arch. Two soldiers heaved on the cranks to pull the arm back, and before it locked into place, four soldiers reloaded the bucket from the stockpile of rocks. From the east tower, the massive ballista loosed twelve six-foot-long bolts. Near the western watchtower, a second catapult launched a volley of rocks.

Dozens of gnomes shrieked and fell, but the army pressed closer, trampling their dead comrades underfoot.

Tranas grabbed a long shield and climbed onto the battlement. "Come and get some!" he bellowed as several bolts ricocheted off his shield.

When the gnomes neared the base of the wall, the overhanging torches revealed what had looked like upside-down canoes from a distance. Three groups of gnomes each carried three huge ladders: one directly over their heads and two on the sides. Light armor plates were wedged between the spindles to protect the gnomes on their approach as arrows rained on them. All at once, the ladders came apart. The gnomes drove the ladders into the ground while others used long poles to thrust the ladders against the wall. Behind the ladders, a large group of gnomes released another volley of bolts to keep the soldiers pinned behind the battlement as nine ladders careened between merlons. A bolt struck one brave soldier high in the chest, slamming him to the back railing of the wall walk. *219.*

Gnomes scrambled up the nine ladders as bolts flew up to the battlement and arrows rained into the clearing. The first gnome up a ladder carried a small wooden shield and a single-hand crossbow. As he neared the battlement, he shot an archer in the armpit. The soldier fell outside the wall to his death, taking two climbing gnomes with him. *218.* The ladders bounced precariously beneath the weight of the ascending gnomes, but for every gnome shot off a ladder, a dozen more waited to climb. Roaring battle cries drowned out the screams of death.

Morgan used her Trannalun cloak as a shield and dragged the first wounded soldier back to a waiting stretcher. "Hurry!" she shouted to two porters. "Not that way!" She pointed. "*That* stairwell is for going down!" After helping load two more stretchers, Morgan approached the battlements, trying to get used to the intensity. Although not trained for battle, she knew her prowess with a sword would soon be called upon.

A bolt had struck the first casualty beneath the chin and was lodged in the man's head. Julie gasped before pointing and checking the next person.

"He's dead," Gloriana said. "Go!"

Gloriana was at the next stretcher examining a soldier who had been struck in the face. The thick shaft of bolt protruded from his cheek.

"Dead. Go!"

Julie leaned over the next stretcher. "Dear God," she breathed. A bolt protruded from the man's shoulder, and after a quick examination, she saw little blood loss. She followed this stretcher to her makeshift operating table where she spent the remainder of the night as Gloriana ran triage.

With a pair of shears that resembled bolt cutters, Julie snapped the tip and pulled the shaft clear. The soldier flinched and grunted through clenched teeth. "Let me get a few stitches in there before you go," Julie said as the soldier tried to get up.

Morgan whipped her head to the side as a gnome carrying two small handheld crossbows leapt over the battlement. He was struck in the chest with Tranas's battle-ax before he could aim. Another gnome followed and shot a small narrow bolt, striking Tranas in the shoulder but failing to penetrate his thick leather armor. Tranas spun and struck the gnome in the face with the butt of his ax handle, sending the gnome in a high dive off the wall.

Most gnomes had extra crossbows hanging from their belts. As they approached the top of the ladder, they shot two or three before pouncing onto the wall with the two remaining crossbows in each hand. Choosing targets quickly, they shot again, then exchanged the crossbows for two short swords before jumping onto the wall walk. *217. 216. 215.* Shouts erupted as dozens of Striker Company soldiers exchanged their bows for shields, pikes, and swords. The archers were slowing the enemy attack, but several bush gnomes gained the wall walk in a crazed rush, only to be cut down. *214. 213.*

Rowe leapt onto the battlement near a ladder, his face guarded beneath the cowl of his hood. Several bolts struck his Trannalun cloak. His sword flashed, striking three gnomes dead before he lost his footing. A massive ballista bolt knocked more gnomes from the ladder, and Rowe fell into the arms of two soldiers. Gaining his feet, he continued slashing as several gnomes rushed over the battlement. *212.*

Morgan continued to lead the effort to help the wounded, keeping them sheltered with her cloak as she got them off the wall walk. Suddenly, she shouted as five gnomes landed on the wall walk ten feet from her. They wore light leather armor beneath baggy forest garb, and their hair was long and wild. The dark war paint on their cheeks contrasted with gnashing teeth and flashing eyes. Their short swords blurred in the shadows as two soldiers tried to fend them off. Despite being a few inches shorter than an average man, the bush gnomes had wiry, nimble limbs.

The soldiers killed two gnomes, but three more stabbed their backs. *211. 210.* Morgan lunged, driving her sword into the nearest gnome as Tranas jumped beside her, his ax cutting another gnome in half at the waist. A soldier at his side stabbed the fifth with a long pike.

Wiping sweat from her face, Morgan sheathed her sword and grabbed a fallen soldier beneath the arms and dragged him toward the waiting porters along the back railing. A bolt deflected off her cloak, but she paid little heed as she rushed for another soldier.

The catapults continued launching rocks into the darkness, and the ballista shot as close to the base of the wall as possible. For three unrelenting hours, the battle raged, and nearing the fourth, it was obvious the defenders of the South Crow Gate were losing. Morgan's arm and leg muscles burned as she struggled to keep up with the distressing number of fallen. *209. 208. 207. 206. 205.*

Rowe and Tranas fought side by side. With his powerful battle-ax, Tranas looked like he was chopping wood, only in this nightmare he was splitting skulls. He had stopped shouting taunts, and his swings were lower. A bolt found a gap in his armor and lodged in his shoulder. Another sunk into his hip. Still, he continued to fight as soldiers fell around him. *204. 203. 202.*

Rowe edged close to the battlement, and a bolt struck his left calf as his cloak flew up.

"I'm hit!" Rowe cursed as he dropped to his knees, gritting his teeth. He sprang to his feet, sword arching with deadly accuracy.

"We're all hit, princess!" Tranas bellowed.

Shouts and clashing metal filled the air as the gnomes pushed ever forward, up and over the ladders. *201. 200. 199. 198. 197. 196.*

Morgan noticed Illious's students, Dadore and Kydaris, cowering with shocked expressions. "I could use some extra hands over here!" she called.

The young students joined Morgan as she helped another wounded soldier onto a stretcher.

"It should have ignited by now," Dadore muttered.

"Maybe I made the glass too thick," Kydaris said.

"What are you two talking ab—" A powerful explosion cut Morgan's words short. She stumbled, then glanced at the two students, who were both grinning.

The fighting on the wall came to an abrupt halt as a blast of heat rose from the outside base of the wall. Bows, crossbows, and catapults ceased firing.

Morgan and the students rushed to the edge of the battlement. Massive cones of white-hot flames shot from the four holes of Dadore's *ordinance*. One cone of fire set five ladders and the gnomes on them ablaze. Another cone ignited two ladders at the west end of the wall near the cliff. Liquid fire splattered against the wall and ignited dozens of small fires on the ground. Screams filled the air as gnomes plunged to their deaths from the burning ladders.

The other two cones sprayed streams of fire two hundred feet into the clearing. The heat of the flames scorched and scattered hundreds of gnomes who had been waiting to climb the ladders. But as quickly as the eruptions of intense fire had exploded in every direction, the ordinance went dark.

Rowe was the first to react. Rushing to the back guardrail, he grabbed a bow and a handful of arrows and returned to the battlement. "Archers ready, and release at will before they can regroup!"

The soldiers followed his lead, and before the gnomes on the remaining ladders moved a single rung, they found themselves beneath a hail of arrows. At the base of the ladders, burning gnomes rolled on the ground, trying in vain to extinguish the liquid flames. But the more they rolled and brushed themselves, the more the flames spread.

As soon as the ladders were empty, soldiers heaved them up and over the wall. The gnomes who survived the flames retreated across the clearing to the mouth of the thoroughfare, abandoning their dead and dying. The enormous arm of the center catapult flew up, sending a final volley of rocks into the fleeing gnomes.

Illious marched across the wall walk, waving a bloody mace at his two students. "That…that…was *that* what you carried in your wagon?"

Dadore and Kydaris looked sheepishly at one another and shrugged.

"You could have killed us and a hundred others!" Illious continued, spittle spraying as he spoke.

"You did ask for light at the base of the wall," Dadore said.

Kydaris's boyish features cringed. "Not what he wanted to hear."

Tranas ambled between them, his face splattered with blood. He squared up close to Illious. "Why don't you leave them alone and make yourself useful by going to get me something strong to drink!" The big man scowled, and Illious took a few short steps back, too scared to defend his honor, then disappeared into the crowd.

"Well done, lads!" Tranas said as he worked his cramped hands free of the ax handle. He leaned against the railing and examined the bolts in his shoulder and hip.

Rowe limped over and sat beside Tranas, the bolt still lodged in his calf. "Blasted barbs."

"Impossible to pull out," Tranas said with a grimace.

Four young children approached and offered mugs of water and bowls of steaming stew.

"This is no place for them," Rowe said as the children served other soldiers.

"The nightmares will pursue them to the grave," Tranas grumbled.

✦

Morgan helped carry a stretcher with a bleeding, unconscious soldier to the bottom of the stairs.

"Give me that other clamp!" Julie shouted as she and two maidens worked on a soldier lying on his side. One maiden gasped as Julie leaned in with a long stainless-steel clamp that she'd taken from Lady Minto Hospital back in Cochrane.

"Hold him still!" Julie snapped as the soldier writhed in pain.

Five tables were occupied by seriously wounded soldiers. Julie and Gloriana offered assistance and instructions as the volunteers did their best to remove bolts and stitch bloody gashes. Every cot was in use by recovering soldiers with bandages and fresh stitches. A group of porters loaded the bodies of several soldiers onto a wagon set aside for the dead.

Morgan relinquished her grip on the stretcher to a porter who stepped in to take her end. Exhausted, she grabbed a large platter of cheese and fresh bread and trudged up the stairs. She stepped past a wounded soldier and fought back tears when she saw Rowe bleeding beside Tranas.

"You can set that down right here, sweetie," Tranas said, eyeing the cheese and bread.

Morgan resisted the urge to respond to what was probably an unintentional patronizing comment. She grimaced at Rowe's leg.

"Not to worry there, Morgan. A real man would have pulled it out," Tranas said with a wink. "Like I did. See, princess?"

Rowe laughed.

Morgan handed the platter to Tranas and knelt beside Rowe. She drew a knife from her boot and cut away part of his pants. "It's lodged in the muscle," she said with a long sigh. "These bolts are like fishhooks with all the barbs they put on the shaft beneath the tip."

"How'd they hit muscle on that chicken leg?" Tranas said with a mouthful of cheese.

Rowe grabbed several pieces of cheese and stuffed them between two chunks of bread.

"Just pull it," Tranas smirked.

"I'd pull half his leg apart," Morgan snapped. She touched Rowe's skin around the protruding arrow before gripping the shaft with her other hand. She pushed the bolt ever so slightly and Rowe stiffened, but not nearly as much as she'd expected.

"The barbs are almost through," Morgan said.

"You sound like you've done this before," Rowe said through clenched teeth.

"More times than I care to admit." Morgan wiped her forehead with the back of her bloodstained hand.

Tranas reached for the bolt. "Here, let me help."

Morgan slapped his knuckles, but Tranas grinned. She glanced up at the dark-gray sky. "How much time do we have before dawn?"

"I don't think they'll attack again tonight," Rowe said, his voice quavering.

"Shades! I can't imagine what they'll hit us with after a long day to prepare," Tranas said. He took a long drink from his mug.

"Tonight will look after itself," Morgan said. "For now, we need to get this bolt out of you so you can sleep."

"Morgan, sit for a moment before Tranas eats all the cheese and bread," Rowe said.

Tranas chuckled, then lifted his head. "Illious!" He shouted. "A word, if you will."

The master alchemist shuffled over to them.

"Should I be thanking you or those two students of yours?" Tranas asked.

Illious steadied himself with a deep breath. "The boys were lucky that worked as well as it did. I had planned on saving my wiles until day three, maybe day four, but—"

"Not sure if you're keeping score, Illious, but we just had our backsides handed to us!"

"And tonight will be another long night," Rowe added, washing his food down with a large gulp of water.

"I think your two lads need to be loosed," Tranas said.

"Definitely," Rowe agreed. "Give them their heads and see what they come up with."

Illious's jaw flexed. "Fools, the lot of you, if you think those younglings should be given their heads!"

"Are you that dense?" Tranas asked. "Why bring them here only to clip their wings?"

"They have no business dealing with such power!" Illious spat. "Imagine if that ordinance erupted while the gates were open? Then where would we be?" He spun with a flourish of his cloak, muttering as he stormed away. "Blockheads!"

"Is he terrified of what Dadore and Kydaris are capable of, or is he just a crusty old bugger?" Tranas asked.

"I hope neither, because we need those students," Rowe said.

Two barn swallows flew overhead and chased each other playfully, singing to the morning. Morgan marveled at the tiny display of beauty and freedom surrounded by the ugliness of war.

"Keep an eye on the two students, Tranas," Rowe said. "Make sure Illious doesn't cage them."

The smell of meat and eggs from the makeshift cooking area below wafted up to the wall walk, reminding everyone how hungry they were. Children scurried up and down the stairs, carrying as much food and water as their little hands could manage.

Despite wanting to help Rowe, Morgan stepped back as he pulled himself to his feet. His legs trembled.

"Rowe," called a soldier. "We would like to switch out the arm for one three-feet shorter to create a better angle."

"How long will that take?" Rowe asked as he limped beside Morgan.

"Four hours."

"Do you have everything you need for the refit?"

"Everything and more, sir."

Rowe gazed out at the clearing. "Set up for the refit but don't begin until you can see clearly across the field."

"You think they might resume their attack this morning?"

"I doubt it; gnomes cannot survive long in the sun. But let's be sure."

The soldier bowed and returned up the short set of steps to the elevated section of the wall, which was littered with rocks. Another soldier cranked a winch and pulley carrying a large basket of rocks from a wagon buckling beneath the weight of its load.

Morgan groaned as she looked out beyond the wall. The dim light revealed the grim result of hundreds of arrows and rocks, not to mention the modified Illious Fire. Between the smoldering corpses, dozens of gnomes searched for survivors.

Rowe craned his neck and called to Tranas. "I don't want any shooting today."

"Why not?"

"Let them tend to their wounded in peace."

"They wouldn't show us such grace," Tranas grumbled.

"Probably not. But who are we to judge those worthy of mercy? Our current reality is not lost on me, but doing the right thing is not always simple. Good men do not take potshots at others—even their enemies—while they care for their dying friends."

Tranas rolled his eyes and nodded. "You're a better man than I."

When they reached the bottom of the steps, Morgan met her mom walking out from beneath the wall walk and wiping her hands with a towel. Blood saturated her apron.

"Mom!" Morgan said. "You look…amazing, considering…"

Julie smiled. "It was a good night, Morgan. We saved a lot of lives."

The women embraced. Morgan clung to her mother as she realized how many lives had been lost. If the gnomes had broken through and killed her mother, she could not bear the loss. She silently vowed to protect what remained of her family as long as she had strength within her.

Julie pulled away and scanned Morgan from head to foot. "You, on the other hand, look like you need to rest your feet."

"I've never been so tired in my life, Mom."

"And then there's Rowe," Julie added with a heavy sigh. "The man who never rests." She frowned at him when she noticed his bleeding leg. "How are you?"

"I see where Morgan gets her fire," Rowe said.

Morgan smiled. She'd always admired her mother's determined spirit.

"Let's get you on the table and remove that bolt," Julie said.

Around them, the South Crow Gate slowly recovered from the shock and terror of the night. Volunteers collected bloodied linens and washed utensils in pots of boiling water. Many of the helpers were old, moving at a slow but unrelenting pace as Gloriana led the effort to reset the entire operation in preparation for the next attack. Three wagons were leaving the South Crow Gate, two with empty loads, while several dozen returned from the town of Rainia and the Crow's Nest. On the south side of the wall walk, soldiers extinguished lanterns as the dawn of a new day overtook the darkness. A few clouds drifted lazily in the blue sky. It promised to be a nice day were it not for the advance force of the South Gnome Army preparing their next assault.

Morgan helped Rowe onto the only empty table. "I can read the concern on your face like one of your open books in the Records of Time," she said.

"Thinking about Will," Rowe said. He winced as his foot slipped and the bolt in his leg banged against the table. "His leg was far worse than mine last time I saw him."

Morgan nodded as she washed the sweat, blood, and grime from his forehead. "When I first met Will…well, to be honest, I thought he was a mess. He was an awkward, misunderstood loner in a town where people only give you one chance before they decide if you're in or out. But look how far he's come, how far we've all come. There's a fire in him, to steal a phrase from you, Rowe. Somewhere along the way that boy done grow'd up." Morgan flashed a smile at her mother.

Julie laughed softly. "We used to talk like that when Morgan was a little girl," she explained to Rowe. She slipped on a fresh pair of latex gloves and reached for the scalpel she'd been using all night. Wiping it dry, she grimaced at the smell of the cleaning solvents. She scraped a low stool across the hard-packed ground. "All right, let's have a look."

"I can't believe how much energy you still have, Mom," Morgan said.

"Roll onto your side," Julie told Rowe. "You kids were the ones doing the heavy lifting last night."

Rowe looked at her and, seeing the smile on her face, shook his head. "You share the same sense of humor."

"Rest your head on the pillow and try to relax," Julie said, adjusting his leg. "Mussa," she called to a woman, "can you bring over a fresh basin please?"

An older woman wearing an apron like Julie's brought a shallow basin from another table. "Here you are, Julie. Do you want me to help?"

"No, thanks, Mussa. This will be an easy one. How's Gunther?"

"We had to cut off his leg above the knee, and the surgery didn't go well. He hasn't woken yet."

"I'll check on him when I'm done here. Any problems with his IV?"

Mussa shook her head. "I changed the bag like you showed me and it's working well."

"Very good, Mussa." Julie was about to speak to Rowe but noticed he was sleeping.

"See, he does sleep," Morgan said.

Rowe jerked awake suddenly. "How long was I sleeping?"

"Easy, Rowe," Morgan said, running her hand through his hair. "Ten seconds, maybe."

He leaned on an elbow and looked around.

"Who are you looking for?" Morgan asked.

"Has Tranas come off the wall?"

"He's coming down now," Julie said, pointing.

"Tranas," Rowe called.

The councilman hobbled over and stood next to the table.

"We need to send a few carpenters to the North Crow Gate," Rowe said.

"Why?" Morgan asked.

"To remove the gates," Tranas said, staring at Rowe.

"But, why?" Julie asked.

"If we fail to hold this wall," Tranas explained, "the gnomes will break for the North Crow Gate to hold it against the Marauders until the main gnome army arrives. If they succeed, the Crow's Nest will be lost."

"You don't think we can hold the wall?" Morgan asked.

Tranas held Rowe's stern expression as if the women were not present. "I'll send some men."

"Be quiet about it," Rowe said.

"Rowe, answer me," Morgan said.

"That was some bad business last night," Tranas offered.

Rowe's eyes flickered to Morgan. "Better pray, Morgan, because those gnomes need to breach this wall as much as we need to defend it."

CHAPTER 20

CLOVER FIELDS

The rear gate of Will's wagon prison squealed on rusty hinges and crashed open. A strong hand gripped the ankle of his broken leg and pulled. Will flinched. The nauseating crunching of shifting bones reignited the agonizing spasms. Now fully awake, he cried out, kicking with his other leg. His upper back and shoulders scraped across the weathered wooden planks, collecting several slivers before he dropped to the stony ground. The wind exploded from his lungs.

After a few hacking coughs and gasps for air, Will squinted to adjust his eyes to the sunlight. He peered into the deep hood of the gnome tormentor standing over him. He had only encountered the cruel gnome once, at night, but he'd recognize that ugly wart and vicious sneer anywhere.

Grudum's lips tightened into a menacing grin as he pulled back his hood, as if trying to intimidate the feeble human. The gnome was as tall as an average man, but it was hard to determine his mass because of the layers of clothing he and all gnomes wore. He was definitely stockier than the average man. Long, greasy hair spilled around his grubby face. His pointed ears reminded Will of the Elf Queen who had saved his life in the miraculous healing tent, but Grudum's bulbous eyes and flat face were anything but elvish, and far from regal.

"Mornin', Sage," Grudum snarled. Although the gnome sounded simple, Will sensed Grudum was more intelligent than he looked. "Welcome you be to the Clover Fields."

Will moaned, trying to mask the searing pain in his broken leg and hand. He coughed several times as his lungs, thick with phlegm, fought to recover from his sudden impact with the ground.

A group of gnome soldiers marched past, towing six humans shackled at the neck and connected by clanking chains.

"You be part of the latest batch of slaves to be processed, Sage. Best get on those feet or drag you I will to the compost pit. Vile a place it be to spend your final moments in this world."

Will rolled onto his side, trembling. He sucked a sharp intake of air that made his chest crackle, then inched into a sitting position.

Grudum bent down and feigned a backhand. Will cowered and reached to break his fall, but the broken bones in his hand shifted under the pressure and he cried out.

"Grudum! Worthless sack of rot you be," someone shouted.

Grudum kicked the dusty ground, and Will coughed and raised his good hand to his stinging eyes. Grudum shuffled away, grumbling under his breath.

Between labored breaths, Will slowly regained his awkward sitting position. Such a simple task sapped his energy. He struggled against his desire to lay in the dirt and sleep.

"Here, drink you must," a female gnome said.

The kindness in her eyes contrasted with the hatred and anger in Grudum's. Will discerned few other features because of the heavy full-body clothing and the large hooded cloak she wore. But kind eyes were all he needed to calm his nerves, at least for the moment. The way she studied him reminded Will of the other gnome who had offered him water during the night on their journey to the Clover Fields. *Panigim*, she had answered when he surprised her by asking her name.

A gloved hand holding a dirty wooden cup appeared from the folds of the gnome's cloak. Strands of linen covered the skin on her outstretched arm. Will extended a shaking hand and accepted the cup of cloudy water.

The gnome leaned closer and lowered her voice. "Mixed in some tevan root extract I did, to ease your pain."

Will didn't move.

"Worry not, Sage. There be no ill will in me."

Will ventured a few sips and discovered he was having difficulty swallowing.

"That be your cloak up there?" she asked, pointing.

Will followed her finger to a long pole attached to the wagon he'd traveled in. He choked on the water, sputtering as he realized his Trannalun cloak was so close. He longed for the healing magic of the garment, could almost feel its warmth, but with his broken leg and weakened condition, it might as well be a hundred miles away. When he turned back to the gnome, her eyes had narrowed, as if considering whether he would survive another day.

"Thank you," Will said, clearing his gravelly throat and putting on his bravest face. "For the water."

Several gnomes passed by. They were slightly larger than the gnome sitting next to him. Will struggled to recall Panigim's words about the difference between highland gnomes and bush gnomes. She had derided him for not knowing but didn't instruct him either. Will had a sense that if he were to survive, he needed to pay attention. The gnome soldiers were slow and clumsy, unlike the graceful way in which Panigim and the gnome he was speaking to moved. Panigim had spoken harshly of bush gnomes, so Will surmised that the soldiers were bush gnomes. In fact, he realized as he glanced around, most gnomes in the area seemed to be bush gnomes. One other obvious distinction he noticed: the bush gnomes' unkempt appearances and unpleasant smell made them easy to identify, even from a distance.

"Getting familiar with your new home?" the highland gnome asked. "Need this you might." She withdrew a short, crude crutch from within her cloak and dropped it beside him. "Join that line to be processed you must," she added, pointing to a long line of humans leading to a large tent. Without waiting for a response, the gnome scampered away to the next wagon as another group of bush gnomes approached. She offered water to another prisoner who had been dragged from his rolling cell, then she moved to the next wagon.

Will surveyed his surroundings. The only buildings were a dilapidated wooden barn to his left and three large but simple stone structures to his right. The three buildings might have been cattle barns long ago. A tent city sprawled out in front of the three buildings. Although organized, the canvas tents were filthy. Many were packed in so close together it was difficult to tell where one tent ended and the other began. Scraps of rotten food waste and small bones littered the paths and roads. Beyond the tents and buildings was a beautiful sprawling valley marred by scores of human slaves working in acres of vegetable fields. Along the sides of the valley, herds of small, long-haired cattle grazed in lush green meadows.

The humans able to walk on their own wore collars with chains connecting them to other prisoners. All of them were clothed in matching filthy gray pants and shirts. Will suspected that many prisoners had once been soldiers, although there were a few women and children among them.

Several people lay next to the wagons near Will. Some looked dead, while others were so broken they could hardly move. A group of gnomes carrying stretchers collected those who couldn't stand. A man tried to push a stretcher away, but he was beaten unconscious and carried off. The cracking of wooden clubs against fragile bones and skull reached the workers in the fields, who paused only a brief second.

Will's stomach turned at the sound, but he determined not to suffer the same fate. He grabbed the crutch with his good hand and drew a long breath. His lungs rattled. Flashes of tiny stars filled his vision, but within a few agonizing seconds, he was standing on his good leg with the support of the worn-out crutch. His eyes slowly focused on two groups of gnomes carrying stretchers laden with unmoving prisoners. Will gritted his teeth and leaned bravely on the crutch, fearing what Grudum had called *the compost pile*. One harrowing step at a time, he hobbled toward the long line of prisoners. Not his preferred destination, but at least the people in that direction stood on two feet.

As he approached the end of the line, Will felt like a character in a postapocalyptic movie, in a scene where the camera panned the miserable survivors to depict the hopelessness that had befallen the new world. But this was real. The characters in this scene actually suffered and died, and the bad guys were truly violent. Despair slithered into a dark hole in Will's heart. Rowe would probably not show up any moment to save the day. There would be no Joe arriving to cast a magic spell and protect him from the monsters that threatened to kill him. Will was alone.

Back in Cochrane, loneliness was his friend, but if he remained alone in this bleak place, he would certainly die. He had to make friends, or at least allies. He suppressed a horrible-sounding cough, afraid of spreading his sickness to others, but soon heard many coughs that sounded as bad or worse than his.

The line moved faster than Will had expected. Of course, he couldn't imagine the need for long interviews to assign menial tasks to slaves. As he waited for his turn, Will examined his broken leg. Both feet were dirtier than they had been after a week of summer camp when he was young. But his right foot was significantly more swollen than the left. From his knee to his ankle, ugly patches of dark bruises clustered like reddish-purple storm clouds.

The person in front of him left the line, leaving Will face-to-face with a short gnome who sat behind a rickety table littered with parchment. Will noted the gnome's layered clothing: a heavy wool shirt with wide stands of linen wrapped around his arms and chest. On his hands he wore thin gloves that allowed his fingers the flexibility to write. Will unclenched his teeth and loosened his grip on the crutch. Perhaps this highland gnome might offer him a grain of mercy as the other two had.

The gnome grimaced beneath the wide brim of a green leaf-woven hat. Large dark goggles covered his eyes, but Will sensed the gnome was appraising his condition.

"I'm fine," Will said in a deep, raspy voice.

The highland gnome looked up and down Will's body, shaking his head. "Ask how you were I did not."

A gnome soldier appeared at Will's side.

Will stiffened. "I'm…a Callum Sage," he mumbled.

The gnome at the desk leaned to one side and peered past the line behind Will. He frowned. "Told I was they sent you to the depot. Useless half dead you be."

Will seized his only hope. "I can write faster than you can talk."

The gnome scoffed. "But for how long? Walking near death you be."

The soldier grabbed Will's arm.

"I'm ready to write whatever you need," Will said. "Even if I only live three days, that's three days less work for you."

The gnome behind the desk adjusted his goggles. "Wait," he said to the soldier. "Send him to the main depot. Deal with him they can."

"To what end?" the soldier sneered. "Survive the short walk he never will."

"The Shadowfallen wants Callum Sages brought to the depot until his return. And what matter is it to you?" the gnome snapped. He reached behind the desk, grabbed a set of filthy rags that vaguely resembled a pair of pants and a shirt, and handed them to Will. "If you grunts stopped torturing our slaves, simpler this would be! Unless back to working the soil you wish?"

"Bah!" the soldier barked, jerking Will so quickly he nearly went down.

After two hurried hops on his good leg, Will stopped beside the soldier who pointed at the three stone structures fifty yards across a field of clover. "Middle structure be the main depot," the soldier said. He shoved Will, and this time his feet failed him.

Will strained his weary muscles to find a sitting position, but he lacked the strength to stand again. He hung his head, pressing his forehead against his left knee. Tears streaked his dusty cheeks.

But he knew unsympathetic eyes watched him, so he unbundled the dirty clothes and dressed himself.

"Now would be a good time for a heroic rescue, Rowe," Will whispered. He glanced past the line of prisoners to his wagon cell and noticed his cloak was no longer hanging from it. His throat tightened. Every symbol of hope was disappearing.

Will swiped at a fly that buzzed around his chin. His hand settled on his neck, and he thought of the symbol of hope that used to hang around it. Ryowyn needed him, loved him. Somehow, she had stayed alive for him; he vowed to do the same for her.

He pushed his broken hand through the shirtsleeve and slipped the tattered garment over his head. The rough material brushed the back of his hand like tiny hammers. He held both hands in front of him. The broken left hand seemed to balloon with each throbbing beat of his heart. In contrast, the pain in his broken leg was still sharp but sporadic, at least when he kept still.

"They're coming for you," said a man behind him.

Will lifted his head. An old man, possibly a soldier at one time, stood over him. A thin, bruised arm stretched out from filthy rags, offering Will a helping hand. The man clasped Will's right forearm and pulled him to his feet.

"The next time you go down will be your last," the man said before a gnome shouted at them to move apart. "Good luck."

"Thank you," Will said, overwhelmed by the simple act of kindness. "All right then, Mr. Owens," he mumbled to himself, "time to punch a clock."

Will took the first in a long series of labored steps toward the depot building, the crutch bearing most of his weight. A few other humans wearing similar ragged clothing passed him, but everyone kept their eyes to the ground. The old man who had helped him stand was unique. He tried to think of a prayer of thanks that Morgan might offer, but all that came was a simple thank you.

There were few large trees in the area, but Will passed beneath the shadow of a single large oak and paused, savoring the sudden coolness. "Thank you, oak," he said.

As he stood in the shade, Will noticed a person following him less than twenty yards away. The young man stumbled a few steps and fell. Will groaned, wanting to return the help others had offered him, but he was too far away.

Near the wagon Will had arrived in, Grudum turned his attention to the fallen man. The cruel gnome gave a sharp whistle, and two dogs sprang from the old barn and were by his side in an instant, jowls frothing. The dogs reminded Will of his neighbor's Rottweiler. Every soldier near Grudum scattered, but Grudum knelt between the dogs and grasped their chain collars as they sniffed the air. He pointed to the fallen man struggling to gain his feet. Both animals growled. Grudum looked around, then released their chains, and the beasts bolted for the helpless man.

Will froze. The man stood, but his knees buckled and he fell again. Will took a step toward him but came up short, knowing he lacked time and ability to help. Even if he did, what good would he be? The snarling dogs closed the gap in seconds. Will's chest thumped as he limped toward the tree. Its lowest branch was within reach, but with only one good hand, any hope of climbing was futile.

The first dog careened into the man with such momentum they both tumbled through the clover. When the second dog landed on him with its considerable mass, the man cried out, but the vicious creature silenced his screams with a series of terrifying bites. Six gnome soldiers on horseback galloped toward the chilling scene.

After bowling over the man, the first dog rolled a few yards before it came to its feet. It yelped at the other dog tearing into the man, then noticed Will. Without hesitation, it bounded toward him. Will spun and hobbled toward the oak, ignoring the shooting pain in his leg. The footfalls pounded in his ears like those of a charging bull. He would never reach the tree in time, let alone climb to safety. Will reared and raised the crutch, pressing the wide end tight against his shoulder. He squeezed his eyes shut and screamed at the top of his feeble lungs.

With jowls opened wide, the dog ate the end of the stick before it could turn its head. The force of its weight threw Will backward several feet. Writhing on the ground, Will tensed and covered his head, preparing for the terrifying attack. But instead of snapping teeth, he heard galloping horses and shouting gnomes. He opened his eyes, slowly at first, then wide with shock. The dog lay dead not three feet away, with the wide end of the crutch protruding from its bleeding mouth. Tears of disbelief pooled in Will's eyes. With the last of his strength, he crawled to the dog and jerked the crutch free. Will shivered at the sound it made, like pulling a boot from clotted mud.

The gnomes on horseback gathered around him. Behind them, three riders chased the other dog back to the barn. Before it entered the building, the dog turned. Despite beads of sweat rolling down Will's face, an icy chill tickled the length of his spine.

"Gods be damned!" a gnome rider said with a loud, raspy laugh. "The luck you possess!"

"Try such a thing a thousand times you could only to end up dead every time," another said.

Will leaned on the crutch and stood. His legs were shaking so much he would have fallen over without support.

"Here." A third gnome rider tossed Will a waterskin.

Will inhaled a few deep breaths, trying to settle his frantic heart before it exploded. He was uncertain if his voice would cooperate, but he pushed his luck. "Do you have any food?"

"Stones he has, and right where they belong," the first gnome said. The three riders burst out laughing.

The second soldier tossed a small sack of mixed nuts at Will's feet. "Earned at least that much you have, for killing one of Grudum's monsters."

The riders reared their mounts and returned to the prisoner wagons.

For the third time in less than a few minutes, Will wanted to cry. Until now, the only reason Grudum had to hate him was that he was human. Now the gnome's hatred would be personal, and Will could not imagine the cruel vengeance to follow.

By the time he reached the main depot, the sun was straight above him in the cloudless sky. Sweat poured from his body, but he could not stop shivering. He crossed a wide, hard-packed road in front of the depot, walking straight and tall, at least in his mind. But even through his fever, he knew he must look drunk as he swayed and hopped across the hot surface.

Two gnomes sat at a long table in the shade of the depot's gaping doorway, pointing at Will and snickering.

"Seen ghosts in better shape I have," one gnome said.

"The Callum Sage, you be?" the other asked, pointing to a red bundle lying beside the table.

Will nodded as he hobbled close.

The gnomes leaned back in their chairs as if expecting the sickly human to crash into them. When he didn't, one gnome cleared his throat, and two gnome soldiers joined them.

"Take him to a pen before he dies where he stands," a gnome said.

A soldier grabbed Will's upper arm and pushed him toward a nearby wagon. Will's peripheral vision was failing; the world around him grew dark. A cage door creaked open, and the hand that gripped his arm shifted to his head.

"Bend down you must to get in, fool."

Will stopped. "Can you…well, just tell Ryowyn…I'm sorry," he mumbled.

"Tell her yourself you can." The gnome sniggered. "In the next life."

Will stumbled forward, catching himself with his good hand before collapsing face-first into moldy hay. He rolled over and yielded his weary and broken body to the rough bedding as it carried him into unconsciousness.

CHAPTER 21

THE IRON MINES

Joe stood on a narrow path along the jagged ridgeline of the Siodin Mountains north of the Niasa Sea. He gazed into the cloudless afternoon sky and waved goodbye to the giant eagle and to Shaey, the elven eagle rider. He felt as awkward as an adult waving at a childhood rock 'n' roll idol. But in all his years in the Fourwinds, he had met no one who had the privilege of riding a giant eagle, let alone meeting an eagle rider. Now, in less than a week, he had ridden twice. And both times with Shaey.

As the eagle disappeared behind the mountains, Joe drew deep, slow breaths and leaned on his walking stick to help his footing as he navigated the treacherous terrain. The cool winds off the Niasa Sea soothed his flushed face as he approached the sharp dogleg in the trail that bent south, leading him to his first view of the sea in decades.

Now that he was back on solid ground, Joe's thoughts turned to General Raric, the Druid Margrave, and the dragon hide melding. The smell of burning flesh permeated Joe's clothing, his hair, his skin. He would welcome a hot bath and a change of clothes in

Fairbay. When Margrave had finished fusing the dragon armor to the general's skin, Joe had carefully encased the hideous wounds in ice to give Raric a fighting chance when he awoke. The precise density and mass of each layer was a tedious but necessary procedure. The wounds must stay frozen for at least thirty-six hours. Even with the ice and the extensive magic used to help Raric, Joe and Margrave were under no illusions as to the general's chances of awakening, let alone surviving to face Uluk the Shadowfallen.

With nothing more for Joe to do in the Druid Forest, Margrave had summoned Shaey to expedite Joe's passage to the Niasa Sea. Elves were reluctant to respond to human affairs, and eagles even less so. Fortunately, Shaey shared Margrave's concern about Uluk's secretive activities in the Gryton Mines.

Joe was especially interested in the welfare of the Niasa Sea. Before leaving the Fourwinds, he had lived in Fairbay, the sleepy fishing village that was a haven for travelers, healers, and merpeople. But now as he approached the sea, a sense of longing pressed against his chest. His friends, he knew, were now ghosts—except for Ryodan Ayoust, king of the merpeople. The Gryton Mines were on the way to Fairbay, so Joe decided to take the secret path through the Siodin Mountains, a path that descended to the bluffs overlooking the town of Gryton.

What the Siodins lacked in size, they made up for in rugged beauty. Most of the range was unclimbable due to the jagged rock. For fifty coastal miles, waves crashed against the bluffs, patiently carving intricate sculptures in the rocky outcroppings hidden just beneath the surface. A narrow pass provided the only commonly known entrance to the inlet, a small patch along the shoreline that had once sheltered the small mining town of Gryton.

Until recently, the inlet town had been abandoned, the four

main entrances to the mines dark and quiet. Deep within a massive rocky shelf that jutted out of the mountains, the Gryton Mines possessed a rich vein of iron ore known throughout the Fourwinds for producing strong steel. Despite the high quality of the iron, transporting the raw material through the Siodins was difficult, and trade negotiations with the merpeople prevented transport by sea. In time, the mine had closed due to high transportation costs.

Joe maneuvered each step down the path. He crossed a narrow field overrun by brambles and boulders, then stepped onto the bluffs. His pulse quickened as the vast expanse of the sea materialized before him. The sound of crashing waves brought him to tears, the sweet melody a forgotten song. He breathed in the familiar salty blend of the Niasa's unique marine life. Now that he stopped walking, sweat beaded on his brow; he rolled up his tunic sleeves and unfastened the top two buttons.

Scanning his surroundings, he noticed a human soldier creeping along the bluffs directly across from him. Joe ducked behind a boulder, out of sight. Still a few hundred yards away from the man, Joe watched as two more soldiers moved stealthily between rocks. Given their vantage point, it was obvious they were also spying on Uluk's mining operation.

The soldiers climbed down a steep section of rock to a thin ledge two hundred feet above the town. Joe lowered himself onto his belly and crawled to the edge of the bluff. The mining town sprawled across the inlet. At the base of the far bluffs were six rows of small cottages. Closer to the gaping mine openings was a large structure that housed the main smelter. A stone smokestack towered fifty feet above the center of the building. At first, the smelter looked dormant, but as Joe stared, a thin line of steam rose from the stack. The wind shifted slightly, and a moment later, a pungent, indiscernible odor reached his hiding place.

Joe covered his nose with a small kerchief and moved to a comfortable position. Over the next two hours or so, he studied the transformed shoreline. Drawing on his experience as a police investigator in Toronto, he gathered clues that might reveal Uluk's criminal activity. Three warehouses dominated the area. Between two warehouses, a single catapult was aimed at the mountain pass. The large swing arm was cranked down and loaded with a giant flask filled with a cloudy liquid. Whatever Uluk was doing in the mines, he clearly meant to defend the operation. *Clue number one.*

A set of railway tracks led from the smelter into the warehouses, and more tracks sloped down from each warehouse to the water's edge. A tremendous amount of work must have gone into the construction of huge, rocky beds to support the rails over the water where they ended twenty feet from the shore. Joe pondered the rails for a few minutes. With no piers or docks, and with waves constantly breaking on the shore, it would be impossible to get a ship near the warehouses, which made the rails seem like a futile project. *Clue number two.*

The strangest part of the entire scene below was the hundreds of gnomes hard at work during the heat of the day despite being allergic to direct sunlight. Covered in layers of clothing to protect their skin, the gnomes struggled for each step, keeping to the shade whenever possible. Workers pushed mine carts from tunnel openings to the smelter. Each cart was full, not with chunks of iron ore, as Joe expected, but with the powdery tailings from the mines. A steady stream of carts emerged from the far end of the smelter and traveled down a track that appeared to pass through all three warehouses before completing its loop at the mine entrance. Joe couldn't see what the carts contained when they left the smelter, but they were empty when they left the warehouses. *Clue number three.*

As he tried to make sense of the strange operation, Joe caught sight of the corner of another catapult that was mostly hidden beyond the farthest warehouse. Like the other catapult, the arm was loaded, but this one was aimed in the opposite direction, pointed at the sea. Joe was perplexed. He knew the merpeople well, and a single catapult would be useless to defend the beach if a battle began. What kind of weapon would Uluk point at the powerful merpeople? *Clue number four.*

The gentle onshore breeze shifted as a low cloud masked the late-afternoon sun, and a warm wind flowed from the mountains. This slight change in climate signaled the unveiling of Uluk's mysterious operation. A dozen human soldiers appeared from hiding along the far bluffs, quietly scurrying to the catapult aimed at the mountain pass. Three soldiers carried bows and quivers of arrows. Seeing them reminded Joe of Will's story about a similar flask transported by a storm giant that Will had burst with an arrow. Will had said the flask contained a deadly gas called Guilliad that destroyed all living things in its path. The gnomes here at the mine must have planned on using Guilliad to defend against an attack from the pass. But they would need the regular onshore breeze to carry it up into the mountains, away from their mining operation. If the soldiers intended to destroy this flask now, the rare offshore breeze would carry Guilliad directly into the operation, destroying the gnomes, the buildings…and the second catapult.

Joe's heart beat faster, and he rubbed his sweaty palms together. He needed to know what was in that second catapult. The safety of Uluk's army of gnomes was of little concern, but if Guilliad—or something worse—threatened the home of Ryodan and his people, Joe refused to be a spectator. Scooting back from his perch, he followed the narrow path to a chasm in the bluffs, then down a precarious set of switchbacks that led to the water's edge. The last time he was crazy enough to complete the decent, he'd been a teenager. Now that his body was old and frail, he drew a deep breath and took the first of many difficult steps.

At the bottom of the harrowing trail, Joe followed a rocky ledge that remained perpetually damp from the water breaking just beneath it. He rounded a corner, and the warehouses came into view. He was now closer to the second catapult but still could not see the contents of the bucket. Before he could move, there was a loud crash, and he knew immediately that the soldiers had shattered the flask containing Guilliad.

Deep guttural screams filled the air, and clusters of bush gnomes raced toward the warehouses. Many gnomes were cut down by arrows from the bluffs. Joe ducked behind a large rock. The warehouse doors flung open, and gnome workers pushed mine carts along the tracks toward the sea. One after another, the carts splashed into the water, quickly covering the surface with thick black sludge.

Gnome soldiers rushed to the warehouses as the expanding Guilliad gas disintegrated the catapult. Within seconds, the smelter building began to crumble as the mountain breeze carried the destructive gas toward the sea. Gnome cries grew frantic as their powerful weapon turned on them, pinning them between Guilliad and the grisly, dark water. In a few minutes, life in the inlet would be snuffed out.

Joe was contemplating an icy spell to stop the sludge from poisoning the merpeople's habitat when suddenly, beyond the black sludge, the sparkling water churned. About thirty mer soldiers clad in dark-blue coral plate armor exploded from the depths, sailing effortlessly over the contaminated water. As their tails transformed to legs in midair, they launched their tridents into the gnomes, who were caught defenseless. The mer soldiers landed near their victims and pulled their tridents free, then made a frantic dash for the catapult facing the sea, cutting through the ranks of gnomes with savage intensity.

Joe craned his neck for a better view and finally saw the payload in the catapult's bucket: a translucent glass flask, at least six feet in diameter, filled with a murky liquid. Inside the flask, thousands of tiny minnow-like creatures swam furiously, struggling to escape their prison. Three gnomes leapt onto the catapult to release the stop pegs. Another gnome shouted and tugged on a long rope. The enormous swing arm lurched forward, shaking the deck. The flask sailed in a high arc. For a moment, the shouts and fighting on the shoreline stopped. Joe's stomach clenched as the final piece of Uluk's plan fell into place. The flask struck the water and shattered. What followed was a nightmare.

The water around the broken flask roiled. Dozens of mer soldiers who were nearby slapped at the tiny creatures, then screamed uncontrollably. Seconds later, the entire bay was frothing. Joe shouted as a mer soldier swam toward him, jerking from side to side. The soldier screamed and dropped beneath the surface. When he came up, a dark, minnow-like creature slithered into his nose. Scores of the tiny creatures covered his head and chest, their razor-sharp fins slicing the soldier's flesh. Many slid into his ears, nose, and mouth. More mer soldiers sprang from the water, shrieking and tearing at their own flesh as they struggled to remove the creatures.

Joe stumbled backward against a rock, his breathing coming in sharp gasps. Scores of mer soldiers exploded from the water in a desperate attempt to escape, only to plunge back into the lethal water filled with the tiny nightmares. Those who reached the shore were fighting wildly as the tiny creatures slithered into their noses, ears, and eyes. The rocks and sand were a bloody mess. The shocked gnomes fled along the beach as far from the mer soldiers as possible, but the cloud of Guilliad was wafting toward the beach, slowed momentarily by the large smelter.

Helpless, Joe had no choice but to flee. Spinning around, he crossed the wet ledge and started up the set of crude steps carved into the rock, struggling for breath. For a minute he was sure he was having a heart attack as he clambered up the rocky path as quickly as his old bones would allow.

When he reached the first switchback, he stopped and nearly emptied his stomach when he looked back. A mer soldier was pulling himself onto the shelf Joe had been on moments ago. Bloody claw marks covered the soldier's face. He gnashed his teeth and glared at Joe with wild black eyes. Driven by something Joe could not comprehend, the mer soldier climbed after him. After a few steps, the soldier fell to the ground, twitching and rolling as his moist blue skin turned a dry, sickly gray. He screamed and clawed the rock with bloody fingers that resembled talons.

Joe turned and continued up the treacherous path without a second glance. At the top of the ridge, he looked down at the shoreline. The entire mining operation—smelter, cottages, warehouses, and gnomes—had been converted to a rocky wasteland. The sea was a gory nightmare of mer soldiers and sea creatures writhing in agony.

Without hesitation, Joe turned south to warn the people of Fairbay.

CHAPTER 22

RECOVERING AT THE SOUTH CROW GATE

Without a sound, Rowe removed his Trannalun cloak and dangled his legs off the operating table. He sat up and stretched with a quiet yawn. Fresh, brilliant-white bandages were swathed around his lower leg. Between Julie's surgical expertise at extracting the gnome bolt from his calf, and the reviving capacity of the cloak, there wasn't a hint of blood. Despite the quick healing and four solid hours of sleep, he was exhausted. He looked enviously at Morgan sleeping quietly on a cot next to the table. Throughout the triage area, soldiers, porters, and medics slept within the shade of the South Crow Gate.

Rowe tossed his cloak over his shoulder and tested his weight on the bandaged leg. Standing was painless. He took a few steps without a limp, breathed a grateful sigh, and climbed the stairs to the wall walk.

The midday sun beat down on the uncovered wall where soldiers hid behind the battlement with arrows nocked, wide-eyed. Strange, Rowe thought, it was too early for the battle to begin. He wandered over to the ballista. Dadore and Kydaris stood back near the guardrail within earshot of Tranas and Illious in the midst of an impassioned argument. The boys wore sheepish looks, like children who had been caught lighting fires where they shouldn't have.

"Gentlemen." Rowe climbed the steps to the platform, raising a hand to shield his eyes from the shimmering sunlight.

"Rowe, they've been shooting at us, if you can believe the gall," Tranas said.

Rowe donned his cloak and approached the battlement. In the clearing below, gnomes were still carrying off their wounded, but at the center of the battlefield was a semicircular wall of timbers protecting a small troop and a ballista. A bolt ricocheted off Rowe's cloak, and he backed away from the battlement.

Tranas was smirking. "I suppose the grace you spoke of was lost on the gnomes."

"I guarantee it meant something to the wounded who didn't have to bleed alone on foreign soil as the sun slowly burned the life from them."

Illious glared.

"I never said you couldn't shoot back at them," Rowe said with a yawn.

"And I never said we didn't," Tranas countered. "But our arrows won't penetrate their blockade."

Dadore ventured a step toward the men. "Begging your pardons, but we do have—"

Illious flashed a threatening frown that cut off his young student.

"Why the short leash, Illious?" Rowe asked calmly.

"They do not comprehend the potential repercussions of their actions!"

"So why did you bring them?" Tranas pressed.

Illious's face turned a fiery red. "I brought them to support me in my work, but evidently they had other ideas!"

"I'm not sure if you've been keeping score, Illious, but—" Tranas began.

"There's as much blood on my hands as yours, Councilman! But if these two are not restrained, they could do infinitely more harm than good."

Rowe stepped between Tranas and Illious. "There won't be anything left to harm if we don't come together and find a way to get through another night," he said. "Shades! Listen to that commotion." The distant rumbling of timbers being moved and the thumping of sledge hammers in the thoroughfare echoed across the clearing.

"They've been at it all morning," Tranas said. "They mean to end this quickly and then prepare to hold the North Crow Gate against the Marauders. In the meantime, they've got us trapped up here."

"Take a stroll, Illious, and let me talk to those boys," Rowe said.

"How dare you speak to me with such a—"

Tranas wrapped a massive arm around Illious's shoulders and directed him away from Rowe. "As much as I enjoy our banter, Illious," Tranas said, "you'd be well served by minding that tongue of yours. In case you haven't noticed, this isn't a place of *learning*; this is a place of *doing*. So, you'd best leave the doing to those that do best."

Illious huffed. "Very well. But their actions will be on your heads." He glared at Rowe, then stormed away.

Tranas waved Dadore and Kydaris over. "Mind telling us why Illious is so angry with you?"

Dadore glanced at Kydaris and then at Illious as he lowered

his voice. "Illious is a Master Alchemist and perhaps the greatest instructor ever. He walks around the Alchemist Hall like a god, and perhaps he should. His problem with us is, well—"

"We've learned everything he knows in half a term, and everyone recognizes it—except him," Kydaris interjected.

Dadore nodded. "For whatever reason, Kydaris and I excel at alchemy, and doubly so when we work together."

"It infuriates Illious," Kydaris said. "Whereas he creates his famous Illious Fire a drop at a time, we produce it by the gallon."

"So why did he bring you here?" Rowe asked. "Why not kick you out of the Alchemist Hall and be done with you?"

"He tried, but the other masters protested," Kydaris said. "So Illious insists on keeping us, well...*leashed*, as you say."

Rowe looked at Tranas, who shrugged.

"All right, then," Rowe said, scratching his chin. "If we removed your leash, could you make that barricade out there go away?"

Dadore's eyes brightened. "Could we utilize the ballista?"

"If I said yes...?"

"We have two wagons with us," Kydaris said. "Can we access them without fear of reprisal from Illious?"

"I'll see to it myself," Tranas said.

"How much time do you need?" Rowe asked.

"To make that go away?" Dadore wore a mischievous grin. "Not long...if we can use the ballista."

Rowe nodded. "Get at it, then."

"What about Illious? He can be mean," Dadore said.

"The brutal type of mean," Kydaris added.

"Tranas will have a conversation with Illious in a manner he will understand," Rowe said.

The boys exchanged an apprehensive expression.

Tranas chuckled. "Believe me, boys, he won't so much as swivel his beady eyes in your direction when I'm done with him." He patted their shoulders and went to find Illious. Dadore and Kydaris raced down the stairs to their supply wagon.

Rowe gazed across the Rainia Valley to the Crow's Nest. The castle was a much better fortress than the South Crow Gate, but the distance between the two was significant. If the gnome army breached the wall, Rowe realized the defenders of the valley would never make it to the safety of the castle.

A lone rider approached. At first Rowe thought it was Morgan but soon realized it was Julie. While removing the bolt from his leg, she had spoken of her desire to check on Ryowyn in the Records of Time.

As he watched Julie dismount, Rowe wondered how long Ryowyn could survive away from her home in the Niasa Sea. Somehow, Will's love sustained her. Was it conceivable that her love was simultaneously keeping Will alive? Remembering the beating and the violent way Will had been captured, Rowe despaired. But Will was beyond his reach now. Morgan had said Will was resilient, but slave runners were ruthless and bush gnomes were merciless. If they beat him so he was incapable of working, the gnomes would have no use for him at the Clover Fields. Rowe swiped at a tear, unwilling to imagine his friend dying alone.

Death had become commonplace in Rowe's world. But what troubled him most was that, within a few days, his friends had been dispersed across the Fourwinds. He had been so confident when Will and Morgan were restored in the elven healing tents. Even General Raric had been healed, although to what extent, Rowe was uncertain. That left his age-old and elusive friend, Bremer. Surely, the rogue had left the elven outpost by now, but where would he go? Would he find his way to the South Crow Gate to help, or would he vanish for months the way he sometimes did? They could certainly use his blades here. But the rogue preferred to choose his own battles. Maybe he decided to return to the Waerdreath to finish off Queen Sidara. But Will had killed her, hadn't he? Or had she simply fled, only to rise again and fight another day? The questions tumbled in Rowe's head like leaves in a gust of wind until a sharp whistle startled him.

A soldier manning the ballista shouted: "Mind your ears!"

Dadore, Kydaris, and two soldiers knelt beside the weapon with hands over their ears. A soldier pulled the rope to launch the ballista. There was an emphatic thump and the large bolt whooshed into the battlefield. When it struck the gnome's wooden barricade, an explosion rattled the wall. The soldiers and the two junior alchemists rushed to the battlement to see pieces of the barricade raining down. A resounding cheer erupted as the surviving gnomes fled to the mouth of the thoroughfare. The clearing was empty, at least until dark.

Rowe stared at Dadore and Kydaris. "That was fast," he said.

"That was easy," Kydaris said.

"Can you do more of that when the gnomes attack tonight?"

"How much more?" Dadore asked.

"Can you blow up the whole cursed clearing?" Tranas asked.

"That would take someone more powerful than any alchemist we know," Kydaris said.

Dadore lowered his voice. "Illious confiscated most of our really fun stuff back at the Alchemist Hall, but we still have a few ideas."

"Very good, then, what do you need to prepare?" Rowe asked.

"We could use a few soldiers."

"Four would be appreciated," Kydaris added.

"You," Rowe said, pointing to the four nearest soldiers, "get these two whatever they need, and be quick about it."

"Yes, sir," they said, following the boys.

The late-afternoon sun cast lengthy shadows along the wall walk. Morgan made her way to Rowe and Tranas, staying clear of busy soldiers bringing rocks for the catapults and massive bolts for the ballista. Others were hauling kegs of water. Bundles of arrows lined the battlements, and dozens of bows leaned against the railing. The South Crow Gate was well stocked for a protracted siege, but ordinarily there would be a substantial army to defend it.

Morgan stood a few paces behind Rowe and Tranas, waiting for a break in their conversation.

"I think we should lock and barricade the gatehouse," Rowe said, muffling his voice.

Tranas shook his head, leaning against the west tower catapult. "If we do that, you'll be saying that you believe we'll lose the wall tonight."

"I realize that, Tranas, but what happens if even a small group of gnomes gets inside the gatehouse? It wouldn't take long for them to figure out how to release the locks, and if that portcullis rises and the gate is opened, we would never get it closed again."

"I know." Tranas hung his head. "I've been hoping all day that by some miracle the Marauders might arrive early."

"I think our best hope tonight is in those two students."

"Do we send all the maidens and aged back to the Crow's Nest?"

Rowe shook his head. "We need them."

"I suppose you're right. And besides, I don't expect any of them would leave."

Morgan moved closer. "You're right: no one is leaving."

They both turned to face her, and Tranas cocked an eyebrow at Rowe. "I have work to attend to," Tranas said. "I'll see you at the briefing." He brushed past Morgan on his way to the gatehouse.

"Morgan. You look…" Rowe faltered. "I was going to say *rested*, but…" He looked down at his feet. "Uh…pleasing. You look…pleasing."

The soldiers who had been working on the catapult left for another load of rocks, leaving Morgan and Rowe alone.

She flashed a smile. "When did you learn how to speak to a lady?" She stepped closer. "Just kidding. I wish I could say *you* look rested, but… I like the new scar on your cheek—makes you look tough."

Rowe glanced around, and his face turned a light shade of red. Before he could respond, she pressed against him. He stepped back and bumped into the catapult.

"Gotcha," she said as he swallowed hard and looked down at her. She leaned up and kissed the corner of his mouth.

He glanced at the gatehouse as if expecting the soldiers to return at any minute. His hands rested on her waist, keeping her from getting too close, but the look in his eyes suggested he was longing for more of her at the same time. He leaned to kiss her, and she kissed him back as her hands worked through his tangled hair. His warm tongue touched her dry lips and ignited a fire within her. She drew her head back slightly and gazed into his eyes. He pulled her closer, and her lips caressed his ear.

"Forget everyone," she whispered. She kissed his ear, then returned to his lips.

For a brief moment, *she* forgot everything except the sparkle in his eyes and the warmth of his body against hers.

Thumping footfalls beyond the gatehouse burst the magical moment, and they parted. The soldiers returned and dumped three small wagonloads of rocks for the catapult.

Morgan jogged over to the dogleg part of the battlement that overlooked the Misty Gorge. Rowe followed her until they could no longer see the soldiers. She seized his hand, and they stopped between two merlons. The rectangular gap in the battlement was just wide enough for them to press close together as they leaned over the wall. A warm breeze brushed her cheeks. Rowe put his arm around her, and she studied his face as he gazed into the stunning gorge. After a moment, he turned, and she wished she could stop time.

"I love you," he said suddenly, then turned again to the sun-soaked vista. "I've loved you since the moment I removed your boots that first night in the Records of Time. Since we first drank elven mead together as I waited for you to awaken. Since the first time you spoke my name."

Morgan stood in silence as his first three words lingered in her ears. It was more than she'd expected, but somehow, hearing his expression of love felt natural.

"Whatever happens tonight," he continued, "I have to say this now. Morgan, I…" He took a deep breath before the words poured from his lips. "Of all the words I've read in the Records of Time, none come close to capturing the depths of what I'd like to say. And this view… it's magnificent, vast, mysterious, and wild, but I cannot take my eyes off your face. Of all my experiences as a Callum Sage, and the friendships I've formed, none compare to the bond I feel with you. I know we've only known each other for a brief time, but all my longings and pursuits find meaning in my relationship with you."

The wind tousled her hair, blowing it across her face. He smoothed it back and held his hand a moment longer. He lifted his other hand and buried his fingers in her hair, massaging gently. She closed her eyes and smiled as the tension in her shoulders relaxed. He kissed her forehead, her brow, her cheek, and then her lips. She lost track of time, surrendering to the fire inside, lost in the sweetness and wonder of his intoxicating mouth. He slaked her thirst better than elven mead, and she could not drink enough.

The sound of another load of rocks crashing onto the catapult pile nearby caused them both to flinch. Their lips parted, but he held her cheeks. The sincerity and intensity of his gaze filled her with a calm assurance, and her words came naturally.

"I love you too," she whispered.

He smiled and released a contented sigh. A moment later, his eyes shifted to the catapult, and his familiar frown returned. "I must address the soldiers before battle, but I don't know what to say to them."

"The words will come." She took his hand and fixed her eyes on his. "They look to you because you're good, and you're strong. They'll follow you and they will fight for you, and together we will defend this wall."

He straightened, and his eyes brightened as if her words momentarily dispelled his fear and doubt.

"You will not fail, Rowe. You don't know how." She hugged him tight, and he kissed the top of her head. "I love you," she whispered into his chest.

"How many do you have?" Rowe asked as the sun crept toward the western horizon.

"Kydaris is preparing the last one," Dadore said. "So, three."

"Will they throw as much fire as the one last night?" Tranas asked.

Dadore shook his head. "The explosion should spray liquid fire in a wider radius than last night. If we had known what to prepare for, we could have brought more, but we struggled to hide this much from Illious. We'll bring them up one at a time and clear the top deck before each launch."

"Good luck," Rowe offered as he and Tranas went to meet the soldiers near the gatehouse.

"Illious is in a wickedly foul mood," Tranas said, shaking his head. "But he won't hinder those lads tonight—maybe not ever. I may have gone at him a little hard."

"Any chance of him trying to outshine his students?"

"Here's hoping," Tranas said with a short salute. "I just hope we haven't given those younglings enough rope to hang us all."

Rowe supervised the vast amount of work occurring behind the wall. Soldiers and volunteers were making final preparations as the sun disappeared.

"Is the gatehouse secured, Tranas?"

"It is, but I don't like it." Tranas stood his ground near the side entrance of the gatehouse. "If they want the gates open, they'll do so over my dead body!"

Rowe offered only a few words of encouragement to the less-than-two-hundred surviving members of Striker Company. "And in addition to your skilled bows and blades," he concluded, "we have another fiery surprise for our enemy tonight!"

The soldiers cheered, but each man wore fatigue like a heavy, constricting cloak.

"Wait until we hear them coming before lighting the watch fires," Rowe said. "It won't be long now."

CHAPTER 23

Day 2 on the South Crow Gate

Morgan took up her position on the wall walk as soldiers lit the massive overhanging watch fires one by one. She ventured closer for a better view. Although she couldn't hear gnome voices, there was movement in the dark clearing. Apprehension among the soldiers swelled until Tranas shattered it with the hum of his bow. The peaceful night gave way to war.

A volley of arrows descended silently into the thunder of footfalls. The light from watch fires revealed hundreds of foot soldiers led by the familiar canoe-shaped attackers. Last night, the initial assault had brought three groups, which broke into nine ladders. This attack would bring thirty ladders crashing onto the battlement within minutes.

"Send it!" Rowe shouted to Dadore.

The young alchemist tugged a long rope and tripped the catapult lever. The arm slammed forward, launching a large flask toward the approaching army. Dadore dove behind the cover of a merlon.

"Down!" Rowe shouted.

The soldiers dropped behind the battlement, terror flickering across each face.

The shattering of the flask caused a roaring vortex that sucked air from the clearing to feed the abrupt, horrifying explosion of fire that obliterated gnomes in an eighty-foot radius. Beyond the epicenter, liquid fire rained down another hundred feet out. Screams filled the night as gnomes tried to brush fire from their bodies, only to spread it to others. A hail of arrows followed from the wall.

Four of the approaching ladder groups burst into flames. But despite the mayhem, the flask overshot the main group of ladders. Spurred by the panic behind them, the six remaining ladder groups broke apart and redoubled their efforts. Behind them, gnomes gave the inferno a wide berth as they sprinted toward the wall. Of the eighteen ladders that struck the wall, only four were knocked aside by a large ballista bolt. The remaining fourteen were out of the ballista's range, and gnomes scrambled upward like an army gone mad.

Soldiers released volley after volley of arrows, and soon gnome bodies littered the base of the ladders. The liquid fire slowly died out and the smell of scorched flesh permeated the air.

Although shaken, the gnomes had strong leadership and quickly reformed battle lines. Crossbowmen assembled in the clearing and shot at the wall. The arrows from the battlement slowed. *195. 194. 193.*

Gnomes rushed up the ladders until they were close enough to shoot their smaller handheld crossbows. *192. 191.* Many of the soldiers exchanged their bows for long lances and small shields that they strapped to their arms to defend against the bolts.

"Shields up! Here they come!" Rowe shouted as sharp lances pierced the gnome advance. Half the soldiers released arrows into the swarming masses below while the other half engaged the gnomes at the top of the ladders. *190. 189.* Battle cries gave way to the clashing of metal as the first wave of gnomes fought to scale the battlement.

Two hours into the battle, the defenders had stalled the gnome assault when they came within reach of the lances. But at such close range, and with daunting numbers, their bolts slowly cleared a passage to the top of the battlement. *165. 164. 163.*

After the third hour, the first gnome dropped onto the wall walk and was quickly cut down. A fresh burst of bolts followed. *143. 142. 141.*

A flurry of bolts whizzed around Rowe. *140. 139.* While reaching for a freshly stocked quiver, Kydaris reached up and tugged his cloak.

The young student crouched next to Rowe and shouted over the wailing of dying gnomes and soldiers: "We have one more ready!"

"I thought there were three!" Rowe shouted back while nocking another arrow.

"The last one failed, but Dadore is working on something else!" *138. 137.*

"Launch it!" Rowe bellowed. Several soldiers formed a defensive circle of shields for Kydaris, and two soldiers carefully loaded the flask of modified Illious Fire into the catapult bucket. *136. 135. 134.* All at once, they scrambled from the catapult. Kydaris crouched beneath a shield and, with eyes squeezed shut, pulled the rope. The catapult arm sprang forward, but only halfway, stopped short by chains that soldiers had hooked to the bucket. The moment the flask took flight, the soldiers around the catapult shot at it as the battle raged around them. One arrow struck its mark. *133. 132.*

The flash lit the clearing, illuminating a sea of gnome archers advancing toward the ladders. At the center of the gnome offensive was an enormous wood-framed structure as high as the wall, with four ladders surrounding a broad platform on top that could accommodate twenty gnomes. Dozens of shielded gnomes pushed and pulled the structure across the clearing over a sequence of rolling logs. The momentum they had already gained would have carried the structure crashing against the South Crow Gate within minutes if not for the explosion halfway between the wall and the rolling structure.

⁂

Morgan gasped and almost dropped the end of the stretcher as the writhing soldier lying on it shielded his face against the sudden brightness in the night sky. "Keep moving!" Morgan shouted to the porters ahead of her carrying two more stretchers.

At the bottom of the stairs, Julie looked up, blood splattered across her face and apron. She shook her head and pointed toward the barns. Two porters grabbed the stretcher and left with the soldier she had been operating on.

Morgan lowered her stretcher onto the table, and Julie handed her a waterskin. "Stop bringing down anyone who's about to die," Julie whispered.

Morgan took a deep drink, then rubbed an aching shoulder. "But—"

"We only had two bombs, Morgan, and that was the second. We need to concentrate on those who can return to the fight." Julie's eyes were wide and full of fear.

Despite the powerful explosions, Morgan knew their numbers were dwindling. She gripped the hilt of her sword. "I promised I would keep my sword sheathed until the final hour, Mom. But that hour has come." Tears burned her eyes. "Do you still have the long knife I gave you?"

Julie nodded, pointing to the tray of bloodied instruments beside her. The women embraced, tight and quick. "I never imagined what those fencing lessons were preparing you for, Morgan." A gentle smile touched her lips, erased by battle cries above. *131. 130. 129. 128. 127.* "Coach would be fighting beside you, kiddo, and he'd be proud as punch."

Morgan studied her mother's face a few more precious seconds. "See you soon, Mom." She took a final drink, tossed the empty skin aside, and strode up the stairs. Her sword hummed with a magical intensity that tingled down her arm, igniting her adrenaline as she held it high.

⚜

As Kydaris's experimental fire rained down, spreading through the gnome ranks, the remainder of Striker Company strengthened their efforts to take advantage of the confusion. The explosion had engulfed the large platform and those around it in flames, scattering the gnome army. Some huddled in small pockets, launching their heavy crossbows at the wall, but the catapults stifled their efforts with a barrage of rocks. More than half of the South Gnome Army retreated from the growing inferno. Gnome commanders roared over the shrieks of death, yelling for those able to continue to push toward the ladders. The gnomes already on the ladders assumed a defensive position beneath shields, but the dead piled up at the base of the wall.

The lull was short-lived. When the gnomes focused on the wall to escape the fires consuming the clearing, they charged the ladders like a panic-stricken mob. Bolts flew up, dozens at a time, as the ladders buckled under the massive weight. *126. 125. 124. 123. 122.*

Rowe stood in a crenel on the battlement with his cloak wrapped tight for protection in the vulnerable gap in the wall. He jabbed a lance at the gnomes, killing several as bolts ricocheted off his cloak. One bolt glanced off his shoulder and struck the soldier fighting beside him in the neck. *121.* A few gnomes landed on the wall walk. Some were hacked down, but their numbers were overwhelming. *120. 119. 118.* Rowe hurled his lance down through a gnome and withdrew from the wall, his sword flashing in the firelight.

The battle for the South Crow Gate raged for several long hours. A few fearless gnomes stood atop the battlement, shooting several bolts with devastating results. *98. 97. 96. 95.* A half dozen soldiers armed with lances wrenched shields from the clutches of fallen gnomes and sacrificed themselves to knock the gnome archers off the battlement. *94. 93. 92. 91.* More gnomes crested the wall and forced soldiers into hand-to-hand combat on the wall walk.

The soldiers faltered near the gatehouse, and Rowe fought his way toward it through a frenzied wall walk. *90. 89. 88. 87. 86.* Thrusting his sword repeatedly, he stepped over bodies in an exhausting struggle to reach Tranas and the vulnerable gatehouse. Human and gnome bodies littered the wide landing around the gatehouse as Tranas swung his battle-ax, defending his station like a cornered bear protecting her cubs. *85. 84.*

Rowe had almost reached Tranas when a small bolt, fired at close range, plunged into the big man's chest. With a roar, Tranas hacked the gnome archer's shoulder. His ax and the gnome's arm landed on the wooden planks at the same time. Tranas stumbled back against the locked door to steady himself. Three gnomes rushed him as several more leapt off the battlement, desperate to breach the gatehouse.

Rowe threw a knife and killed the first gnome, but before he could catch the other two, they drove their swords into Tranas's exposed chest. With outstretched arms holding him firm between the jams, another sword plunged through his abdomen, striking the door behind him. A few soldiers witnessed the attack on Tranas and attempted to reach him. *83.* Rowe bore down on the gnomes, killing them with two quick slashes. Tranas flashed a zealous grin at Rowe, then fell to his knees.

Rowe tried to rush to his friend's side but found himself hemmed in by gnomes. Spinning on his heels, he parried and struck with a revived fury, his red cloak sweeping behind him. Morgan and four other soldiers charged into the fray, steel clanging against steel. Another wave of gnomes surged over the wall. *82. 81. 80.*

Tranas slumped onto the floor, and a gnome slipped past him, kneeling in front of the gatehouse door with pick tools in hand. With each step toward the gatehouse, Striker Company lost ground to the gnome horde. *79. 78. 77.*

"Blow the horn!" Rowe cried, tears and sweat streaming down his face.

A single burst of a horn blared over the fierce clashes of metal to signal that the gatehouse had been lost. *76. 75.*

The casualties mounted quickly as gnomes reached the battlements, standing above the fighting as they unloaded their crossbows at easy targets. *74. 73. 72. 71.*

The gnome picking the lock gave a shout and shoved the gatehouse door open. About to rush in, the gnome was thrown back by a small chunk of metal.

Illious strode through the doorway wielding two long-handled maces. The master alchemist's arms blurred as the spiked iron balls lifted gnomes off their feet, barring unwanted entrance to the gatehouse.

After two more hours, neither side had secured the gatehouse. *59. 58.* Illious must have added something to his weapons because the gnomes he struck were dead on impact. Even so, there was little his magic could do at this late hour. The gnomes surged for another assault on the gatehouse before dawn. Rowe was near Illious when a bolt pierced the alchemist's neck. *57.* Desperation set in. Rowe slashed with renewed intensity while deflecting bolts off his cloak, shielding himself and as many soldiers as possible. Morgan fought nearby, as swift and fluid as any Callum Sage Rowe had ever fought alongside. *56. 55.* But his muscles ached, and his grip weakened on the hilt of his sword. *54. 53. 52.*

Rowe was fighting near the back railing when he heard the familiar high-pitched scraping sound of the portcullis slowly rising. Volunteers and medics below screamed. There was no way to stop the gate from opening now, but Rowe had to protect the defenseless. One group of soldiers fought near the catapult, somehow holding the elevated section of the wall. *51. 50.* Another small group of soldiers struggled to block the far stairwell. *49. 48. 47.* The only remaining soldiers were those rallying around Rowe. *46. 45.*

"To the portcullis!" Rowe shouted as he ran down the stairs. Morgan and eleven soldiers followed.

As the massive iron grate inched its way up, Rowe shuffled to Morgan's side. Scores of gnomes shrieked and pounded the other side of the thick wooden gate behind the iron portcullis. The battle raged above them on the wall. *44. 43. 42. 41.* Morgan's soaked hair clung to her head, and her face was flush. But she seemed to ignore the threat on the other side of the gate as she watched her mother and Gloriana remove a bolt from a soldier's arm. The women were indomitable in their care of the wounded.

When the portcullis was about three-quarters of the way open, Julie and Gloriana stopped their work. *40. 39. 38.*

"What do we do now?" Julie cried out. *37. 36. 35.*

Gloriana grabbed a knife from the table. "Die well," she said with a resolute nod. *34. 33.*

A thunder of pounding footfalls suddenly overpowered the shouting and clash of swords. *32. 31. 30.* From the darkness of the Rainia Valley, a new horde emerged.

"It's Dench!" Gloriana cried.

Seconds later, the half-orc's massive form materialized, broadsword in front of him. He bellowed a vigorous battle cry, and a deafening surge of shouting erupted behind him as more half-orcs raced into the firelight.

"Dench!" Rowe called. "We have to close the portcullis!"

Four half-orcs seized the bottom edge of the partly opened portcullis and heaved it down. Others jammed short timbers through its gaps to keep it closed.

"To the gatehouse!" Rowe shouted.

Morgan and the soldiers followed Rowe, with Dench and his band of half-orcs close behind. At the top of the stairs, Rowe pulled Morgan out of the way as Dench swung his broadsword in a wide arc, cleaving three gnomes with a single slice. The other half-orcs were almost as deadly, hurling themselves into the fray as they howled deep, guttural battle cries. Together they slashed, kicked, and punched their way to the gatehouse. *29. 28.*

Rowe sheathed his sword and pried his fingers from the hilt. Grabbing a bow and quiver from the back railing, he shot into the gnomes standing on the battlements. The surrounding soldiers followed his lead, standing clear of the half-orcs' blood rage. Their arrows quickly cleared the battlement, and the bolts eased off.

Dench blazed a gruesome trail straight to the gatehouse. A moment after he stepped inside, four gnome bodies flew out the door, one in two pieces. When the half-orc strode back outside, he was holding a gnome by the throat high above the wooden planks. With a thunderous roar, he flung the gnome a dozen feet over the battlement.

Dadore appeared beside Rowe, his face animated as he shouted, "Get us to the ladders!"

Rowe nocked another arrow. "Where were you three hours ago?"

"I couldn't get it working," Dadore said as Kydaris joined them. "But I found a solution to clear the ladders!"

Rowe released the arrow and glanced at the small pails and brushes in the students' hands. "Dench! Help me get these boys to the ladders!"

Before Dench took his first step, Kydaris was struck dead by a bolt. *27.* Rowe caught him in his arms and snatched the pail before it spilled. He laid Kydaris on his back and moved in front of Dadore, shielding him with his cloak. The half-orcs had decimated the gnomes on the wall walk, but it still took several minutes of brutal fighting to get within reach of the nearest ladder.

"Brush some on the wood!" Dadore said.

Rowe reached out with the brush and two bolts bounced off his cloak. He wiped the wet brush over the right support of the ladder, and Dadore shouted that it was enough. Rowe stepped back and gaped as the wood turned dark and withered. The blight spread down the right side of the ladder, and before Rowe was at the second ladder, the first disintegrated, sending dozens of gnomes to their death.

Dench shouted at three half-orcs to guide Dadore to the other ladders. The young alchemist was wide-eyed and trembling at the large creatures, but he kept his feet moving. The three half-orcs devastated any gnome within reach.

As the last ladder crumbled, the first traces of light peeked over the Hillron Mountains. The fighting raged on for another hour as both human and half-orc cleared the wall walk of the remaining gnomes. With that immediate threat removed, soldiers manned the catapults, firing again at the retreating gnome army.

There was no cheer from the beleaguered soldiers on this morning. Only a collective sigh as the remnant of Striker Company discarded weapons to help their wounded and dying friends.

Rowe searched the wall walk for any surviving gnomes, then whirled around to see Dench. He barely managed a smirk before the half-orc lifted him off his feet in a tight embrace.

"My friend," Rowe muttered, the words snagging in his throat.

Dench lowered Rowe and grinned. "Me almost too late."

"You saved us, Dench." Rowe leaned against the battlement, breathing in the cool morning air. "We were done."

"No, you never done, Rowe."

Rowe simply shook his head before wiping his eyes with his right hand, his left one numb from gripping the hilt so long.

Dench frowned. "Me took too much time to bring help. Only one tribe join me. Ninety-one fighters."

Rowe felt as though someone had punched him in the stomach. So few! Too drained to worry about it now, he nodded and beamed at his old friend and personal guard. "I'm grateful for what we have, Dench. Thank you."

"You go sleep. They no fight again today. We be ready for tonight." Dench offered his hand and lifted Rowe to his feet. "Where Morgan go?"

"When the fighting stopped, I saw her go downstairs. I imagine she went to be with her mother."

Dench arched his bushy eyebrows. "Mudder?"

"Yes, my friend. We have some stories to tell you."

As they walked toward the stairs past the resting soldiers, Rowe realized with a terrible sinking feeling that even with Dench's formidable troop, they were far less than two hundred. Half-orcs were deadly in hand-to-hand combat, but they were not the best archers. If the gnomes scaled the wall again, they would take the valley.

At the top of the stairs, they met Dadore. His shaggy hair was a sweaty mess, his eyes wild. In the light of day, Rowe realized this young alchemist who'd helped save the South Crow Gate was an awkward boy whose lanky body had not yet caught up to his large feet.

"Well done, lad," Rowe said with a smile. "That's twice you saved the day."

Dadore's mouth hung open. "What a crazy night… They just kept coming… All I wanted to do was run but we couldn't let you down, not after you loosened Illious's constraints on us, and then—"

"Easy, lad. Slow down and breathe a little," Rowe said.

"I feel like burning off some of this energy," Dadore said, his gaze shifting among the soldiers along the wall walk. "Where did Kydaris go? I need to find him."

Rowe placed a hand on Dadore's shoulder. "I'm sorry, Dadore, but Kydaris didn't make it." Rowe pulled him in and wrapped his arms around him. He read Dench's sympathetic gaze and remembered the day the half-orc's best friend, Ruint, was slain by one of the duke's guards.

"Wait, where is he? Where's Kydaris?" Dadore cried out, but Rowe held him fast. "Let me go! I want to go to him!"

Dench took a knee and spoke with a gentleness that surprised Rowe. "You no want to see him now. It will be too hard. Me clean him, then you see him properly for goodbyes."

Dadore wept, fighting against Rowe, who held him tenderly but securely. "I'm so sorry, lad," Rowe said. "He gave his life for us, as did many others." He watched a large tear roll down Dench's clenched jaw into his braided beard. "But that doesn't diminish the sharp sting of saying goodbye to our friends."

CHAPTER 24

THE NORTH GNOME ARMY

West of the Hollowtangle, the North Gnome Army prepared for their march to Dwenlin Thah. As the sun dipped below the Aerodice Mountains, gnome soldiers emerged from the sea of pup tents scattered among the trees. A week had passed since a storm rolled eastward from the Habina Ocean, and the days grew warmer. The sun made it difficult for gnomes to travel by day, but the heat made it impossible. And so, they marched at night. The cool, moonlit sky made the journey less arduous, but knowing that General Raric's reassembled army was close cast a somber cloud over each weary gnome.

Commander Yossar stood on the hillside overlooking the awakening camp. His bulbous brown eyes blinked often. The tall highland gnome wore no armor but dressed simply in common gray homespun. He carried no weapons. His tapered ears, nicked and scarred, poked upward through well-groomed, ponytailed blond hair. A tended, gray-streaked beard reached to his chest. Amber-toned, weathered skin testified to years of training and battle under the sun.

As commander of the North Army, Yossar carried a heavy yoke. Despite having the human army dramatically outnumbered—with the onus on Raric to engage—Yossar's doubts were growing. A band of Raric's army had captured and closed the Stoneberg gate less than three weeks after Yossar had led his army through it on their way to attack Hammerclaw. After the victory at Hammerclaw, the gnome army had stayed near the Clover Fields, recovering and restocking. There, Uluk had divided the army into two separate forces. Yossar had led one force back to recapture the Stoneberg. But before they'd arrived, Uluk had ordered them north to Dwenlin Thah. They'd marched for one night but were waylaid west of the Hollowtangle due to uncertainty surrounding Queen Sidara. Uluk was not seen for days. The gnomes had grown restless. Eventually, Uluk had returned with news of General Raric's unexpected arrival at Dwenlin Thah. But the Shadowfallen had said nothing of Sidara.

The loss of his main supply line west of the Stoneberg, the mystery surrounding Sidara, and Uluk's infrequent visits gave Yossar much to brood about. But that wasn't the lot of it. The day he had taken command of the six giant flasks of Guilliad was the last he had slept for more than an hour at a time. In his opinion, a deadly gas capable of disintegrating everything in its path had no place in the Fourwinds. But the decision to use such weapons was out of his control.

Yossar had witnessed the effects of Guilliad firsthand at Hammerclaw. What concerned him more, however, was the mysterious weapon his army carried, a weapon even Queen Sidara feared. They had infused the vile elixir, aptly named Phyriad, into over two thousand small, carefully wrapped pieces of maple syrup candy. The toxic candies were packaged tightly in a crate and transported in a plain two-wheeled cart.

"Set before us be a long night."

The quiet voice startled Yossar, but he maintained his composure as he turned to see his chief overseer. "Pleased I am to have you back with us, Panigim. What news have you?"

"Pleased I am to see you too, Commander. But not pleased to report that the last of the Callum Sages has been captured by bush gnomes. At the Clover Fields he is. Or *was*."

Yossar stuck out his bottom lip. "Let him live, they did?"

Panigim swallowed and gazed out at the army breaking camp. "Barely alive when I saw him. Survive the Clover Fields he will not—especially under the cruel hand of Grudum."

"Grudum." Yossar spat on the ground. "That scum. Miserable, sun-scorched days these be, Panigim. Great reconcilers the Callum Sages were."

"The last bond between humans and we highlanders our esteemed Ellywick was." She closed her large eyes. "And murdered him the bush gnomes did."

Yossar studied the overseer's face for a moment. "Careful you must be in speaking of our allies, Panigim. Bury your feelings you must."

Panigim opened her eyes and nodded curtly.

"And what news of our queen, Panigim? So many rumors surrounding Sidara there be."

"Nothing at all, Commander. Only of Uluk do our allies speak."

Yossar growled. "Yes, assumed general command the Shadowfallen has. Moving faster now we are."

"The orders, have they changed?"

Yossar shook his head. "Press on to Dwenlin Thah we will."

"The scouts report that mobilize Raric has not."

Yossar raised his eyebrows. "More good news, Panigim. Set a

hard pace this night, reach the northern Hollowtangle we must before the sun is upon us. Tomorrow we travel beneath the shade of the Hollowtangle. Expect this of us Raric will not. Should we push beyond the Hollowtangle, at our backs the wind will be."

Panigim grasped the frayed edges of her hood between the thumb and index finger of her slender hands and uncovered her head. The evening breeze whisked her long white hair from her guarded features. "Raric's restraint I fail to understand. If first we be to reach the Nameless Forest beyond the Hollowtangle, a better position we will secure to wage war."

Yossar nodded. "Without equal Raric's lineage is, and numerous the victories he has seen. Yet see the walls of Dwenlin Thah we will, due to simple mathematics. Outnumber the humans we do. And…" Yossar tightened the muscles in his face. "Guilliad we possess. If the west winds continue, sweep through their ranks it will, before an arrow be fired."

"Nature herself is with us," Panigim agreed. "Comfort I find in this."

Yossar puffed his chest. "Defeat Enders Brigade we will. Then on to Dwenlin Thah."

"And still the somber face?" Panigim observed.

Yossar exhaled, unable to shake the weight of war from his shoulders. "How many battles have we fought together, Panigim?"

"Too many to count."

"On the eve of any of those battles, never have I felt so agitated." Panigim was quiet.

"Vomiting I've been the last two days, and not from sun sickness."

"Nerves," Panigim suggested. "Uneasy have I been too. At the onset of this war, expanding our lands was the goal. And keep the sprawling nature of humankind in check." She smiled. "Recall our conversation when returned to us our lands were? All those crops we can grow again?" Her smile faded as the breeze swept some hairs across her cheeks. "Changes on the wind there be."

Yossar folded his arms. "Bent on destruction, the Shadowfallen is. So little we know about Phyriad, and so much it frightens me. The end of all humans that elixir could bring."

"Part of our plan, this is not."

"Out of our hands, the plans are now, Panigim."

The overseer placed her hands on her hips, and the wrinkles around her eyes deepened. "Yours to command, the army is."

Yossar hissed through his teeth. "In truth? Drifting closer to the precipice are humans and gnomes."

Panigim lowered her voice. "Let us return home, Yossar."

Yossar raised a finger to his lips. "Vigilance, Panigim. Broaden our understanding we must before contemplation of such thoughts." He stepped toward the camp. "Until then, keep apprised of that cursed wagon carrying Phyriad. Many miles before us lie."

CHAPTER 25

When Reading Saves

Will lay on his back, knees bent, staring at wispy white clouds flecking the blue sky. He longed to take a morning walk back home around Lake Commando and breathe the freshness of a new day. But he dared not inhale too deeply now, dreading the onset of another violent coughing fit.

Yesterday's events replayed in his mind like a nightmare: the brutal welcome to Clover Fields, the misery of the other slaves, the growing infections in his leg and lungs, the near-death encounter with Grudum's vicious dogs, and the threat of being dumped in the compost pit if he failed to perform his duties. As he struggled to a sitting position in his crude but solidly built cell and looked around, Will's nightmares became his reality.

The cell—more like a large dog cage—was one of many that stretched along the front of the three stone buildings the gnomes referred to as *depots*. Surrounding the cages were many tents where gnomes sought relief from the vexing sun. Each depot had wide open gates at both ends and stone side walls. In the center depot, a massive caravan of wagons was pulling away. Dozens of humans cleaned sparse racks and stalls inside the depot, while others scribbled on parchments, probably taking inventory of what little remained. A large gnome stood among them. Initially, Will thought it strange that the gnome guard was unarmed, but then realized it was a harvester disguised as a gnome.

Three cages away from Will's, a prisoner groaned. The man lay motionless on his side as a gnome wearing a leaf-green cloak, hood drawn, worked the lock of the cage. The gnome wore tight gloves and his arms were wrapped with layers of light-brown fabric. Behind him, a taller gnome with large tinted goggles waited, arms crossed at his chest as he tapped his foot on the ground. After some effort, the lock snapped open, and a horse pulling a single axle wagon stopped in front.

"Why, during high sun, must we deal with such matters?" the gnome working the lock complained as he swung the cage open.

"Better now while he be breathing," the other answered. "An awful stink a dead body becomes in this heat."

"I'm fine," the man mumbled, lifting a trembling hand.

The gnome grabbed the man's arm and pulled.

"I just need a little rest." The man's death-rattle voice gave Will a shiver.

"Plenty of time to rest on the way to the compost pit," a gnome said.

The man was almost out of the cage when he kicked at the gnome and grasped the door.

The gnome wearing goggles bent low and punched the man's head, silencing his efforts. He glared at the other gnome. "No help, saying such things to prisoners."

Together the gnomes lifted the limp body and tossed the man

into the wagon. They grimaced and buried their noses in their elbows.

"Gods be damned, you carry a stink!"

The wagon driver coaxed the horse forward, and the iron-banded wheels creaked to a stop in front of Will's cage. "This one coming?"

"Well, look who be up," the shorter gnome said.

The two gnomes walked to his cage, and Will pulled his pant leg down to cover the severe bruising. He opened his eyes wider, tightened his cheek muscles in a forced smile, and carefully cleared his wheezing throat.

"Why bring me this far only to throw me away?" Will had hoped to sound alert and confident, but his crackly voice betrayed him. He sat up straighter to face the gnomes and noticed that someone had hung his Trannalun cloak atop a tall pole.

The gnomes bent at the waist and peered into Will's cage as if he were a rare snake. "Dead we thought you would be by now."

"I'm the Callum Sage," Will said, pointing at his cloak that flapped like a flag in the breeze. "I hear you're in need of my writing skills."

The shorter gnome snorted. "You be the one that killed Grudum's dog?"

Will hesitated, but Grudum didn't seem to be popular with the gnomes he'd met so far, especially with the highland gnomes. After an awkward silent moment, he nodded.

"Killed a bear that dog did. A big one," the taller gnome said, then lowered his voice. "Vile creatures, Grudum's dogs."

"I care not for the dogs," the shorter one said. "Why they bring Callum Sages here? Too many slaves already. Stoneberg be lost to us, and that be the last caravan of arms, equipment, and food that left this morning. And that shipment be late!" He wagged his head. "Shut us down Uluk will."

The tall gnome jabbed his partner's shoulder. "Not your decisions. If Uluk wants the Callum Sage, spare him we will."

Will stiffened at the thought of interrogation by the Shadowfallen.

"Away with you," the tall gnome snapped to the driver.

The driver nodded and cracked a short whip, steering the old wagon along a worn path carved between lush rolling hills.

The tall gnome leaned close to Will and shook his fist. "If try to escape you do, not a tree to hide behind for miles. Catch you we would, and straight to the compost pit for you, no questions."

"I understand," Will said.

⁂

Within an hour, Will had been given a bowl of oat-based mush and a cup of water he choked down. After that, he was taken from his cage to the center depot. The human slaves were still working while the gnome-harvester monitored their progress. Will flinched as his gnome guard escorted him past the harvester to a small table near the back of the depot. Another gnome dropped a thin leather-bound book on the table and slapped a stack of blank parchment beside it. He added a bottle of ink and a quill with a crusty dark-red plume.

"Copy the logs in this book by end of day tomorrow, or your final day it will be."

Will wanted to tell the gnome about the harvester but didn't know what kind of trouble that would create, so he simply nodded. "Thank you."

The gnomes chuckled and left him alone. Will breathed a

sigh of relief but kept a wary eye on the harvester who seemed to ignore him.

The inkwell was stopped with a small cork that proved difficult to remove with his broken hand, so he gripped the bottle between his knees and with effort popped the cork without spilling. He examined the quill for a few moments before dipping the tip in the ink. He'd never used a quill-and-ink set before, but he'd seen them used in movies.

The writing process was slower than using a ballpoint pen, but after copying half a page, his speed increased. After the second page, his hand cramped and his broken leg ached from sitting too long on the ironwood bench. He set the quill down and rubbed his leg. Considering the size of the logbook and the fact he could only write for a few minutes at a time, Will panicked. His breaths came in quick intervals as his chest tightened. Sweat stung his eyes. If he didn't finish this simple task, the gnomes would drag him to the compost pit, regardless of what they said about Uluk's interest in Callum Sages.

Will was not alone in his despair. The human slaves moped about their tasks, shuffling their feet, wearing hopelessness like the filthy rags on their backs. One point of consolation for Will was the lack of a military presence at the Clover Fields. There was no need for trained soldiers or stockpiles of weapons. After they beat the slaves and broke their will to live, the gnome guards simply waited until death came to claim each wretched human.

Grudum, however, was impatient. He seemed to revel in human agony. So, when the bush gnome rode into the shade of the depot on a mule, Will tensed and reached for the quill.

"Why you be here?" the harvester-gnome growled.

Grudum removed his goggles and locked his eyes on Will, grinning. "Know who he is, I do. Here to tell you."

Will set down the plume to keep it from shaking. He glanced at both ends of the depot, searching for a highland gnome who might intervene. But he and the few human slaves were alone with the bloodthirsty bush gnome and an unnerving harvester.

"Say your piece and be gone," the harvester said with a dismissive wave.

Grudum rummaged through his saddle pack, pulled out a handful of nuts, and shoved them into his mouth. "A Callum Sage he be." Bits of nuts and spittle sprayed from his thick lips.

"Knew that already we did."

"Then aware of the value he be to Uluk."

"Yes, yes. Wasting my time you be, Grudum."

"Here on the morrow Uluk will be."

The harvester glared at Grudum as though seeing him for the first time. "On the morrow? This be true?"

Will's stomach churned, threatening to reject his mushy breakfast. Grudum must have seen a change in his expression because the cruel gnome's grin broadened as he nodded.

"Said your piece you did, Grudum. Now off with you," the harvester said.

"Remember who told you that Uluk be coming," Grudum said as he turned the mule.

Will feared the gnome, especially after killing his dog, but the harvester terrified him. He resisted looking directly at the creature, trying to think of it as just another gnome. If the harvester knew Will saw its true identity, it probably wouldn't wait for Will to die on the compost pit.

"What difference does it make if Uluk is coming tomorrow?" Will asked, trying to sound brave.

"Pay handsomely for a Callum Sage he will. Fly you to the Waerdreath himself he will."

"W-what?" Will stammered.

"As a simpleton soldier, your value to Uluk be this." The harvester stuck a hand out waist high. "As a scribe…" The hand raised to shoulder height. "But as Callum Sage…" The harvester reached high above its head.

Will's breathing slowed. If the harvester wanted to please Uluk, there was a good chance it had no interest in killing Will—for now.

"To the cage with you, and bring your work," the harvester snarled. "If it be true that Uluk be arriving soon, find you locked up safe he will."

Will collected the parchments. "Why would Uluk take me to the Waerdreath?"

The harvester scowled. "That be between Uluk and the Dark Queen."

So Sidara was still alive. Or at least that's what her minions believed. Will wanted to ask more, but the low growl in the harvester's throat indicated he'd already asked too many questions. He gathered his writing project and crawled into his cage.

⁂

Unable to write more than a page in the tight confines of the small cage, Will lay on his side, easing the pressure from his broken leg and wondering how he might die. There was a time, back in Cochrane, when he wished death was as imminent as it was now. But since coming to the Fourwinds, Will had found hope, friendship, and love. Now he wanted to live. He sniffed and let the tears come.

There were many possible ways for him to die at the Clover Fields. First, the gnomes might kill him. Although he had received mercy from a few gnomes, every one of them wished him dead.

Second, his injuries and sickness could overtake him. Infection in his leg might eventually kill him, but the onset of pneumonia would likely come faster.

Third, the harvester might turn on him. He had seen how quickly a harvester could kill a human, but this one's fear of Uluk seemed to override its hatred for humans. *Harvesters obey the strongest master*, Rowe had once said.

Fourth, there was the threat of Uluk the Shadowfallen. The name struck fear in the hearts of all who heard it. Rowe had described Uluk as part fallen angel, part vindictive human. Fear was an appropriate response. Will had survived standing in Sidara's presence, but he couldn't imagine the wrath of the winged demon. And if Uluk took Will to the Waerdreath to face Sidara again, it would be a doubly slow and tortuous death.

Then there was Grudum. Of all Will's enemies, the bush gnome wanted to destroy him, the sooner the better. And of all the end-of-life scenarios, dying at the hands of a disrespected, heartless brute was the worst way to go.

A tray of uneaten slop, now covered with ants, lay beside Will's cage. No one so much as looked his way all day except the slave who had brought the food. Will wiped his nose with the sleeve of his rough, grimy tunic, and sat up to cough, trying to clear the congestion in his upper chest.

"Your bark reminds me of my dog you killed."

Grudum sat atop his mule in the depot entrance. The shade masked his features, but his large form cast an ominous shadow into the depot. Ironically, it was the shadow of Will's Trannalun cloak hanging from the pole that provided Grudum shelter from the sun.

The mule clopped across the hard-packed ground in front of the depot and halted next to Will's cage. Grudum dismounted and removed his goggles. His large eyes narrowed, and his lips drew back to reveal a snarling, yellow-toothed grin.

"My poor dog." The gnome's voice rumbled. "A mercy it be I had two."

Will kept his eyes low, expecting no mercy, but knew he had nothing to lose. "It whimpered like a worthless mutt," he mumbled.

Grudum lunged forward and grasped the pitted, rusty lock with his meaty hand. He glanced from side to side, but there was no one to yell at him this time. The harvester had left the main depot, taking the slaves back to their respective cells in a secondary depot.

"Shutting down this operation they are," Grudum said. "Cleaned out this depot they have…but still need to dispose of remaining scum. That be *my* task."

Will swallowed hard, wishing he'd had more to drink of the muddy water offered to him earlier. "Uluk wants me alive tomorrow; you said it yourself."

Grudum shook the lock. "Changed my mind I have! When Uluk see your cloak, enter the depot he will, and find you dead." He drew a short sword from beneath his tattered cape. "I only wish I could be around when Uluk kills every gnome here for letting you die."

Three gnome soldiers emerged from the depot. Grudum released the lock and stepped away, then moved to the next cage and grabbed its lock as if pretending to be inspecting the cages. Will wanted to cry out for help, but Grudum was close enough to stab him through the cage. The gnomes noticed him but continued to the next depot. Grudum maintained his charade, making his way around four cages, pulling and prodding at locks and bars. One of the gnomes paused at the other depot's entrance and stepped out of the direct sun, watching Grudum with a curious look.

As Will gazed at the gnome, hoping he would stay and foil Grudum's murderous plan, he noticed the shadow of his Trannalun cloak was gone. He turned to confirm the empty pole, and when he looked back, a flash of steel behind the gnome caught the sunlight. The gnome buckled at the knees, crumpling to the ground. His cry was cut short as a lanky three-foot-tall creature stepped from the darkness and smashed a mace into the gnome's head. The goblin's coarse dark hair bristled as his narrow purple eyes glared in Will and Grudum's direction, large nostrils flaring. Strands of leather held a shock of black hair atop his head. He was clothed in dirty rags. The goblin tugged the mace handle several times and yanked the weapon free from the bloody mess.

"Urk," Will breathed. He peered through the cell bars with misty eyes, hopeful yet guarded. "Hadn't expected you."

The two gnomes who had entered the depot ahead of their dead partner raced outside but did not see the goblin. Urk was leaning against the wall by the doorway, resting the mace casually on his shoulder. The goblin gave a sharp whistle. As the gnomes spun around to face the depot, two arrows struck them both high in the chest. The gnomes hit the ground hard, grim gurgling sounds escaping their lips as blood pooled beneath them.

"You're all dead," Will wheezed.

Urk stepped back into the depot and reappeared carrying two large sacks. He scurried to the tents encircling the prisoner cages, pouring the contents of the sacks around the base of each tent.

Grudum wasted no time. He donned his goggles, raised his

sword, and took a few quick strides toward the depot entrance, then stopped suddenly.

A man stood in the doorway holding two empty handheld crossbows. He was dressed in black: loose pants lined with pockets, short boots, and a sleeveless shirt. A brace of knives was strapped around his midsection, the blades glinting in the sunlight. A leather scabbard dangled from his left hip, and a second hilt was visible behind his left ear.

The sun glistened off Bremer's bald head as he tossed the crossbows to the ground.

Grudum bent down as though adjusting his boot and scooped a handful of sand. Will opened his mouth to warn Bremer, but a coughing fit stifled his voice. Grudum stepped toward the man in black and raised his chipped sword, flashing a vicious smile. The gnome shuffled forward, faster than Will had thought possible. Grudum lunged, throwing the sand into Bremer's face with one hand while thrusting his sword with the other. It happened so fast Will was certain Bremer would be blinded and stabbed in the stomach.

What the bush gnome failed to see was the long knife his opponent held hidden behind his wrist. Bremer closed his eyes and leaned to the side, timing the knife perfectly to deflect Grudum's sword a few inches short of its mark. Grudum stumbled, then shuffled to maintain his footing. His bulbous eyes widened as Bremer came at him like a ravenous wolf. Before the gnome could draw back his sword, Bremer punched him in the neck and kicked the back of his knee. Grudum's back slammed onto the hard ground. Gasping for breath, he raised his sword in defense. There was a blur of movement and then Grudum's arm flopped to the ground, hand still clutching his sword. A circle of bright-red blood swelled around the gnome's severed arm as he lay on his back in shock. In one easy motion, Bremer slashed down with his sword, opening the gnome's neck.

Two more gnome soldiers ran through the entrance. Bremer spun on the ball of his foot and launched the knife in a smooth underhand motion. The blade sunk into the chest of the nearest soldier. Bremer's sword flashed, deflecting the second soldier's short sword with a quiet flourish. The rogue spun around in a blur, carving a clean red line across the gnome's neck.

Urk finished knotting up the drawstrings to each tent entrance and crouched next to a dark trail of powder, sparking a flint several times. The powder flashed, and within seconds, flames licked the sides of the tents. A few screaming gnomes sliced gaps in their tents, diving through the flames, but Urk stopped them with his mace. The goblin then raced from cage to cage, smashing each lock and flinging open the prison doors.

Bremer rushed to Will's cage and dropped a small pack on the ground. He pulled out the Trannalun cloak, shoving it through the cage. With two tiny pick tools, Bremer had unlocked the gate before Will could unfold the cloak. He swung the gate open and offered his arm to Will. Once out of the cage, Will threw his arms around Bremer's neck and clutched him close. His body convulsed in a muddle of terror, relief, and joy.

"Good to see you too, kid," Bremer whispered as he pried Will's arms from his neck. "You've smelled better, though." He took the Trannalun cloak, shook it open, and draped it over Will's shoulders. "We need to leave, Will. Now." Bremer jerked his hands away as the cloak instantly became too hot to touch; its magic flared to life in response to Will's overwhelming need.

Will trembled beneath the euphoric currents of magic surging through him. He stumbled against the cage, then arched his back, sucking air into his rapidly clearing lungs. He hacked and spat a mouthful of green phlegm. Wheezing, he doubled over and vomited.

Bremer grabbed the reins of Grudum's mule as shouts and roaring flames spread through the Clover Fields. The flames from the tents leapt over to the depots and flickered up the doorposts. Bremer tried to help Will into the saddle, but the heat of the cloak made it uncomfortable to touch. He grasped Will's filthy head. "Get it together, Will!"

Will tried to focus on Bremer's eyes, but his head was spinning. "My leg's broken," he muttered.

"Okay, kid. Lean on me and put your right foot in the stirrup." Bremer grunted as sparks arced between them, but he slowly lifted Will into the saddle.

Gnomes appeared at the front entrance with buckets of water.

Bremer shoved a large leather sack into Will's lap and leaned close. "Follow your shadow east, and when you reach the river, follow it south—to the right—until you come to a stone bridge. Cross there and continue east." He grabbed Will's jaw, forcing him to meet his wild dark eyes. "Do you understand?"

Will nodded slightly. "Yes, but don't leave me, Bremer!"

"I found you here, didn't I, kid?" Bremer said with a steely look. "Don't worry. I'll catch up to you."

Bremer slapped the mule's rump, sending it off through the rear entrance.

As the animal trotted from the encampment, Will turned to see a sword in each of Bremer's hands as gnome soldiers circled him.

CHAPTER 26

DAY 3 ON THE
SOUTH CROW GATE

On the morning after the second night of fighting at the South Crow Gate, Morgan was finding it difficult to sleep despite her exhaustion. Many soldiers had died, including Tranas, Illious, and Kydaris. In silent numbness, Morgan and Rowe helped lift Tranas's body onto a wagon to be taken with the rest of the fallen to a burial site in the northern valley. When they were finished, they wandered over to Dadore's multicolored wagon.

The three alchemists' wagons were backed together with the rear entrances facing each other, forming a tight triangle. Ramps connected each entrance, probably making it easier for Illious and his two students to interact and share supplies. But Illious and Kydaris were dead now, leaving Dadore to manage all three wagons.

Rowe stepped inside, but Morgan lingered at the entrance. Wide counters on the inside walls dominated the traveling workshop. Almost every available surface was covered with flasks, tumblers, and measuring devices in an assortment of sizes and colors. Hoses interconnected some of the flasks, and shards of broken glass and spilled liquids littered the counters. Books and parchments were crammed together on floor-to-ceiling shelves. Under each counter was a massive storage locker and numerous cubbies, some locked, and some without doors.

At the far end of the wagon, the young alchemist, Dadore, sat on the edge of his bed, unable to find an elixir capable of stopping his incessant tears.

"Kydaris was my best friend," he mumbled. "I have few memories that don't involve him."

Rowe sighed and folded his hands in front of him, giving space to the young man grappling with the death of his companion.

"It's like he's still with me, urging me on." Dadore stood slowly.

"What would he say to you?" Rowe said quietly.

Dadore sniffled and cocked his head to one side. "I'm going to find out." He sprang to his feet and strode across the wagon, brushing past Rowe. He turned back and tugged Rowe's cloak. "Come along."

Morgan and Rowe followed Dadore into Kydaris's wagon.

"You and Kydaris have been an invaluable part of this effort," Rowe said. "Your version of Illious Fire saved us the first night, and that dissolving solution you created to destroy the ladders brought an end to the fighting last night. More of either of those would be welcomed tonight, but I am confident you will come up with something."

Dadore seemed lost in thought, fumbling through bottles and parchments, mumbling to himself. His puffy, bloodshot eyes brightened when he found a notebook that caught his interest. "All right, Kydaris. What tricks did you leave behind to help us tonight?"

"Well," Rowe said, clapping his hands once. "I'm glad we had this talk. We'll leave you to it, then."

⁂

Hours later, Morgan stood next to her mother and gazed across the sun-dappled ripples of Rainia Lake as their horses enjoyed a well-deserved drink. The mares had taken Morgan and Julie to the Crow's Nest to check on Ryowyn and now, on the return trip to the South Crow Gate, they needed a rest from the hot sun.

If she'd had her smartphone with her, Morgan would have taken a panorama shot. Instead, she closed her eyes to capture the scene in her memory: clear blues of the lake and midday sky; bold greens of willow and alder mixed with the odd red maple; creamy white flowers in the nearby shrubs with orange-and-blue butterflies dancing among them. All this beauty refreshed her like an afternoon nap, rinsing the mire and murk of suffering and death from her mind. She knew the stains would remain and she wondered how her mom was taking all this. As a veteran nurse, Julie had been through enough trauma and seen far too much violence to expect complete cleansing.

"The irony of Ryowyn's condition," Julie said, "is that as she sleeps peacefully, her vital signs perfectly normal, hundreds of soldiers are dying a few miles away. And the survivors long for a taste of the sleep that sustains her. Ryowyn rests, unaware that her every breath depends on the courage of a few soldiers."

Morgan opened her eyes to see two butterflies chasing each other in a haphazard flight pattern near the shore. "I've been wondering about Will," she said. "Who's watching out for him? Assuming he's..." She trailed off, refusing to think about his fate.

Julie smiled as the sun lit her face. "The best we can do for

Will is to care for Ryowyn. I saw a flicker of life and hope in him when he was with Ryowyn—the misunderstood boy who lost so much and was shunned by the town that should have cared for him. I don't know what's become of him, but there's always hope for another miracle."

Morgan closed her eyes again and inhaled deeply, trying to rest in the comfort of her mother's words. When she opened her eyes, something caught her attention. Fifty yards along the main road, an old woman hobbled toward the South Crow Gate, leaning on a walking stick with each step.

Morgan and Julie remounted and rode slowly behind the woman, off to one side to avoid startling her.

The woman was clothed in rags, with a weathered shawl draped over her snow-white hair and hunched shoulders. She glanced at Morgan and Julie, and her wrinkled forehead smoothed. Her eyes were as clear and blue as Rainia Lake.

"Oh, I'm sorry for being in your way." The woman's gritty voice quivered, matching her slight frame. "These old bones don't seem to move the way they once did."

"No need to apologize," Julie said. "We were just resting by the lake and didn't notice you."

The horses came to a stop and Julie's snorted through its nostrils.

"Don't worry about me," the woman told the mare. "I'm harmless." She raised her eyes to Julie. "I wasn't always so easily missed."

There was something familiar about the grandmotherly woman, Morgan realized, but she couldn't recall seeing her before.

"I'm sorry," Julie said as the woman squinted up at her, shielding her eyes from the bright sky. Julie dismounted, took the reins, and walked beside the woman. "I don't believe we've met."

The woman gave her a warm smile. "Perhaps we have. Or maybe I remind you of someone you once knew?"

Morgan cocked an eyebrow.

"Age has a way of changing what people see on the outside," the woman said. "But some see beyond appearances." The woman reached out a fragile hand. Her fingernails were yellowed and curved inward, with dirt beneath each one. "Are you able to look beyond appearances?"

Julie accepted the woman's hand as Morgan studied the stranger. She was frail and faltering, yet somehow, she had walked two miles south of Rainia by herself. Morgan puzzled over the woman's question. Was she implying that they should look beyond frailty for danger, or beyond danger for acceptance?

The lack of clear answers increased her mistrust. "Where are you going?" Morgan asked.

"The South Crow Gate, of course."

"Why? You should be back at the Crow's Nest, safe with the others."

"Perhaps I want to be part of the last great adventure."

Julie snorted softly at the idea. "I've spent the last two days there. There's no adventure to be had, believe me. There's only war."

The woman smiled. "Then perhaps I've come to help—if these old bones will carry me just a little farther."

Morgan drew her head back slightly, suppressing a laugh. The woman was spunky at least. "What's your name?"

The woman hesitated. "Well, I've been known by many names— as you might expect from someone as old as I."

"Do you have a favorite?" Julie asked.

"Oh my, what a charitable question!" Her eyes shone, clear but unfathomable as sunlight sparkling on the sea. "Nyrianne.

That name would please these feeble ears, my dear. And how are you called?"

"Julie," she answered as the old woman stumbled on a rock. "Oh dear! Would you like to ride? We still have a mile to go. You must be tired."

"No, thank you, Julie. My feet have served me well, but I'm afraid my hips need a good smith." She gave a soft chuckle. "Or maybe another miracle," she added with a wink at Morgan.

Julie appeared to remain wary of Nyrianne, holding the reins loosely as if ready to remount should the need arise.

Morgan tried to keep the conversation light. "Where are you from?"

"My journey began long ago…" Nyrianne pursed her lips and gazed into the sky for a moment. "I cannot say where it began." Her mouth moved, testing the words before discarding them. Her frown transitioned to a bright smile as if a dark cloud had suddenly cleared from her memory. She patted Julie's hand. "It is not often I am greeted with the kindness of company, especially from a dear child who has endured much suffering the last few days."

Julie started. "How do you—"

"Such responsibilities you have, and still you take the time to walk with an old crow at a pace that would test the patience of a snail."

Julie brushed strands of windswept hair from her face. "Actually, I welcome the interlude."

"Interlude? Yes, change can add such flavor to a stew. And chance encounters all the more, wouldn't you agree?"

Morgan's mind swirled as Julie nodded her agreement. Nyrianne sounded half crazy, but there was something about her, something as fleeting as a forgotten name so near the surface. Morgan stared at the old woman, who lowered her gaze as they plodded closer to the South Crow Gate.

Julie wiped sweat from her forehead and removed her leather vest, exposing the knife sheathed at the back of her belt.

"Tell me about your knife, child," Nyrianne said without slowing her shuffle.

"I've never worn a knife before coming here."

Nyrianne flashed a smile at Julie. "And yet knives are so comfortable—and safe—in your hands."

Julie was speechless. She had said nothing about her work here, or in Cochrane as a nurse, handing scalpels to surgeons. The old woman's interest in knives made Morgan uncomfortable.

"And you are no stranger to war and brutality on foreign soil," the woman continued.

Morgan's head swam with memories of her mother's stories of treating war victims in Nigeria.

"Or to strange, evil creatures," Nyrianne added.

Julie stopped as if she'd walked into the side of a mountain. She backed away from Nyrianne. Morgan was suddenly aware that they were alone with this stranger. How much did the woman know about her father and the harvester that had killed him? Morgan casually placed a hand on the hilt of her sword. They were still a few hundred yards from the South Crow Gate, and the wagons following the main road were ignoring them, pushing hard to deliver supplies before sunset.

Morgan lowered her voice. "I don't know how you—"

Nyrianne ignored Morgan and focused on Julie. "Oh, dear. Please forgive me. I do not wish to alarm you or cause you more suffering. Now, please, let us not speak of our dark histories."

They walked in silence for a few minutes as Morgan's heart rate returned to normal.

"How about you, Nyrianne?" Julie cleared her throat. "What finds comfort in your hands these days?"

"Oh, dear child, a great many things," she said, eyes animated. "I picked a flower this morning that was so beautiful it set my heart to racing like a newborn foal in a cool green field."

Julie gave a soft laugh as she rolled up the loose sleeves of her light-green shirt. "That must have been a pretty flower."

Nyrianne knit her thin gray eyebrows into a steely scowl. "There was a time when simple beauty eluded me… It was a barren place where beautiful things are forbidden, where light cannot penetrate"—Nyrianne glared at Julie as if she were looking right through her—"where life chokes on the foul air."

Once again, the dark cloud passed, and the old woman's countenance brightened. "I'm sorry to have frightened you again, dear child." Nyrianne's cheeks rose slightly. "My life has been long, with many chapters. Some were dark and difficult, but not all. The bad ones were written in blood—some of it mine—but most of it belonged to others. This current chapter has been short but sweet, perhaps the best of my days combined. But please, do not be frightened of me. I do not think I could bear it."

Nyrianne took Julie's hands suddenly and stepped to within six inches of her face. The hunger in her eyes reminded Morgan of one of her mother's many emergency room stories. A drunk driver, desperate and full of regret, had begged Julie to save the lives of three kids who were in a car he had T-boned.

"Please," Nyrianne pressed. "It has been some time since I've experienced the kindness of another without condition. Despite what has been and what could be, I could never harm you, dear child."

A tear pooled in Nyrianne's eye. When it spilled over, a tear trickled down her mother's cheek.

"I—I don't understand," Julie stammered.

"Well and good that you do not. Those who do are dark, hollow vessels."

The image of Morgan's father flashed into her mind: *a dark, hollow vessel.* In those final days, when darkness finally overtook him, Morgan had felt so abandoned, wounded and unloved. But there was one thing her mother used to say to her.

"You are loved," Julie breathed.

Nyrianne stared, her eyes swimming.

Julie released herself from Nyrianne's tight grip and wrapped an arm around her shoulders. When the old woman's feet shuffled forward again, Morgan exhaled a long-held breath.

They continued in silence until they reached the South Crow Gate.

"This stronghold is like a sepulchre," Nyrianne said quietly, giving Morgan a start. "A place of great loss and despair. I'm familiar with such places."

"Why are you here?" Morgan asked.

"A fair question," Nyrianne said. "I know what it's like to lose so much, to cling to the slippery edges of life. Not long ago, I was offered a chance to live again. I never expected to understand why, but I have gained clarity today."

Morgan smiled and nodded, not because she understood but simply to appease the old woman.

"Wait here while we find Gloriana," Julie said. "I'm sure she'll find a place where you can help."

As they left the old woman, Morgan thought she heard Nyri-anne say, "Perhaps."

Morgan's muscles ached as she followed Rowe up the iron ladder bolted to the side of the gatehouse. On the roof, Dench was leaning against the battlement, surveying the aftermath of two days of war. The tall platform the gnomes had built was a pile of charred rubble. Catapult rocks and patches of burnt objects marred the ground. On the wall walk, human and half-orc worked side by side on final preparations for the night's assault. Bows, bundles of arrows, spears, and shields of various sizes leaned against the battlements. Rocks were piled beside both catapults and a stack of large arrows lay beside the ballista.

"I still cannot believe you're here, Dench," Rowe said.

"Me wish more came, but you know how stubborn we be."

"Our final count this morning—including your troop—came in at a hundred and nine soldiers."

Dench's lips flapped as he exhaled. "Big wall walk for only a hundred and nine."

"We should never have survived the first night," Rowe said. "The odds were worse the second night, but thanks to you, some of us saw the sunrise."

"Can we do it one more time?" Morgan asked.

Dench nodded. "How many times we face terrible—no, not de right word—impossible be better word. How many times we face de impossible and still win?"

Rowe shook his head. "We've never stared *these* odds in the face, Dench."

The half-orc's wide forehead wrinkled. "How many times you tell me: *always darkest before dawn?*"

"Sure seems dark now."

"Me know." Dench's face twisted into a smile that revealed enormous flat teeth. To a stranger, the smile would have been a terrifying thing to look at. "Big brawl coming, and my kin like a good brawl."

"I'm tired of fighting, Dench."

Dench's smile faded. "What will you do when dis war be done?"

Rowe didn't hesitate. "Remember that small lake up past the Skran Bluffs?"

"Branit Lake?" Dench said with a nod. "Me always know how much you like dat place."

"There's a beautiful spot on the east side next to the water, and most of the land is flat enough to farm," Rowe gazed into the distant hills beyond the Misty Gorge.

"Me help you build your home," Dench said.

"*Our* homes, Dench. I want our kids playing together every day."

Dench laughed softly. "Good hunting dare. Me like de ruffled grouse."

"And we've caught our fill every time we've fished up there," Rowe said.

"Dat be wort fighting for."

Morgan looked out over the Rainia Valley and smiled as she listened to the old friends talking. A steady flow of wagons approached, buckling under the weight of fresh supplies. A few hundred yards out, the blue-and-gold colors of a single rider flapped behind him as his horse galloped toward the wall.

"Messenger from de Marauders," Dench said.

At the base of the wall, the rider jumped off his horse and

bounded up the stairs. Rowe led him into the gatehouse and shut the door behind them. When they reappeared moments later, the messenger raced back into the valley as quickly as he had arrived.

All eyes were on Rowe. A murmur spread through the sparse crowd.

"When dey come?" Dench asked.

Rowe put on an optimistic face, but Morgan sensed he was trying to be brave. "The Marauders have been on a hard march for five days," he said, "stopping less than six hours a day to rest. They've pushed horses to death and soldiers to near madness in their haste to come to our aid." He faltered as he scanned the despondent faces. "They won't be stopping through the night… but still won't arrive till shortly before dawn."

The murmur rose again, but Dench snuffed it out. "What orders did dey send?" The half-orc sounded positive.

Rowe shook his head. "They know the numbers are against us, Dench. If this wall falls tonight, the Crow's Nest will fall with it."

"Why we no fall back to de castle?" a half-orc in the crowd asked.

Morgan felt as if Rowe had explained this a hundred times, but he remained composed as he spoke. "Once the gnomes breach this wall, they will only need to hold the North Crow Gate a few hours, stopping the Marauders from entering the valley, until the main body of their army arrives from the south. Last we heard, they are over twelve thousand strong. That's more than enough to defeat the Marauders and then kill any survivors in the Crow's Nest."

The silence that followed was a heavy, suffocating thing. Even the most optimistic soldier could only shake his head in bewilderment.

"Sun high and hot," Dench said, pointing up. "Gnomes get sick and no fight well in de hot sun. Do we attack dem?"

Rowe put his hand against Dench's broad back. "I know that

waiting for a battle to come to you is a foreign concept, but there could be a thousand gnomes around that corner."

Another half-orc spoke up. "We no see anudder sunrise from dis wall, so why not die on *our* terms."

Rowe rubbed his eyes with the palms of his hands. The half-orc was right, of course. If they managed to hold the wall an hour, it would be a miracle. But they had to protect the Crow's Nest. "Every minute we stall the gnome army is a minute gained for the Marauders to reach the North Crow Gate," he explained.

A few soldiers shuffled their feet, and a half-orc coughed. Morgan surveyed the grim faces of human and half-orc, young and old, man and woman. No one wanted to die, but the thought of abandoning the wall was unthinkable.

"Your final act of valor may save many lives," Rowe said, but his voice cracked with uncertainty.

Slowly, the crowd dispersed. Soldiers returned to preparing the catapults. Dench and the half-orcs congregated along the largest section of the wall walk, discussing ways of killing gnomes by the dozens. Rowe caught Dadore's arm before he trudged down the stairs to his wagon.

"I'm sorry," the alchemist said before Rowe could speak. "There isn't time to create anything substantial. I'll do what I can, but I'm afraid I can't promise any miracles."

※

As evening approached, Morgan and Julie walked arm in arm through a field just north of the wall, trying to relax in the short reprieve. They were reminiscing quietly over their first family camping trip to Thunder Bay.

"It rained so hard the first night the tent collapsed, and we had to sleep in the car!" Morgan said. "The second night started out picture perfect until the mosquitos came out, thick as clouds, forcing us back into the car."

When Julie stopped laughing, she wiped a tear from her eye. "You get your tenacity from your father, you know."

"Tent collapses? Fix it. Mosquitos overtake the camp? Build a huge fire and smother it with leaves to smoke them out. Don't catch fish? Hmm... Remember when he drove to town and came back with frozen fish sticks?"

Julie burst into another bout of laughter. "I've never met such a patient cook."

Morgan stretched her arms out and let the tall grass weave between her fingers. "When did you know you loved him?"

"The first time I laid eyes on him." Julie was still smiling. "He was building a game for a youth retreat at the church he was interning at. He was holding a nail between his teeth and hammering boards together. His hair was long back then and always messy, like a surfer dude. He was wearing an old white T-shirt with paint stains and a plaid shirt wrapped around his waist. I remember a half dozen awkward teenaged boys with him, trying to help. He drew them in with joke after joke. I came in carrying a tray of water balloons, and when he looked up, I knew it that moment."

"Really," Morgan said. "I always assumed that he finally wore you down after chasing you for a couple of years."

Julie laughed. "I suppose that's not entirely untrue. But that day I knew he was the one." She plucked a blade of grass. "So tell me, young lady, when did you know you loved Rowe?"

Morgan stopped. "What makes you think it's love?"

"I see the way you look at him."

Morgan picked at a cracked thumbnail. "This will make me

sound like a sucky romantic, Mom, but I think I fell in love with him the first night I arrived in this crazy place. I woke up in the middle of the night and we ended up talking for hours. In the end, I was over the moon."

"I get it, kiddo."

Morgan hung her head. "But I guess none of that matters now."

"No, Morgan! It's always worth it to love, whether it's for a lifetime or only a few weeks."

"You seem awfully calm about tonight," Morgan said.

"Far from it." Julie pulled Morgan close. "I'm so scared for you."

Morgan hugged her back.

"If I thought there was a chance of talking you into running back through the Gateway, I'd get on my knees and beg."

"But I'm my mother's daughter," Morgan said with a sniffle.

"You certainly are that. Stubborn to the core."

Morgan shook her head. "*Formidable*, Mom. I will be a force on that wall, and *that* I get from you."

They returned to the wall, and Morgan stood near the 109 soldiers gathered around the gatehouse. The sun inched ever closer to the western horizon. Everyone was silent, allowing Rowe to address them without raising his voice.

"The gnomes need to breach the wall as much as we need to defend it, and they are short on time. With that in mind, I suspect they've been building ladders all day hoping to overpower us with sheer numbers. They won't be moving up one careful rung at a time behind shields while loaded crossbows are passed up to them. They will fly up the ladders with little protection. We need to cut them down as efficiently as possible, so pace yourselves. Keep on the bows as long as possible. Once they breach the wall, get out of the way because Dench and his band of brothers will offer them a bloody warm welcome. Find a sheltered place and let arrows fly on the ladders. I suggest the catapults or atop the gatehouse. When the gnomes clear the battlement, make certain they step into a hail of arrows while the half-orcs introduce them to their axes.

"Do not scatter and do not panic. Stay in tight groups. If you hear a single trumpet sound, we've lost the wall. From there, leave it all on the battlefield."

Rowe raised his sword to offer one final word of encouragement, but the old woman, Nyrianne, elbowed her way between two soldiers, and he stopped. Her frail, hunched form contrasted with the strong, alert men, but then she lifted her head to face Rowe. In her eyes, Morgan saw a confidence and fierce determination that matched the bravest soldier.

A distant shout from the thoroughfare caught everyone's attention, and Morgan peered across the clearing. When she looked back, the old woman was gone.

CHAPTER 27
MUST KEEP MOVING

Plumes of dark smoke billowed from the Clover Fields. Will's vision was blurred by the combination of a fever, the healing magic of his Trannalun cloak coursing through him, and the unsteady jostling of Grudum's mule. He clung to the saddle horn, knowing that if he fell, he lacked the strength to remount—assuming the mule would even wait for him. Will struggled to focus on the shadow in front of him. Bremer had told him to head east, but Will couldn't resist taking constant glances over his shoulder. He half expected to see Bremer, and possibly Urk, hurrying after him. But such hope was difficult to trust, given the atrocities of the past week. With the luck he'd had since returning to the Fourwinds, it was more likely that a horde of furious gnome guards would appear behind him.

Despite his pessimism, Will had enough history with Bremer to imagine the fate of the slave camp. He had been with the rogue after he single-handedly slaughtered a group of harvesters and guards near Acttun, dozens of slave runners in Fairbay, and a handful of mysterious stone guards in Sidara's castle. In the Epping Forest,

Bremer and Urk slew an unbelievable number of holgs, although Will had been unconscious for most of that day. So, a few lazy bush gnomes in the Clover Fields would be a walk in the park for Bremer and his unpredictable companion.

The eastern pastures of the Clover Fields turned into rolling hills. Will tried to keep his eyes open, but he wandered close to the edge of an irresistible sleep. Each time he sagged in the saddle, he jerked awake, catching himself before he fell.

After a mile or two at a surprisingly steady pace, the mule slowed beside a river that meandered southward through the rocky grasslands toward a distant forest. Will's shadow disappeared; it would be dark soon. He rubbed his burning eyes, then squeezed his nose with his fingers and blew out as hard as he could to pop his plugged ears. It didn't help. Despite the cloak's magic permeating his entire being, Will felt wretched and longed for a bed and some Advil.

"So…you must be the river Bremer mentioned," Will mumbled. "But didn't he say somethin' about a bridge?"

Leaning back in the saddle, Will swayed as the mule descended the short embankment and stepped into the water. While the mule drank, Will tried to recall Bremer's instructions. *Follow the river.* But which way?

"Get up," Will said, pulling the mule's head from the water.

Instead of moving back to the shore, the mule stumbled forward over the river rock. Will was surprised by how deep it was so close to shore. His bare feet dipped beneath the surface as he floundered in the saddle. The mule's eyes flared. It drew back its lips, reared its head, and let out a loud *wheeeheee-haaww*! Will pulled on the reins to stop their advance, but the current carried them downriver as the mule struggled to maintain its footing.

They finally got closer to the shore when a four-legged creature leapt from the riverbank, piercing the evening air with a terrifying snarl. Will cried out as he realized the creature was Grudum's second dog. It crashed into the mule, forcing it back into the river, and sending Will headlong into the water.

The river exploded with turbulent splashing as the mule scrambled to its feet with the dog clinging to its back. Wild-eyed, the dog sunk its teeth into the mule's neck. The water bloodied as shrieking mule and snarling dog went down again. The mule almost regained its feet, but the dog took another chunk from its neck. With deep red claw marks on its rump and legs, and blood gushing from its neck, the mule dropped awkwardly onto its side in two feet of water. The dog pounced and proceeded to tear flesh as if it hadn't eaten for days.

As the sickening sounds echoed off the river, Will dragged himself out of the water and crawled up the bank. When the thrashing stopped, he looked back. The dog lowered its head and growled at him, baring its bloody teeth. Will drew his hood over his head, then wrapped the cloak around him, trying to cover his legs and feet. He considered searching for a weapon in the pack Bremer had given him, but there was no time. The dog barked viciously, then growled and crouched, ready to pounce. Will turned away, bracing for the impact.

Suddenly, the ground shook, and a pair of enormous hooves thudded next to Will. The shadowy form spun in a blur and kicked a hind leg at the leaping dog. The crunching sound of hoof hitting ribs was as gruesome as the dog ripping at the mule. In a single powerful jump, the animal landed beside the dog. Both front hooves hammered down, crushing the dog's skull and hindquarters.

Will blinked several times to clear his failing vision, but there was no denying what he was seeing. To refer to the creature before him as a horse would be like calling a dragon a lizard. Enormous black wings folded against its dark hide. Its long mane cascaded to the side as its head slowly turned to face Will. High on its forehead was a jagged stump, the remains of what was probably a large horn that once crowned the majestic beast. It stomped once and huffed. Will recognized the familiar sound from his recurring dream.

"It's you," he mumbled.

The great creature took a few steps toward Will and nickered softly as if it were trying to communicate with him. A torrent of images played in Will's mind like a disjointed movie in fast-forward. As he relaxed, the images morphed into coherent subjects. There was a large room with a bed. There were two stands next to the bed. A glass pitcher of clean water rested on one, and a platter of fresh vegetables on the other. A beautiful woman who shone like a star hovered over the person in the bed. Will blinked several times, and the vision focused on the sleeping form in the bed. It was him!

Will bolted upright and looked at the creature. "Can you take me there?"

The creature nickered again and closed the gap between them, its hooves pounding the earth. It kneeled with regal elegance, and Will clambered onto the creature's back. Although his bones were slowly mending, the cloak's magic was doing little to reduce his raging fever. Half starved and broken, Will realized that, despite the power of his Trannalun cloak, he was dying.

When the creature rose, it was six hands larger than any horse Will had ever ridden, with shoulders of pure muscle. Will's head spun as he looked at the ground. The creature waited until he was settled, then moved without the need to be guided. This was fortunate because Will was in no condition to lead, even if he knew where he was going. And so, he closed his eyes and clutched the mane, placing his trust in the mysterious beast. The last thing he remembered before losing consciousness was a gentle lurch in his stomach as he was lifted off the ground, followed by a rushing wind whipping his hair.

***

Will lay between a set of clean sheets, a soft pillow beneath his head. His cloak hung on the bedpost. On a side table to his left was a pitcher of clear water. He turned his head slowly to the right and saw a plate of colorful vegetables. His head had stopped pounding and his vision was sharp. Someone had been caring for him. Overflowing with gratitude, he wept softly.

The curtain of a large window rustled, and he inhaled the salty breeze through clear nostrils. Outside, the sound of creaking rigging mingled with the laughter of children and the call of seagulls. Will leaned up on his elbows and scanned the room. The aged tongue-and-groove wood paneling, the pitch to the roof, and the tapestry of a seascape confirmed the familiar location. Not only was he back in Fairbay, but he was convinced this room was in the Recovery Ale House and Inn. Will straightened his arms and stretched beneath the sheets, tears of joy and relief trickling onto his pillow.

There was a soft knock at the door, followed by the iron handle lifting quietly. When Jessman stuck his head in, Will fought back another swell of emotion.

"There ya be, laddie. Glad yer awake." The long-haired, bearded bartender and part-owner of the Recovery stepped into the room, one hand hidden behind his back. "Tough coupl'a days ya had."

Will sat up. "Is this real, or am I dreaming? Am I dead?" He was surprised by how good his voice sounded. Not only was the fever gone, but his congested chest had cleared.

"No, this is all real, and yer alive and well." Without revealing what he had behind his back, Jessman poured a cup of water and handed it to Will. The first sip soothed his cracked lips and dry throat.

"I acquired this some time ago in the event you returned." Jessman flourished a bottle of elven mead. They shared a laugh as he popped the cork and filled two small cups.

"Now, don'tcha tell anyone about this," he said, raising a finger. "The healers would have me in stocks."

Will sipped quietly, enthralled by the lingering flavor. "How long have I been here?"

"The healer's been fussin' over ya for over a day, laddie. Had us all in a fret, ya did."

"I don't remember how I got here." Will took another sip.

"You were in a bad way, lad. No one thought ya were gonna make it. Yer a good hand at cheatin' death."

Will ran a hand through his clean hair. He remembered the slave camp, Bremer's rescue, the nightmare at the river, and then…

Jessman winked. "Ya have some interestin' travelin' companions."

"Did I…" Will paused as Jessman's teeth peeked between his bushy beard and mustache.

"Thaudas brought ya here, and had I not seen it with these two eyes, I would never have believed such a thing possible."

There was a gentle knock at the door and Jessman jumped. He snatched the mead, drove the cork back in, and shoved the bottle under the bed just as the door opened. Wide-eyed, he tipped his head back and drained the cup. Not needing any encouragement, Will did the same.

"Jessman!" A young, fair-haired woman hissed the moment she saw him. "I warned ya!"

"Beggin' yer pardon, but I—"

"Beggin' nuthin', ya stiff-necked simpleton!" She jammed her fists against her hips. "She's on her way here! Now!"

Jessman's face blanched.

"Out the winda!" she squawked, pointing. "I'm gonna bust a cauldron over yer head for this!"

Jessman rushed out the window, cup in hand, in a fluid motion. Apparently, this wasn't the first time he had made a hasty exit from an upper room.

The young woman strode across the room and sniffed the air. She grimaced. "You didn't," she said, squaring herself toward Will. She plucked the cup from his hand, sniffed it, glanced around, then dropped to her knees and reached under the bed.

"I'm gonna cut off his knackers the next time he falls asleep!" She lifted the hidden bottle triumphantly and stood. "Is there anythin' else I should know about?" She started lifting the sheet, but Will slapped it down. "A whore beneath the sheets, perhaps?"

Will was unconcerned with the woman's private battle with Jessman but wanted her to calm down. "Who's coming here?"

She flashed him an odd look as if he should know, then dashed out of the room. The door closed solidly behind her, leaving Will with a myriad of questions. He stretched out beneath the sheets and for the first time realized he was naked. And clean. The setting reminded him of the elven healing tent where he had recuperated after his confrontation with Sidara at the Waerdreath castle. What was it about people in the Fourwinds leaving patients naked?

A moment later, the door opened without a knock. Will sat upright as a beautiful woman in a sparkling gown glided to the edge of the bed, her white hair cascading over her shoulders to her waist. Her skin, tight against her lean form, was the color of the sea. Although her physical features reminded Will so much of Ryowyn, it was her sparkling-blue eyes and gentle smile—full of kindness and understanding—that convinced him she was Ryowyn's mother.

Without warning, a crushing wave of sorrow overwhelmed him. "I-I'm so sorry," he stammered. Tears gushed from his eyes as sobs wracked his body. He wrapped his arms around his chest. He had not experienced such a deep ache since the day the police had arrived at his house to inform him of his father's suicide.

She sat on the edge of the bed, patiently listening to his painful cries. He looked at the wall, the window, the door, his knees—anything to avoid her eyes. And yet, despite his remorse, he felt vulnerable and safe in her presence.

"If it weren't for me…if…if I'd been more careful," he spluttered, searching for words to articulate how sorry he was for what had happened to Ryowyn. "I wanted to keep her safe…but I"—he choked on a sob—"I couldn't reach her…like I couldn't reach Mom…or Dad, when he…" He clenched the edges of the sheet in tight fists. "Why? Why do I keep losing the ones I love?" He wept freely now, forehead pressed against his fists.

The delicate touch of her hand in his hair reeled Will back from the precipice of despair. His convulsions slowed and eventually stopped. She touched the back of his hand, and he flinched, tightening his grip. But as she wrapped her soft hands over his knuckles, the tension dissipated. He sniffled several times, wiping his eyes with the sheet.

"Your sorrow and guilt are misguided." Her voice was quiet, melodic, and it stole his breath. "You are not responsible for the suffering and loss of those you love." She looked and sounded so much like Ryowyn it hurt. "Sometimes storms blow into our lives with such force we wonder how we could ever rebuild. But the storms are not your fault, Will Owens. Nor is it always possible to know why the storms come. It's how we weather them, how we rebuild, and how we live on that makes the difference for us and for those who remain." She reached down and took his hand. "Let go of the guilt you hold, Will. No one blames you for what happened to your loved ones…or to Ryowyn."

Another round of sorrow seized him, and the woman waited until the flood of tears subsided.

"Ryowyn spoke of your courage, your selflessness, and your affection for her. You touched a part of her with the fire that burns within you."

Will looked into her radiant eyes and, seeing so much of Ryowyn looking back at him, he groaned, wondering what had befallen her.

"My name is Almithara Ayoust. I was away on the day you saved this village, but I heard the stories. I would have enjoyed meeting the young warrior who rescued my daughter."

Will snorted. "A weeping warrior."

She disregarded the self-deprecating remark. "You are exactly as I imagined."

He shook his head, fighting back the threat of more tears. "Your daughter would be well and at your side right now had it not been for me. I'm so sorry."

Almithara smiled as she filled a cup with water. "She has been taken from you, Will, the same way she has been taken from us." She handed him the cup and waited as he drank.

"Do you love her?"

Will lowered the cup. "I would die a thousand deaths to wake her."

"Is your love for her any less than mine?" She raised an eyebrow. "Of course not, Will. Listen well. I bear no ill will toward you. Neither does King Ryodan. If either of us could go back in time and alter the course of events that led to you meeting our beloved daughter, we would not. The depth of happiness you brought her was something Ryodan and I would never want to take from her.

"So," she continued with a smile that lit up her face. "You must open your heart and find a way to forgive yourself for the transgressions you feel you have committed. When you do, you will realize they were not transgressions at all. We live in a broken world where bad things happen. We both know you would die a thousand deaths for Ryowyn, but the real question is: Will you let your guilt die? Can you forgive yourself and live on, for her sake?"

Will had assumed he would bear the yoke of guilt to the end of his days, but the mere thought of forgiveness lightened his spirit. Actually, he had never thought of relief from despair in terms of self-forgiveness. It would take time, but Almithara had opened the door a crack.

"You have endured enough heartache to last a lifetime, Will, and at such a young age. Let the guilt go. Do not let your past define your future. You were destined to change the world the moment you took your first breath. Let nothing take that away from you."

Will stared at the cup in his hands.

"Look at me, Will."

He raised his eyes to meet hers.

"Ryowyn is not yet lost to us."

Will leaned forward. "What…what do you mean?"

"When we learned she was in the Records of Time, Ryodan made the journey to see her."

"Why didn't you go too?" As soon as the words escaped his lips, he regretted them.

The mer queen's eyes narrowed, but she maintained her poise. "I begged to go with him."

Will cringed. "I'm sorry, I didn't mean—"

"The journey is challenging for our kind, and through a land ravaged by war. Ryodan told me that his heart could not bear to lose another of his beloved, so I remained. Additionally, we agreed that it was imperative for me to stay while our son, Wrathan, leads a patrol at the north end of the sea, near the Gryton Mines."

She turned toward the door. "We have not yet heard from the king, but I have not given up hope for Ryowyn."

Will wiped his nose with the back of his hand. "May I ask you a question?"

"Of course."

"What is…Thaudas?"

"Now there is a question I'm sure your friend Rowe would find compelling." She tucked her hands behind her back. "Let me see, where does one begin? Thaudas…is a creature of faerie. There have always been winged horses and unicorns among us, although to call either rare would be a serious understatement. A winged horse is an incredible gift in times of war, while a unicorn, through the magic ingrained in its horn, has the ability to heal. Thaudas is both winged horse and unicorn, and the only creature of its kind known in the Fourwinds. History is vague on the details, but hundreds of years ago, Thaudas's horn was stolen."

"I saw the stump," Will said.

"So much time passes between sightings that Thaudas is considered a myth. There are few tales about the creature, but the most common story is that Natas severed his horn during a fierce battle. Thaudas has been searching for the horn ever since."

"So, why did Thaudas come to *me*? He first appeared in my dreams, then he saved my life and brought me here. Wouldn't he be more valuable in the war, even if he's lost his ability to heal?"

"I came to ask you the same questions, Will."

Almithara stood in regal silence as Will searched his mind for a reasonable explanation. If he were half the man her daughter had described, he would come up with something. "I suppose he brought me here because he couldn't heal me without his horn, and this is a place of healing. But why would he want me healed? Or did someone send him to find me? I don't understand it…yet. But maybe Thaudas wants me alive for a specific task."

Almithara lifted her eyebrows and nodded as the edges of her lips curved down. "I suppose that is possible."

"I hope he doesn't want me to fight in the war. I need to get back to help Ryowyn. Maybe if Thaudas had his horn, he could—" Will stopped short and stared at Almithara. "That's it! If we found his horn, could he heal Ryowyn?"

Almithara's eyes became misty. "The legends tell of Thaudas restoring many from the brink of death. But that was a long time ago."

Will leaned forward and slung his legs over the side of the bed. "Thaudas must know where his horn is! And maybe he believes I can help him get it!"

"How can you be certain?"

He nodded, chewing on his bottom lip. "There must be something he knows about me that makes him think I can get it back. And if I'm right, he might be able to help Ryowyn. Is he still here?"

"Thaudas is waiting out in the plains. It is most unusual."

Will started to lift the sheets but remembered he was naked. "Did I have a pack with me?"

Almithara reached down at the foot of the bed and handed him the leather bag. Will flipped it open and gasped. Resting in its holster was his Springfield 1911.

"Bremer." Will chuckled to himself, shaking his head slowly. "How does he do it?"

"I'll be waiting with a hot meal below." Almithara pointed to a dresser in the corner. "You will find fresh clothes in there." She paused and smiled the way his mother used to before an important basketball game. It felt like pride mixed with unconditional love, regardless of the outcome. She sidled through the doorway and closed it behind her with a soft click.

CHAPTER 28

THE SOUTH CROW GATE

Morgan leaned against the back railing of the wall, taking in an otherwise picturesque sunset. She had tried to remain hopeful all day, drawing strength from those around her. But now, as the sky slowly darkened, she realized that the fate of the South Crow Gate and its brave defenders was in the hands of an army of gnomes stomping an incessant battle rhythm in the thoroughfare. Hope seemed to have hitched a ride with the sun, and it was fleeing fast. Morgan wrapped her arms around her chest and trudged down the stairs to see her mother, one last time.

"Did you notice Nyrianne up on the wall walk during Rowe's speech?" Julie asked.

"Yes," Morgan said. "What was she doing there?"

"I don't know, but there's something about her…"

Morgan had seen that look on her mother's face before. "Good? Or bad?"

Leaning against an operating table, Julie fidgeted with a small knife. "She seemed so sweet, and I believe she was sincere, but… there was something just beneath the surface."

"Do you think she's"—Morgan glanced up at the wall walk and lowered her voice—"a harvester?"

"I don't think so, Morgan. It would have killed us. And remember, I lived with a harvester." Julie choked back a sob. "There wasn't an ounce of sweetness in him."

Morgan put her arms around mother as she cried silently. "I know. I'm sorry, Mom."

After a moment, Julie sniffled. "All the same, I think we should keep an eye out for that woman, and let the others know."

Morgan nodded. "I agree. I'm just heading to see Rowe, so I'll tell him. He was meeting with Dadore above the gatehouse."

Julie blew her nose into a handkerchief. "I love you, kiddo."

Morgan soaked in her mother's presence like a sponge. "I love you too, Mom—to the moon and back."

⁂

As she waited for Dadore to climb down the ladder from the gatehouse roof, Morgan sensed the eyes of soldiers and half-orcs watching her. She grieved silently for them as she scaled the ladder. These men would not have the luxury of a final farewell to their wives and daughters. The injustice of war smothered them all, sucking the life from their vibrant communities.

At the top of the ladder, a breeze ruffled her hair. The V-neck of her thin, collarless shirt fluttered beneath her Trannalun cloak. She gathered the crimson garment around her chest and realized that the top two clasps on her shirt had come undone. She reached up to fasten the clasps but seeing Rowe alone near the battlement with his back to her, she hesitated, then left her cloak open.

Rowe spun around at the sound of her approach. The failing light of the sun highlighted his dusty hair and straggly beard and smoothed the distressed lines on his wonderful face. She sauntered toward him, suppressing a grin as they shared an admiring gaze. *Yes*, Morgan thought, *I've loved him from the moment we met, just like in the storybooks.* But this particular story was not getting a happily ever after.

She stepped close, and he inhaled deeply, his chest pressing against hers. She kissed his neck. "You look like you've seen a ghost," she said.

The thin line of his lips yielded to a smile. "Your beauty is a haunting thing." He caressed her cheek with a calloused finger, scanning her brow, eyes, nose, and lips with a gentle gaze. After a moment, he took her hand and they walked along the battlement.

"What do you need me to do?" she asked.

Rowe sighed as if a new burden had settled on his shoulders. "Have a wagon ready. When we lose the wall walk, I need you to force your mother and Gloriana, and as many of the volunteers as you can, into that wagon and break for the Crow's Nest."

"But—"

"You asked me a question, and I answered it, Morgan." He released her hand. "There is a small group of older men at the main gates, awaiting your word. Once inside the curtain wall, tell them to lock the castle. From there, head up to the Records of Time. Just remember to release the warding magic before touching the locks."

The ladder rattled and creaked as someone made their way up to the roof, and Morgan turned away to fasten her shirt hooks.

"Did you see that old woman on the wall walk earlier?" she asked.

Rowe nodded. "Do you know her?"

"Mom and I met her earlier today, on our way back from visiting Ryowyn."

"I saw you coming up the valley together."

"Mom's worried about her…" Morgan shook her head. "Not *worried*, but—"

"I think I know what you mean. I saw her earlier, and when our eyes met…well, she's certainly more than she appears."

"Do you think she's a harvester?"

"I don't. Harvesters are far better at hiding their true identity. Although I wish Will were here to confirm that. I tried to find the woman after the briefing, but she was gone."

"Are you concerned?"

Rowe laughed softly. "If she means trouble, Morgan, she'll have to wait behind a long line of gnomes."

She jabbed him with her elbow as Dench crested the top of the ladder.

"Have room for me?" he asked.

"Of course," Rowe said.

"Me still no believe you not dead."

Rowe smiled. "Seems I'm always surrounded by those who help keep me alive."

"Always been dat way wit' you."

Morgan took a small step away, watching the two who looked so different but acted as if they were brothers.

Dench gazed out at the clearing. "Me feel Ruint wit' us."

"He was the best in battle." Rowe patted Dench's massive arm. "No offense."

Dench smiled. "Deese I brought from de high country fight like Ruint."

"They cut through gnomes last night like an ax through rotten apples," Rowe said.

"Is there no hope for that tonight?" Morgan blurted.

Rowe shook his head. "If we can hold the wall at least until the wee hours, the Marauders will have a chance to reach the Crow's Nest. That would be a significant victory."

"One that you're not around to share in," Morgan said.

"If the Crow's Nest falls, Morgan, your world could fall with it."

Morgan drew her cloak tighter. "Only two harvesters have made it through the Gateway, and look at the mess they made. Now two more have gone though, possibly carrying Phyriad—"

Rowe clasped her shoulders. "We can't do anything about that now, Morgan. But tonight, we can try to make sure no others make it through the Gateway."

"What you always say before every big fight?" Dench asked.

"It will go the way it has to," Rowe said with a nod.

"Good enough for Dench."

Morgan gave Dench a heartfelt hug. "Take care of him," she whispered.

<hr>

Rowe paced the wall walk, his hands opening and closing as he wrestled with the madness of this battle. There might be a better way to defend the valley, but it was far too late to consider new options now. He observed Dench interacting with the half-orcs, a roast turkey leg in one hand and his broadsword in the other. Each half-orc wore overlapping layers of banded armor over their coarse hair.

Rounding a catapult station, Rowe caught himself midstride before bowling into the old woman. There was a glimmer of anger in her eyes, and then her features softened.

"You love her," she said suddenly.

"Pardon me?"

"Julie's daughter, Morgan. You love her."

Rowe shifted his weight from his heels to the balls of his feet and tightened his jaw. Despite his cause for concern, he offered a short nod.

"Julie is kind and her love is unconditional." Her lips pursed in a stern expression.

Again, Rowe nodded.

"Violence begets violence, I have been told, but I do not see another way. I will not allow harm to come to Julie."

Rowe stared at the wrinkled face, trying to decide if these were the ramblings of a madwoman or an oracle.

She shook her head and stomped her walking stick. "I will *not* allow it!" She shuffled along the wall walk and down the main stairway.

Someone tapped Rowe's shoulder. "Begging your pardon?"

Rowe turned to find Dadore watching the woman leave.

"I'm sorry, sir, but there's something not right about her."

A shadow covered them as the sun suddenly disappeared beyond the horizon, jarring Rowe into action.

"Agreed." Rowe planted his hands on his hips. "Are you ready?"

Dadore nodded. "I've laced the beams with an incendiary agent."

"How long will the men have after the trumpet blast?"

"Not long. I'll ignite the main beam midpoint, and the fire will spread along its length at a fast walking pace. I've covered the crossbeams more sparingly, but once they start burning, the wood planks will catch quickly. By the time the flames are lapping between the planks, the entire wall walk will be on borrowed time. From there, I'll slip back and watch the gatehouse. If it's breached, I'll send in a flaming arrow."

"How long will the gatehouse fire last?"

"A week, at least. In that time, the controls, gears, and pulleys will meld together into one big mess. I don't think the portcullis will ever be raised again."

"Remind me never to get on your bad side," Rowe said, placing a firm hand on the boy's shoulder. "Just remember to wait until you hear the single trumpet blast."

Dadore nodded. "Of course."

"Well done, Dadore. It has been my pleasure to serve with you." Rowe squeezed his shoulder.

"I could have done so much more…"

"We all could have. But tonight, we get one last chance to right our wrongs." Rowe released his grip and Dadore scampered away.

⁂

"Rowe!" Dench shouted from the gatehouse battlement. "Come see dis!"

"What is it?" Rowe said as he and Morgan ran to Dench's side.

Twenty yards into the clearing, almost unseen in the dim light of dusk, the old woman hobbled directly toward the thoroughfare. The stomping and shouting of the gnome army was intensifying, but there was still no sign of an initial attack.

"Have the gates been opened?" Rowe shouted, shattering the heavy silence that had befallen the stronghold.

"No," someone shouted back. Soldiers and half-orcs crowded the battlement for a closer look.

"How did she get out there?" Rowe asked.

"Me go check de gate," Dench said as he started down the ladder.

"How did she get beyond the wall?" Rowe shouted. He rushed from side to side of the gatehouse battlement, echoing his question and receiving similar confused responses.

Morgan rushed to the back wall. "Mom! Come up here—quick!"

"Once she rounds that cleft in the mountains," Rowe said, "she'll come face-to-face with a thousand gnomes poised to attack."

Julie climbed the gatehouse ladder and squeezed between Morgan and Rowe.

She gasped, despite being out of breath. "Oh no! What is she *doing*?"

"I was hoping you could tell us," Rowe said. "I spoke with her earlier, and she seems to know you."

"How did she get out there?" Julie asked.

"Does she know the gnomes are right around the corner?" Morgan said.

Julie nodded. "She does, Morgan. She asked me and Gloriana all sorts of questions about the last two nights, so she knows."

Rowe turned to Julie, glowering. "To what end?"

"Pardon me?" Julie asked.

"Why did she want to know about the last two nights?"

"I don't know," Julie said, rubbing her temples.

"Crank the catapults!" Rowe bellowed. He turned back to Julie. "Did she sound like she might be a scout working for the gnomes?"

"A spy? N-no, not at all," Julie stammered. "She just seemed like a…like a lonely old woman who wanted to talk."

"She seemed a bit crazy," Morgan added.

"I doubt that," Rowe said as he watched the woman hobbling ever forward in the fading light. "She managed to slip through the wall, and anyone capable of that is of sound mind. And anyone of sound mind would not walk into an enemy camp, unarmed and alone. She has to be with them and armed with the knowledge of how thin our numbers are."

"She'll be killed," Julie mumbled.

"We'll *all* be killed," Rowe said.

"Wait a minute!" Morgan snapped. "She isn't on their side. She can't be."

"Then she'll be dead in a few minutes," Rowe said. "Either way, the gnomes will be here in short order."

Rowe climbed down the ladder to address the men and half-orcs on the wall walk. "Don't be distracted by the old woman! Prepare for battle!" He walked the length of the wall walk, checking stations and catapults. When he returned to the gatehouse roof, the clearing was a misty gray.

"Can you still see her?" he asked.

"She's just rounding the corner," Morgan said, her voice nearly failing her. "There! She's around it now."

Rowe paced, wringing his hands, but Morgan stared across the clearing, confused by the unexpected turn of events. It was dark enough that the gnomes should have launched their attack by now. Were they consulting with the woman? Or were they deliberately trying to induce fear by prolonging their assault?

⁂

It came from beyond the bend as a single powerful voice, filling the night sky.

The shrill cry was followed by a fierce wind that blew across the clearing and howled up and over the wall, knocking every human and half-orc to their backs. When they caught their breaths, soldiers cried out, covering their heads as they curled into fetal positions.

The mountains groaned as massive sections of rock broke away, crashing to the ground. Explosions of granite sounded like the world was coming apart. Boulders fell from thousands of feet above as several avalanches splintered from the mountains, thundering down into the valley. The South Crow Gate shook. Great cracks opened in its thick mortar lines. The few soldiers able to gain their feet soon fell to the wooden planks again as a large portion of the back guardrail collapsed.

Morgan lay next to Rowe, clutching him in stark terror. Rowe was on his back, sprawled out to stop them from falling off the shifting gatehouse.

As suddenly as it had started, the earth stopped shaking. Rock slides continued for several terrifying moments until the heavy breathing of soldiers and half-orcs was the only sound.

Morgan kept her eyes shut, fearing the worst. *Was this an attack? Was the wall still whole?* Rowe's grip on her arm loosened, and she sighed, relieved he was still alive. She opened and closed her mouth wide several times to clear the pressure in her ears.

Rolling his head to the side, Rowe blinked at Morgan, relief reflected in his gaze. As the rush of dizziness ran its course, she rubbed her ears and tilted her head sideways to hear beyond the wall. If gnome ladders started crashing into the battlements, it would be a terrifying few minutes.

"I can't get up yet, Morgan," he said. "I hit my head, and everything is spinning."

Morgan stood and peered over the battlement. "The men are looking this way," she said. "What do I tell them?"

"Light the watch fires," Rowe mumbled.

Morgan shouted: "Light the watch fires!"

There was a rustle of activity below. The first watch fire hanging over the wall flared to life. Someone lit the others, and the area glowed beneath the flickering flames. The wall was damaged but whole.

"What else?" Morgan asked.

"Send a volley of flaming arrows," he said, and immediately Morgan shouted out the order.

"Ready! Release!" someone shouted, and a dozen flaming arrows fluttered into the night sky. Some landed with a heavy *thunk*, while others pinged off rocks. None struck the soft flesh of gnomes.

"What do you see?" Rowe whispered as he trembled.

"Nothing," she said, rubbing her eyes to help them focus.

"Is anyone standing at the catapults?" Rowe asked.

"Yeah," Morgan said as she took her mother's hand to help steady her. "Both are manned."

Rowe pushed himself to his knees, gulping air. Slowly, he stood and leaned against the battlement.

"The arrows are burning out," he said, "which means the gnomes have not attacked. What are they waiting for?"

"Maybe they bore the brunt of that…whatever that was," Morgan said.

"Was it an earthquake?" Julie asked.

Dench appeared at the top of the ladder. "Me tink it's too quiet." He walked to the edge of the roof. "Set de rope ladder," he called to a soldier on the wall walk before starting back down the gatehouse ladder.

"What are you doing, Dench?" Rowe asked, rubbing the back of his head.

Dench didn't answer. Down on the wall walk, he approached the rope ladder that had been slung over the wall. Without a word, he dropped his broadsword over the edge, clambered over the wall, and carefully descended the ladder. At the bottom, he called for light, and a soldier dropped an unlit torch. He scooped up his sword and started across the dark clearing.

Knowing that gnomes could see well in the darkness, Dench

didn't bother crouching or trying to hide as he approached the thoroughfare. He strained his ears, but all was silent as he neared the cleft in the mountain. A thousand gnomes, even if trying to be as quiet as possible, would be detected this close. The moment he came around the bend, he would have a clear view of the thoroughfare for a solid mile. He was now only a few feet away but still heard nothing. He pressed his back against the mountain face, listening to the silence, then peeked around the corner.

Gasping in astonishment, Dench blinked several times to be certain of what he was seeing. He lit the torch and stood before the twenty-foot-wide thoroughfare. But the thoroughfare was gone.

Moments ago, a thousand gnomes had stood poised to attack, but now there was only a gaping dark hole. Dench stood a few feet from the dizzying drop. His broadsword clanged to the ground as he stumbled backward. After one more look, he grabbed his sword and sprinted back to the South Crow Gate.

⁂

Morgan held Rowe's hand, barely able to contain her questions as Dench climbed the ladder and hoisted himself over the battlement. The half-orc was instantly surrounded.

"Dey gone! Road all gone." Judging by the grin on his face, Dench was panting more from excitement than the sprint back to the wall. "Me serious. De whole ridge gone, no more road, just a big drop for a long way."

Morgan squeezed Rowe's hand.

"So, it's over?" a soldier asked.

Dench nodded. "No more gnomes. Me guess dey all buried at de bottom. Me saw a long way, and it looks like de road gone all de way back to de first bend. No more way trew."

"It's over," someone echoed as an infectious smile spread from face to face.

"What about the main gnome army coming up the thorough-fare?" someone asked.

Dench shook his head. "It would take twenty years to build a bridge."

"Let's get some archers out there with flaming arrows to see how much of the ledge is missing," Rowe said.

"So, we can open the gates?" a soldier asked.

"Dis wall no more need to be here," Dench announced.

"Open the gates!" Rowe shouted, his voice cracking. Soldiers rushed to the gatehouse to raise the portcullis while others raced down the stairs to open the gates.

"I trust your word, Dench, but I need to see this with my own eyes," Rowe said, grabbing a torch. He shared a tentative smile with Morgan.

Minutes later, Rowe, Morgan, and Dench led six archers across the clearing. After the trauma and loss of the past two days, a cloud of doubt lingered. Victory seemed too good to be true.

When the group rounded the cleft in the rock, Morgan stood stunned. Stepping up to the ledge that had once contained a wide road, Rowe raised his torch high above his head, revealing only rugged cliffs. The thoroughfare was completely gone, as Dench had said.

"Release the arrows!" Rowe shouted.

The archers lit their arrows from his torch and released. The tiny flames grew smaller as they fell into the hole until the darkness extinguished them. Another round was released, this time farther out. Archers hopped with excitement as the flames revealed noth-ing but darkness for a hundred yards. Without waiting for Rowe's command, the archers pulled bowstrings as far back as they could, aiming higher this time. Despite the distance, the thoroughfare was gone for at least three hundred yards. Beyond that, it would require daylight to confirm the extent of the damage.

The whooping and whistling from the small group soon reached the South Crow Gate. When they returned through the gates that could now remain open, Rowe took several minutes to quiet the crowd. They were laughing, weeping, and chattering about a night of celebrating.

"We have twenty-five hundred men arriving in a matter of hours," Rowe said, "and they've been on a hard march for days. Let's get word to them right away."

Three soldiers mounted horses and raced north to deliver the news.

"We'll have hot stew for them," Gloriana said as several older women cheered. "Where shall we set up?"

"I suppose…the Crow's Nest," Rowe said, inciting another hearty cheer. People hugged anyone within reach.

Morgan took Rowe's hand again.

"I just can't believe it," he said. He picked her up off her feet in a tight hug and spun around.

Morgan laughed. "Nobody can," she said.

"You tink de old woman do dis?" Dench asked.

Rowe released Morgan and stared at his friend. "In all the excitement, I forgot about her, Dench."

"Who was she?" Dench asked as they walked behind the main group of people climbing onto wagons.

"I spent some time with her," Julie said. "She was full of mystery, but I just shrugged it off, assuming she was a lonely old woman with a complex history."

"Did she tell you her name?" Rowe asked.

"Oh, sorry," Julie said. "I thought I told you. She said she preferred the name Nyrianne."

Rowe stopped as the others continued a few paces. His arms fell to his sides and his mouth hung open as he gaped at Julie.

"Do you know her?" Morgan asked.

Rowe nodded. "I know that name well."

Julie and Morgan exchanged wide-eyed glances. "Who is she?" Julie asked.

Rowe spoke slowly. "When Nyrianne arrived as a six-year-old girl at the Academy in Acttun, the wizard brothers, Addolay and Marlay Bonicle, had no idea she would become the Dark Queen Sidara."

CHAPTER 29

From Fairbay to The Maidstone

The Recovery Ale House and Inn was a whirlwind of activity. Hansla was cooking in the kitchen, rattling pots and turning slabs of sizzling bacon in large pans, while Jessman helped Homas work the tables. The smell of bacon permeated the pub as the morning rush subsided. When only a few patrons remained, Jessman hung a sign on the front door that read *Closed till Supper*, to prevent any late risers from coming in. It wasn't necessary; six mer soldiers stood guard at each entrance.

When the pub was empty, Jessman asked Homas's two sisters to finish a final clean before sending them home.

Ten mer soldiers descended the stairs, surrounding Queen Almithara. The soldiers' dark-blue coral armor appeared black in the dim light of the pub, but their tridents gleamed. At the bottom of the stairs, they divided into pairs and moved to various parts of the room. Two remained beside Almithara.

"Please," Jessman said, opening his arms wide, "the Recovery is yours to search. We desire nothing less than the best security for the queen."

The mermen did not speak as they looked under tables and opened cupboard doors. After they inspected the main eating area, two went through the swinging door to the kitchen while four others searched the cellars. Two assumed positions by the front door.

Jessman and Homas put the final touches on the center table, which was simply but colorfully prepared. They arranged several bowls of fresh fruit, from the queen's favorite—strawberries—to an assortment of sliced green, red, and yellow melons. Each bowl they garnished with fresh bright-green seaweed. Jessman filled a fine goblet with sparkling yellow juice, then pulled out a tall, padded chair from the head of the table. Almithara acknowledged his bow with a slight nod before sitting gracefully on the chair. Jessman and Homas departed to the kitchen.

Will stood quietly in the shadows at the top of the stairs, watching the formalities. He rolled up the sleeves of his fitted green shirt and straightened it over his pants, which he had tucked into a pair of brown leather boots that reached halfway to his knees. The Trannalun cloak over his shoulders flowed behind him like a cape. He took a deep breath and limped down the stairs.

Almithara set her goblet down and looked up. "How do you feel, Will?"

"My leg's really stiff, and I think it's gonna be a while before my hand stops aching." He flexed his left hand, which had been unusable two days ago, and sat across from the queen. "I still can't believe I'm alive…and here in Fairbay…with you. A lot can change in a day."

She smiled. "Are you able to eat?"

Will inhaled the aroma of bacon and fresh-baked bread as he

surveyed the melange of fruit on the table. "It seems like a long time since I ate something I recognized, something without ants crawling all over it."

Almithara filled his goblet with fresh juice as he piled his plate with fruit. Unable to hide his delighted groans, he closed his eyes and savored each bite.

Jessman emerged from the kitchen carrying a plate of scrambled eggs, fresh bread, and thick slices of bacon. Will pushed his plate of fruit aside to make room for the steaming entrée. Before returning to the kitchen, Jessman flashed a proud smile and winked at Will.

As Will devoured his breakfast, Almithara placed her elbows on the table, folded her hands, and leaned toward him. "I have been thinking about my family, Will. We have never been separated until recently. Wrathan has been up near the Gryton Mines for seven days. Ryodan has ventured to the Rainia Valley, hoping to find Ryowyn and bring her home. In their absence, I have borne the extra duties demanded of our family." She leaned closer and frowned. "I fear that our people will soon be forced into the war, and I have seen enough war to last a hundred lifetimes."

Will risked a nervous glance at the two soldiers standing by the front door. He recognized one from the group that had accompanied Wrathan when they'd confronted Will on the beach shortly after Will had rescued Ryowyn from the hands of the slave runners. Will forced down another mouthful of eggs.

"We love to tell stories of gallant deeds done by heroes," Almithara continued, "yet we speak little of what led to their victories: sleepless nights before battle, exhausted efforts against impossible odds, lifelong scars, self-doubt, failure…the loss of family and friends. All the things that stop most people midstride are the very things that separate a mere mortal from a hero."

Will drew comfort from her genuine confidence in him. "Well, all those things describe my life, but I don't know about the *hero* part. Still, you have a way of making a guy believe he can do anything." Looking at the queen's face made him long for Ryowyn. If he succeeded in helping Thaudas find his horn, the creature might heal Ryowyn. Of course, the opposite was also true. Yet Almithara spoke with a simple conviction that defied their present reality.

"Since coming to the Fourwinds," Will said, "I've been scared to tears more times than I care to admit. I've been beaten and imprisoned, and I've come up short in nearly every battle I've been part of. I've required protection and saving almost every day. I'm often overcome with anxiety, and I never really know what I'm doing." He set his fork down. "But somehow, I'm doing it.

"We needed to purge the Crow's Nest of harvesters for the refuges, and we purged it. In the Epping Forest, vicious gorilla-like creatures ambushed us—*holgs*, Rowe called them—and we escaped. We came to Fairbay just as it was being sacked by slave runners, and we killed a dark elf and freed the town. I saw Ryowyn being taken by a group of slave runners. They ended up dead, and I fell in love. I faced the Dark Queen, Sidara, on her own turf, and lived to tell the story…although I don't know what became of her. When Ryowyn was hidden in the depths of Lake Commando, far from anyone's reach, I found a way to her. Now I'm teaming up with a legendary flying unicorn, and hopefully wake Ryowyn from whatever spell she's under. This is just another day at the office where I have no idea what to do, but somehow, I get through it. One thing I'm beginning to understand: I can do *none* of this without help. You talk about heroes, but I'm hopelessly lost on my own.

Will gulped down some juice as the queen watched him in silence. He thought she might have smirked.

"I guess this is my way of telling you that you don't need to worry," he said. "I'll have Ryowyn back to you soon."

"Do I look worried to you, Will?"

His fork stopped a few inches from his mouth, and the peaceful look on her face took his breath away.

"I know you will bring her back to us, but hear this. You must take care of yourself as you do so." She placed her hand over his. "You are family now, Will; the second son of a king."

Will's fork clattered onto his plate.

Before he could find his voice, there was a commotion outside. A mer soldier's face appeared in the small window set high in the door. He nodded once, then twice, before the two soldiers opened the door partway. There was a hushed conversation, and Will's spine tingled with apprehension.

Almithara was on her feet, and the other eight mer soldiers assembled around her.

A soldier closed the door and spun on his heels. His voice was low and shaky. "A Callum Sage has arrived with a report from the Gryton Mines."

"Rowe?" Will said.

"Bring him here at once," Almithara said. "And do not let him speak to anyone but me." She tapped a long, slender finger against her lips as her eyes narrowed.

The soldier rushed outside and relayed the orders.

Almithara sat in her chair, frowning again. "Word from Wrathan should come from a merman, not a human."

Will sat and picked at his food as the soldiers angled their tridents at the door.

When the door swung open, Joe staggered into the room with mer soldiers supporting both arms, half carrying him.

Will shot to his feet.

Joe's mouth hung open as he panted. His face was filthy, and his frizzy white hair was tangled with twigs. His clothes were torn and dirt-smudged. But it was his eyes, dark and drawn, that gave Will the most cause for concern as the soldiers helped the old man into a chair.

"I know you," Almithara said as Will handed Joe a goblet of water.

"And I you, Your Majesty," Joe managed with a raspy voice. "I am Johanissan of the River Country."

"Please drink, Johanissan," Almithara said.

"What…are you doing *here*?" Will asked, glancing at the door. "Are the others with you?"

Joe drained the glass and wiped his mouth. He kept his eyes on the queen. "Begging your pardon, ma'am, but time does not allow for pleasantries." He accepted another goblet of water.

"Clear the room," she said, and within seconds, the three of them were alone, save for her captain, who stood with his back to the door.

"Speak freely," she said.

"The Gryton Mines—" Joe coughed and took another drink. "Rangers—I believe from Enders Brigade—destroyed a large flask of what I assume was the deadly gas called Guilliad. The flask was in a catapult meant to defend the single mountain pass against a land attack. They set off the catapult from the cliffs, after the wind had begun outflowing from the mountains, which carried Guilliad back into the gnomes. Had I not seen with my own eyes what followed, I would not have believed it." He paused again to drink. "The mining operation had been a ruse to lure your people in. When the Rangers destroyed the Guilliad flask, the gnomes raced toward the sea to escape the vapor that was disintegrating everything in its path. In the confusion, your people attacked. Unfortunately, they were unaware of a second catapult hidden next to a warehouse close to the beach. The moment your people attacked, the gnomes launched another flask into sea. It was filled with…with…" Joe fell short, tears forming in his dark eyes. "It was filled with some type of tiny black fish—millions of them, and they…"

Joe turned away from Almithara, staring at a window. "The instant the flagon shattered in the sea, the water churned as the tiny creatures attacked, burrowing themselves into anything living. I can still hear the screams from your soldiers as they fought bravely. There were too many of the creatures, and they moved like lightning through the water. The soldiers went mad, clawing at their own flesh. It was horrifying. One soldier climbed onto the shore as I fled. His skin…his beautiful skin was turning gray."

Almithara gasped.

"Nothing could stop these deadly creatures. Anyone attacked turned mad with rage, transforming into… I don't know what they are." Joe faced the queen. "But I'm afraid they will soon find their way here."

The room was uncommonly silent. After a moment, Will spoke in a quiet voice: "How much of the sea will be affected?"

"Unless we stop these creatures, they will infect the entire Niasa Sea.

"How much time do we have?" Will asked as Almithara stared at Joe.

"Judging by what I saw…five days, perhaps less."

Almithara's eyes widened, but she remained composed.

"I'm sorry, but you need to leave the sea at once. Please do not hesitate," Joe said.

Almithara spoke in a slow, sad tone. "If you are correct in your assessment, Johanissan, we have just lost two-thirds of our army, including"—she choked on a sob, and two tears pattered on the table—"my son."

She raised a trembling hand to summon her captain. "Send the gulls with word to the king at once."

The captain nodded but remained statue still.

"We evacuate immediately, and unless you hear otherwise, our destination will be Rainia Lake. Keep your message short. I will announce the evacuation at the pier myself, so make sure our human friends are also there. We will require a tremendous joint effort to make this effective. I expect an actionable evacuation and travel plan before I make the announcement."

"It will be as you wish, Your Majesty," the captain said before leaving in a flourish.

"You, Will Owens, must leave at once," Almithara said, her voice distant, strained.

"Leave for where?" Joe asked.

"I think I know how to save Ryowyn," Will said. "Thaudas is waiting to take me to the Maidstone."

Joe gaped. "The Maidsto—"

"Will you stay with us, Johanissan?" Almithara asked. "Our need is great."

"Most assuredly, ma'am," Joe said, watching Will as he stood.

"Fairbay has recently suffered the untimely death of one of its chief elders," the queen said. "There has been a power struggle between the surviving two elders and councilmen. I have difficulty trusting any of them. I need the wisdom of an experienced Callum Sage to take control and organize a caravan of covered wagons to escort my people to Rainia Lake."

Despite the weary look on his face, Joe straightened his back. "I will coordinate with the captain."

"Now, Johanissan, please eat. You must be famished from your journey."

Joe immediately filled a plate with fruit and a large slice of bread.

Numb from the torrent of bad news, Will simply nodded and stood. The guards at the door parted. One held the door as Will exited the Recovery, possibly for the last time.

The sea of swaying grass on the gentle rolling hills contrasted with the deep-blue sky. Thaudas stood on a hill, majestically dividing the grasslands from the sky. The creature was a commanding presence.

Will's pounding heart helped take his mind off the lingering pain in his leg. His mind swirled as if trying to complete a puzzle with missing pieces. He didn't understand how Joe was at the Niasa Sea, and he'd had no time to ask what had happened to Rowe, Morgan, and her mother. Joe hadn't responded when he said he was planning to help Ryowyn, so he assumed she was still in the Records of Time.

The scene at the Gryton Mines must have been horrific to have rattled Joe. Will had seen the effects of Guilliad, but he wondered about the other flask and the tiny black creatures. Rowe had described the transforming power of the elixir called Phyriad that Sidara planned to use as a weapon. Bremer had learned of the mysterious potion from Fadua, an alchemist imprisoned by Sidara in the Waerdreath dungeons. And Bremer had seen people transform during his terrible night at the Stoneberg. Had Uluk infected the tiny black fish with Phyriad to use against the merpeople? It was plausible. In fact, it was the only thing that made sense. If Uluk had intended to strike before Ryodan engaged in the war—and while he was absent—it had been a well-executed plan. The Niasa Mer had once been a mighty nation, but with over two-thirds of the army decimated, and the kingdom potentially lost, the mer army would be taken out of the equation.

Will pushed his confusion aside as he crested the knoll, and Thaudas came into full view.

The creature nickered and ruffled its massive wings. A clear vision of riding Thaudas flashed in his mind, as if the creature were communicating the thought to him. Although Will had ridden him already, he had little memory of the experience because of his fever. There was an undeniable sense of urgency in Will's pace, but his breathing became labored with every step.

Thaudas watched Will, unmoving. Despite the creature's magnificence, Will realized that Thaudas needed him. This understanding offered him a measure of courage, mixed with trepidation. He ventured closer, and thoughts of Ryowyn's need lightened his heavy steps.

Dry-mouthed and shaking, Will rubbed a finger absently over the grip of the 1911 beneath his cloak. Thaudas lowered his head slightly, and a vision of what was to happen flooded Will's mind. He braced himself as Thaudas unfolded a massive wing, black feathers rustling quietly. Will stepped behind the wing and reached out to touch the creature's side. It was as cold and solid as stone. Thaudas slowly raised his neck. Will lifted a foot and, testing the feathers, placed some weight on them. The wing hardly budged. He grasped the mane and pulled himself up with a grunt. Flinging his leg as high as he could, he winced as his groin stretched while straddling Thaudas's wide back.

Thaudas walked along the ridge, heading west at a relaxed pace while Will tried to settle himself. When he stopped moving, Thaudas began an easy trot. Will gripped the mane, bracing himself for liftoff. He leaned forward and lowered his chest until it was touching the mane. Thaudas rolled into a gallop, gradually gaining speed as his fluid stride increased. The thunder of hooves filled Will's ears. Thaudas opened a stunning wingspan, and Will squeezed his eyes shut, burying his face in the mane.

After several minutes, Will risked a peek at the ground below. They were soaring high above the Niasa Sea, heading straight toward a dense forest on the distant shoreline. Will closed his eyes again. The next time he opened them, a sparkling river cut through the forest. Thaudas banked gently and flew upriver. Overcome by the contrast of deep greens and dazzling blues, Will kept his eyes open. Thaudas approached a gully where the waters became choppy. He descended, and Will tightened his grip as they flew gently toward the sound of roaring waterfalls and a wall of mist.

The ravine rose around them. Will pressed his knees against the creature's sides to brace himself against the turbulent descent. They flew over the mist and dropped a dozen feet as Thaudas banked to set up their final approach. Suddenly, they hit a calm section of air, and Will loosened his white-knuckled grip. He cried out when Thaudas flared his powerful wings, and his arms and legs flexed to prepare for the sudden drop, but it was less than a foot to the ground.

Will leapt from the creature's back, landing in a low crouch with the rushing waterfalls behind them. He rolled onto his back, stretching his arms. After a moment, his muscles relaxed and his breathing returned to normal. When he recovered, he opened his eyes to find Thaudas watching him.

"What are you thinking right now?" Will asked.

He stood to look around. They were at the entrance of a chasm, just beyond the mist. There was a familiar bend in the trail that Will recognized as the place where he, Morgan, Bremer, and Rowe had roped themselves together when they had passed through on their journey to the Waerdreath about three weeks ago. Will spun around and found a Y in the trail. He held his breath and peered up through the mist, tracing a less-traveled path up to a gloomy, uninviting tower: the Maidstone.

"Why do you need me to go up there?" Will asked.

A vision of a massive black horn materialized before his mind's eye.

"Are you sure it's up there?"

Thaudas turned and, looking up, released a great guttural huff.

Will nodded his understanding. "I wonder why people are so intimidated by that place." The sight of the tower didn't jar him nearly as much as he'd thought it would. What troubled him most was the precipitous trail weaving along the cliff wall. He groaned. The hike would take him hours.

"Despite wanting to vomit on my boots right now, I have to admit: there's something good about us being here."

Thaudas huffed, looking up at the Maidstone.

"Okay, okay. I'm anxious too. But let me savor the moment, Thaudas. All the dreams, all the adventures…everything leading to this moment. There's a weight to it, isn't there? We're both nearing the end of long journeys."

Thaudas was silent.

Will ran his fingers through his hair. "I realize you want me up there, so why can't we just fly up and get started?" He bent down to a small pool, scooped a handful of water, and splashed his face. "The thought of something keeping a powerful creature like you away is a little worrisome."

Thaudas walked toward the head of the small trail and Will followed, the roaring water of the falls becoming louder.

"Last chance to change your mind, Thaudas," Will said with an uneasy smile. "I'm guessing there's a good reason you can't land up there, but if I fall off that ledge, I hope you can catch me."

Thaudas's bobbed his head and nickered.

"Well, that's comforting…sort of."

Will looked up at the sky and estimated it would be dark when he reached the top. "I'll be back, I guess, when I get back."

The dizzying flight and the incredible task ahead made him light-headed, almost drunk. He rubbed Thaudas's cheek. As he stepped onto the narrow path, he frowned. "I hope you're right about this."

The path led along the riverbank several feet above the frothing water. Ahead, it seemed as though the river swallowed the trail as it hugged the cliff. Glancing back, he saw Thaudas in the same spot he'd left him, watching. He took courage from the creature and continued along the narrowing path until only a few feet remained between the river and the cliff.

A gust of air created a vortex of water before him. He wiped his face and pulled his cloak tight, taking one precarious step at a time. He peered down at the churning water and swallowed hard. If he fell in, he would either drown or be crushed at the base of the waterfalls. He was still puzzled by the way the trail disappeared ahead of him. He stopped for a moment, then remembered Rowe telling him that the trail was a series of switchbacks up to the tower. What he thought was the trail's end was actually the first switchback.

A section of the trail had washed away, forcing him to search for handholds and footholds on the cliff wall. The constantly swirling mists made the wall slippery, but he found a few deep crevices for his hands and feet. Pressing his chest against the wall, he passed the washed-out area, only to find the trail even narrower on the other side. He stayed close to the wall and soon arrived at the first switchback in the path. He slid his hands along the ledge and stepped around the sharp bend.

Will shook his shoulders to release some tension, but the persistent buffeting of wind and mist made it difficult to stay calm. At the end of the second switchback, he hesitated again, considering turning back. It made more sense to start this climb at dawn, yet Thaudas had wanted him to go immediately.

He rubbed his sore leg and pressed ahead, remembering why he was here: the night he had spent on the beach with Ryowyn replayed in his mind. He slid his feet sideways as his hands continually probed the wall for places to grip and steady himself. In his mind, Ryowyn smiled and held his hand.

When he came to the third switchback, he glanced down, and immediately regretted doing so as a rush of vertigo distorted his vision. He tipped his head back and squinted. Nervous laughter burst from his lips when he realized he still had a long way to go. Determined to press on, he sang a few bars of a Van Halen tune his dad used to sing in the car: "Right Now."

"Well, Dad," he said aloud, "here I am, living in the moment. Right now? Huh. I'll bet Eddie never had to climb a trail like this."

He climbed around the fourth switchback. He was growing

wetter and more tired, and his muscles ached. "You're a loooong way from home, Will Owens."

The sun dipped below the ridge line, and soon he was relying on his hands and feet to guide him through the shadows. At the next switchback, he found a wide landing. Overcome with exhaustion, he leaned his back against the cliff and slumped into a sitting position. His ankles hung over the edge of the trail, giving him enough room to lie down against the cliff without fear of rolling over and falling to his death. He curled up, covering most of his body with his cloak. Minutes later, the warmth of the cloak and the constant rushing sound of the falls lulled him to sleep.

⁂

Will lingered in the warmth of his cloak until the persistent rumbling waterfalls reminded him of his task. He sat up and removed his hood, and the cool mist in the morning sun washed his face. From his pack he withdrew a waterskin and took a long, leisurely pull, then slowly munched on some slightly soggy bread and a handful of dried fruit. He took another drink and stood.

Four waterfalls roared over the cliffs near his resting place. As he stared through the water plummeting down, he spotted two massive metal arms that jutted straight out from the cliff. Between them was some type of turbine, its blades blurring from the force of the cascading water. Will studied two other falls and saw similar turbines. The fourth also had a turbine, but it wasn't moving because several blades were missing.

"What is this place?" he whispered.

It was early afternoon when the path ahead widened just beyond a tangle of exposed tree roots along the wall. Will turned around and released a long sigh as he gazed at the swirling mist now behind him. The waterfalls thundered below, but their dangerous bluffs were no longer an immediate threat.

In the shelter of a lonely, weathered fir tree about twenty feet away, a few chickadees darted and called to one another. Will brushed wet hair from his face and ascended the final length of trail. The small signs of life revived him, propelling him on to face… He realized he didn't know what to expect. Despite a vivid imagination and a sketchy recurring dream of this place, nothing prepared Will for what he was about to see.

CHAPTER 30

THE MAIDSTONE

Will reached above his head and grasped an overhanging root, pulling himself from a squatting position. The final leg of the trail was wider than the previous switchbacks, but here a canopy of gnarled roots and vines forced him to crawl on his hands and knees as he inched along the narrow ledge. When he could stand again, he peered around the corner. An enormous cleft in the escarpment, nearly two acres wide, provided a place of refuge between the treacherous waterfalls below and the inhospitable surrounding cliffs. Along the inside edges of the area, a few hemlock trees towered above the jagged ridge line. The exposed roots of the ancient giants twisted and clawed the soil over mossy boulders. Scraggly overgrown currant bushes, woven together with thorny, arching blackberry canes, bordered a field of tall grass flecked with bright-yellow dandelions. It was the most unusual, incongruous place Will had ever seen.

The Maidstone stood in the center of the field, not far from the cliff. The round tower was about two hundred feet tall, topped with a conical slate-shingled roof. Crooked vines traced the mortar lines and spread their dark-green leaves over the weathered and mossy stone blocks. Not a single opening was visible from where Will crouched. He rubbed his burning thigh muscles and crept through the field for a closer look. As he rounded the tower, an archway of blocks came into view, protruding from the base about six feet. Shadows veiled the narrow, arched entryway, obscuring any hint of a door.

The grass near the entryway was crudely cut in a wide swath, and a large, flat rock provided a primitive path to the tower. Stretched out on a spindly, sun-bleached wooden bench was a woman lying on her back. She wore a short beige-colored sleeveless dress that was so torn and threadbare that most of her pasty-white skin was exposed to the full sun. Her long brown hair straggled over the edges of the bench. Around her neck was a dirty leather collar. Her eyes were closed.

Will took two quiet steps toward the tower, then froze. Thirty feet to his right, a naked body dangled from the branch of a massive cedar rooted to the rocky cliff. The man's scrawny legs were bent awkwardly, his arms limp and lifeless. His skin was gray and tight against his bones. Around his head was a crude iron cage linked to the tree branch by a rusty chain. At first glance, he appeared long dead, but then the cage slowly turned. Will shuddered as he stared into glassy red eyes.

The man's body twitched, and Will ducked behind a large boulder. He dug into his pack and whipped out the 1911. There were ten rounds in the gun, with an extra clip in the holster. He opened his cloak and fastened the belt around his waist, then strapped the holster to his thigh and eased himself to his feet. The caged head followed his movement as he crossed the field. The man didn't seem to pose a threat, so Will continued toward the Maidstone, the roaring waterfalls muffling the crunch of dead leaves and twigs beneath his feet.

Will had barely taken ten steps when a gaunt, bald man carrying a large wooden box stepped out of the tower's shadowy entryway. He wore a grimy pair of overalls with no shirt and large leather boots. His gray eyebrows formed a menacing V, and his shockingly large white teeth gleamed in the sunlight. Around his neck hung a long black horn on a crude leather necklace. He glared at the woman on the bench like a starving dog. She flinched, and her eyes shot open, wide and unblinking, full of terror. Neither of them noticed Will, who stood still in the long grass.

Before Will could choose his next move, his options were taken away when the bald man's eyes settled on him and his mouth opened wide. A blood-curdling scream pierced the waterfall's white noise as the man lifted the box over his head and took several quick steps toward the woman. Will brought the 1911 up to eye level. He squeezed the trigger, and the slug struck the crazed man just as he was about to slam the box into the woman's head.

The woman twisted sideways, craning her neck as the toolbox grazed her head and crashed through the fragile wooden bench. A thin bright-red line marked her cheek. Will wondered why she hadn't moved more, then noticed that her collar was chained to a spike in the ground. He took a few steps toward her, and the bald man sprang from the ground. Blood covered his chest. He glowered at Will, then stumbled into the dark entrance of the Maidstone.

The woman stared at Will like a trapped wild animal. He suddenly felt like an actor who had been given the wrong script on opening night and the curtain was up, a spotlight shining in his eyes. As he gazed at the woman, she morphed into the beautiful shape of Ryowyn, sleeping peacefully on the settee in the Records of

Time. The sound of stomping hooves and a snorting horse caused him to glance over his left shoulder, but the field was empty. When Will looked back at the tower, the vision of Ryowyn was gone, and the wild woman was staring at him again as she clutched the edges of the old bench.

Will blinked hard. "Get a grip, Will," he told himself.

The woman recoiled as he holstered the gun and approached her with palms open before him.

"I'm here to help," Will said, his mouth parched.

A small measure of wildness retreated from her eyes, but her mouth hung open as she panted.

"Can I take your collar off?"

She stared at him as if no one had ever asked her what she wanted.

Will kept his hands raised. "It's time for you to go home."

Her eyes flicked to the caged hanging man, then back to Will. "Seer," she hissed in a husky voice that didn't match her slight frame.

Will turned to meet the hanging man's deathly gaze.

"Natas sees what he sees!" Her voice was deep and gravelly, as if she had something caught in her throat.

Will dropped his hands to his sides and narrowed his eyes as her words registered in his foggy mind. A few missing pieces of the Maidstone puzzle fell into place. He remembered the peculiar sense of being watched when he, Morgan, Rowe, and Bremer had passed by the Maidstone on their way to the Waerdreath. It made sense, Will realized. Natas had been watching him as he journeyed across the Fourwinds. Had the Iron Dragon actually seen them at the Stoneberg as he'd flown past? They'd all assumed he had ignored them, but maybe Natas had known they were heading into his trap at Sidara's castle, anyway.

If Natas is watching through the eyes of the hanging man, Will thought, *it's time to blind those eyes.* He took several strides toward the hanging man, raised his gun, and fired into the cage. He raced back to the woman, his heart beating with a renewed sense of urgency.

"I'm gonna take that collar off now, and I'll get you home once my business here is finished."

She whipped her wild hair side to side.

Will raised his hands. "It is up to you. You can stay here while I go inside."

"Don't!" she groaned. "Don't go in there! Don't leave me here, I beg you! Please! Kill me now while you still can!"

Will took a deep breath. "I'm going to remove that collar while you tell me why I shouldn't go inside. Does that sound reasonable?"

She nodded, barely able to move her head more than a few inches.

"Is it okay if I reach around to the back of the collar?" Will stooped to his knees.

She blinked once.

Taking this as permission, Will bent close to look at the collar. "Why shouldn't I go inside the tower?"

"He will kill you over and over. That cursed horn be damned to the deepest hell. There is no end to the pain he will cause you. You frightened him, but when he comes back, he won't be scared anymore."

The hairs on the back of Will's neck tickled his skin. "Actually, I've come for the horn."

She gaped at him as if he had just told her he was about to swallow the tower whole.

"I will leave this place with that horn."

"The horn is part of his body, like an arm or a leg. It sustains him."

"Who is he?"

"He is called Illume, and he's from the old world."

Will reached around her neck and slowly worked the buckle. "Old world? What's in there?"

"A city from the old world…filled with things Illume calls *machines*. It's the most frightening place in the Fourwinds."

"How long does it take the horn to heal him?"

"Not long. He's been alive far too long, and the fits of rage get worse each time. It's unnatural." Her eyes grew large.

Will gently removed the collar from her neck and glanced toward the entryway. The woman bolted as fast as a caged bird whose door had just opened. He stood to follow her, but she was too fast. "No! Wait!"

She stumbled toward the cliff and, without a sound, ran over the edge.

A dark hole opened in Will's heart. He had intended to free her, to save her life, but instead he'd sentenced her to death. Nothing he could say, no weapon he wielded, no act of heroism or bravado, could have saved her from the darkness that possessed her.

But there was no time for Will to stay in his dark hole. Illume stumbled at a half run from the Maidstone. He flung himself to the side of the doorway as six humanoid creatures emerged from the shadows behind him. They hunched over, arms bent and clawed hands scratching the air as they squinted at the sunlight. Their dry dark-gray skin was almost scaly, their eyes as red as the hanging man's were before Will had obliterated them with a single blast. Dried blood was splattered across their arms and chests, and clumps of hair fell away as a wind gusted up from the waterfalls. They moved as a tight herd and lurched toward Will.

"Holy crap!" As soon as the words escaped his lips, Will recalled the first time he had faced harvesters in the halls of the Crow's Nest. His fear had paralyzed him then, but afterward Rowe had encouraged him: *You chose to use your gift to help instead of using it to save yourself.*

Barely managing a semblance of control, Will raised the 1911 to eye level. He fired six rounds in rapid succession, blowing holes in each creature. They crumpled to the ground, and Will sprinted toward the Maidstone.

Illume stood in the entryway. His wild eyes widened when he saw Will running toward him. He croaked something unintelligible and stepped back into the darkness. Will fired a desperate shot that somehow hit the man, sending him sprawling into the darkness. Will followed.

The entryway was so dark Will couldn't see an inch ahead. He slowed and traced one hand along the block wall, gripping the gun in front of him with the other. The entryway was remarkably quiet, muffling the waterfalls. Will pressed forward, desperate to reach the man with the horn before he disappeared.

Spurred on by the possibility of more creatures attacking from the darkness, Will strained his ears, holding the gun high and ready. The rough stone wall transitioned to something smooth, cold, and metallic. Will stopped. It felt like a metal doorjamb, but he had never seen steel doors in the Fourwinds.

When he passed the doorjamb, he followed a smooth wall to the left. His footsteps on the solid floor echoed in what he imagined as a large foyer. He listened again, thinking he was hearing the muffled sounds of the waterfalls outside, but then recognized it as the droning of turbine engines. If he had not seen them earlier through the falls, he would never have believed his ears.

The sudden presence of multiple footfalls caused him to shrink down to the base of the wall as they rushed by. Will imagined more of the creatures were searching for him. He shivered. Whatever they were, they hadn't noticed him sitting in the darkness.

His eyes had adjusted so he could see their ghostly forms exiting the main entryway behind him. Will sat still, trembling as he strained his ears for any hint of a straggler.

The occupants of the Maidstone had been alerted to his presence, but that was only part of his problem. Since he had cut off Natas's method of monitoring the Maidstone, he assumed it was only a matter of time before the dragon paid a personal visit to the tower.

A single set of footfalls suddenly ran back into the entryway. In the dim light cast from outside, Will saw movement. He rose to his feet and raised the gun with hands shaking so badly he nearly dropped it. The form stopped, and Will pulled the trigger. The explosion echoed in the darkness, alluding to the room's size. Will's ears were ringing, but there was a distinct groan and a glimpse of movement. Whoever it was crawled deeper into the tower.

Frozen with fright, Will listened as the footsteps stumbled down a set of metal steps. If it was Illume, Will imagined the man was trying to flee until the horn healed his gunshot wound. Will had to stop him. He slammed a fresh clip in the 1911 and ventured into the darkness, but quickly bumped into a smooth wall. He pressed his hand against it, following the footsteps and heavy breathing until he felt a cold metal handrail. As he inched his feet forward, seeking the next step, the person tumbled down what sounded like another set of stairs. Will followed slowly, gun raised.

The groaning increased, and Will quickened his pace. The person stumbled down more steps. Will came to a platform, and a metal latch clicked loudly below him. The handrail led to the right, and he carefully descended another flight of stairs. At the bottom, a red light glowed softly above a large metal door that was inching open. Illume knelt in front of the door, his bloodied hands slipping on the polished metal. A dark pool was forming around him.

"You…have no…business…here!" Illume might have been trying to shout, but with a devastated lung, the words came out in a hollow gurgle.

Will pointed the gun at Illume's head. Assuming the man was almost dead, he reached down for the horn around his neck. Illume reared like a caged animal, then lunged. Will dodged, and the man's hands smacked the floor. The horn swung from Illume's neck, and Will snatched at it, but the determined man reared back and made another helpless but terrifying grasp at him.

Despite his fear of the strange man, Will's anger flared white hot. He stepped close and pulled the trigger point-blank. The report in the confined stairwell set Will's ears to ringing anew. Illume's body flopped to the floor. Will seized the black horn and snapped the leather necklace from Illume's neck.

"On the contrary," Will said. "I have very important business here."

The moment the horn was free, Illume's body shriveled.

Will recoiled in horror as the body dissolved into a pile of blood and bones. He was thankful the dim light spared him the details.

A sliver of light radiated through the narrow gap beneath the door. Despite the terror swelling in his chest, Will was too curious. He opened the door and peeked inside.

The lighting was dim but brighter than the stairwell. The hallway reminded Will of a hospital lab, empty and sterile, except for the streaks of blood on the white walls. The floor was a nightmare of human remains. At the end of the hallway, a group of scaly humanoid creatures with heads and claws like dragons trudged through the carnage.

Will slammed the door shut and scrambled up the stairs, retracing his steps to the main entryway. He didn't understand how Thaudas communicated with him, but with every step, Will spoke the creature's name as he clutched the cold black horn. He prayed for a miracle, that somehow Thaudas would come for him before Natas arrived. If he didn't, there was little hope of surviving the treacherous journey back down the trail.

The entryway took shape ahead, and Will slowed, expecting to encounter more of the unnerving creatures he had shot outside. With the 1911 in one hand and the horn in the other, Will slid his back along the smooth wall, which soon became a rough stone wall. He leaned forward, searching for signs of creatures outside as he listened for sounds of others who might be pursuing him from the stairwell. If too many monsters appeared, he would quickly run out of bullets. But he only knew of one way out. Will paused as his eyes adjusted to the light. He took the final few steps and peeked beyond the dark entryway.

Thaudas stood tall and majestic, the bloody remains and severed heads of a dozen creatures strewn in a wide circle around him. He nickered as Will emerged, then whinnied and reared on powerful hind legs when Will raised the large black horn.

"This belong to you?"

CHAPTER 31

WILL OWENS

The caravan of wagons meandered north through the Rainia Valley from the South Crow Gate to the Crow's Nest. Some wagons carried people, but most were laden with supplies no longer required at the South Crow Gate. Many people chose to walk; others skipped, sang, and danced. Everyone smiled, celebrating the miracle of their unexpected victory.

High above the caravan, Will leaned slightly, and Thaudas banked left. It had taken time, but Will had become confident in the great winged unicorn's ability to keep him from falling. Thaudas soared toward the Crow's Nest in a rapid descent. Will was unclear what the caravan was, but there was activity near the castle's curtain wall.

A few older men along the wall pointed into the sky. Will straightened his back and waved at them, but no one shared his enthusiasm. Thaudas approached a secluded patch of grass a few hundred yards from the road leading to the Crow's Nest. Will clutched the black mane with both hands. A moderate breeze allowed Thaudas to draw in his wings slowly for a gentle touchdown.

Will slid from the creature's back and ran up the road toward the Crow's Nest, his brilliant-red cloak fluttering behind him. He hadn't yet come to the base of the road when someone shouted, "It's Will!"

Rowe was riding a chestnut mare through the Gauntlet when he saw Will. He yanked on the reins and came to an awkward stop. His hands hung low, and his face was a mask of unreadable emotion. He smiled, then frowned, then he raised his eyebrows, which made him appear sad.

Morgan hid none of her emotion. She screamed with excitement as she raced past Rowe and bounced into Will's outstretched arms. "I can't believe it's you!" Morgan sobbed into Will's shoulder. "You're alive!"

She stepped back. Although tears smudged her dirty face, her smile was as brilliant and beautiful as the day they'd met on Nineteenth Avenue.

"It's so good to see you, Morgan!"

Her smile faded. "And what is *that*?" Morgan gasped. Thaudas stood about thirty feet behind Will.

"You won't believe the story I have for you." Will was happier than he remembered feeling in years. Looking up the road, he waved at Rowe and then at Dench, who was running from the castle.

"And you won't believe ours," Morgan said.

"Why is Rowe hanging back?" Will asked. "He looks…sad. Well, you all look exhausted, but—"

"Listen, Will," Morgan said as they walked back to meet Rowe and Dench. "Rowe feels like he let you down, and it's really eating at him. He was just leaving to try to find you. We've been trapped here fighting gnomes since you were taken; otherwise, he would have gone as soon as you were captured by the slave runners."

Will shook his head, too confounded to speak. "Fighting gnomes?"

Rowe dismounted and took a few steps forward. Will ran, quickly closing the gap between them, and Rowe's mouth opened in a huge grin.

"Buddy!" Will cried as the two men hugged. "Rowe, my good friend!"

"It's so good—" Rowe's voice cracked.

"Man, do I have a story for *you*!" Will said.

Dench arrived and enfolded them in his massive arms, lifting them off the ground with a shout. "Me no think me see you again, Will!"

Morgan stood a few feet away, beaming through her tears.

"It's so good to see you all!" Will said as Dench lowered them. "You won't believe what happened after the slave runners took me away."

"We all have incredible stories to tell," Rowe said, looking past him toward Thaudas. "But I think we should begin with yours." His eyes widened. "Thaudas? But…his horn…"

"I got it back for him," Will said. "And you'll never guess where we found it."

"That means—" Rowe began.

"He can break the spell over Ryowyn! Is she still up in the library?"

Rowe nodded but kept staring blankly at the winged unicorn.

"C'mon!" Will said. "Help me bring her down here!"

Will was running so fast that by the time he arrived at the main gates, he had to stop to rub the aching cramp in his side. Dench ran past, punching him in the shoulder and grinning.

"Let's go, let's go, let's go!" Will shouted as he waved his arms and raced after Dench toward the keep. Dench swung the door open for Will as Rowe and Morgan caught up. Together, they made their way toward the Records of Time, creating a stir as they rushed past clusters of bewildered people.

Will slid to a stop in front of the small stairwell.

"What is it, Will?" Morgan asked, breathing heavily.

"What happens if this doesn't work?" he asked, his voice heavy.

"Impossible," Rowe said. "After what you did for Thaudas… Will, this is unbelievable."

Will hung back as Rowe climbed a few stairs.

Morgan waited with Will until Rowe turned. "Trust your heart, Will," Rowe said. "You have the instincts of a true Callum Sage. Come, let's go get Ryowyn."

Will smiled anew and laughed as he bounded past Rowe. "I love you like a brother, Rowe." He scrambled up the stairs with abandon. When he reached the top landing, he ran through the open door and nearly collided with Julie.

"W-Will?" Julie stammered. "How—"

Will gasped.

Ryowyn sat on the edge of the settee, gazing at the room with her mouth open and her arms folded tightly around her shivering body. When her eyes met Will's, they widened with recognition. With effort, she opened her arms wide.

Will never wavered and ran into her gentle embrace.

Morgan put her arm around Rowe's waist. "This is a good day," she said.

"I…I don't understand," Julie said.

"Come with us, Mom. We'll show you."

The moment Rowe, Morgan, and Julie entered the stairwell,

Julie started asking questions. "How was Ryowyn healed when Will returned?"

"Just wait one second, Mom. I want to show you something." Morgan led her mom across the great hallway at the bottom of the stairs to the embrasure that had provided her initial view of the Fourwinds. Julie squeezed beside her.

"Look there," Morgan said, pointing into the valley.

After a moment, Julie inhaled sharply when she spotted the huge black horse running with its wings extended. A few strides later, the majestic creature took flight.

"Lord, have mercy! This place is…"

"A trip?" Morgan suggested.

Julie nodded. "I can't believe what my eyes are seeing right now. What is that creature?"

"Thaudas is part winged horse, part unicorn," Rowe explained. "He has been searching for his broken horn for five hundred years, and somehow Will found it. The horn has healing properties, so I assume Thaudas healed Ryowyn just by being close."

"I'm sorry," Julie said, rubbing her forehead. "These days have been such a blur, I haven't had time to process this strange place." She gazed out the embrasure. "Where are we, Morgan? How did we get here? And what happened to the Will Owens I knew in Cochrane?"

"We don't understand it either, Mom. All I know right now is that the Fourwinds is somehow linked to our world. Will was insignificant and friendless in Cochrane. But here—"

"Insignificant?" Rowe interrupted. "Are we talking about the same Will?"

"Interesting, isn't it?" Julie said as they watched Thaudas circling in the clear sky.

"What's that, Mom?" Morgan asked.

"I wonder if Will would've found the horn if not for his abduction? It's funny the way things work out sometimes." Julie stepped back from the embrasure. "Ryowyn is healed because that creature was healed, and Will is fine." She pushed a finger into Rowe's chest. "If you had gone off to rescue him…well, I doubt we'd be here right now. What we assumed was a devastating loss turned out to be a great gain."

"We've suffered incredible loss at the South Crow Gate," Rowe said, "and this war is not over."

"Yes, I know," Julie said. "But Will has given us something to celebrate. Let's hold on to that tonight."

Rowe and Morgan nodded.

"And you two aren't fooling anyone, especially me," Julie continued. "I see the way you look at each other. I used to worry about the men who would come knocking at our door for my daughter. But I see the way you care for her, and for me, for Will, for Dench, and for those who fought at the South Crow Gate."

Morgan wiped her eyes and sniffed.

"I—I don't know what to say," Rowe stammered.

"You don't need to say anything, Rowe," Julie said. "Your actions say it all."

"Moorrr-gan!" Lillie squealed as she ran through the hallway with Gloriana following twenty feet behind.

Morgan stretched out her arms to catch the little girl. "Someone smells like a princess!"

"Gloriana gave me a baff."

"Thank you, Auntie Gloriana," Morgan said.

Despite her years and her failing body, Gloriana's eyes twinkled with a vitality Morgan envied. "And did she ever need one!" Gloriana said. "This little rascal was out running around with Tara and Avery *all* afternoon!" Gloriana's smile smoothed many of the dark lines beneath her eyes.

"Can I sleep with you in the big bed?" Lillie asked.

Morgan laughed. "Of course you can, sweetie. I was gonna come find you, but a dear friend returned to the castle."

"Who?" Lillie asked.

"Do you remember Will?"

Lillie scrunched up her face. "I don't think so."

"Well, you'll meet him soon enough," Morgan said. "I have to talk to Will before I come to bed, so can Auntie Gloriana tuck you in until I get there?"

Lillie beamed. "I'll warm up the bed this time." She draped her arms around Morgan's neck.

"I love you to the moon and back," Morgan said, winking at her mom.

"I love you to my room and back," Lillie said proudly.

"All right, little one, time to get you tucked away," Gloriana said, reaching for her hand. Before she could snatch it, Lillie jumped over and wrapped her arms around Rowe's leg. He crouched until he was eye level with her.

"What are you going to dream about tonight?" Rowe asked.

She wrinkled her nose and shrugged. "Can you tell me again? I like it when you tell me what I'm gonna dream."

"Tonight," Rowe said thoughtfully, "tonight you will dream of riding your old horse Blackie. But in this dream, Blackie will have wings."

Lillie's eyes widened before giving him a big hug. He held her tight a moment before turning her around toward Gloriana. She continued spinning and shot at Dench, who caught her up into a tight embrace. A few of his beard braids tickled her cheek, and she giggled.

"Night night, Dench."

"Night night, little one."

Gloriana almost caught Lillie's hand before she leapt into Julie's arms.

"Your hugs are my favorite," Julie whispered into Lillie's ear. "But don't tell anyone."

⚜

When Rowe, Morgan, and Julie returned to the Records of Time, Ryowyn was stretching out on the settee, wearing a light linen robe. Will massaged her feet. They were speaking softly to one another as Morgan peeked inside the library.

"May we come in?" she asked.

"Please," Ryowyn said.

Rowe filled a cup of water from the serving table and offered it to Ryowyn.

"You are Morgan's mother, Julie," Ryowyn said, holding out her hand.

"So pleased to finally meet you," Julie said, taking her hand.

"I was telling Will that, despite the state I was in, I could still sense things around me. I remember you massaging my arms and legs and washing my body. It felt wonderful. Every time you rolled me onto my side, I was so relieved."

"It was my pleasure, Ryowyn." Julie smiled and took a moment to feel Ryowyn's forehead and check her pulse. "If I hadn't seen it for myself, I'd never guess you spent the past few days in a coma—or whatever it was."

Ryowyn's eyes were bright and animated. Her skin, the color

of a tropical ocean, shone. Even her white hair looked neat, full and flowing. She sipped the water while looking at each of them as if she didn't have a care in the world. Will was speechless and hardly seemed to notice anyone else.

"How do your muscles feel?" Julie asked.

"Good," she answered. "My feet are especially happy." She gazed at Will. "The rest of me feels lazy."

"That's understandable. How about your joints? Any joint pain?" Julie asked.

"A little, but I haven't tried to get up yet."

"I would take it slow," Julie suggested as the others dragged chairs next to them.

Dench walked in and closed the door as the others sat in a semicircle around the settee.

"Do you feel like talking?" Will asked.

Ryowyn nodded. "I really do."

"I wish this could wait," Rowe said, "but there are a few things you should hear sooner than later."

Ryowyn shot an apprehensive glance at Will but nodded.

"Will can give you the details later, but for the moment…" Rowe inhaled sharply. "Your people have been attacked, Ryowyn—but your parents are fine."

Will flinched as her body twitched as if Rowe had struck her.

"Do you recall your father's concern about the Gryton Mines?" Rowe asked.

"Yes," Ryowyn said. "The Shadowfallen had reopened it."

Rowe blinked slowly and nodded. "The attack was launched from there. When it happened, your father was on his way here to find you. Early this morning, he received news of the attack from the gulls. As much as your father wanted to stay here with you, he left at once. The reason I'm telling you this now is because we are sending a caravan of covered wagons to Fairbay. It's leaving shortly."

"To what end?" Ryowyn asked. She pulled her legs away from Will and turned around, so she could lie against his chest. Taking both his hands, she wrapped his arms around her.

"The Niasa Sea may be lost," Rowe said. "If it is, your people may have to live in Rainia Lake until your father can determine when it's safe to return."

Ryowyn trembled. "I need to be on that caravan," she breathed.

"I'll be traveling with you," Will said.

"You look exhausted," she whispered.

"I'm not leaving you again."

"We're covering as many of the wagons as possible should we need to bring your people here, so you can ride in one of them," Rowe said. "I'll have a down mattress added so Will can catch up on sleep. Dench will drive your wagon. I wish I could make the trip with you, but we have to shore up our defenses at the North Crow Gate in anticipation of the South Gnome Army as they journey around the Misty Gorge."

They were all silent for a few moments, allowing space for Ryowyn to process the news.

Morgan cleared her throat softly. "Mom and I need to check on some patients before we turn in."

"Can we get you anything before we leave, Ryowyn?" Julie asked.

"Something to wear would be much appreciated."

"I brought up a few sets over there," Morgan said, pointing to the table. "I'll have some food prepared for the two of you. Dench, will you stop by the kitchen on your way out?"

The half-orc nodded as he opened the door. "Look for me by de wagons," he said to Will before leaving with Morgan and Julie.

When the door closed, Will's eyes settled on the large duffle bag he had brought from Cochrane.

"It's all there," Rowe said. "Even the…um…shotgun."

"Thanks, Rowe. I was in Fairbay when Joe brought word about the attack on the sea. Sounds like it might be rough, so I'll be packing a lot of heat for this trip."

Ryowyn slid her legs off the settee, and Will held her as she took a few moments to steady herself.

"Take your time, Ryowyn," Will said. "I'm just going to go through my bag. No need to get up yet."

Rowe stared at Will. "You were in Fairbay? And Johanissan was there too?"

Will grinned. "I told you I had some stories to tell. In a nutshell: I spent two days in the Clover Fields before Bremer and Urk helped me escape." Will held up a hand, stifling any questions. "Yes, Bremer. Then Thaudas found me and carried me to Fairbay where Queen Almithara nursed me back to health. That's when Joe arrived, but there wasn't time for me to hear his story. Thaudas flew me to the Maidstone where I found the horn and came straight here."

Rowe's mouth hung open as his head rocked gently back and forth. "You went to the Maidstone?"

Will flicked Rowe's chin and his mouth snapped shut. "Careful, buddy, you'll catch flies with that thing."

"Bremer helped you escape?" Rowe said. "For some reason that does not surprise me. But the Maidstone? We need to talk about that."

"All in good time, I'm sure."

"And I thought *we* were busy defending the South Crow Gate against twenty-five hundred gnomes."

This time, Will's mouth popped open. "You fought twenty-five hundred gnomes? *What?*"

"We could have used these weapons of yours," Rowe said as they hefted the duffle onto a table. "But I do not understand how they work."

"We'll need more than one night for stories, Rowe. But we've got to get ready to go." Will unzipped the bag, pulled out the shotgun, and inspected it. "My precious," he whispered with a chuckle. "Remington Nitro Mag short-barreled shotgun with oodles of three-and-a-half-inch super magnum double-aught buckshot."

Rowe arched his eyebrows. "Sounds dangerous."

Poking through the duffle, Will retrieved a skinny black flashlight that clipped to the rail beneath the barrel, and flicked it on and off to test the battery. Despite its size, the flashlight seemed as bright as the sun. He pulled an additional eight shells from a full box and loaded them in a sidesaddle mounted to the right side of the gun. Next, he found his green cartridge belt and fed the empty slots with shells. The holster he wore on his hip also carried an extra clip for his 1911.

"I cannot imagine…" Rowe said, shaking his head.

Will stepped over and gave him a hug. Rowe hugged him back then pulled away, smiling.

When Rowe left the room, Ryowyn rose slowly to her feet. "You care deeply for him," she said.

Will took her hands, surprised to see how well she was doing. "Look at you," he said. "You'll be running and jumping before long."

"And look at you, my Will. You smile, but those same eyes, those beautiful eyes, speak to how exhausted you are."

"I'll sleep well tonight," Will said with a nod.

The sun had almost set when Will and Ryowyn walked through the front gates of the castle. The caravan of thirty-four wagons was already moving. Marauders Brigade had arrived at the Crow's Nest earlier that day, and despite being travel weary, a hundred light cavaliers were riding out with the caravan. The battle at the South Crow Gate was a victory, but the war was far from over.

Dench waved at Will from the driver's seat of a large canvas-covered wagon, then cracked a whip. The two draft horses trotted forward and stopped next to Will and Ryowyn. Dench pulled back the long brake lever and jumped down to lead them to the back of the wagon. Will climbed up and through the opening while Dench held the canvas flap open. He tossed his gear inside, then took hold of Ryowyn's hands as Dench lifted her.

"Thanks, Dench," Will said with a yawn. "How long will the trip take?"

"About tree days."

Ryowyn stood up straight with room to spare between her head and the top, but Will had to bend his knees and hunch. The front canvas opening was already cinched tight, and now that Dench was tying down the back, it was dark inside.

Will removed his cloak as he waited for his eyes to adjust.

"Feel how thick and soft this bed is," Ryowyn said, unable to hide the joy from her voice. "And look at the food and water over here."

"You be ready now," Dench called out.

Ryowyn sat on the bed a second before the wagon lurched. Will reached up and steadied himself on a wagon bow above him as they lumbered forward. As they adjusted to the gentle rocking,

Ryowyn bent and unlaced Will's boots. He sat beside her, suddenly realizing how tired he was. She pulled back the blankets as he kicked off his boots and watched the outline of her body in the dim light, enthralled with the slow, smooth way she moved. She kneeled on the bed and faced him. Her warmth was exhilarating, and he breathed in her exotic scent.

"Reach for all that is good and well in the world," she whispered, her lips tickling his ear. He raised his arms, and she pulled his shirt up and over his head. Before he lowered them, her cool fingertips touched his chest and coaxed him onto his back.

CHAPTER 32

PRODUCTION AT THE NORTH CROW GATE

The next morning, Morgan and Rowe stopped at a large field on their way to check on the progress at the North Crow Gate. Fresh burial mounds cut dark swaths in the tall grass. Morgan waited on her horse as Rowe slid from his saddle. He strolled past several graves before locating the one they had come to visit: a small stone marker he had personally chiseled for his good friend.

"You weren't supposed to leave me this soon, Tranas," Rowe said. "Maybe we should have killed the duke sooner...but who's to say, really?" He cleared his throat and rubbed his freshly shaved jaw. "I'll be sure to cast a line for you from time to time, as long as you promise to watch over me, old friend. If this war gets more difficult... Shades! How I'll need your wisdom." He scanned the burial field. "You're in good company, Tranas. I'll come visit every chance I get."

Rowe mounted his horse and they continued on. Morgan said nothing, wanting to give him space to grieve. They made one final stop before arriving at the North Crow Gate. The three colorful alchemists' wagons were backed close to one another with planks connecting the rear entrances to each, as they had been at the South Crow Gate.

Dadore rushed out from one wagon on his way to another but stopped midstride when he noticed Morgan and Rowe. The alchemist's hair was wild, and the dark lines beneath his eyes suggested he had been working through the night.

"I was beginning to wonder if you were alive in there," Rowe called out with a friendly wave. They rode closer, and Dadore's haggard appearance became clearer. His cheeks were pale, and his head twitched as he glanced around, hands trembling.

He looked at Rowe, shifting his weight from foot to foot without going anywhere. "I wonder that myself sometimes." His eyes darted between Rowe, Morgan, the North Crow Gate, and the burial field.

Morgan and Rowe dismounted and walked between two wagons. Morgan winced at the smell of Dadore's pungent body odor.

"May we come up?" Rowe asked.

Dadore nodded, then shook his head rapidly. "Just don't go in either of those," he said, pointing at two wagons.

"Why not?" Morgan asked.

"That one was my master's wagon, and I've since turned it into a processing lab. There's enough Illious Fire in various stages of production to give us all an unfortunate start to the day. That one there was…was Kydaris's…and…" He trailed off.

"You want nothing touched," Rowe said. "We understand that, Dadore. We just visited my dear friend, Tranas, over at the grave site. Already, I miss him so much it's all I could do to get up this morning. Life without him doesn't seem…natural."

Dadore nodded.

"I saw the way you two worked together," Rowe said. "You seemed more like brothers than fellow students."

"We grew up in the same orphanage. Hardly a day went by we weren't together." Dadore stared at the ground. "Maybe we *were* brothers."

Morgan studied the young man's face. "Why don't you take a break?"

"That would be good," Rowe agreed. "Let's go out to the grave site. I'd like to show you how we honored Kydaris."

Dadore hesitated, his head hung low.

"Come," Morgan said. "He would have wanted you to visit."

Dadore's feet seemed set in stone, but as Morgan and Rowe led their horses into the long grass still wet with dew, Dadore moaned and jumped off the wagon. He quickly caught up, and they walked together in silence. It was about a quarter mile back to the grave site, but the cool air put a spring in their steps. The day was young and fresh with hope.

"You have an exciting life ahead of you, Dadore," Rowe said. "You remind me of myself when I was your age. I believe your life will be marked by grand adventure.

"We have suffered terrible losses the last few days, and now is the time to mourn. Tomorrow might be a little easier. The day after that, a little easier. One day, you will wake up feeling almost whole again."

"I can't imagine ever being whole again," Dadore said with a sniffle.

"I can't either, but that's why I said *almost* whole. When our friends and loved ones die, part of us goes with them. We'll never be the same. But our wounds can experience a measure of healing if we are willing."

"I don't want to feel this pain anymore." Dadore kicked a stone. "I want it all to go away. It hurts too much."

Rowe slowed his pace. "I know. But there is much to live for. Just don't allow yourself to become comfortably numb."

"What does that mean?"

"Well, it's a phrase our friend Will once quoted. I think he heard it from a popular bard where he comes from…" He glanced at Morgan and shrugged. "Or something like that."

Morgan smiled and nodded.

Rowe stroked the mare's cheek and continued. "I think it's an appropriate phrase for us, Dadore. In my experience, I've seen people bury their pain, never opening their hearts to the possibility of healing. They devote their time to work, training, or studies. They tell themselves how important it is to press on until they can no longer see straight. Soon they are not eating properly or sleeping well. I've seen men turn to strong drink or excessive use of tevan root or other mind-numbing herbs. They do all this to keep their pain buried deep, to numb the wound. Some people can do it for years. They appear to be living comfortably and at peace, but all their activity and overuse of elixirs and herbs has only deadened the pain. They're comfortably numb. Outwardly, they appear to be functioning like everyone else, but beneath the surface, the wound festers." Rowe stopped. "I'm not judging them. Believe me, I understand why it happens and that it could happen to me." He placed a hand on Dadore's shoulder. "But I do not want this for you."

"I don't think that will happen to me," Dadore said, gazing into Rowe's face. "Although I can see how easy it would be…especially for someone like me. I could create a powerful comfortably numb elixir."

Rowe smiled. "I'm sure you could."

"How do I prevent what you described from happening to me?"

"Well, there are no guarantees, but you could start by saying farewell to your friend." Rowe led him to a small burial mound marked with a memorial stone nearly three feet tall. A thin border surrounded the words, each letter painstakingly carved, the detail done in loving memory:

Here lies Kydaris
A powerful force in the battle at the South Crow Gate
Giving more than he took, he was a true friend and brother

The floodgates opened, and there was nothing Dadore could conjure to stop it. He buried his face in Rowe's shoulder and wept like a child.

⁂

It was still early in the day when Morgan and Rowe arrived at the North Crow Gate. Two walls—each just over a hundred feet long and thirty feet tall to the base of the battlements—stretched between the Hillron Mountains and the Misty Gorge. The walls were undergoing an extensive renovation. Work crews concentrated on the outside wall, deepening the wall walk and building a peaked roof over the entire length. The front of the roof had a sharp overhang intended to protect soldiers from bolts being lobbed in while also providing shade from the sun. After his experience at the South Crow Gate, Rowe assumed the gnome armies would attack at night, but the soldiers would need shade during the day as they rested and prepared for battle.

Brigadier Twell Henowing of the Marauders was giving final instructions to a few messengers, who then rode off in various directions.

"Good morning!" Twell called. He wiped a finger across his forehead and used the sweat to smooth his thick gray nests above each eye. The commander was a tall man with broad shoulders and an infectious smile. Despite the promise of a warm day, he wore dark-brown pants and a long-sleeved shirt with a leather vest cinched tight across the front. He paced like a tiger in a cage.

"Good morning, Twell," Rowe said, dismounting. "Are we still on schedule?"

"Everyone has set hand to plow, Rowe. Three crews are heading to the South Crow Gate to dismantle both catapults and the ballista. The barracks, the barn, and the makeshift hospital are already torn down, since they're no longer needed there. The wood will be put to good use on this wall. Twenty catapults are in various stages of construction—some for here and some for the Crow's Nest."

Three wagons rambled by and Twell paused until the clamor had passed. "Those wagons are bringing broken shale from a mountain slide for the new building footings. The three-level barracks that had been started before the duke shelved the project will finally be finished. And the horse barns are getting a thorough mucking and resupply."

"What about weapons, Twell? We used up a huge number of arrows at the South Crow Gate."

"The two blacksmith shops in Rainia have six forges between them, and they're working at capacity until the new forges are completed. The town's only arrowsmith now has a crew to expand his manufacturing efficiency tenfold. Three fletchers are busy making arrows until more arrowheads are ready."

"What about food?" Morgan asked.

"We have farmers bringing in the winter wheat, beans, and a few other crops that are ready. Out on the lake, fishing boats are coming in low to the water from the weight of their catches. The smoker has been processing fish like it did years ago."

Rowe gazed across the valley to the large lake. "When Ryodan returned to Fairbay the other day, he left a dozen mer soldiers to explore Rainia Lake at length. I hope they find it suitable."

Twell laughed. "Well, I hear there's a number of fishermen pretty excited to catch the odd glimpse of those majestic creatures."

"The soldiers under your command work like an army of ants," Rowe said as they walked past a crew of shirtless men hoisting the arm to a catapult.

"They do, but I'm also impressed by those under *your* command, Rowe. Look at that man there." Twell pointed to an older man shuffling along, sweat rolling off his bald head, while carrying a tool pouch in one hand and a bag of nails in the other. Beside him walked a boy of no more than six years old, holding a second pouch of nails while following the old man to a catapult that was nearing completion.

"There's a spirit that burns deep inside a person who has lost everything," Rowe said. "We call them refugees, but we should call them heroes."

Twell snorted a laugh. "And you do, Rowe! I've heard you use that word several times. That's what I like about you: you inspire people. My men work because they know if they don't, this boot will provide a memorable motivation. *Your* people work because they want to. There have been times the past two days you reminded me of General Raric—and that's something I don't say lightly."

"I don't know about that," Rowe said. "I just like people—always have."

"It's far more than that," Twell said before shouting orders to his crew: "Hey! Someone grab the other end of that beam—now!" He turned to Rowe. "See what I mean?"

They went a little farther, and Morgan noted the vast reinforcements to the wall. "You're planning for more than a siege," she said when they were beyond the earshot of anyone.

Twell nodded, his weathered face tightening. "News from Enders Brigade has not been good. That said, if they weren't a thorn in the side of the North Gnome Army, Rainia would be one of the last human towns left."

"What's the news?" Morgan asked.

Twell furrowed his brow, and his narrow eyes almost disappeared. "I will share this with you for two reasons. First, General Raric himself declared you both trustworthy. And second, I have seen the way you carry yourselves these past few days." Twell looked around and lowered his voice. "Enders Brigade discovered that the North Gnome Army is transporting Phyriad. Raric had been hoping they could engage the gnome army before they received it. They believe the gnomes have hidden Phyriad in a small two-wheeled cart, which will be difficult to find, given the size of the North Gnome Army."

Rowe scratched his chin. "If the attack on the Niasa Sea was Phyriad, as the reports suggest, a similar assault on Dwenlin Thah will be devastating." Rowe fixed his gaze on Twell. "Which is why you intend to seal this valley off from the Fourwinds, isn't it?"

Twell shrugged. "General's orders."

"So, what will he do?" Rowe asked.

"The North Gnome Army is also in possession of at least two flasks of Guilliad. The General plans to destroy them at all cost because one flask was enough to wipe out Hammerclaw. Imagine what two or more flasks might do in Dwenlin Thah…or here."

"But if Raric can destroy the Guilliad flasks," Rowe said, "we could hold this valley for years. By then, hopefully Phyriad dies out or we find a way to stop it." He gazed at the impressive North Crow Gate. "I hope that caravan gets to Fairbay and back as soon as possible."

Hurry home, Will, Morgan thought. *Once the refugees start pouring through this gate, we'll need your eyes to help us keep the harvesters out.*

CHAPTER 33

FAIRBAY

A steady flow of wagons left Fairbay for a staging area in the high plains east of town. Most of the wagons were owned by shopkeepers who were carrying as much stock and equipment as they could gather in a short period. Everyone worked together. The elders of Fairbay had heeded Queen Almithara's recommendation to evacuate. The citizens assisted merpeople before any creatures infected with Phyriad reached the village. All efforts were encouraged by the knowledge that the renowned Callum Sage, Johanissan, had confirmed the terrifying report of Phyriad, and was overseeing the exodus.

Despite Joe's attempts to get wagons started on the journey to the Rainia Valley, some people were taking too long. It seemed as if they were reluctant to come to terms with his account of the horrors at the Gryton Mines. Those not overloading wagons filled the air with the sound of hammering as they boarded up their dwellings and shops. Joe shook his head in dismay. These people had seen the fallout of war; they should know better than to hope for a quick return to status quo. Nevertheless, Joe directed wagon traffic, keeping a close eye on the sea, expecting hordes of deathly creatures to arrive any minute.

He removed his straw hat, wiped his forehead, and tightened the leather strap around his ponytail to keep his long white hair off his face. His dark, weathered skin was no stranger to the sun, but these days the heat tired him more than it used to. He was coming to terms with his aging body, but the hard work and hiking in the past week left him pining for a relaxing weekend on the couch. His feet blistered in his unyielding leather boots. He smiled at the thought of his old Merrell hiking shoes he used to love.

A wagon slowed near him.

"Johanissan, I don't know how to thank you." Jessman was driving the largest of three wagons from the Recovery.

"You just did," Joe said, tapping the wide brim of his straw hat.

"I doubt even a single wagon would've left Fairbay if not for yer ability to move people. Shades! If only you could've filled the vacancy left by Akia Tibers as our third elder! I can't imagine how organized our little town would've been."

"We do well when we do what we're created to do." Joe scratched at a week's worth of growth beneath his chin.

"Well, I hope to see ya at the new Recovery, wherever that might be. You'll always have a drink and a meal on the house." Jessman cracked the reins and proceeded along the road. His wagon groaned against the weight of the custom whiskey still that had made their pub such a popular place. Hansla rode in the second wagon carrying the ale-making equipment, along with most of the dishes from the pub. He said nothing, still devastated at having to leave this beloved town and the grave where he had buried his parents. Homas drove the third wagon, bearing a heavy load with all the linens and memorabilia from the rooms. Dozens of people on horseback followed the caravan out to the staging area, along with an escort of a dozen armored cavaliers.

Joe grimaced at the number of possessions people tried to jam into wagons. When horses were unable to pull the weight, people simply abandoned what items they could live without along the roadside.

"Johanissan," shouted a soldier on horseback as he trotted over. "The main road is becoming too congested for wagoners to navigate, and people are getting hot and angry."

"Bring me a dozen soldiers with good backs," Joe said.

"Why more soldiers?"

"People are grieving the loss of their homes and livelihood. Let's help them load the last of their goods before we push them too hard, or this day will not end well for anyone."

The soldier nodded. "I suppose you're right. Yelling seems to slow people down."

Near the beach, several covered wagons formed a long line just before the sand. Joe realized it was time to stop loading wagons with belongings and get people out.

"One more thing," Joe said to the soldier. "Direct all new wagons to the seashore so we can get the merpeople out. We're running out of wagons, horses, and time."

Approximately two thousand mer soldiers had set off weeks ago to investigate the Gryton Mines, but only six had returned. The last two had arrived only five hours ago, and Prince Wrathan was not among them. The stories the six survivors carried with them were much worse than Joe had described. But Ryodan Ayoust had come home several hours ago from Rainia Lake and was rallying his people with a good report of their new home.

Along the waterfront, nearly five hundred mer soldiers loaded large pieces of carefully wrapped coral into covered wagons. They had filled every bucket in Fairbay with seawater and loaded it into every nook and cranny they could find, hoping the coral would survive the trip to the Rainia Valley. If it did, there was hope of a new life in the depths of Rainia Lake.

Joe maneuvered through the busy soldiers and approached the mer king.

"Johanissan," Ryodan said with a short nod, causing the king's long white hair to shake. "My son is out there, somewhere. Nonetheless, I do not believe time allows for us to wait or to load more wagons."

"I was thinking the same thing, Your Majesty. How long do you need?"

"I will sound the call in a moment," Ryodan said.

"I was hoping for more time," Joe muttered.

"Time is not ours to extend, Johanissan."

A loud commotion in town captured their attention. Through the crowds, Ryowyn sprinted toward them. Ryodan stumbled and placed a hand on Joe's shoulder. A scream rang out above the excitement as Almithara spotted her daughter and they rushed into each other's embrace.

Ryodan's fierce glacial eyes softened and his strong grip on Joe's shoulder loosened. Ryowyn had not yet seen her father, so the king called to his commanders to get the wagons rolling at once.

Joe worked his way through the streets, directing people on wagons to take what they had and proceed to the staging area. He turned on a less-crowded street near the water before heading back to find Will and the others who'd traveled with them from the Crow's Nest. On the far pier, a young man was leaning over the water six feet below him. Something exploded from the water, and a second later, a trumpet blast filled the air, sounding the order for everyone to leave at once.

Joe gasped and leaned on his walking stick to steady himself as a creature sailed over the pier, slamming into the young man before he could move an inch. Crushed against the railing, the man screamed. The creature raked with its claws, then scooped up the man's body and plunged headlong into the sea. Blood and water soaked the wooden planks.

"Was that a mer soldier that attacked that man?"

Joe turned to see an elderly woman standing next to him. "I…I believe at one time it was a mer soldier," he answered.

"But his skin wasn't blue," she said.

She was right, Joe realized. The former soldier's skin was rough gray hide. Most of the coral armor was only sharp edges jutting from his body. His hands were thick claws, and his face was longer, his mouth full of sharp teeth.

Joe hurried down the street to the sound of more screams. The mer soldiers on the beach waited by the sea, tridents poised. Another creature burst from the water toward them. Half his tail was missing, and his skin was gray with fragments of coral armor dangling from his chest. Arms outstretched, he crashed into the beach several yards short of the stunned mer soldiers. His tail didn't transform, so he clawed his way forward.

A soldier shuffled over and drove his long trident through the creature's head. When he removed the weapon, five more creatures tackled him, clawing his chest and limbs. Within seconds, the five hundred mer soldiers on the beach were joined by hundreds of part mer, part… something else. Their skin reminded Joe of the dragon hide the druid Margrave had melded to General Raric's skin, except it was gray. Their shrieks echoed Raric's cries of pain.

Ryodan charged into the sea and stopped knee deep. Hundreds of mer soldiers accompanied him and formed a defensive wall along the beach, struggling to protect the merpeople and villagers fleeing to the plains. They cut down the vicious hordes with ruthless abandon, their tridents a blur. Some creatures resembled the mer soldiers, making it difficult to discern friend from foe. All of them slashed with thick, sharp claws.

Dozens of human cavaliers rode along the water's edge, hacking the strange creatures, but small, lizard-like creatures swarmed the horses, digging claws deep and bringing riders down.

Ryodan and his men fought like caged animals but quickly lost ground. Forced from the water, the king stepped behind his soldiers who formed a defensive perimeter. He thrust his massive trident into the sand and took a deep breath, expanding his chest. Ryodan closed his eyes, raised his hands, and began a slow chant.

Will's eyes shot open. In his dream, Ryowyn was attacked by a harvester, and she had screamed for him. He slid his arm across the bed but could not feel her lying next to him. He sat upright. The high-pitched scream came again, but this time it was real, and it was followed by loud shouts and rumbling wagons.

Dench bellowed his name, and Will stumbled to the back flap and opened it a few inches. A warm breeze ruffled his already messy hair. He lifted his arm to shade his eyes and squinted as dozens of wagons crammed with people and supplies hurried past. The screams came from ahead of his wagon. He was about to jump out but remembered his lack of clothing. Diving across the bed, he threw on his pants and shirt as the screams grew louder. He cinched his belt and adjusted the holster at his hip, making sure to fill the slots with two extra clips. His tall leather boots proved difficult to slide on once again, but he got them laced almost to the top. The shotgun was already loaded and leaning in a corner, so Will grabbed it and leapt from the wagon. A wagoner shouted something at him, but Will's head was still fuzzy, and his eyes were adjusting to the bright sunlight. Merpeople crowded on the flatbed wagon with no cover. Dozens of humans and merpeople ran alongside the wagons. Everyone wore frightened looks.

"Dey coming from de sea!" Dench roared, his sword held low as he ran toward Will.

"Stay here and protect the wagon, Dench! I'll be back soon!" Will said.

"Me come wit you!"

"No, Dench. I'm coming back with Ryowyn and her parents, but they'll need a covered wagon, so stay here and make sure someone doesn't take it."

Dench tilted his head and nodded.

"I'll be right back!" Will shouted as he ran.

Will raced forward, but there were so many wagons and people fleeing for the plains, he was swept back to the hillside protecting Fairbay from the winds off the plains. He climbed the hill for a better view. At the top, he recognized the ridge as the same one that he'd stood on during his first visit to Fairbay. He massaged his leg and gasped at the terror below.

Transformed mer soldiers exploded from the sea and attacked those defending the beach. The creatures slashed wildly, heedless of deadly tridents. Those they slew writhed in the sand but did not appear to die. Some changed color as their bodies mutated. Will could only imagine he was witnessing the terrifying effects of Phyriad. Among those fighting the mad horde, Will recognized King Ryodan.

He stumbled down the path, remembering the direction he and Bremer had taken when they'd pursued the dark elf, Onathe Wyeth. He traced his way through two alleyways toward the beach, his cloak flying behind him.

Will rounded a cluster of cottages and saw Almithara loading children into a wagon. Ryowyn appeared at the far side of the wagon, a small mer child in each arm. She lifted the crying children onto the crowded wagon deck and reached for another child. The driver yelled and cracked a whip, and the wagon jerked forward.

A group of creatures broke through the defensive line on the beach, tumbling over one another to reach the wagon. Joe appeared and swung an arm out as he shouted, launching a huge cone of icy shards into the transformed mer soldiers. The spell penetrated their thick hides but only slowed the onslaught.

Instinct took over and Will pumped his shotgun, rushing between the beach and the wagon, gun raised. Ryowyn leapt back with a scream.

"Run!" he shouted before pulling the trigger five times in rapid succession. The explosions overpowered the battle cries on the beach. Each double-aught buckshot sent nine steel pellets from the short-barreled shotgun in a wide grouping.

Bodies were blown apart as forty-five pellets stopped their advance. The creatures flew back, some in pieces, from the hail of hot steel as Will fired three more shots. He slammed eight new shells into the barrel.

Ryowyn, her mother, and most of the mer soldiers retreated with the wagon. Will rushed toward Ryodan, who now stood apart from a few remaining mer soldiers, his massive trident spinning in his hands.

Sparks of electricity lanced from the trident, killing those creatures nearest the king as he prepared to unleash hell on the advancing hordes. There were too many emerging from the sea for Ryodan to fight alone, so Will took a deep breath, planted his feet, and fired eight rounds. The powerful buckshot devastated a dozen creatures at such close range. When the shotgun clicked, Will flipped the sling over his shoulder and drew his 1911. He squeezed the trigger, making slight adjustments to his aim as the gun jerked in his hands. Again, the bullets thrust mangled bodies back into the sea. The 1911 emptied and Will jammed it back into its holster. He fumbled at the extra shotgun shells looped in his belt and reloaded, desperate to help protect Ryodan.

The king's eyes blazed bright as a welding arc. He shouted in a language Will didn't recognize, keeping his arms raised as he spun the trident in wide circles. In response, a fifty-foot wall of water shot up from the sea, cutting off further access to the beach. Scores of creatures were caught up in the spell and launched backward into the sea. The mer soldiers slew those that had already gained the beach.

Ryodan remained still, his trident held high, eyes wide and unblinking. His chant diminished as he altered the direction of the trident. The sea pulled back from the shore just beyond the wall of water. In the distance, a tidal wave was growing. It was still a mile away, but it was getting taller and moving faster by the second.

Ryowyn grabbed Will's shoulder. "We need to run! Now!" she shouted, shaking him.

Will turned and saw Ryodan's eyes returned to their normal blue color, his hands at his sides. Two mer soldiers braced him beneath each arm to help him escape with the others. He appeared power-less to move on his own, so they swept him up and ran toward the plains. The giant wave raced toward them.

"Come!" Ryowyn screamed to get Will's feet moving. "Now!"

They were the last to leave Fairbay. Once past the final row of cottages, Will and Ryowyn jumped onto the wagon that Dench already had in motion. The half-orc whipped the reins, and the horse sped down the road to the plains. A great rushing sound thundered close to shore.

A few minutes later, the wave struck the beach. It blew through Ryodan's defensive wall of water like a freight train through a single-pane glass window. The wave smashed the fishery and the buildings facing the sea to splinters. It then lay waste to the entire village, slowing only when it crashed into the hillside. Seawater splashed across the plains for twenty yards. Everyone who had already escaped covered their ears against the explosion as the wave shook the hillside.

Will and Ryowyn were knocked from the wagon and clutched at each other as a surge of water flowed along the road toward the open plain. The turbulent waters swept them off their feet. Ryowyn grabbed Will and swam hard for the surface, allowing Will several breaths as they tumbled in the temporary river.

The water quickly receded. Will spat and coughed as Ryowyn held him close. He lay in the wet grass beneath several inches of water, amazed to see he was still holding the shotgun in a death grip.

Beyond the hill, the water pulled back, taking everything the wave had pillaged with it into the sea in a single powerful rip cur-rent. Most of the infected hordes were carried several miles from shore. From there, they swam off in every direction.

Sopping wet, with hair covering his eyes, Will let out a harsh sigh. Ryowyn stood beside him, watching as the parched plains soaked up the water. Her parents were next to Joe, and a few villagers helped Dench get his wagon upright.

"That was my favorite place in the Fourwinds," Will said, spitting salt water from his mouth.

Ryowyn dropped to her knees and brushed the hair from his face. She took his cheeks into her hands, smiled, and kissed his mouth long and hard.

The sound of spongy footfalls pulled them apart. Ryowyn's parents approached, holding hands. Despite all that had happened, Ryodan managed a slight smile. Ryowyn stepped up to embrace him. A foot taller than his daughter, the king gazed out beyond the hillside with a distant look in his eyes.

"Are you thinking about Wrathan?" Ryowyn whispered as she leaned her head against his chest.

"I am," Ryodan sighed.

"Me too," she said.

Ryodan wrapped his arms around Almithara and Ryowyn. "The sea gives life, and the sea takes life. But through it all, the sea is our life."

Almithara reached down and helped Will to his feet.

"My Will," Ryowyn said within the folds of her father's embrace.

The king and queen opened the circle and invited Will in. "*Our Will*," Almithara said.

CHAPTER 34

TREE PERCH

At the edge of the Nameless Forest, north of the Hollowtangle, a late-morning breeze rustled the great willows, and thousands of narrow leaves clashed like tiny emerald swords. High above the forest floor, the thick, crooked branches of the towering trees twisted and knit together, making it impossible to tell which branches belonged with which tree. Captain Culthison of Enders Brigade's Second Dragoon Company studied the dense canopy as he thought back on his briefing with Commander Bayard and General Raric.

"It's vital you and your rangers reach the Nameless Forest before the North Gnome Army, Captain," Commander Bayard had said. "I will need a full report of the capabilities of their army. We already know they outmatch us in terms of numbers, so we must outwit them."

"Remember, Captain," General Raric had added, "this is the army that razed Hammerclaw. They are operating under the command of Uluk the Shadowfallen and plan to unleash their powerful weapons on Dwenlin Thah. We need descriptions and locations of those weapons if we are to destroy them."

Commander Bayard had raised a warning finger. "Be on your guard, Culthison. Like us, the gnomes will send scouts ahead of their main army. Before you find an optimal vantage point to study the army, you will have to deal with the scouts first."

As Bayard had suspected, the gnome scouts had reached the Nameless Forest ahead of the fifty rangers of Second Dragoon Company. Because Culthison was expecting them—and because his rangers outnumbered the gnome scouts five to one—the skirmish had been thorough and brief. Culthison was sure that not a single scout had escaped. But the North Gnome Army would arrive shortly.

Throughout the day, Culthison and his rangers crawled high in the trees. It was a tedious process, spreading out among the broad branches, seeking shelter for what might be an extended reconnaissance. If the gnomes discovered even one ranger, General Raric's outlandish plan would fail. And so they moved in small clusters, working carefully not only to prepare the way for Enders Brigade, but to ensure they had a way to escape the gnome army after it passed beneath them.

The rangers had settled high in the giant willows when Culthison whistled a sharp birdcall warning. Uluk the Shadowfallen soared above them, circling the Nameless Forest. Even in the bright sunlight, the winged creature looked as dark and mysterious as death. Despite the thick canopy over the rangers, no one dared to breathe. The Shadowfallen made several passes, then disappeared to the south.

"I'm sure he didn't see us," Culthison said. "If he had, we wouldn't be alive."

"Good thing we hid the bodies of the gnome scouts," a ranger said.

A collective sigh rustled through the willow branches with the afternoon breeze.

Commander Yossar of the North Gnome Army dabbed a bead of sweat from his forehead with the cuff of his sleeve. His simple gray homespun clung to his body, but he sat straight and proud in his saddle. The army had fallen behind schedule, so Yossar forced the gnomes to march the final few miles to the Nameless Forest beneath the blazing afternoon sun. The soldiers scowled but were careful not to complain.

The army followed the Endrow River into the forest of willow trees, quickly dispersing to find shelter from the sun. Gnome soldiers crowded beside the water's edge to soak their heads. The river here was shallow, with a few pools amid the many rocks and gentle current. Many of the soldiers walked into the river without disrobing, groaning loud sighs as the water soothed their hot skin. Despite their hooded cloaks, the sun had taken its toll; the sound of vomiting disturbed the peaceful forest.

Overseer Panigim guided her horse next to Yossar's. "First to arrive we needed to be, and first we are, Commander," she said. "Yet troubled you are."

"Our scouts sent to the forest have not returned."

"But other scouts report that miles away and stopped for the night is Enders Brigade. Reach the large field at the edge of the forest before them we will."

Yossar frowned. "More scouts have I just sent into the forest."

"Defeat ten Enders Brigades this army could, Raric or no Raric," Panigim said.

"Tell me what has become of our scouts and smile with you I will."

Panigim scowled. "Find them we will," she mumbled.

"Have the men form up. Push through the forest we must. Secure the high point of the field, then rest we will."

<hr>

Thirty feet above Yossar and Panigim, a ranger stretched out, still and silent along a wide tree branch. He peered through a gap where the limb forked. Branches and leaves covered all but his eyes, which he blinked only when he was sure no one was looking up. The skilled ranger drew breaths through his nose and exhaled through his mouth, noting troop numbers, supplies, and, most importantly, cargo.

The foot soldiers, mostly highland gnomes, marched two abreast. After about an hour, there was a gap in the line of soldiers, followed by a squad of bush gnomes. Even from high in the trees, the differences were clear: the bush gnomes wore no armor beneath their dirty cloaks. Most had long, unkempt hair that tumbled from the cowl of their hoods. Their arms were covered with dirty, tightly layered linen to hide their skin from the sun. Most wore thick goggles. Their eyes scanned their surroundings as they led the first light catapult pulled by a team of four mangy workhorses.

Behind the catapult came a large, flat deck wagon carrying a sturdy timber frame. Connected to all four corners of the structure with heavy rope was a giant flask. A translucent light-green liquid splashed within the flask, which was at least six feet in diameter.

Thirty bush gnomes walked close to the wagon, armed with loaded crossbows.

Over the next hour, five more guarded wagons with identical flasks went by, each twenty minutes apart.

A hundred yards behind the last wagon came a small two-wheeled, one-horse cart driven by an old man. Beside him was an old, frail-looking woman and behind them sat two young children beside a large wooden crate. Clothed in little more than rags, the humans traveled in utter silence. The ranger held his breath as the cart rolled past. On the back of the cart was a small sign that read *Maple Syrup Candy.*

The ranger watched the strange cart until he could no longer see it. The cart and cargo looked like a tinker's wagon heading from one village to the next, trying to sell whatever goods they carried. But this tinker traveled in the center of a war machine. Even more confusing were the gnome soldiers giving the tinker such a wide berth.

By the time the gnome army stopped to set up a defensive perimeter beside the Nameless Forest overlooking a large, gently sloping field, the sun had dipped below the trees. Darkness settled in quickly in the dense forest, but the gnomes needed no watch fires. The only light in the entire forest came from the cooking fires.

"Still no word from the advance scouts," Yossar grumbled.

"Yet flew above us this afternoon Uluk did," Panigim said. "No ill news has he brought."

"Trust the Shadowfallen I do not, Panigim. This you know. Why Queen Sidara does I understand not. More precious in their eyes be the weapons we carry than the lives of our army."

"The power of Guilliad have we seen, Commander. But a mystery is Phyriad. Only here and the Gryton Mines be such weapons. Although rumors there be that some was sent to Acttun."

Yossar scowled. "More scouts have I sent to the Gryton Mines, but fearful I am of their report. If Uluk used Phyriad against the mer…sick I am at such thoughts, Panigim."

"Waded too deep we have." Panigim sighed.

Too deep indeed, Yossar brooded. He shared most of his thoughts with his trusted overseer, but one secret he guarded: the harvesters. Before leading the attack on Hammerclaw, Sidara had held a private conference with Yossar. She had given him strict instructions to ensure the four harvesters and the small two-wheeled cart made it safely to Dwenlin Thah. Yossar wished the queen had not told him that the harvesters had infused a crate of maple syrup candies with Phyriad. The thought of children eating them made his stomach churn. He had considered sending word to General Raric the moment the cart left the Waerdreath, thinking he might have a way of dealing with it. But it was too late for that now.

⁂

A ranger watched from high above as the gnomes set up cooking fires. He paid careful attention to what they ate and how they prepared to feed the large army. Large pots of water boiled as gnomes diced soft and wrinkled potatoes and moldy cabbage. Others sliced slabs of salted meat and dumped the pieces into the pots. A short, round-faced gnome sprinkled in spices, stirred, then dipped a wooden ladle into each boiling pot, tasting the contents. The cooks processed wagon after wagon of food, adding to the pots that occupied nearly an acre of forest.

The ranger caught sight of another gnome who seemed to

move slower than the others, but her head never stopped shifting. She carried a pail from one vegetable wagon to another, casually making her way closer to the cooking pots.

She approached the pot beneath the ranger and lowered a large waterskin from her shoulder. A cook came over to empty her bucket into the pot, then returned to the wagon for more vegetables. The gnome glanced about as the others worked quickly around her, then she took a few steps toward the pot and squirted part of the contents of her waterskin into the pot.

"Too close you be!" someone shouted at her. "Off with you! Wait like everyone else!"

The gnome feigned a nervous start before walking away with a pronounced limp that the ranger had not seen earlier. No one offered her a second glance save for the ranger who shifted slightly so he could see her hobbling to the next pot. Waiting for an opportunity when no one lingered, she once again squirted something into the pot before being shooed away. The ranger crept along the massive limb, watching the woman repeat the strange process at every pot she passed until he could no longer see her. Through the darkness, the ranger began a careful journey along numerous branches, desperate to get word to Commander Bayard.

❧❀❧

By midmorning the next day, gnome scouts reported that Enders Brigade had crossed the Endrow River seven miles due east. Yossar was ready. His plan was to dig in and see what Raric had in mind. The humans would probably not attack such a defensible position, but there could be no telling with someone like General Raric. Six catapults were loaded with the flasks of Guilliad and spread out near the edge of the forest. Throughout the Nameless Forest, fifteen thousand gnomes waited, armed and ready to fight.

Late in the afternoon, Brigadier Bayard rode out into the field, surveying the battle grounds. The winding Endrow River bordered the north side of the field. A half mile to the south, the grasslands met a series of steep knolls and rocky outcroppings. Ahead of Bayard, to the west, the knee-high grasses and wildflowers swayed in the field along a gradual incline to the incredible willows that bordered the Nameless Forest. The landscape was pristine, were it not for the rows of gnome soldiers standing beneath the shade of the willows, and farther back into the trees as far as Bayard could see.

Behind the commander of Enders Brigade came First Battalion made up of two hundred armored cavaliers, a hundred archer cavaliers, five hundred foot soldiers, a hundred lancers, and a hundred longbowmen. Second Battalion followed, stretching across the tree line they had just come through. Third and Fourth Battalions marched out last, with two hundred longbowmen, two hundred lancers, and six hundred foot soldiers each. Bayard had been clear to stretch out the ranks as much as possible to give them the appearance of having larger numbers than they did.

Second Ranger Company, two hundred strong, trailed behind but was nearing the Nameless Forest. A hundred archers from First Dragoon Company had moved in quietly, spreading out along the Endrow River, with a hundred light armored cavaliers staged a few hundred yards back. The only troop yet to arrive was Second Dragoon Company, which had been stationed near the Gryton Mines. They were due to arrive late afternoon with a hundred armored cavaliers, fifty rangers, and fifty longbowmen.

Captain Culthison rode beside Bayard. "We've lost the exact location of the suspicious two-wheeled cart my ranger reported last night, sir."

Bayard glowered. "Everything hinges on that cart, Captain. We don't know for certain that it contains Phyriad, but the general was confident the gnomes are transporting it. Nothing else in your ranger's report suggests Phyriad would be anywhere else."

"Yes, sir. We'll find it, sir."

"In the meantime, let's proceed with Raric's plan. Have the chairs brought out to the middle of the field."

Culthison relayed the instruction to three unarmed standard-bearers. Two proceeded to carry out two chairs, while the third bore the Enders Brigade banner. When they returned, two gnomes also brought two chairs to the center of the field.

Bayard dismounted and strolled through the grass.

"How can you appear so calm?" Culthison whispered, stepping alongside the brigadier.

"They never taught courses at the Military Academy about what we are doing here today," Bayard said, a wry smile crossing his face. "But they did teach us to maintain a calm exterior in the face of the unexpected."

"Are you certain this will work?" Culthison asked.

"Raric was."

Culthison groaned. "That sounds about right."

Enders Brigade grew quiet as all eyes watched the commanding officers.

The sun ducked behind the Nameless Forest, and two gnomes started down the gentle slope. The chairs were set ten feet apart. Enders Brigade's chairs were ornately carved, high-back pine, and the gnomes' chairs were lower to the ground, made of a dark teak and simple to look at.

The four leaders faced one another, standing in front of their respective chairs.

"Panigim my name is, overseer of the gnome army," said the female gnome, offering a short bow. "Commander Yossar this is."

"My name is Brigadier Bayard, of Enders Brigade, and this is Captain Culthison."

They all took their seats.

"I have requested this parley," Bayard said, "because Captain Culthison has recently returned from the Gryton Mines. His report was alarming, and I wanted him to tell you as he has told me, so you'll hear it firsthand, no translations. Everything he is about to tell you, he has witnessed with his own eyes. I have asked him to speak freely and truthfully. Do you have anything to say before he begins?"

"It behooves me to ask, with respect, why at the Gryton Mines was he?" Panigim said.

"A sound request," Bayard said with a short nod. "I have to admit, the Gryton Mines have intrigued me. At the onset of this war, it made sense for you to occupy the mines—even if they're not yours to reopen. But then we received reports that Uluk was often seen in the area. Now, why, we wondered, would something like a Shadowfallen be interested in a simple mining operation? Captain Culthison was there to find answers. If it was a simple mining operation, his instructions were to shut it down. Evidently, it was not."

The gnomes remained expressionless but turned their eyes to the captain.

A thin line of sweat ran down Culthison's forehead as he told the tale of the destruction and massacre at the Gryton Mines. He spoke for nearly ten minutes without pause. Bayard watched the gnomes' expressions and was certain this was new information. When Culthison finished, a long silence followed.

A short trumpet blast sounded from Enders Brigade. Bayard turned and saw a messenger standing a dozen yards into the field.

"The importance of this parley is not lost on anyone," Bayard said. "But the fact that one of my messengers saw fit to interrupt us is disconcerting. If it pleases you, perhaps we could reconvene after I have heard his report?"

Commander Yossar was quiet for long moments, his face unreadable. "Remain here we will," he said.

Bayard and Culthison rose and walked back to the messenger.

"They didn't know about the Gryton Mines," Bayard said when they were beyond earshot.

"I was thinking the same thing. So where do we go from here?"

"I'm not sure how much more news I can bear," Bayard said as the messenger met them.

"I bring word from the Stoneberg, Commander," the messenger said.

Commander Yossar sat stunned as he digested the news about the Gryton Mines. "Began this war effort we did under the guise of wanting better lands to farm, Panigim. Years of drought left us with little choice. If survive we would, expand our lands we must. But diplomacy failed and to war we went."

"Battle for land should not annihilation of a species seek," Panigim said.

"Hated the humans for what they did to her, Sidara did, and

for leaving us with so little farmland. But never did she speak of genocide. But Uluk.…Without boundaries is the Shadowfallen's rage."

Brigadier Bayard was returning—only, he was coming with the messenger instead of Captain Culthison.

"The truth you believe he speaks?" Panigim said quietly.

Yossar nodded. "And you?"

"If dissension they wanted to create, why such an outlandish story? And confirm such a story we can."

"Soon will our scouts return from the Gryton Mines," Yossar said.

"As you know," Bayard said as he approached, "we sent a company of rangers to lock down the Stoneberg to disrupt your supply chain. This ranger has just returned from the wall. Would you like to hear from him?"

Yossar nodded.

"Just tell them what you told me," Bayard said.

The grimy-faced messenger took a long pull from his waterskin. "I was on watch atop the Stoneberg when they first appeared from the west, far beyond the wall. At first, we thought it was a confused supply caravan, but as they neared the Stoneberg, we knew something was not as it should be. Hundreds of gnomes were traveling afoot, at a slow, awkward run…in broad daylight. What little clothes they wore were torn and did little to protect their skin from the sun. They wore no hooded cloaks, no hats, nothing. They should have all died from exposure."

He paused for another drink. "The gnomes, well…they weren't gnomes anymore. When they reached the base of the wall, they tried to climb it until their fingers were bloody stubs, and still they scratched the wall. I watched them over the course of two days until I was certain of what I was seeing."

The messenger gazed at the gnomes' stunned faces. His hands were shaking. "They hadn't simply changed… They were in the *process* of changing. Scales formed on their skin like a terrible rash. Over time, the scales thickened. Then they grew darker. Their eyes had no white to speak of and were like chunks of polished coal. Around their eyes, they seemed to have cartilage growing out like…like…small horns. Their teeth had fallen out, replaced by jagged fangs. Those with darker gray scales had strange growths along the back of their shoulders, something forming from their bones. They were slowly evolving, and it appeared to be a painful experience. Many of them were writhing, some much worse than others. They ignored one another as they stumbled about.

"Their faces had the most dramatic changes, their noses and jaws seemed to protrude as their skulls changed. Some had faces that looked more animal than gnome. At first it looked as if they were morphing into lizards, but there was more to it than that. We watched through the arrow slits, so we were only a few feet away. We all came to the same conclusion: they weren't morphing into lizards, but rather something closer to a dragon. When we figured this out, I had the fastest horse, and so here I am. But before I left, I went up on the wall and saw more coming—hundreds of them."

Bayard already had time to consider this news and was the first to break the uneasy silence. "May I offer a thought?"

Yossar looked up as though seeing him for the first time. He barely managed a nod.

"When we rescued General Raric from the Waerdreath, we learned a few things about a dangerous elixir called Phyriad. We know that your queen, Sidara, did not in fact, create it, although she had a healthy fear of it. The general believed that the creature, Natas, was the architect of the vile substance, but we could not fathom the purpose for it. We assumed that it was a contagion that would spread through a population, killing those that became infected. With this news from the Stoneberg, my question is this: Is it possible that instead of *killing* a population, maybe Phyriad is meant to transform gnome, human, mer—and possibly any living creature—into the image of its creator?"

For a moment, no one spoke, and Bayard wondered if the gnomes had understood, because the messenger had talked so fast.

"Where be General Raric now?" Panigim asked.

"When we rescued the general, we found him nailed to a cross atop the Waerdreath. Beaten and starved, he had one foot planted firmly in the grave. We nursed him back to health, but there were complications. Although his hands had healed, the nail holes in his feet have become infected and there are signs of rot."

"Much information you share," Yossar said.

Bayard sighed. "General Raric believes you are being led down a road you never agreed to travel. And I agree. There has been too much violence between our people throughout history, but at no point has either race tried to render the other extinct. When this war began, you were fighting for land. That made sense because we humans have an insatiable appetite to settle new lands and we often use violence to make that happen. With all due respect, from where we sit, you have become pawns.

"Instead of fighting one another," Bayard continued, "I think it may be time for us to take a deep breath. We may have a common enemy that means to turn us all into something we were never meant to be. Shades! You heard what Phyriad did to the mer. Despite the carnage of this war in the Fourwinds, we would never condone infecting one of your cities with a plague like that. Never."

"If in our chairs you sat," Panigim said, "think how outlandish your claims would sound."

"With respect, you no longer have a home to return to," the messenger interjected. "While your soldiers are fighting here, everyone you know back home have been turned into monsters! And…and…we're all next!"

Both gnomes looked as if the messenger had physically struck them.

Bayard spoke quietly, trying to defuse the tension without taking away from the reality they all faced. "We have shared all we know."

"To save Enders Brigade from the impending battle and certain defeat?" Panigim said.

Bayard huffed. "Please do not mistake our sharing this information as a sign of weakness or fear. You know General Raric. Although his body is damaged, his mind is sound. Should you deem it reasonable to continue the fight to Dwenlin Thah, few of you will leave the Nameless Forest." He pointed a finger at Panagim. "Our sole purpose here is to provide you with a clear understanding of what is happening. Should you come to the same conclusion—that Uluk the Shadowfallen is, in fact, the real enemy—then we are prepared to kill him for you."

"Bold words you speak," Panigim said.

Bayard clenched his jaw and leaned forward, gripping his knees. "Uluk tortured General Raric for over a year. That creature *will* die on this field of battle as sure as we sit here. Will you allow your people to die here as well? Or will we all work together to stop the spread of Phyriad, or perhaps even find a way to reverse its effects? In the meantime, we have shared all we know to be true, as outlandish as it may sound. While we wait for your response, we will refrain from attacking."

The gnomes rose and bowed to Bayard's back as the men stormed away. Panigim started to leave but noticed Yossar sit back down. Panigim sat and watched in silence until the men had returned to their troops. Yossar stood and, without saying a word, walked back to the forest.

"Scouts we have returning soon from the Stoneberg," Panigim said. "Confirm or deny this story they will."

"And return on the morrow Uluk will," Yossar said with a deep sigh. "Find out his intentions we must, but difficult for us to do without his knowing. On the precipice we stand. Cost us dearly will any mistakes."

Panigim tilted her head. "Believe you do in what the humans said?"

"This Bayard…" Yossar paused. "Laid waste we have to much of his lands, killed thousands of his fellow soldiers, yet understanding in him there be."

"If in his boots I stood, hot with anger would I be."

"Deceived he believes we are, Panigim. And speaking for Raric he was. Yet listened closely to his voice I did. Telling the truth he is."

"Tired of war he is…like a commander I know," Panigim said softly.

"Tested very soon will their stories be."

"Speak of destroying the Shadowfallen so easily he does."

Yossar smiled. "Mad he is, or more to the stories there be. Either way, make haste and confirm what can be confirmed."

Panigim turned to leave, but Yossar added in a low voice, "And check on the cart carrying Phyriad. Remain with us it must until confirmed the human stories be."

"For what purpose?"

"If Phyriad does what their stories depicted, destroy it we

must. Guilliad our best option may be to do so, lest infected we all become."

Panigim considered taking a horse to the thicket deep within the forest where the cart had been hidden, but she opted to make the journey afoot to be alone with her thoughts. If the humans' stories about Phyriad were true, and if the gnomes had been pawns this entire time, there would be weighty decisions to be made.

Her thoughts drifted to her husband, who had lost a leg in battle and remained with their two young sons on the family farm, which helped feed the army. It had been nearly two years since Panigim had risen to fill the position of overseer under Commander Yossar. It was an administrative role initially, until the army mobilized for war, and Panigim proved herself a brilliant strategist. Now Panigim longed to be with her family. What had become of them? She choked back a sob and kept her eyes low to the ground.

As she walked through the meadows lined with pup tents, several gnome soldiers emerged from their tents, coughing loudly. Their eyes were bloodshot and faces clammy. They had bedded down after a hot bowl of soup and they all looked as though they had caught the same illness. A seasoned military gnome, Panigim had seen the way sickness could sweep through an army that worked, slept, and ate in close quarters. But this was different. Not a single gnome looked well. Those gnomes waiting to enter the tents after a long shift in the hot sun didn't look much better. They finished their wooden bowls filled with soup and ducked into the tents despite how sick their comrades seemed.

Except for one or two days, the sun had been hot in cloudless skies, so Panigim could only assume that, in their weakened state, the soldiers were catching illnesses they wouldn't normally catch.

Panigim crested a hill and peered through the darkness at a sea of blackberry bushes covering a narrow ravine. There were no sources of light here, and even with her keen eyesight, she could see little. As she took the first steps along the path cleared by soldiers, she was surprised to see none of the twenty gnome guards charged with the cart's security. The hairs on her arms and legs prickled. She settled a hand over the hilt of her short sword. Not a sound could be heard, even when she stopped along the path to strain her ears. With a shift change underway, it was possible that the guards had returned to their tents while the night watch prepared to come down into the ravine. But this was not procedure. Heads would roll if the soldiers were becoming so undisciplined.

Panigim slowed to a stop. The way before her was silent and lifeless. There was a profusion of sound from the forest as the army completed the shift change, and the coughing increased. But here in the dense ravine, Panigim felt alone and vulnerable.

She was close now to the cart. It radiated evil. Panigim considered lighting the cart on fire the moment she found it. If Phyriad was half as dangerous as the humans described, that was reason enough to destroy it. She dismissed the thought. She would never do something so rash without conferring with Yossar. But the temptation dogged her.

She slipped her sword from the scabbard with scarcely a sound. Something was wrong. Everything inside her screamed a warning to run, but her sense of purpose reeled her in. She stepped into the area where they had left the cart until the battle with Enders Brigade was over.

The cart was gone. Panigim squeaked a gasp. In the spot she

had last seen the cart lay a pile of bloodied and broken bodies. Frozen in place, Panigim felt a pinch in her back. Before she could register what had happened, she looked down and saw the tip of a spear protruding from her stomach. She widened her eyes and tried to scream when the spear jerked back through her body.

In shock, Panigim felt nothing. A chain rattled, and had her mind been working properly, she would have identified the sound as a mace being swung through the air.

The spiked iron ball struck the top of the overseer's head, crushing her skull.

A dark form reached down and dragged the body to the pile. Another dark creature snatched the fallen sword. After examining it a moment, the creature tossed the blade onto the pile of bodies and limped back into the thicket.

Brigadier Bayard was exhausted by the time he entered the Battle Wagon. Elias looked up from his desk and adjusted his thick spectacles that had slid down his nose. The scribe leaned back in his chair as Bayard drained a full mug of ale.

"Does your hand ever get tired?" Bayard asked.

The old scribe sighed wearily and shrugged. "It's what I was born to do."

"Any word from the general?"

"Nothing since hearing that he survived the melding."

Bayard poured himself another mug of ale and flopped into a padded chair, sipping in silence.

"Stewing will get us nowhere, so why not tell me how your conversation with Commander Yossar went? I need to get it down on parchment while the details are fresh." Elias wiped the tip of his quill with a cloth. "Unless you have somewhere else you need to be."

Bayard shot him his best stern look of authority, but the grin on the old man's face disarmed him.

"There is a lot going on and none of it good," Bayard said.

He proceeded to recount the details of the meeting. Elias wrote as fast as Bayard spoke, so the commander left nothing out. When he concluded, he peeled off his shirt. He sniffed his armpits and shrugged; he was too tired to find hot water.

"You're sleeping here?" Elias asked.

Bayard sat on the small cot and nodded.

"Well and good. I'll get this report filed and I'll be turning in myself."

Long before Elias finished writing, Commander Bayard was snoring.

CHAPTER 35
THE NAMELESS FOREST

The Battle Wagon rocked gently, and a thin blade of predawn light slashed across Brigadier Bayard's face. A ranger had entered and was whispering something to Elias. On the desk, a small lantern glowed, but there was enough natural light for Bayard to see the grim expression on the ranger's face. Elias glanced at Bayard and shook his head slowly.

"You'll want to hear this," the scribe said. He motioned for the ranger to sit as he took up his quill and parchment.

Bayard pushed away his blanket. He climbed into his dark-brown pants and rose with a groan. The mug from his evening ale was close at hand, so he poured fresh water into it and nodded for the ranger to speak.

"This I have seen with my own eyes lest you mistake what is about to be told." The ranger pursed his lips and cleared his throat. "I was posted above the gnome cook stations and my view was unobstructed. I watched them prepare the soups—which is all they seem to eat—until a female gnome caught my eye. She didn't seem to belong."

"What makes you say that?" Elias interrupted.

"Her fingernails were dirty, and highland gnome cooks would kill her for preparing food with unwashed hands. And there was something about the way she moved that was different from the cooks. She circled around the cooking pots several times, clutching an old waterskin. When she was alone beside a cauldron, while the cooks walked back to the tables for more ingredients, she opened the waterskin and squirted something into the cauldron. It happened so fast that had I not been careful, I would have missed it. She repeated the process with all the pots—or as many as I could see. She did this at great personal risk because if anyone caught her adding something to the soups, she would have been sliced and diced by all the cooks walking around with knives."

Bayard stared, his mouth dry despite having downed a full mug of water.

"I was deep inside the Nameless Forest," the ranger continued, "and it took me all night to make my way clear. I was there for morning shift change and saw the gnomes who emerged from the tents. They looked terrible. They were coughing, deep and raspy, and many spat phlegm so thick we could hear it hitting the ground from way up in the trees. Their eyes were red, like they'd been taking tevan root for a week. Their skin was sweaty and clammy, and by the way they moved, it was clear they were burning up with fever."

"Phyriad," Bayard said.

Elias dropped his quill as the ranger continued.

"Impossible to say for certain, sir. Unfortunately, it gets worse— much worse." The ranger accepted the goblet of water Bayard offered and took a quick sip. "Fourteen rangers are missing—the ones charged with watching the cart we suspect contains Phyriad. The last update we had from them was yesterday, midday."

"And the cart?" Elias asked.

The ranger shook his head. "We cannot see into the thicket where they kept it."

Bayard cursed. "If they snuck it out last night, they have a day's head start."

"With two horses pulling that cart, it will be difficult to catch them before they reach Dwenlin Thah," Elias added.

Bayard grabbed his shirt. "I need to speak with Yossar."

"I'll have your horse saddled," the ranger said as he stood and left the Battle Wagon.

✦

Bayard rode to the edge of the field at a gallop. He slid from his mount as Captain Culthison ran from the opposite direction.

"What is it?" Culthison asked. "What's happened?"

"Walk with me," Bayard said. The moment they were beyond earshot of the soldiers, he continued. "I believe the gnome army may have been infected with Phyriad. Have the entire brigade prepared to leave at once. We may need a hasty retreat."

Culthison stumbled over a rock as he tried to keep up with Bayard.

"Three short trumpet blasts, count to ten, three more, then count to ten again, then one final blast."

"How can this be?"

"Everyone knows what the signal means, Captain, but you need to ensure that the men are ready to retreat at a moment's notice. Don't worry about supplies or anything. If I call for that signal, it means we run lest we get infected ourselves." Bayard stopped and faced the captain so they were inches from each other. "And, Culthison: if Phyriad is as contagious as we think, we will be running for our lives." He continued walking. "Keep those on watch out along the tree line but have horses ready for them. I want everyone else with their boots laced and ready. That's all, Captain!"

Culthison turned back as Bayard marched out to the four chairs in the middle of the field. The dew-laden grass soaked his boots and pants to the knees. The morning sun had yet to crest the trees behind him. Smoke from the watch fires that had burned themselves out drifted like a gentle haze across the field. Soldiers stood to attention as their commander made a beeline to the chairs. His hair was messy, and his clothes looked as if he'd slept in them, but he didn't care. He clenched his jaw and fists.

Bayard stood alone beside the chairs. Within the willows, gnomes were moving en masse, and Bayard briefly considered the possibility they were preparing to attack. His heart thumped, but a moment later, Yossar stepped out from the forest. The gnome commander took long strides, as Bayard had. Behind Yossar, the sound of coughing and hacking pierced the morning air.

"On my way to find you I was," Yossar said. "And here you are."

"You have a serious problem, but I guess you already know that," Bayard said.

"Troubled I am that you know this, Commander Bayard." The gnome's eyes narrowed. "If close enough your rangers were to know of our dilemma, perhaps it was *you* who poisoned us."

Bayard's jaw slackened. "If we poisoned you, I'd be leading my troops in an attack on your weakened army right now instead of meeting with you."

Yossar raised his eyebrows as he nodded.

"Why aren't *you* sick?" Bayard asked.

"Segregated my inner circle is, something we have always done in the event of sickness in the ranks. This morning, infected is over half my army already."

Bayard noticed pain in the gnome's large eyes. "Is it…Phyriad?"

"So little we know, but if someone means to infect us all, Phyriad it could be. Decimated will both our armies be if—"

"Shades!" Bayard said, rubbing his forehead.

The gnome's shoulders slumped. "One more thing: your rangers at the Stoneberg allowed one of our scouts a view beyond the wall. As you described, it is."

"I'm sorry, I…"

"Homeless we are now."

"Not completely," Bayard said. "Do you still have the cart?"

Yossar shook his head. "Killed many gnomes something did last night, without a sound it was. When alerted we were moments ago, the cart was gone. Where it was hidden, gnomes lay broken, including…my good friend…" Yossar's bottom lip trembled.

"No!" Bayard exclaimed, too afraid to speak Overseer Panigim's name. "I am truly sorry, Commander."

Yossar's eyes flared as he held out pleading hands toward Bayard. "Tell me the means you have to destroy the cart! Stop this madness we must!"

This time it was Bayard who shook his head. "I've dispatched riders, but unless there's a miracle, they will never catch the cart before it arrives at Dwenlin Thah."

Yossar's hands fell to his sides.

After a moment of silence, Bayard spoke. "Have you heard of the Rainia Valley?"

Yossar nodded. "Report I have that our bush gnome army can

no longer access the South Crow Gate. Rerouted they are. Well protected that valley is."

"Do you understand why your queen wanted the valley?" Bayard asked.

"A time there was when I thought I knew, but now…"

"I think you *do* understand, Yossar. They mean to infect the Fourwinds with Phyriad. First Hammerclaw, then your lands west of the Stoneberg…. Next will be Dwenlin Thah and the Rainia Valley.

"That valley has, or *had*, only two ways in. Now there is only one way, and that is protected by the North Crow Gate. It is a sprawling, highly defensible valley. If Phyriad is indeed released across the Fourwinds, well, there's a chance we can survive behind the North Crow Gate. If those infected gnomes could not scale the Stoneberg, they will never get past the North Crow Gate."

Yossar stiffened, turned his head slightly, and narrowed his eyes. "Why tell me such a thing in light of what we have done?"

"I received a report this morning. Because of the attack at the Gryton Mines, the Crow's Nest has sent a caravan to help move the remnant of merpeople from the Niasa Sea to Rainia Lake. I'm prepared to seek similar permission from the Crow's Nest for your people."

Yossar's lips parted. "But…"

"Like you," Bayard continued, "we have been deceived into thinking your queen, Sidara, was leading the campaign against us to expand your lands. Now it's clear there is more at work here than any of us could imagine. There was a time when I suspected the Shadowfallen was behind all this, but General Raric was certain of one thing we all missed: we are witnessing the work of Natas."

"A myth that dragon is," Yossar scoffed.

Bayard shook his head and waved his hands in front of him. "I used to think the same thing, Yossar. But recent evidence has shattered my unbelief."

Yossar nodded, his hands folded together in front of him. "How can you make such an offer to our people?"

"I have not come to this decision lightly, but General Raric believed your people were caught up in a lie that's been years in the making. That said, we still have to ensure that whoever comes with us is free of this plague. If we were to make it back to the Rainia Valley…well, that's when the real work would begin. There would have to be agreement among the races before you were granted clemency. General Raric was prepared to speak on your behalf. If he cannot, I will. From there, we will see how deep fear runs."

"This is"—Yossar paused—"not who I thought is General Raric."

"Torture by the Shadowfallen will change a man."

Yossar went to his chair and motioned for Bayard to sit in his. Instead, Bayard sat in the low gnome chair beside Yossar.

"An enigma you are, Commander Bayard."

Bayard chuckled. "I've been called many things in my life, but never an *enigma*."

"The compassion you speak with is lost on your crown."

"Our king was assassinated by his own family. Now his daughter, Alarra, a vile shell of a person, rules. At least she *did*. General Raric now controls the army, and I suspect our queen's days are numbered. General Raric believes that you were justified in going to war against our crown, and he is certain you did not comprehend the true purpose of the war. Our queen is also deceived about what is happening across the Fourwinds. Besides, most of our people do not hate other races; that is a posture set forth by our queen."

"In the—" Yossar was interrupted by a deep swooping sound overhead.

Both commanders jumped from their seats and looked up. A massive winged creature materialized like a nightmare in a dreamy blue sky.

"Can your army still fight?" Bayard asked.

Yossar shook his head. "Most cannot even speak, and like fire the fever burns."

"Send word to those not yet infected to prepare to ride hard. We'll draw the Shadowfallen into a brawl, and the moment that happens, I want you to lead your people north of the Endrow River, then east to the Mofard Flats. I'll send a contingent to meet your there. You met Captain Culthison yesterday; he'll be at the helm. Remember: those showing symptoms of illness must be left behind. Anyone who was near a sick person needs to be isolated until we are certain they were not infected. Our understanding of Phyriad is that it is highly contagious, so keep to smaller groups, and be vigilant. If anyone has so much as sniffles when we meet up at the North Crow Gate, no one will be allowed in."

Yossar stared at him, visibly shaken. "The words I do not have."

Bayard glanced up as Uluk circled high above. "We have a long way to go and a short time to get there, Yossar." The dark speck was taking shape as the Shadowfallen bled altitude.

"Several hundred gnomes capable of fighting we still have," Yossar said.

"No! You can ill-afford to lose anyone lest your people become extinct. Focus on getting to the Mofard Flats as quickly as you can."

"Very well," Yossar said.

"Good luck, my new friend."

The moment Bayard started back toward the tree line, he lifted a hand with three fingers raised. A moment later, the trumpet blast sounded.

Culthison ran out to meet Bayard. "Commander!" he shouted. "Raric is coming through the ranks as we speak!"

Bayard stopped midstride as though physically struck. "Raric? How is he?"

"He's stumbling through the forest like a drunkard. Apparently, he's behaving so erratically the men are staying clear of his path."

Bayard ran with the captain. "Is he…wearing the armor?"

Culthison nodded. "The men said it was like looking at the sun, the armor's so bright."

"When will he arrive?"

"The way he was shambling around, he could be another thirty minutes."

"I hope he's ready for a fight," Bayard said as they reached the tree line. "First Battalion must be ready to back up Raric, but I want the remainder of Enders Brigade gone the moment the fighting starts. The only gnomes not infected are preparing to leave for the Mofard Flats once the Shadowfallen has landed. That will leave thousands possibly infected with something that is highly contagious. If they end up evolving into something half as aggressive as we've heard, it will not bode well for anyone left in the field."

Culthison broke away, shouting orders to officers who rushed back to their commands to spark the men to action. Uluk was still soaring a few hundred feet up as if taking careful stock of what he was descending into. Bayard made his way to a small table with his battle gear carefully laid out.

Soldiers and cavaliers emerged from the forest. Swords rang, horses stamped and whinnied, and chains and spears rattled. Enders Brigade was ready for war.

As he often did before battle, Bayard disregarded the activity around him and withdrew into himself. His thoughts drifted across the histories, reminiscing over hard-fought battles. Some had gone well; others gave him nightmares so terrible he would wake in a shivering sweat. But the Shadowfallen was unlike anything Bayard had ever faced. If Raric was not of sound mind, the men would look to him to lead the bloody brawl. A thousand men against Uluk, with little hope of success.

A galloping horse approached from the eastern forest, and Bayard glanced back to see Tonna, his most trusted messenger, riding in on his indefatigable mare, Interrupted. Tonna was clear of his saddle before Interrupted had stopped.

"The general is coming this way, sir," Tonna said, his chest heaving.

"How does he look?" Bayard asked.

"He wouldn't respond to my voice, sir. He's definitely heading this way, so there must be intelligence left in him, but it's hard to say." Tonna inched closer. "I wouldn't expect much from him."

Bayard nodded and slid on freshly laundered linen pants and a soft undershirt. Next came a pair of leather pants with chain mail embedded into the fabric. A few light plates overlapped the front and sides of the pants down to his knees. He slipped into the tall leather boots and secured the side buckles, then tightened the long-knife sheath strapped to the boot.

Next, he put on the chain-mail shirt and cinched the buckles at his wrists. Tonna helped him with the armor plate that covered his upper body, strapping it to the backplate. Once that was buckled, Bayard reached for the leather belt and scabbard. On the right side of his belt was a small sheath with a long-knife. Bayard pulled on a pair of tight leather gloves and lifted his sword from the table.

The highly polished blade gleamed. The cross guard was a simple thing to look at, extending a few inches from the grip.

"How will the Fourwinds look tomorrow?" Bayard muttered rhetorically to Tonna as he marched out to join his army.

A dead calm had settled over the field as the Shadowfallen descended, his wings a vast expanse of darkness.

A great murmuring swept through the ranks as Uluk swooped above the trees over the perimeter of the field. Bayard could now see the huge black feathers of the Shadowfallen's enormous wingspan behind his broad, muscular back. His long legs dangled in the wind. Uluk leveled and dove across the field until he reached the midpoint where his wings flared. His body shot up several feet, then crashed his thick-taloned feet onto the two human chairs, scattering pine splinters into the long grass.

Despite that which had descended upon the field, there was little movement along the tree line of the Nameless Forest. The ranks of gnomes Bayard had seen earlier had thinned. The only constant throughout the forest was the coughing. Bayard hoped Commander Yossar was leading a remnant of healthy gnomes from the forest as the balance of his own men were now retreating to the Rainia Valley.

Uluk looked huge soaring above, but standing less than a hundred yards from Bayard, he was a giant. His wings folded tightly behind his round, broad shoulders. Large purple eyes surveyed the army before him. Hairless, and wearing only a pair of tight leather pants, he turned in a semicircle, as if displaying his considerable muscle mass for all to see. Uluk stood nine feet tall and, despite the wings, looked like a man with skin darker than anyone Bayard had ever seen. He carried only a five-foot-tall set of scales that resembled a cross with small swirling flames fluttering from either side. Uluk dropped the strange apparatus to the ground with a loud *thunk*.

The flames hanging from the scales mesmerized Bayard, reaching out to him. One misstep and it would all be over before it had begun, and he knew it. He swallowed to be sure he still had command of his tongue.

"Do what you can to get Raric here," Bayard said, but it was obvious Tonna heard nothing, his wild eyes fixated on the Shadowfallen.

Bayard grasped Tonna's arm and looked into his eyes. "Tonna, I need you to make sure Raric finds his way to this field. Then take another messenger with you and ride like the wind to the Crow's Nest. Tell Rowe of the Nest what you've seen here, and that most of the North Gnome Army has been infected with Phyriad. And that more infected gnomes have been sighted at the Stoneberg. The gnome commander now sees that Uluk has deceived them and means to destroy them. We have formed an alliance with Commander Yossar and the healthy remnant of the North Gnome Army. Tell Rowe that General Raric himself requests clemency and sanctuary for them."

Tonna was wide-eyed but responsive. "Yes, sir."

"I will join you after we deal with Uluk, bringing Enders Brigade to the safety of the Rainia Valley."

Bayard spun the messenger around, and Tonna leapt onto Interrupted's back and was away.

"Run off, has he, your beloved commander general?" Uluk's voice rumbled like rolling thunder. "There is wisdom in such fear."

Horses huffed and stamped, and the soldiers settled them as best they could.

Uluk crouched and gazed at the scales for long moments, then shook his head gravely as he rose to his full height. "Raric has been found wanting!" Uluk shouted. "A terrible sentence for a general. This charge is punishable by death. Bring me General Raric and you all may leave with your heads."

Bayard stared as the creature's words hung over the army like an ominous cloud. Raric had assured him he would arrive in time to deal with Uluk, but there was still no sign of him. Even with a thousand cavaliers at his side, Bayard was doubtful they could defeat such a creature, not to mention the threat looming behind it. The six catapults armed with Guilliad were abandoned, but the infected gnomes would soon attack others. If the contagion reached the human ranks, the battle would come to a decisive end.

"The two-wheeled cart you seek is approaching Dwenlin Thah even as we speak," Uluk announced, his voice deep and unnatural. "What little hope you may have had was foolhardy. My gift to your beloved capital city will soon be within the curtain wall."

The words struck Bayard so hard he stepped backward. He raised a heavy arm and signaled with two fingers, then four.

Anchored in the back of wagons, six large ballistas rolled out behind Bayard, twenty yards apart. Soldiers aimed the long iron bolts at the middle of the field.

Bayard swept his arm down, and another trumpet blasted. He took a step toward the Shadowfallen, and the cavaliers formed ten groups of a hundred riders each.

The Shadowfallen watched, unflinching, as the field came alive around him.

Bayard climbed into the saddle of his horse, stalling as much as he could, hoping General Raric would arrive. His hands trembled. He had given little thought to addressing Uluk, but he needed more time.

"Look at you, all full of wind and fire!" Bayard shouted. The fierce sound of his own voice surprised him and ignited his spirit.

Uluk reared, eyes narrowing. He crouched and grasped the thin chains of the scales with both hands. From each chain, a swirling ball of fire less than a foot in diameter dangled, too bright to behold. He raised both hands and spun the chains. They extended outward until the expanding balls of fire scorched the ground. Uluk threw his arms wide, the force sending both fireballs across the field in high arcs. They were eight feet wide when they struck the ground with terrific explosions. The field shook, and tongues of fire lashed in every direction.

Riders shouted, guiding their horses clear of the fire that rained down from the explosions. They pressed forward in a great concerted effort to overwhelm the Shadowfallen.

Uluk fixed his eyes on Bayard, a fierce smile across his tight lips. The chains pulled back the fireballs toward the center of the field, sizzling the grass in broad swaths until all that remained was blackened soil.

The ballistas released long iron bolts in a low trajectory, and the archers followed with a volley of arrows.

Uluk jerked the chains, and the fireballs flew at him with blinding speed until both exploded together, consuming Uluk in a firestorm. The iron bolts glowed bright orange before disappearing into the fire. The arrows burned up long before reaching the Shadowfallen, who disappeared within the flames.

Bayard drew his sword and eased his horse forward. The cavaliers joined him. Despite the distance, Bayard shielded his face against the heat. The rumble of hooves filled the air as the riders picked up speed, spreading out into a wide circle along the edges of the clearing as they prepared another volley.

As quickly as the fireballs had slammed together, they came apart once again. Uluk twirled the chains, flashing a menacing grin of sharp fangs. He lifted one arm up, spinning the weapon like a fiery mace and chain, then launched it. Countless soldiers leapt from their horses as the flames spread. Screams drowned out the pounding hooves. Bayard tumbled from his saddle and pressed his face into the dirt. The blast of heat flew several feet above him, killing his horse instantly. He scrambled to his feet, snatched up his sword, and charged the Shadowfallen, dodging small ground fires, fallen soldiers, and terrified horses. Chaos reigned around him.

The Shadowfallen took his eyes off Bayard and jerked the fireball back while sending the other into the nearest group of cavaliers.

The six ballistas thumped, sending more iron bolts into the fray. Three missed their mark and three were about to slam into Uluk, but the Shadowfallen shot a hand out. The iron bolts ricocheted off an unseen force and crashed against the south bluffs.

Bayard was less than ten yards away when a dozen cavaliers lowered their lances and rode straight at Uluk. The fireball jerked back, crashing through the attackers, and riders went down hard. Bayard dove to the ground. Flaming horses ran wildly in every direction before collapsing. He struggled to his feet and rushed between infernos.

As Bayard raised his sword, Uluk glanced over to see the attacker bearing down on him. A blade like pure lightning appeared in Uluk's hand and one fireball died out. His other hand brought the second fireball around in a high arc to keep the riders at bay.

Bayard shouted a battle cry and lunged at Uluk with surprising speed. Uluk parried, and the moment their swords struck, a jolt of electricity blew Bayard back ten yards. Bayard forced his eyes open, but the rest of his body was inert. He tried to rise but could not feel his legs. He willed his arm to reach for his sword, but his arm did not respond. He lay helpless as the battle floundered around him.

Uluk brought the ball of fire around in a continuous orbit, keeping the remaining attackers at bay. A group of cavaliers almost broke through his defenses but checked their horses short of the extreme heat.

Throughout the field, corpses burned. A quarter of the cavaliers were dead or dying. The survivors rode out near the tree lines to regroup. Some noticed their fallen commander and fled east into the forest. Others slowed their mounts, waiting for Bayard to rise. At the same time, several gnomes staggered from the Nameless Forest, their hollow eyes staring at the living.

From the eastern forest, something lumbered toward the battlefield.

The juggernaut arrived, red as a blood moon, shaking the earth with each powerful stride. Soldiers recoiled from the sudden appearance behind them. The red blur stumbled headlong into a tree, snapping the trunk with a crushing impact. Riders scattered for cover as the falling fir crashed through the limbs of other trees before hitting the ground with a terrific thud.

General Raric stood, his dragon armor shimmering so bright in the sunlight that Uluk's fireballs paled in comparison. Thick red hide covered in scales formed a tight helm around his head with a visor of white bone over his brow. Razor talons lined the back of both arms, and short horns protruded from his shoulders. Clawed hands slashed at the air. A row of curved horns ran down his spine, dividing the crimson scales enveloping his torso. His legs, layered with smaller scales, bulged with muscle mass as they propelled him forward.

He almost toppled over a few times but somehow kept his feet beneath him. He appeared disoriented and had yet to notice the Shadowfallen. When he slowed long enough to rise to his full height, Raric was every bit as tall as Uluk.

The moment his eyes fell upon the Shadowfallen, Raric stretched his arms wide and roared. Uluk stumbled backward, soldiers covered their ears and cried out, and the infected gnomes stopped in their tracks. Bayard widened his eyes but was still unable to move.

The Shadowfallen shot his arm up and spun the fireball. Raric had no time to react before the weapon hit him. The explosion rained fire in a wide swath, and Raric disappeared in the flames.

After a long moment, a roar escaped the firestorm, deeper and louder than the first.

Uluk leapt, enormous wings propelling him upward.

Raric sprinted from the flames with eight-foot strides. His appearance was now more dragon-like than human. The helm he wore covered his face and extended in a long snout. Large fangs flashed as he roared again, pursuing the creature that had taken so much of his humanity. He hunched suddenly, writhing as if in pain. His shoulders shook, and a pair of leathery wings unfolded.

The Shadowfallen gained altitude, and it seemed Raric was too late. He leapt into the air. There was a brilliant flash of light followed by a boom so powerful that many riders were thrown from their saddles. Raric—looking more like the Red Dragon that Bayard remembered from the Dragon War—shot through the air toward Uluk the Shadowfallen.

His wingspan was at least four times the size of Uluk's, thrusting him upward with inconceivable power, closing the gap in seconds. Raric's colossal head shifted, gnashing at the Shadowfallen's wings.

Uluk banked and launched several bolts of white lighting. Raric's body jolted against the impact and plunged downward before his wings caught a current. Without hesitation, he shot forward again. The Shadowfallen banked from side to side. Raric circled.

With a final terrific thrust of his wings, Raric reached out with razor-sharp claws. He plucked the Shadowfallen from the sky as if he were a tiny songbird, piercing his feet like spikes driven into a cross. Uluk shrieked as he dangled upside down. Raric wrapped his other claw around Uluk's chest and squeezed. The Shadowfallen came apart in two gruesome pieces.

Raric tossed Uluk's remains above him, then reared his head back with a neck that seemed to extend unnaturally. A blast of fire exploded from his mouth, incinerating the Shadowfallen. Fine ash floated down from the blue sky.

Raric soared higher, then released a second eruption of fire that streaked ahead of him. Moments later, the Red Dragon melted from view. Bayard's eyes fluttered, and the battlefield went dark and silent.

※

"Tranton, what was that?" a ranger whispered. He peered through the trees without giving his position away to the sickly gnomes below.

"Stay on task, Mio," Tranton hissed.

Another roar filled the air.

"Sounds like a bloody dragon," Mio said.

"When I woke this morning, of all the ways I pictured this day going, I never came close to this nightmare."

Mio shook his head. "Some gnomes have fled, but many are still down there."

"I heard they might be infected with Phyriad," Tranton said.

On the massive branch between them was a large pile of rocks wrapped in a fishing net. A group of gnomes approached a wagon beneath the net. The gnomes coughed and hacked, barely able to walk as they moved toward the horses harnessed to the wagon. The flask of Guilliad mounted on the wagon was directly under Tranton and Mio. If the wagon moved even a few feet, their painstaking preparations would be in vain.

"Should we wait for—"

Before the ranger could finish his sentence, a low trumpet blast sounded. There was no questioning where the signal had come from. The rangers were about to make this nightmare a lot worse.

"Strangest day ever," Mio said.

Tranton rose to his knees as Mio worked the knife in quick slices on the thick rope. Below, a gnome fumbled with the wagon harness. A second before the wagon lurched forward, two hundred pounds of rock fell from forty feet above. The two rangers watched the rocks fall despite knowing they should have been fleeing.

Several gnomes cried out, but it was too late; the rocks shattered the flask of Guilliad. Liquid splashed around the wagon, instantly transforming to gas. A thin cloud of smoke rose, and the wagon and the grass beneath it disintegrated. The leather harnesses dissolved, allowing the horses to run. Shouts rang throughout the forest as the rest of the rangers dropped similar nets filled with rocks. All six flasks of Guilliad shattered within seconds.

Many of the infected gnomes were only now emerging from their tents, but they were so delirious they failed to notice the surrounding danger. The gnomes that had the wherewithal to realize what had happened shouted for their comrades to leave the tents and run.

Mio and Tranton scurried along the branches, jumping from

one tree to another. Trunks disintegrated, toppling one giant willow at a time. Throughout the forest, trees collapsed into dust as a warm breeze spread the ever-expanding Guilliad. Crashing trees blended with screaming gnomes, and the rangers fled from tree to tree until they cleared the forest.

The cavaliers heard the rocks shattering the flasks of Guilliad and prepared to ride eastward. Hundreds of gnomes tumbled from the forest, wailing and gnashing their teeth. Their bulbous eyes settled on the soldiers and horses. With a dissonant cry, the gnomes stumbled forward in a frenzied horde. The soldiers in the field jerked their reins, shouting at their horses and kicking their flanks, desperate to flee the Nameless Forest for the safety of the Rainia Valley.

CHAPTER 36

The Rainia Valley

Joe sat beside Dench, leaning forward in the driver's seat as the wagon bounced along the final leg of the journey from Fairbay to the Crow's Nest. Nostalgia overcame him, having not seen the entrance to the Rainia Valley in almost two hundred years. Joe couldn't recall the name of this road, but it could easily be *Memory Lane* today. He stretched his aching back, removed his wide-brimmed straw hat, and released his ponytail to allow the wind to blow through his hair. He breathed in the familiar scent of lupines that sweetened the rich aroma of the stately firs of the Epping Forest. It was the smell of home. The procession of wagons ahead had thrown dust in his face for most of the trip, but he smiled in spite of it and all the filth he had witnessed in his long life.

Dench guided the covered wagon through the pass where the road snaked between the Hillron Mountains and the Misty Gorge. Through the trees, the North Crow Gate loomed before them. "Been a long time since you no see her," Dench said with a broad smile. His massive hands rested in his lap with the reins dangling from his fingers. "You be home now."

"It's been so very long," Joe said in his slow, rhythmic way.

Near the gate, they approached a clearing surrounded by fir trees, where refugees gathered under the ample shade. Soldiers were helping them set up tents. Gloriana and a small army of volunteers worked to keep everyone fed and watered. Joe tucked his hair back under his hat and surveyed the weary faces of so many displaced people. This was not the Rainia Valley he remembered.

A horse pulled up beside their wagon and brightened Joe's melancholy. Will was riding a large brown mare with Ryowyn nestled behind him. He wore a broad-rimmed leather hat and the top hooks of his shirt were unfastened. Resting across his lap was his shotgun, which had been unnecessary on the return trip, considering the escort of cavaliers from Marauders Brigade. Ryowyn wore his Trannalun cloak.

Joe burst out laughing. "Looks like Billy the Kid and Little Red Riding Hood."

"Evenin', cowboy," Will said, tipping his hat.

Joe laughed harder.

Ryowyn pulled back the hood of the Trannalun cloak as they rode through the shade. The cloak not only protected her teal skin from the hot sun, but the magical fabric kept her cool.

"Your laugh is contagious," Ryowyn said as Joe's booming laugh subsided.

Joe wiped away a few tears. "Young lady, if you had any idea how far Will has come since I first met him on the bridge that crosses the narrows of Lake Commando, you would be laughing with me."

"You just made a clean spot on your face, Joe," Will said.

This time it was Dench who laughed. "We so dirty," he said.

The half-orc leaned back and spoke through the flap in the wagon cover. "Not long now."

The exotic faces looking back at Dench and Joe were tight, dry, and chapped. The merpeople had used most of the pails of seawater to keep moisturized, and now they admonished the younglings to be patient and not scratch.

"Not long now," Joe repeated. "Almost home."

Will smiled as Rowe approached the caravan riding a black mare. He stood in his stirrups, his eyes scanning the wagons until he noticed Dench and Joe.

"Good to have you back," he said, guiding his horse beside Will's.

"Fairbay's gone, Rowe," Will said in a quiet, solemn voice. "And the Niasa Sea was a nightmare. We saved as many as we could, but—"

Rowe pressed a finger against his lips. "Let's talk about it later, Will. These people have been through enough trauma."

Will glanced around and nodded. "Okay, well, before we set off on your next crazy adventure, how about a little fishing first?"

Rowe smiled. "You've earned more than a little rest," he said. "But there's a favor I need to ask of you."

Will shifted to the side and leaned back to Ryowyn. "I think we should make a break for it before he asks!"

Ryowyn wrapped her arms around him.

"What do you need?" Will asked.

Rowe pointed two fingers to his eyes.

Will clued in to what was happening in the clearing. Refugees were arriving from all over the Fourwinds, but with no way of identifying harvesters, they were quarantined outside the gate. The revelation struck him like a splash of cold water.

"Man, I'm sorry, Rowe. I didn't realize what was going on. Where do you need me?"

Rowe eased his horse closer and kept his voice low. "We need to keep your gift a secret, Will; otherwise, there would be an enormous bounty on your head by day's end."

Will nodded, looking around to see if anyone might have overheard them.

"Morgan and Julie have been working on protocols for allowing people into the valley. For now, our main concern is harvesters. But very soon, we'll have a bigger problem: those infected with Phyriad trying to get into the valley. Some may not even know they were infected, so we're building quarantine areas like this one."

"That's fine, just tell me where you need me," Will said.

"Thank you, Will," Rowe said as the caravan slowed to a halt. "Looks like the first wagon has arrived at the gates. If you and Ryowyn will follow me, I'll take you to the front where we'll get instructions from Morgan."

"Here," Dench said, offering Joe the reins. "If we find harvester, me kill it for Ruint." He reached back for his ax, jumped off the wagon, and marched toward the front of the caravan.

"Sounds like you guys are all ready for this," Will said.

"Morgan and Julie are a driven and intelligent pair," Rowe said. "When it comes to organization, there's no one like them."

Will smiled. "Go ahead, Rowe, we'll catch up." He guided the mare to the back of the wagon, and Ryowyn leaned over and pulled the flap open. Inside, Almithara sat with several grieving families, most of whom had lost husbands and fathers.

"It won't be long now, Mother. Will and I are heading to the gate to help get people safely into the Rainia Valley."

Almithara's eyes were half open and red around the edges, but she nodded and forced a smile.

Will and Ryowyn walked along the side of the road past dusty wagons laden with supplies and travel-weary humans and mer-people. Construction on the wall continued despite the influx of traffic. Hammers pounded on the new shake roof over the wall walk. Morgan stood outside the massive gate, and when she saw Will and Ryowyn, she rushed over to greet them with excited hugs.

"Thank you for helping with this, guys. Rowe just told me you've already been through so much in Fairbay. I'm so sorry about your home and for all you've lost, Ryowyn."

Ryowyn's eyes glistened. "I'm thankful my parents, and many of our people, survived. We have many lost ones to grieve, but for now, we must get the survivors to the water to prevent further loss."

Morgan nodded. "The mer soldiers your father left to explore Rainia Lake have reported that there's an old settlement your ancestors once had along the western shores. They believe that will provide a suitable place to rebuild. But we need to be careful...," She glanced at Will.

"Yes, Rowe explained the situation," Will said. "But he mentioned you have a plan to help things go smoothly?"

Morgan handed Will a roofing shake, a large piece of parchment, and a quill. "I know this is unusual for us, Will, but you can use the shake as a clipboard, and this is the best I could find since we didn't bring pens and paper from home."

"It's okay, Morgan," Will said, groaning as he took the quill. "I have some experience with these."

"Okay, you'll have to tell me about that some time," Morgan said.

She directed them to an open space near the wall where she lowered her voice. "Here's my plan. We'll check each wagon, and if you see nothing that alarms you, pretend to scribble something important. I'll write a random number on the side of the wagon and off they go. If you see anything that concerns you, write a brief description of the harvester. When I read that, I'll write two sevens on the wagon. We'll allow that wagon through the first gate where Rowe and Dench will deal with the harvester."

"That makes sense," Will said. "Wow. Beauty, brawn, and brains. I'm glad you're on our team!"

"Very funny, Will." Morgan leaned closer, and they almost bumped heads. "Have you seen any harvesters yet?"

Will shook his head. "Not since the Clover Fields."

"Perfect. Let's get going so we can introduce these people to their new homes." Morgan turned on her heels, waved at Rowe standing inside the first gate, then marched toward the first wagon with Will and Ryowyn trailing behind her.

⚜

The sun was setting behind the surrounding firs when the final wagon from Fairbay passed through the North Crow Gate. The small group of refugees were also cleared to enter. Will was thankful he had only identified one harvester, and Rowe and Dench had discretely killed it.

"Lock the gates," Rowe shouted.

Soldiers collected supplies and tools and prepared to close the thick wooden gates. Iron chains rattled above as soldiers in the gatehouse lowered the portcullis.

"Wait!" Rowe shouted as two riders charged up the road. Their familiar red-and-gold tunics hung open, flapping in the wind. "It's Tonna!"

The horses stopped in a cloud of dust. "Rowe, we bring news from Enders Brigade," Tonna said.

Morgan and Will offered them their waterskins, and the riders drank. Dench and Joe approached, eyes fixed on Tonna.

"Speak freely, Tonna," Rowe said.

"Enders Brigade met the North Gnome Army at the edge of the Nameless Forest, beyond the Hollowtangle. Brigadier Bayard has formed an alliance with their commander, Yossar."

"To what end?" Rowe asked.

"A sickness broke out in the gnome ranks, infecting most of their army. Yossar agreed that Uluk the Shadowfallen has been using them and intends to destroy the gnomes. General Raric requests that Yossar and the healthy gnomes be granted sanctuary here in the valley."

"You spoke with General Raric?" Rowe asked.

"Not directly. I saw him—rather, a form of him—just before he reached the battlefield. When I left, Commander Bayard and Enders Brigade were facing the Shadowfallen, waiting for the general to arrive." Tonna shuddered. "Uluk is an intimidating presence, Rowe, but what the general has become would frighten a dozen Shadowfallen."

"He has become the Red Dragon," Joe said in a low voice.

Everyone turned their heads to the elder Callum Sage.

"Druid Margrave said there can be only one soul that lives in a dragon's hide." Joe closed his eyes and bowed his head. "If Raric has transformed, he has lost his soul, even if he defeats Uluk."

Rowe shook his head. "No. *No!* We can't lose him again." He turned to Tonna. "What about the two-wheeled cart that was said to carry Phyriad, Tonna? And the flasks of Guilliad?"

"We assume the cart has been taken to Dwenlin Thah. If so, it's already inside the curtain wall. As for the flasks, if they survived the battle with Uluk, we had rangers ready to destroy them.”

“What else, Tonna?” Rowe asked.

“A messenger from the Stoneberg reported seeing gnomes from the west who might have been infected with Phyriad. As I travel, I hear rumors of a strange sickness spreading throughout the Fourwinds—in the west, the north, and even among the South Gnome Army.”

Will glanced from Tonna, to Rowe, then to the others as they all stood gaping. After a moment, a raven cawed from a nearby fir, breaking the silence.

“How soon will Yossar and the gnomes be here, Tonna?”

“I estimate within four days.”

“And Enders Brigade?”

“Difficult to say, Rowe. If the battle ends as quickly as I imagine, they could be here in four or five days.”

Rowe placed his hands on his hips. “We will be ready for them all.”

Morgan nodded. “We plan on quarantining refugees outside the walls until we know they are healthy, so both armies will be part of that process. Mom’s working on those details as we speak.”

“If it’s all true, it might be a long time before any of us leaves this valley,” Rowe said.

⚜

The following morning, Will, Ryowyn, Rowe, and Morgan rode out toward Rainia Lake. Will turned his head often to gaze at the massive castle to the north. The Crow’s Nest was row upon row of battlements, embrasures, parapets, and rooflines, offering something new to look at for hours on end. Ryowyn pressed against his back, clutching his waist. A long caravan of covered wagons was moving along the west side of the town of Rainia, which would soon become a small city.

Will leaned his head back. "I can feel you trembling," he whispered.

"With Wrathan gone, my people will look to me, as will my father and mother," she said.

"I've seen the way you treat people, Ryowyn. They're drawn to you."

"I have always preferred the company of common people, but now I will need to tell them that all will be well."

Will rubbed his clammy hands on his thighs. "Do you believe all will be well?"

"I do, my Will. But there is so much to be done while so many of our people grieve. We've lost so much." She rested her chin on his shoulder.

"I love you with everything I am, Ryowyn," Will said.

"You are my safe cove, Will."

"That will never change, Ryowyn." Will paused. "I wish I could tell you how this is all going to work with us, but I have no idea. All I know is that I long to spend the rest of my days loving you, serving you, with all I am. Even though I won't be able to be with you in the depths of Rainia Lake as you settle your people—"

"*Our* people, my Will."

Will tried to swallow, but it caught in a gasp and he coughed.

Rowe's horse drifted closer. "Are you all right, Will?"

"Yes, just a little choked up."

Morgan chuckled, but Rowe gave him one of his classic confused expressions.

"If you follow the northeastern shoreline," Rowe said, pointing past the caravan, "all the way to that village at the mouth of the Foglan River…"

Will squinted, then nodded.

"…that new town is being called Little Hammerclaw. Keep following the lake for half a mile south. At the base of that escarpment is a fine-looking cottage that Tranas once owned. To be honest, to call it a cottage would be a disservice."

"Okay," Will said. "I think I see the area."

"Well, you should see the new owners. A strange couple, really. The woman is as beautiful as a summer's day, and the man is—"

"A bit of a blockhead," Morgan chimed in, grinning. "He was married to her for a couple of weeks before he even realized it." She and Will laughed together as Rowe watched them and arched an eyebrow. Ryowyn wore a slight smile and hugged Will tighter. "She is…poetry in motion," Morgan continued.

"While he dances with two left feet," Will added.

"She came from royalty, and he came from…dragons," Rowe said with a broad smile as if he were suddenly in on the joking.

The smiles faded from Will's and Morgan's faces.

"What does *that* mean?" Ryowyn asked.

"Hmm.…" Will pondered his response. "That part of the couple's story will have to wait for another chapter."

"So…the cottage," Morgan said, changing the subject. "Tell us more, Rowe."

"Only a few steps from the water," he said. "You can see the dock from here. We used to sit out there fishing all day…"

Morgan reached over to touch his arm.

"I miss him. But I believe he's quite happy with what is to become of his cottage." He smiled at Will. "Not to mention the fact that you have a standing invitation to the Crow's Nest and access to anything within the walls, Will. Anything."

"Thanks, Rowe. But I'll be purchasing all my supplies in Little Hammerclaw," Will said.

"*Purchasing?*" Morgan said. "Don't they use gold for trade here in the Fourwinds?"

Will winked at her.

"Does this have anything to do with that quick trip to Timmins you made before we came back to the Fourwinds?" Morgan asked.

"Before I met you, Morgan, I had cleaned out three bank accounts and placed a special order for gold coins. A precious-metals dealer in Timmins was holding it for me—just under seven pounds of solid gold coins." Will grinned. "I carried them through the Gateway in the duffle with my shotgun."

Morgan laughed. "*Like an onion.* That's what Joe said about you, Will, while you were searching for Ryowyn in Lake Commando. *So many layers.*"

Will shrugged. "An Owens always pays his way." He puffed his chest, smiling at Morgan and Rowe, as content as if he'd just finished a Christmas dinner with his family. *My new family*, he thought.

Morgan laughed again, but Rowe's face was solemn. "You've certainly paid your way, Will. We all have," he said. "And I suspect more will be required of us in the days ahead."

"I like the way you said *us*, Rowe," Will said. "Let's try to stick together from now on."

CHAPTER 37

DWENLIN THAH

In the fertile northern plains a hard day's ride north of the Nameless Forest loomed a forty-five-foot-high curtain wall, a feat of human engineering. Each stone block was larger than a vegetable cart, expertly carved and fitted together for four miles around the densely populated city of Dwenlin Thah. Every three hundred yards along the wall, guard towers rose another ten feet, each topped with red conical roofs contrasting with the brilliant-blue sky. Atop each guard tower was a flag marking troop divisions and border patrols. Soldiers manned the wall walks as people arrived for various reasons from across the Fourwinds. These days, most visitors were refugees.

Only one harvest time had passed since Alarra of the House of Aldor had betrayed her brothers, Harroc and Raric, seizing the throne to become High Queen of Dwenlin Thah. She had immediately ordered all but four city gates closed and sealed, with each portcullis locked down against the threat of gnome invasion. The four open gates were continuously congested with lineups, often several hours long, as people journeyed to the safety of the capital. The roads leading to the four gates were fully exposed to the sun, providing a frustrating end to a long journey.

Brynlee Mason, the queen's governess since Alarra's birth, stood at an open window of a castle tower, silently watching the dreary line of refugees far below. Fear of war had driven many of these families to abandon homesteads and land cultivated for generations. Leaving all that was familiar, they also abandoned hope of finding anything remaining should they be lucky enough to return. Their plight was not unfamiliar to Brynlee. Half a century ago, she had arrived at the capital gates with her parents, fleeing the onset of war. Fortune had smiled upon Brynlee, and someone in the king's service had offered her an opportunity to work for the royal family. Now, Brynlee wondered if such kindness still existed within the walls of Dwenlin Thah. She sighed deeply and stepped away from the window, into the High Council chamber.

The large room was furnished only by a U-shaped ironwood table surrounded by twelve armless chairs for royally appointed councillors. At the head of the table, equally dividing the councillors' chairs, was an ornately carved, gold-gilded plush chair—more like a throne—for the ruling monarch. On the walls hung life-size portraits of former kings and queens, ever-present reminders of the kingdom's glorious heritage. Brynlee raised her eyes to the high, buttressed ceiling and imagined the spirits of bygone monarchs and councillors gathered like a cloud of witnesses. She prayed for their wisdom to rain down.

Queen Alarra sat in the gold-gilded chair, poring over the plethora of parchments strewn across the table. The four-hour meeting of the High Council had recently concluded, and the haggard look on the queen's face suggested it had not ended well.

Her knitted brows, crease-lined eyes, and pursed lips made it difficult to discern whether she was angry or completely confused.

"Careful, Your Majesty," Brynlee said as she ventured into the chamber. "I recognize that fretful mien. It disrupts my sleep every time I see it."

Alarra tilted her head toward Brynlee and stiffened but kept her hands on the pile of parchments. For a split second, the queen's eyes narrowed and shifted left and right, then softened.

Brynlee licked her dry lips and wiped her palms on her woolen dress. Trying to combat the slouch and limp that dogged her aging bones, she ambled toward the table. Although she longed for the wisdom of the silent cloud of witnesses she imagined above, Brynlee was not yet ready to leave this life and join them. She pulled the outermost chair from the council table and settled gracefully into the hard seat. With a shaky index finger, she tucked a strand of gray hair behind her ear. She faced the queen, determined to voice her opinion.

"You speak far too much," Alarra said, as if expecting unsolicited conversation.

Brynlee forced a doting smile. "You keep reminding me of that, yet my tongue remains where it has always been."

Alarra sighed and turned her attention to a parchment. "The High Council is creating more problems than they can resolve."

"Remember, my dear: you created the High Council to shirk… er, to relieve yourself of many of your duties as High Queen."

The queen flicked a fiery glance at her governess. "And as High Queen, I can uncreate it."

Brynlee peered at the parchments. "Planning on running the war effort yourself? Perhaps I should ask the maidens to prepare an armored gown for you—something with some blue in it, of course."

"You're unusually biting today." Alarra pulled a kerchief from her sleeve and dabbed a bead of sweat from her pasty white forehead.

"I'm beginning to realize that you will not change before I step into the next life," Brynlee said. "The thought of leaving the Fourwinds no better than when I arrived pains me more than old age ever could."

Alarra glared. "In case your mind is failing you—which I think it is—there's no greater position than serving the High Queen of Dwenlin Thah."

Brynlee's throat tightened as if to warn her against saying too much, but she would not be silenced. "We both know what you did to become queen, and I'm learning to live with that. What pains me is what you have done as queen."

Alarra reclined and placed an elbow on the padded armrest of her throne. "And what is it that pains you so, my dear governess?"

Brynlee inhaled, trying to cool her boiling blood. "Nothing. You've done nothing as queen. Why did you go to such efforts to take something you never wanted?"

Alarra shrugged. "Perhaps I didn't want my brother Harroc to be king?"

"Shades, woman! How I failed you." Brynlee blinked at tears that obscured her vision of the queen. "You could have done so much."

"Which brings us to the present dilemma and why I am considering dismantling the High Council. I want to take command of the army."

Brynlee straightened.

"Could I do any worse than the High Council?"

"I believe you could."

Alarra scoffed. "Perhaps. The High Council is very confused about recent accounts of a battle in the Nameless Forest between Raric's brigades and the North Gnome Army. But if reports of Sidara's demise and Uluk's defeat are true, then maybe we've already won. Imagine ending the war with me at the helm instead of Raric?"

"Just because Raric has returned does not mean Sidara and Uluk are dead."

"If they aren't, they soon will be." Alarra rubbed her temples with the tips of her fingers. "Raric will see to that."

"So, if you believe Sidara is no longer a threat, why did you summon everyone unwilling to heed Raric's call to arms?"

Alarra gaped, as if Brynlee had just asked why a rabbit would dive into its hole when chased by a fox. "To defend me when Raric comes for my head, of course."

"But *all* the field commanders he roused have heeded his call," Brynlee said.

The queen lowered her head and shuffled a handful of parchments. "Well, you mean most commanders," she mumbled. "The old guard—those faithful to the crown—remain faithful to me. And together, they represent many years of experience."

Brynlee smiled but then realized Alarra was serious. "Why do you think those old crows serve in the garrison?"

"I beg your pardon?"

"Most of the men you speak of were terrible commanders in the field, Alarra. Terrible! But because of their family names, the High Council gave them different commands—posts that did not get people killed when the so-called *faithful* commanders made poor decisions."

Alarra huffed and waved a dismissive hand. "Nevertheless, we still control large numbers, and there's a forty-five-foot wall between us and our enemies."

"If we end up with fifteen thousand soldiers within the wall willing to fight by week's end, as you claim, well, maybe you won't end up hanging from the gallows. But we both have our doubts."

The queen raised her chin and tapped a particular parchment with her index finger. "Our strength is in our numbers."

"You had better hope so, because from a command perspective, your brother has a tendency to cut through numbers far greater than his own."

"You forget, Brynlee, that he still has to contend with the gnome army. That is a tall order for our fair general with no wall to fight behind."

"Have you ever known Raric to need a fortress to succeed in battle? That brother of yours is always on the offensive. It would not surprise me in the least if he decimates the gnome army."

"Which is why I insisted to the High Council that we be ready should Raric set his sights on the crown." Alarra hung her head and gripped both arms of her throne. "But they are blind fools."

Brynlee paused, choosing her words. "Raric will not be coming for the crown, Alarra, but for what it sits upon."

The queen shot to her feet and jabbed her fists into her hips. "Why did you even come here? I assume you have better things to do than launch your fiery darts at me."

Brynlee slowly rose to her feet and took a few steps to the nearest window. Sunlight warmed her cheeks. "You should get some rest, Alarra."

The queen sneered. "Yes, Mother."

"No, I am not your mother. You killed her. I'm simply here to get you back into your bed."

Alarra gaped as if Brynlee had just slapped her face.

Brynlee wondered if she had gone too far. Given the queen's

penchant for removing those who defied her, Brynlee might be joining that cloud of witnesses sooner than expected.

While Alarra brooded, Brynlee gazed at the congested roadway that bordered the castle. She noticed a small, two-wheeled cart driven by an elderly man wearing little more than rags. The man's smile and constant waving caught her attention and held it fast. Beside him sat an old woman, and even from a distance, Brynlee could see the woman's arm linked around his. They looked like a couple that had been married for many years. Behind them, in the box of the cart, were two children, filthy, with unkempt hair and ratty clothes. They were far too young to be the couple's children, so Brynlee assumed they were grandchildren. Times being what they were, their parents were probably dead or conscripted into military service.

Despite how impoverished they seemed, all four were all waving, drawing people in as the children handed out something Brynlee could not see because of the distance. Judging by the excitement around the cart, especially from other children, Brynlee assumed they were handing out some type of food. As the cart rolled down the street, Brynlee squinted and saw a sign with bold lettering on the back of the wagon. "Maple Syrup Candy," she read aloud. "You see, Alarra: kindness and generosity are still alive in this city. Such simple acts by common folk will change the face of the Fourwinds."

The queen scowled in silence, but her eyes narrowed, darting from side to side. It was the same look she'd had when Brynlee had entered the council chamber. Brynlee had dismissed the mien as anger or annoyance at the interruption. But now she realized it was something more. The High Queen of Dwenlin Thah was afraid. Brynlee had held Alarra's hand her whole life, but that grip was loosening. Without Brynlee, Alarra would be alone and unloved, if she had ever opened her heart to love.

In truth, the queen's lack of trust in her governess was warranted. Brynlee's loyalty was shifting. But in these cloudy, unsettled days, she was uncertain where her loyalty would land.

For the next two days, the four harvesters, disguised as poor grandparents and their grandchildren, were greeted with appreciative smiles as they crisscrossed the city until the two-wheeled cart was empty. In total, they distributed three thousand two hundred and twenty-seven candies.

Glossary of Terms and Names

Abaddon: harvester who passed through the Gateway from the Fourwinds to the contemporary world

Acttun: \akt-un\ an eastern city in the Fourwinds, home of artists, fortunetellers, seers, wielders, warlocks, magicians, sorcerers, wizards, and more

Acttun Academy: school in Acttun for training wizards

Addolay and Marlay Bonicle: wizard brothers; taught at the Acttun Academy; their dispute over the young student Sidara led to a dual in which Marlay killed Addolay, putting an end to the Academy

Aerodice Mountains: western range in the Fourwinds that separates gnome and human realms

Akia Tibers: elder in Fairbay

Alarra: of the House of Aldor, High Queen of Dwenlin Thah; Raric's sister

Almithara Ayoust: mer queen of the Niasa Sea; Ryowyn's mother

Arden Forest: fictional name of the large forest outside Will's home of Cochrane

Arman Bayard: brigadier/commander of Enders Brigade

Blackie: Lillie's horse

Bremer: Rowe's friend; former Callum Sage; rogue

Brynlee Mason: \brin-lee\ Queen Alarra's governess

Coach: Morgan's fencing coach

Crow's Nest, the: castle in the Rainia Valley; home of the Records of Time and the Gateway

CTV: a Canadian television network

Culthison: captain of Enders Brigade's Second Dragoon Company

Dadore: \da-dor\ alchemy student; friend of Kydaris

Dench: half-orc; half of Rowe's personal guard

Devin: helicopter pilot in Cochrane

Druid's Slumber: powerful spell used by druids to put people into deep sleep like a coma

Dragon War: battle in the Fourwinds three years before time of Book 1 in which General Raric killed Scarlas the Red Dragon

Dwenlin Thah: capital city of the Fourwinds; throne of the High Queen Alarra

Elias Ward: chief secretary of Enders Brigade

Ellywick: gnome healer; deceased (Book 1)

Enders Brigade: part of the human army in the Fourwinds; commanded by Twell Henowing; usually based in Dwenlin Thah; insignia is a wolf's paw print

Endrow River: narrow river that flows from the Aerodice Mountains, through the Nameless Forest, and into the Niasa Sea

Epping Forest: wooded area east of the Misty Gorge, stretching from north of the Rainia Valley to the central valley; home of very tall, ancient trees and the tree-dwelling, apelike species known as holgs

Eurynome: \yoor-i-nome\ harvester who passed through the Gateway from the Fourwinds to the contemporary world

Fadua: \fad-wah\ an alchemist imprisoned by Sidara in the Waerdreath dungeons

Fairbay: peaceful fishing village on the southern shore of the Niasa Sea

First Dragoon Company: part of Fourwinds human army; 100 Light Armored Cavaliers and 100 Archers

Gateway, the: magical passageway/portal from the Fourwinds (Records of Time) into the contemporary world (specifically, a cabin in the Arden Forest near Will's home)

Gauntlet, the: three-hundred-foot long entrance to the Crow's Nest castle

Gloriana: worker and friend of Rowe who lives at the Crow's Nest

Grant Finley: Morgan's father; pastor of Baptist church in Cochrane

Grudum: \groo-dum\ gnome guard at the Clover Fields

Gryton Mines: iron mines located along northern shore of the Niasa Sea

Guilliad: \gil-ee-ad\ powerful elixir developed under Sidara's rule; when liquid form is released into the air, it turns into a vapor that disintegrates anything living it comes into contact with

Gunther: soldier who fought at the South Crow Gate

Habina Ocean: \ha-bee-nah\ forms the western border of the Fourwinds

Half-orc: ostracized race born of union of orc and humans living east of the Hillron Mountains; tolerated in the Fourwinds but friends and allies of Callum Sages

Hammerclaw: stronghold city in the south-central region of the Fourwinds; commanded by the Iron Lord

Hansla: works at the Recovery Ale House and Inn

Harroc: Queen Alarra's and Raric's brother

Hillron Mountains: range south and east of the Rainia Valley; home of the half-orc community

Histories, the: books documenting the history of the Fourwinds; studied and preserved by the Callum Sages; kept in the Records of Time

Holgs: apelike creatures that live in the treetops of the Epping Forest

Hollowtangle: large forest west of the Niasa Sea; home of the Druid Forest and the Maidstone tower; former home to the People of the River Country

House of Aldor: royal family line in the Fourwinds

Homas: works at Recovery Ale House and Inn

Illious: \ill-ee-us\ Master Alchemist

Illious Fire: explosive weapon developed by Illious

Illume: caretaker at the Maidstone

Interrupted: Tonna's horse

Iron Dragon: also known as Natas, the so-called mythical creature of chaos

Jessman: bartender at the Recovery Ale House and Inn

Joe Cheechoo: Mushkegowuk; Special Investigator for OPP's Criminal Investigation Branch; Will's great-grandfather; see: Johanissan

Johanissan: Callum Sage from the River Country; see: Joe Cheechoo

Josson: captain of Striker Company

Julie Finley: Morgan's mother; nurse

Kain: member of Duke Renaldi's personal guard

Kinlan Barrett: messenger from Second Silver Hawks (Marauders Brigade)
Kydaris: alchemy student; friend of Dadore

Lessers: small, mischievous demon-like creatures from between worlds that infiltrate the contemporary world; visible only to Will
Lillie: orphan girl in the Crow's Nest; considers Morgan her mother
Little Hammerclaw: new town built on the Foglan River on the northeastern shore of Rainia Lake

Marauders Brigade: part of the Fourwinds army almost trying to defend Hammerclaw; recommissioned by General Raric and sent to help defend the Rainia Valley
Margrave: druid who lives in the Druid Forest (in the Hollowtangle)
Military Academy, the: training facility located in Dwenlin Thah
Mio: Enders Brigade ranger
Misty Gorge: canyon west of the Rainia Valley; Serpentine River flows through it
Mofard Flats; the Flats: area between the Upper Plains of Ashron and Dwenlin Thah; used as army staging/training area
Moonwalker: powerful armored creature over eight feet tall, sometimes used by gnome army; usually wields spiked iron ball as preferred weapon
Morgan Finley: Callum Sage; former fencing champion
Mussa: older woman who helps Julie with healing during the battle at the South Crow Gate

Nameless Forest: small wooded area north of the Hollowtangle
Natas: mythical creature of chaos; also known as the Iron Dragon
Niasa Sea: saltwater home of the merpeople

Nyrianne: grandmotherly woman; see: *Sidara*

Onathe Wyeth: dark elf; deceased (Book 1)

Panigim: Overseer of the gnome army
Phyriad: \fear-ee-ad\ a substance found in the Maidstone and used by Natas to create an infectious elixir that transforms living beings into dragon-like creatures
Plains of Ashron: large region west of the Niasa Sea, divided into Upper and Lower

Rainia Valley: community in the eastern Fourwinds; home of the city of Rainia, saltwater Rainia Lake, and the Crow's Nest castle.
Raric: commander general of the human army; the new Red Dragon
Ravenbell: village southeast of Dwenlin Thah
Records of Time: library tower in the Crow's Nest, traditionally protected by the Callum Sages
Recovery Ale House and Inn: eatery and inn located in Fairbay
Renaldi: duke of the Crow's Nest
River Country: home of Johanissan
Rock Pincer: wild wolflike beast trained to kill
Rok: member of Duke Renaldi's personal guard
Rowe of the Nest: Callum Sage
Ruint: Dench's best friend; half of Rowe's personal guard
Ryodan Ayoust: \rye-o-dan\ mer king; Ryowyn's father
Ryowyn: \rye-o-win\ mer princess

Scarlas: the Red Dragon
Second Dragoon Company: part of Fourwinds human army;

100 Light Armored Cavaliers, 50 rangers, and 50 Archers; sent to the Gryton Mines

Shaey: \shay-ee\ renowned elven eagle rider

Shilo: Raric's horse

Sidara: Dark Queen; see: *Nyrianne*

Siodin Mountains: small range north of the Niasa Sea

Southlands: regions south of the Fourwinds; believed to be inhabited by elves

Spicy Toad, Inn and Tavern: eatery and inn located in Ravenbell

Springfield 1911: a semiautomatic pistol; Will's preferred weapon

Striker Company: restored by General Raric; joined Rowe at the South Crow Gate battle

Stoneberg: wall between the eastern and western regions of the Fourwinds; commissioned by Queen Alarra's great-great-grandfather; key to its iron gate has often changed hands

Tara and Avery: children in the Crow's Nest; friends of Lillie

Tevan root: found in Fourwinds forests, used for medicinal properties (pain relief) and also as a recreational narcotic

Thaudas: half winged horse, half unicorn

Tonna: first messenger of Enders Brigade

Tranas: councilman at the Crow's Nest; close friend of Rowe

Trannalun cloak: worn only by Callum Sages; powerful magic woven into red fabric to protect and heal the owner

Trenton: Enders Brigade ranger

Twell Henowing: first lieutenant of Enders Brigade, promoted to brigadier/commander of the Marauders

Uluk the Shadowfallen: \ew-look\ Dark Queen Sidara's minion; offspring of a fallen angel and a woman

Urk: \erk\ goblin; friend of Bremer

Vanar Mines: \vay-nar\ deep in the northern Chicora Mountains, east of Dwenlin Thah; source of strong alloys used for weapons manufacturing in the Fourwinds

Will Owens: Callum Sage
Waerdreath: \ware-dreth\ castle in the western Fourwinds, on the coast of the Habina Ocean; ruled by the Dark Queen Sidara
Wrathan: \rayth-an\ mer prince; brother of Ryowyn

Yossar: \yo-zar\ Highland gnome commander

Did you enjoy *Beyond the Hollowtangle?*

We're looking for a group of loyal readers who will help us continue writing stories like these.

Honest reviews help bring our books to the attention of other readers. If you enjoyed this book, we would be grateful if you could spend a few minutes leaving a review (as short as you like) at Amazon (or other online retailer) and on Goodreads.

What's Next?

Visit
www.MaidstoneChronicles.com

Featuring:
• Regular Giveaways for Fantasy Book Lovers
• Forthcoming Book Releases
• Author Details
• Details on our "Buy a Book / Give a Book" program
(for each book we sell, we're donating student workbooks
for classrooms in Haiti to help kids there learn to read and write)
• Social Media Links

**Everyone on our email list has a chance to win
in our regular giveaways of popular fantasy books.**

Read Book Three of The Maidstone Chronicles:
Into the Maidstone

Thanks for reading and engaging with us!
— *Shane and Darryl*

www.ingramcontent.com/pod-product-compliance
Lightning Source LLC
Chambersburg PA
CBHW021245200726
48288CB00015B/1580